A Murder in Malta

An Elspeth Duff Mystery

Ann Crew

Also by Ann Crew

The Elspeth Duff Series:
A Murder in Malta, 2nd Edition
A Scandal in Stresa
A Secret in Singapore
A Secret in Singapore, 2nd Edition
A Crisis in Cyprus
A Gamble in Gozo
A Deception in Denmark
A Blackmailer in Bermuda
A Presumption in Perthshire
An Ultimatum in Udaipur
A Legacy on Lewis
A Betrayal in Belgium
A Challenge in Chelsea
A Victim in Victoria

The Portia MacRoberts Series:
A Matter of Murder

To Gim and Ian

with many thanks and love

Author's Note

A Murder in Malta was written in between 2002 and 2004, and the first edition was published ten years ago in 2014. This second edition is being issued in 2024 as a celebration of the book's tenth anniversary in print. The Kirkus Review below proved auspicious as I have now developed eighteen Elspeth Duff mysteries (some yet to be published) and one spin-off based on the characters in this book. Thirteen of the characters in *A Murder in Malta* have become my 'friends', and I have enjoyed expanding their lives over time. I thought now would be time to revise this first book in the series, using all the knowledge I have gained over those years. I hope this new edition will correct some of the original deficiencies, and will remind readers where Elspeth Duff originated.

Praise for *A Murder in Malta (First Edition):*
"Each main character has a rich backstory with enough skeletons in cupboards to provide grist for a number of future novels. An often compelling . . . excursion through exotic locales featuring unusual, complex characters."
— Kirkus Review (2004)

List of Characters

Elspeth Duff, special security advisor to Lord Kennington

Eric, Lord Kennington, owner of the exclusive Kennington hotel chain

Pamela Crumm, his silent business partner

Detective Superintendent Anthony Ketcham, Anti-Terrorist Bureau of the Metropolitan Police in London

René LeGrand, manager of the Kennington Valletta Hotel

FitzRoy Conan, born **Kevin O'Connell**, famed author of historical fiction

Bridget O'Connell, his niece who lives in Rome

Seamus Riley, his driver supplied by Bridget in Rome

Fernardu, bartender in the Kennington Valletta Hotel

Giuseppe, the hotel's chef

Loren Axt a.k.a Alicia Kent, an undercover Interpol agent

Abdul Rashid a.k.a Adam Russell, a young Arab guest

Pietru Parra, the night manager at the hotel

Sir William Gaunt and his wife, from the British Foreign and Commonwealth Office

Two sergeants from Scotland Yard assigned to protection duty for Sir William and his wife

Sir Richard Munro, the British high commissioner to Malta, a friend of Elspeth and her cousin **Johnnie Tay** in their schooldays (see below)

Monsieur et Madame Dumont of Tours and Gigi, frequent guests to the hotel and their dog

Miss Frances Knoll and Miss Joanne Fanshaw, guests who are interested in Maltese archaeology

Mr and Mrs Michael Davenport, also guests

Gianni Lugano from Rome who lists his companion as his wife

A tour led by the Smithsonian Institution in Washington, DC

Dr Kahlil Hammud, a professor of Arabic Studies from the University of Durham

Johnnie, the current Earl of Tay, Elspeth's first cousin

Malcolm Buchanan, Elspeth's fiancé at Cambridge

Detective Inspector Evan Davies-Jones, from Scotland Yard

Lady Marjorie Munro, Sir Richard's now deceased wife

Alistair Craig, Elspeth's ex-husband

Elizabeth (Lizzie) and Peter, Elspeth's children

Margaret, Sir Richard's personal assistant at the high commission

Magdelena Cassar (Aunt Mag), Elspeth's titular aunt, a world famous concert pianist who lives on the Maltese island of Gozo

Mitch, Loren's previous fiancé

Roberto Guerrero, vineyard owner

Detective Inspector Dominick Lapira (Inspector Dom), of the Maltese Police

Marija, owner of a restaurant in Valletta

Anthony, a Maltese taxi driver

Pawl, his brother, another taxi driver

Brian Edgewood, Conan FitzRoy's solicitor in London

Liza, bartender at a British pub in Valletta

Giorgio, the night watchman in the hotel's car park

Maria Gabriella, Beatrice and **Manwel**, members of the hotel's night kitchen staff

Salvadore, the night kitchen manager

Brian Clancy, Bridget's boss, mentor and lover

Ryan Fitzpatrick, author of a book on The Troubles

Part 1

Message intercepted at Government Communications
Headquarters (GCHQ), Cheltenham, Gloucestershire,
Thursday, 22 April 2004, 0514 GMT

*Confirming Pericles staying at Kennington Valletta.
Put plans for exchange in place. Saieda will contact you
morning 25th April with time to begin operation. All
activity must be completed in Malta before 1st May. Timing
and precision essential. —Phoenician*

Prologue

Just before the pain struck, he was thinking of the pleasures of the day: the pleasure of his afternoon and his companion during those hours, the pleasure of the small box that now was safely stowed in his case upstairs, the pleasure of the information he had recently received from Dr Hammud and the pleasure of the single malt whiskey he had just ordered.

The garden where he was sitting was bathed in the evening light and the smell of the Mediterranean Sea. The ornately barred and shuttered windows in the surrounding walls were beginning to show evidence of lights behind them. Someone opened one of the sets of louvres above, and he could hear laughter from within. The scent of the spring jasmine and lemon blossoms filled the air, and the neat flowerbeds showed off the skilful hands of the gardeners who had tended them during the afternoon. He found a secluded bench and stretched out comfortably while waiting for the drink to arrive.

1

"Where the hell is Elspeth Duff? "

Lord Kennington rose from his Chippendale desk, which was not a family heirloom although he often suggested it was, adjusted the gold watch in the pocket of his Savile Row waistcoat and shouted into the adjoining office.

His question surprised Pamela Crumm. She looked up from her computer. "In San Francisco, Eric."

Lord Kennington strode over to the glass wall that served as the barrier between his office, the London skyline and the ribbon of the River Thames below.

It was two o'clock on Friday afternoon during the third week in April in the year two thousand and four of the Common Era, and the sun had decided to shine.

The letter from Scotland Yard that lay on his desk had broken his usually calm end-of-the-week mood. He paced. The sun found its way behind a small cloud as if to hide from his irritability.

"Why is she in San Francisco?" he demanded.

Pamela Crumm rose from her work and entered his lordship's inner sanctum through a door that connected his office to hers. "You sent her there yesterday," she said, her deep voice and elegantly clipped words belying her miniscule, twisted body.

"Why did I send her there?" The Kennington San Francisco was one of his flagship hotels. "Nothing there needs the assistance of my top security advisor when there's a more urgent issue," he roared.

The sun came out again and lit up the hazy sky beyond, but he seemed to ignore it.

Eric, Lord Kennington seldom paid attention to the myriad of small details that kept his hotel empire functioning seamlessly. From the very beginning that been Pamela Crumm's job.

"You sent her there because you thought she was needed to help with the trade meeting between the Japanese and Americans," Pamela said calmly.

"Well, get her back. Get someone else to do the meeting. I need Elspeth here and I need her now."

Pamela came over to where Lord Kennington was standing and looked out at the floor-to-ceiling spandrel glass. The sun continued to shine, and the surfaces of the streets below beamed, catching the spring light and winking at them as each car and lorry crept by twenty stories below.

"I'll make the arrangements but there's no way she can be here before tomorrow," Pamela said.

"Then get her here tomorrow—as early as possible. I need her!"

"Of course," Pamela said.

"Why couldn't Elspeth be on assignment in Paris instead of San Francisco? And why don't we have a hotel in Paris? Mark my calendar to call new purchases on Monday, but not until I've dealt with this Malta thing."

"Malta, milord?" quizzed Pamela. She always addressed him formally when he was upset.

Lord Kennington turned from the window and looked

3

at Ms Crumm. "It's none of your damn business."

Pamela Crumm smiled back at him through large round spectacles resting firmly on top of her prominent nose. Mr Eric Kennington, then Sir Eric Kennington and now Eric, Baron Kennington had been credited from the first with massive amounts of magnetism and creative genius but the older he got, the more irascible he became. Pamela knew from long experience how to deal with this. It would be only a matter of hours before Eric would be informing her of his concerns about Malta, and expecting her to put the wheels in motion that would alleviate the problem. Patience filled Ms Crumm, who on occasion had told Elspeth Duff that sometimes she felt like Eric Kennington's nanny. He dismissed Pamela with an impatient flick of his hand.

Pamela retreated into her office. Abutting Lord Kennington's but less spacious, it offered the same view over London. At the very edge of her side window, she could see the London Eye as it made its almost imperceptible rotation above the river. In the few quiet moments she had during each twelve to fourteen-hour workday, she would watch its pods gain teetering heights, and then with certain regularity come back down to earth. The constant rise and fall of the wheel reminded her of the daily course of her job in the Kennington Organisation.

Pamela crossed to the expanse of slick cherry that served as her desk, especially designed for her small body. She picked up the handset from the telephone control panel that was placed squarely in the lower left corner of the desktop. She punched one of her private lines and rang through to the Kennington San Francisco. She calculated that it was well past six in the morning in California. As she waited for the call to connect, she imagined the morning fog pouring through the Golden Gate. She had fond memories of the Kennington San Francisco hotel.

The receptionist at the front desk in California sounded as if he snapped to attention when he received the call from the central office in London, and immediately put it through to Elspeth Duff's room.

*

Elspeth Duff struggled to consciousness amid a vast sea of pillows. She removed the mask from her eyes and searched for the telephone, not remembering on which side of the bed it sat. Finding it, she spoke into it with sleep in her voice. "Elspeth Duff here."

"What light through yonder window breaks? It is the east, and Juliet is the sun," Pamela greeted her.

"Oh, gracious, Pamela, what time is it?"

"Almost half two."

"In London."

"In London, where his lordship has declared you shall be tomorrow morning."

"But I've just arrived here."

"He requires your immediate return," Pamela made it sound like an imperial edict.

Elspeth propped herself up on the pile of pillows, ran her fingers through her stylish razor-cut but tousled hair and sighed. "What's up?" she said, mimicking her son Peter.

Elspeth was filled with forbearance. Lord Kennington's vagaries kept her job exciting, and he paid her handsomely to respond with alacrity to any of his requests, no matter how unreasonable. But still she was just emerging from her sleep in the muddle she always experienced as she ventured back and forth across the globe for him.

"I'm not certain what's up but it must be very important," Pamela said. "He's over there in his office staring out the window. Something about Malta."

Elspeth had seen her employer stare out the window often enough to know that 'Malta' was disturbing his sense of calm deeply.

"I'm on my way," Elspeth yawned. "What time do I leave?"

"I'll get you here early tomorrow morning if you are willing to change planes in New York. He wants you in his office first thing." Pamela's voice softened. "Get your tea and one of those lovely sourdough rolls. I'll ring back as soon as I arrange for your flight."

Elspeth did not like sourdough rolls, especially at breakfast. "Absolutely," she said, pandering to Pamela's romantic vision about the proper food to consume while staying at the Kennington San Francisco.

After Pamela rang off, Elspeth called room service and ordered a pot of strong black coffee, a banana, freshly squeezed orange juice and a bowl of cream-laden yogurt with sweet, fully ripened organic strawberries that the hotel assured its guests had been picked the day before and still held the California sunshine. She felt this a more suitable breakfast for someone about to face the harshness of intercontinental air travel for the second time in three days.

Elspeth arrived at Eric Kennington's office at precisely nine o'clock the next morning. She hoped she did not look so, but she certainly felt as if she had just crossed eight time zones. She had learned over time to keep fresh clothing at her Kensington flat that could accommodate a swift transition from one location to the next, although the weather in London differed little from the April coolness of San Francisco. This morning she had chosen a tailored grey suit with a cobalt blue silk blouse, knowing her clothing suited her clear Scottish complexion and intense blue eyes.

Wearing exquisitely designed clothes was a vanity that she had been able to indulge since she had started working for the Kennington Organisation. She pleased herself by dressing in a style that flattered her rather than bowing to the current fashion. Her London-based French dressmaker admired her individuality, and indulged her simple taste and love of rich colours and fine fabric. Elspeth always kept her accessories to a minimum and let the clothes speak for themselves.

*

As Elspeth entered his office, Eric Kennington looked up from his desk and admired what he saw. He constantly assessed those who worked for him. In Elspeth Duff's case he was sure he had chosen wisely. Elspeth had entered her middle age with grace, and now walked into his office with her head held high, her carriage arresting and her manner assured. Her clothing and understated style were impeccable. He knew that under her self-possessed façade she had a fearless mind and fierce spirit and she was not afraid to use either. One person trying to dodge her enquiries had described her as politely bulldogged; another, who had been fooled by her calm external countenance, had used less kind words. Eric Kennington tolerated this assertiveness of character in few of his employees, as he preferred more deferential types. Elspeth was a rare exception.

One thing about Elspeth, however, bothered him, despite all her skill and composure, in unaware moments sudden sadness filled in her eyes. He had asked Pamela Crumm the source of it, and she had replied that someone whom Elspeth had loved had been murdered a long time ago and, because the crime had never been resolved, it still haunted Elspeth. Pamela did not give any details, although Eric expected she knew them.

With a sense of deep pleasure, he rose and took Elspeth's outstretched hand in both of his. At times like this he fancied he was half in love with her.

"I see you have journeyed back safely."

"Yes, I arrived this morning," she said and added, "at six."

He nodded, seemingly preferring to take her comment as informative rather than arch, and offered her a chair. "I knew you would be here on time. You always are."

Elspeth did not respond to his compliment. "Pamela told me there was trouble at the hotel in Malta. Why Malta, Eric?"

"Read this." He retreated behind his desk and ran his finger over the neat stacks of papers there. He found what he was looking for and handed her a piece of paper headed *On Her Majesty's Service*, the black ink of the signature having bled through to the back. She took the paper, looked at the bottom and saw the scrawl, which made her cock an eyebrow.

"Scotland Yard," she observed.

"Yes, from a Detective Superintendent Anthony Ketcham, Anti-Terrorist Bureau."

"So it's serious."

"In today's climate, yes, very serious."

She read the letter quickly. It was dated 22 April 2004 and the few words were business-like.

It has come to Scotland Yard's attention that your hotel in Valletta may be the site of an as yet undetermined terrorist activity in the week before Malta's accession to the European Union on the first of May. I should like to meet you in person and your security staff to discuss this matter. Will you please telephone my office at the number above at your earliest possible convenience.

"I saw the detective superintendent yesterday, and told him you would be here this morning. He'll be here in half an hour. Use my private conference room when he comes", Lord Kennington said.

Elspeth read the letter a second time. "Tony won't have contacted you if he could have avoided it."

"Tony?" he asked.

"I knew him when I worked at Scotland Yard many years ago."

Lord Kennington refused to be diverted even temporarily from the topic at hand. Neither Elspeth's past employment at Scotland Yard nor her familiarity with Detective Superintendent Ketcham concerned him.

"When I spoke to the detective superintendent

yesterday, he was very explicit. The day before yesterday, Bletchley Park—or whatever they call themselves nowadays you know, the agency that monitors electronic transmissions, picked up an email coming out of a known terrorist internet site in Saudi Arabia. The message specifically mentioned the Kennington Valletta. Can you imagine the effrontery of terrorists thinking of using my hotel!" Eric Kennington barked. "But the detective superintendent will tell you more when he arrives. But here, read this."

Elspeth skimmed the piece of paper with the message intercepted by GCHQ. "I see," Elspeth said. "Do you want to be in on my meeting with Tony?"

He shook his massive head. "I've already seen him, which is why I brought you back to London."

*

Detective Superintendent Tony Ketcham had his back to Elspeth as she entered the conference room but that did not keep Elspeth from drawing in her breath and swallowing hard. The pain of the old but never forgotten memory tumbled through her. Thirty-five years ago then Detective Constable Tony Ketcham had come to the University of Cambridge, where Elspeth was a first-year student, and told her that Malcolm Buchanan was dead. The moment was as fresh as today. After a long investigation, neither Tony nor his superiors had found Malcolm's murderer. The case was declared unresolved but in Elspeth's heart it was not. She did not blame Tony but she had never quite forgiven him. Although they had met many times over the following years, Elspeth always saw him as he was that day in her tutor's rooms at Girton

College. He had looked at his shoes when he told her that Malcolm had been shot, and made a stifled attempt at sympathy. He said Malcolm probably had not known what had happened. She did not hear his words because her heart had died in that moment just as Malcolm had died when bullets penetrated his heart and head. Only she had gone on living.

"Tony," she said.

He turned from his mobile phone. He was still lean and some would have said handsome, but the years at the Yard had put dark grooves in his face and his suit hung off his sloped shoulders. He smiled at her but his eyes held no humour.

She smiled back. "Are you full time in counter-terrorism now? When did you leave homicide?" She did not care that he did not answer.

"Lord Kennington told me we would be working together. It will be a pleasure, Elspeth," he said.

She did not respond in kind. "Eric showed me the message. As puzzling as it may seem, why do you think it's so important? I can't see any outward threat."

"I can't tell you everything, but the source of the message is what alerted us. It came across a site sometimes used by Al Qaeda and by several Yemeni militant groups. We monitor the site closely because in the past it's given us information that's prevented several bombings in the Mediterranean area. Recently the site's been quiet, but suddenly we've picked up a lot of chatter and among it a message mentioning the Kennington Valletta. We can't ignore it."

"But why the clear text giving the name of the hotel

when the rest of the message is encoded?"

"I've no good explanation," he said. "In this business one has to grasp at every lead."

"The lead seems thin."

"In and of itself, yes. In the broad picture of things, no."

"Surely Malta is a benign place," she said.

"It's at the crossroads of the Mediterranean and an important shipping and banking centre."

"Mmm," Elspeth said. "But a Kennington hotel on a small island? Hardly a place for a bomb attack, and besides, the email said an exchange."

"Think, Elspeth, how many things might be exchanged."

Elspeth's mind filled with the possibilities.

"In any case," Tony continued, "Malta's joining the European Union on May first. A disruption of that process could pit Europe as a whole against our unseen enemy. We have to take this seriously. We can only get rid of terrorists if we're always one step ahead of them. I need your eyes and ears in the hotel in Valletta. There may be some danger."

"Why me?"

"Lord Kennington tells me you are his best roving security officer. I believe it. What's more, Sir Michael Gaunt, the British representative to the ceremonies marking Malta's entry to the EU, is staying at the Kennington Valletta."

"Eric didn't tell me that."

"I've set up a team to go out to Malta with him. There'll be twenty-four-seven coverage of Sir Michael and his party. You needn't worry yourself there. You may want to coordinate with his security detail if you feel it's necessary, but I don't think it will be."

"And my job is?" she asked.

"You know the hotels, their security procedures and the type of guests that usually are there. You'll see anyone who is out of place."

"And if they are?"

"I've sent out people to back you up. Someone from my group at the Yard left London for Valletta on Thursday, and an agent from the Public Safety and Terrorism group at Interpol will be arriving today. I've asked the British high commissioner out there to coordinate the effort from outside the hotel and also to be in contact with you. He'll be in daily touch with me through secure channels. He knows you're coming."

"You know nothing more?"

"Not yet."

"I'll do my best," Elspeth said, although she had no idea what that would entail. "But I still don't understand why the Kennington Valletta was in plain text."

"Either to put us off completely or to convey some last minute instruction that was not part of the code."

"Leaving us all floating in a sea of unknowns."

"Welcome to my new world," Tony responded, his face muscles tightening. "Let me explain my plan so far." He did this in precise, succinct words.

"I must be off," he finally said. He jammed his mobile to his ear as he left. His sympathetic manner had not improved.

Elspeth's interview with Tony Ketcham lasted under twenty minutes, and as soon as he left, she picked up the phone in the room and rang Pamela Crumm. "Is Eric still there?" she asked.

"Hanging on every moment and awaiting your return. He's looking busy, even if it's Saturday, his golf day, but he's told me to interrupt him when you finished with Scotland Yard."

Elspeth hurried across the hallway and into Eric's office.

"Eric, how soon can I leave for Malta? I'd no idea things were so grave."

Lord Kennington had a habit that Elspeth found both endearing and annoying. When he had pre-empted another person's thought, he screwed up his eyes and grinned like the Cheshire Cat.

"I have the company jet ready, and my personal car and driver are waiting downstairs. He'll take you to your flat for your cases and then on to the airport. Pamela has notified airport security, and they'll see you through the formalities as quickly as possible. René LeGrand will have a car waiting for you when you reach Malta. You'll remember René, I think, from some of our briefings here in London. He's been promoted to manager of the Kennington Valletta and in that capacity looks forward to welcoming you. And, Elspeth, keep me and Pamela posted as often as possible as to what's going on there."

Elspeth settled the tension of her back into the soft leather seat of Lord Kennington's Jaguar saloon car, and savoured the richness of its touch and smell. She tried to stop the racing of her mind by concentrating on the car. It was a mobile advertisement of the Kennington hotels, she thought. The side doors were emblazoned with the Kennington Organisation crest, and the words 'Comfort and Service' were neatly painted below.

As the car purred through the London streets and on to the motorway, Elspeth attempted to doze but her meeting with Tony Ketcham rattled in her head. She thought of his warnings. He had stressed that the email had come from a source frequently used by Islamic terrorists. She read over the email's contents again, its obliqueness nettling her.

Confirming Pericles staying at Kennington Valletta. Put plans for exchange in place. Saieda will contact you morning 25th April with time to begin operation. All activity must be completed in Malta before 1st May. Timing and precision essential. —Phoenician

What did it mean? Tony had been as puzzled as she was, and had cautioned her that danger might be involved. What danger?

She wound and unwound the copy of the email message around her fingers several times, as if by doing so she could unravel its secrets. Finally the paper turned to paste under her fingers. She no longer needed to read the words, as she had already committed them to memory. Who were the people whose names were encoded in it and what did they intend to do at the hotel?

Elspeth had made this trip out to the private landing strip where Lord Kennington kept his corporate jet many times. The pilot and crew had been advised of Elspeth's arrival and the plane was ready to depart. Elspeth was the only passenger and the pilot assured her that the three-hour flight would be without incident. Elspeth did not mention terrorism to the pilot. Despite Tony Ketcham's exhortation to be vigilant, she considered herself to be an unlikely target for terrorists just as a few hours before she would have considered the Kennington Valletta hotel to be.

Elspeth chose a recliner near a window and occasionally glanced at the European countryside as the flight progressed. Mainly she thought of her task ahead. She declined a glass of excellent New Zealand chardonnay that had been flown in from the Kennington Christ Church for Lord Kennington's pleasure on his trips. Instead, she accepted a cup of coffee, brewed to the strength she preferred, this information having been logged into the plane's computer during her previous flights. The steward left her alone with her steaming mug and the names churning in her mind—Pericles, Saieda, Phoenician.

As they flew over the white cliffs of Dover, across the Channel and out over the farmland of France, the pilot came back and gave her their flight pattern. They would fly over Paris and Geneva, head down the spine of the Alps to Turin and out over the Tyrrhenian Sea, and then follow a course that would take them over Corsica and Sicily before finally reaching Malta. The weather was forecast to be clear, although rain showers were reported at Luqa Airport outside of Valletta in Malta, where they were scheduled to land.

By the time they reached Corsica, clouds had settled in, and Elspeth drifted into sleep, despite the excellent coffee. The steward woke her to advise her of their imminent arrival in Malta. The pilot landed gently on the mirror of the recently rain-crossed runway and in doing so fulfilled his promise of an uneventful trip. Comfort and Service but at what cost?

Elspeth found the hotel car waiting and folded herself into it. She wondered how many hours it had been since she had left San Francisco, but she decided not to count.

2

Seven days. That was all the time she had if Tony Ketcham's fears about the email were true. To clear her mind, Elspeth looked out of the window as the car sped from the airport, past the stony fields and vast football stadium. The driver slowed as they entered the urban streets, lined with a jumble of unevenly parked cars, deep arcades, and open shops brimming with merchandise. Ahead Valletta stood, the afternoon sunlight from behind the car lighting up the high limestone cliffs that fortified the city. The dark clouds to the east gave its buildings a heroic quality that closer observation might belie. At the brink of the city's bastions stood the Kennington Valletta hotel.

Elspeth had visited the Kennington Valletta before, but never in her official capacity. This, the grandest of the historic hotels in Malta, had its architectural origins in the Baroque era that had flourished after the Maltese drove off the Ottoman Turks in fifteen eighty-six. Fifteen years ago, Lord Kennington had discovered the old hotel that had tenanted the knights' palace, a hotel that had been struggling for two decades, but had failed to maintain an image of bygone grandeur. The charm of an earlier redecoration had slipped into shoddiness. The repairs made after the heavy bombardments by the Luftwaffe and Italian air force in the early nineteen forties had proven inferior.

By nineteen eighty-nine the bathrooms had become as obsolete as the clientele. Lord Kennington had renovated the building in a style more in keeping with the seventeenth century than the twentieth, hired a four-star chef from Rome and made the Kennington Valletta the best of the 'old hotels' in Malta. The prices were significantly higher than other hotels on the island. The quality of the service was superb. The hotel had a first-class fitness facility but no swimming pool. Families didn't stay there; well-heeled honeymooners and money, both old and new, did. As a result, the hotel turned a handsome profit. It was not a place one associated with terrorism but rather with the romance of the Knights of St. John, who had ruled Malta for so many centuries.

As the car pressed on, climbing the steep street up to Valletta, Elspeth admired the hotel's quiet splendour. No other words could so aptly describe the level of care of the exterior restoration or, Elspeth knew, the brilliance of the interior décor. Comfort, yes, but a comfort that only several million pounds could achieve, particularly when augmented by the constant diligence of a large, minutely supervised staff. The hotel's location near the Auberge de Castile, the offices of the Prime Minister, was unique. Most of the other Maltese luxury hotels were located outside the limestone bulwarks of Valletta or in the fashionable suburbs of St. Julian's to the north. The Kennington Valletta was a small but brilliant star in the Kennington Organisation's chain of hotels.

Elspeth took in a deep breath as they reached the hotel; her journey was over but her job had just begun.

Elspeth recognised the lanky figure of René LeGrand.

He paced under the porte-cochère as Elspeth's car drew up to the hotel. His short-cropped dark hair, slim steel-rimmed glasses and immaculate black suit remained exactly as they had been the last time she had seen him in London. He opened the car door himself and welcomed her briefly.

"Elspeth," he said, giving her name a French inflection. "Your arrival is most anticipated."

He whisked her past the doorman and concierge, around the ornate reception desk and finally into the back rooms. Fuelled by his sense of urgency, she gave only a fleeting glance at the grandeur of the lobby.

René's office contrasted with the public rooms. His furniture was made of glass, polished stainless steel, and black leather. Minute halogen lights, suspended from a wavy bar above, filled the room with brilliance far beyond that necessary for normal tasks. Flat-screened monitors lined the wall behind his desk and showed all the main spaces of the hotel. Elspeth noticed that the only bow to tradition was a large oriental rug of intricate design, reds, blues, pinks, greens and whites, its threads pulled by delicate fingers using a method that was one of the most labour-intensive and least high tech in the world.

René waved Elspeth to a chair that looked rigid but proved comfortable. A thermos of hot coffee and another of decaffeinated coffee waited on a tray on a sideboard near the desk. Elspeth was thankful for René's thoughtfulness in providing the coffee, but thoughtfulness was the hallmark of Kennington hotels and it did not surprise her. Elspeth accepted the fine porcelain cup offered to her, declined cream and sugar and turned to business.

René fidgeted and finally spoke.

"I run one of the best hotels in Europe. I cannot have this thing—*terrorisme*—happen here." His voice was agitated and his face glowed with perspiration. "We are at the height of our season and there must be nothing, *rien de tout*, that stops its success."

Elspeth wanted to calm René but false reassurance would not work. Because she reported directly to Eric Kennington she had authority over René, but she also had the sense never to use her rank with Kennington hotel managers. In her five years with the Kennington Organisation, she knew it was better to gain the managers' goodwill and make them feel that they were the leaders of the investigations at hand. As she turned in her seat to give her measured response to René's discomfort, the muted buzz of his desk phone interrupted them.

He spoke rapidly into the handset. Elspeth recognised the strangeness of the Maltese language, which to the untrained ear sounded somewhat like Italian but had soft sibilants and strange glottal stops that made it unique. She had mastered enough words during her many visits to her family in Malta and Gozo to delight shopkeepers, taxi drivers and waiters with a few words, but they were not enough to follow René's half of the phone dialogue.

The phone call, or perhaps his competence in handling it, seemed to restore some of René's composure. He rang off.

"Excuse me, Elspeth. It is but a small matter but one that must be seen to."

Elspeth was glad of both the politeness of the apology and the benefit of the moment's pause the interruption had offered, which had given her time to craft her interaction with him.

"René, you undoubtedly have seen the contents of the email."

He nodded assent.

She continued, "I met Detective Superintendent Tony Ketcham from Scotland Yard this morning in London. He assured me that there will be people here from both the Counter-Terrorist Bureau at the Yard and the Public Safety and Terrorism Sub-Directorate of Interpol to help us find the guest codenamed Pericles. Their job is to unearth that person. I'm to assist you in protecting the other guests in every possible way." After her talk with Tony Ketcham, Elspeth knew her role might be bigger, but she did not reveal this thought to René. "Lord Kennington's directive to us is to deal with this affair so that our guests will have no indication that things are not as they always are every day at every Kennington hotel."

"Yes, yes, yes. Yes, that is as it should be. You have my complete cooperation and that of my staff too. Nothing is more important," he said.

Satisfied, Elspeth turned to more mundane matters. "I'd like to stay in a room off the garden where I can go in and out of the hotel without using the lifts."

"I have already made these arrangements and instructed that your cases be taken there. I will show you to your room myself when we are finished here."

She nodded and continued. "The detective superintendent and I have agreed that most sensitive communications will be handled through the secure communications apparatus at the British High

Commission, but Lord Kennington would also like us to be in constant communication with him. I can help you with this."

"*Oui.* I would be thankful for that. Certainly." René tapped his fingers rapidly up and down on the glass surface of the table.

Nerves? Elspeth suspected so. "Do you have a private room here in your operations centre where I might set up communications to Lord Kennington's office without being overheard?" she asked. Her hotel room would not be secure. People could listen at doors and at the main switchboard. No one at the hotel could be fully trusted, except perhaps René. At least she hoped he could be. For now, she needed to take that chance.

"Of course," he said. "You may use my conference room. It is small but has a secure phone and internet connection. Only I have a key. No member of the staff can enter without my being present."

"That will suit me perfectly. Now tell me about security at the hotel."

"I will give you the brief tour to show you the technology we use. Then I will introduce you to the top people on my staff. They have been here for many years and provide our mainstay of safety, but first you would like to have a short rest. I understand you flew from San Francisco last evening."

Elspeth smiled in acknowledgment of his kindness and consideration. Yes, she had set just the right tone for success in their collaboration. She hoped they were both up to the task. She did not tell him that, other than going through numerous security checks at airports and museums, she had never dealt with a terrorist threat before. She found her current task much more daunting than she wanted him to know.

"A few hours of rest would be a godsend, and then we can meet for a full orientation," she said. "We also need to discuss how we can make best use of your staff. It's late now for the day staff, but I'd appreciate your setting up a meeting with them for first thing in the morning. Since today is the twenty-fourth and the email implies that the twenty-fifth is the earliest time for the operation to begin, I think there's still a small window of safety before our complete vigilance is needed."

René rose and brought an end to their meeting. They left his office and entered the lobby again, this time without hurrying. Elspeth looked up at the grand ceiling, repainted so carefully fifteen years ago, around at the walls, heavily adorned with murals and hung with giant mirrors, and then down at the rich carpeting on the floor, undoubtedly chosen with care by the London office. She knew that this grand façade hid the true modern workings that made the Kennington hotels what they were.

As they crossed the lobby, Elspeth heard a disturbance at the entrance to the hotel. She turned towards it. She recognised a large person coming in through the door and was filled with alarm.

"Quickly, René, get me to my room," she entreated. "Save me from your new guest over there."

But it was too late.

3

Conan FitzRoy, né Kevin O'Connell, had been spending the last two weeks of April at the Kennington Valletta ever since the international success of his epic piece of historical fiction depicting the Axis blitz of Malta during the Second World War. He was not the first or last author to choose this horrendous event in Malta's history as background for a novel but FitzRoy had a talent for exacting detail, fast-paced storytelling and just the right touch of eroticism that made his saga one of the best dealing with that era. Local fans, he was sure, anticipated his visits, and he luxuriated in being recognised on the island and at the hotel. Copies of his book were kept stocked in the hotel gift shop, and every year he would consent to a book signing in return for a discounted hotel room rate.

FitzRoy's financial circumstances varied over time. This year he arrived for his annual visit to the Kennington Valletta in a vast black Mercedes, hired with the advance on his next book. His niece Bridget, whom he had just visited in Rome, had the car detailed so that it shone. She had lent him the services of a driver called Riley when FitzRoy's chauffeur from London became ill. The vast proportions of both FitzRoy and the car invaded the landscape of the hotel's porte-cochère, although unlike FitzRoy the car was sleek and new. The doorman, obviously recognising the famous guest, opened one of the hotel's tall and heavily panelled doors, and FitzRoy paraded into the hotel's embrace. He had decided to make his entrance regal. At moments like this he thought of himself as a king or an emperor and he knew he had the power to make people regard him with a certain awe.

Conan FitzRoy had written this grand script for his life because he knew he was a pretentious fraud. His rise to fame had startled him but he covered his inner feelings by becoming bigger than life, grander in bulk, and more flamboyant in dress than those around him. Inside he was the young man who had once betrayed his brother, his brother's wife and his best friend. That act tormented him every day he was alive. Anyone who knew about this, he conjectured, would now be dead or would have forgotten Kevin O'Connell, but he could not forget or forgive himself. All of his success could not atone what he had done in a youthful indiscretion.

Arriving at the hotel, he felt a sense of relief. Here he felt exonerated. The work he had done in Malta had been original; his research had been solid. No, he could not be faulted on that. This was the reason he returned to Malta every year. Here he was exemplary.

Conan FitzRoy was by heredity inclined to obesity. He loved good food and drank heavily but never got drunk, but the effects of his indulgence were noticeable in his florid face and expanding waistline. Each year he wore a longer and larger cape to cover his vastness. Three years ago he had taken to smoking a large Dunhill pipe despite his doctor's warnings. A year later he added a tall, antler-headed walking stick to his costume. He did not concede that he needed the walking stick to alleviate pressure on his knees; instead he considered it enhanced his visibility.

As FitzRoy entered the lobby, he saw her. Elspeth Duff. Cape billowing, walking stick raised in the air, he hobbled at breakneck speed towards Elspeth with an overflowing feeling of pleasure.

How exquisite an encounter. What a wonderful creature she was. How he looked forward to talking to her. He remembered the past years when their paths had crossed at various Kennington hotels—Venice, Hong Kong, San Francisco—and sighed with pleasure.

"Elspeth, my dear, it is marvellous to see you. I had no idea that you would be gracing this magnificent hotel at this precise moment."

But something was different? Normally she would have smiled at him broadly, probably aware that much of his life was a pretentious act but loving him for it. But now she was distracted, aloof. Did she despise his increasing extravagance, knowing that it hid scars of the early days of his existence when a full meal a day was an unanticipated luxury? FitzRoy cursed the remembrance of his past.

Then the old Elspeth was back. Now her manner seemed natural and he felt a great sense of relief.

"Conan, how good to see you. Meet René LeGrand, the new manager of the hotel. Forgive me, I must be off."

"But you must join me for a drink this evening," FitzRoy insisted.

Elspeth smiled but made no commitment.

"Surely you'll share a dinner of sea bass à la FitzRoy. Giuseppe always makes it for me on my first night here," he persisted. FitzRoy enjoyed having one of the hotel specialities named after him.

Elspeth bowed her head gracefully, which FitzRoy took for a yes. Quickly she made her departure.

As FitzRoy crossed towards the registration desk, he looked around the lobby with a deep sense of gratification. The Baroque grandeur of the space satisfied him. The Counter Reformation seemed the most sensible time in the history of the Catholic Church. As the Protestants inflicted austerity on the north, the Church indulged in opulence and excess in the south. Under both systems most people suffered, but the art and splendour in the south were better, at least in FitzRoy's eyes.

He collected his large key, put it in his pocket, adjusted his cloak, and headed for the lift. As he stood waiting for the cab, he watched an intense young woman enter the lobby. He admired her slimness and angularity and her stylish clothes. Money and diet, he thought. Exercise never crossed his mind. He could tell the woman's money was a new attribute. Underneath there was not poverty, as there had been in his own beginnings, but rather middle class ordinariness. She wasn't Rococo. She was nouveau riche Modigliani, but the more he watched her, the more he thought of El Greco. She became an adoring Madonna. He must make her acquaintance.

*

Something happened when Loren Axt entered the lobby. Later she couldn't describe it to anyone's satisfaction but her own. She had heard that architects always looked up when they entered a room. She did so and saw the frescoes that appeared to have been painted by

Maltese artists hundreds of years before. A Grand Master of the Knights of St. John carrying a blazing sword surged from the clouds to lead his brilliantly arrayed and heavily armoured troops into battle. The colours were gaudy, and the figures elongated in a style embraced by Venetian artists in their heyday.

At that moment Loren knew why she had come to Malta. Like the avenging Grand Master, she was backed by the legions that sought to bring justice and order in the world. The passion of her feelings not only surprised her but also gave her a new sense of purpose. She was sure that the next few days would be a defining moment in her life. This was what all her training and preparation had been about.

She walked with a new sense of confidence. The stone walls of the lobby, in some places a meter thick, held the coolness of the evening. Loren was glad of this, as she was tired from her trip from Lyon.

Loren watched as the hotel staff loaded her luggage on a trolley. She found it ironic that she had brought one of the suitcases she had in Washington before she had broken off all relations with her past.

No, thought Loren, no, I won't think about that. She looked up at the Grand Master figure once again. This was right, being here, doing this thing. It was bigger than the failures of her earlier life, her brother's death in Lebanon when she was a child and the fatigue from her uncomfortable trip. Whatever was here for her was as great as the grandmaster and his legions above her. The past four years that she had spent carrying out low-level assignments were just a precursor to this.

She arrived at the reception desk, feeling the rush of blood in her face. One of the receptionists looked up politely. He did not appear to recognise the avenging knight who stood before him.

"Have you booked a room, madam?" he asked.

Loren drew her confirmation letter from her bag and handed it to him as if he ought to know that she had arrived. How could he doubt?

"Sign here please. Which credit card will you be using?"

Loren produced the one she had been given the day before. The name on it read 'Alicia Kent'.

"Ms Kent. Welcome. This is your first visit, I believe. We are giving you a garden room. I am sure you will find it most comfortable."

Loren did not question the location of the room. As she crossed the lobby, she avoided looking up at herself in one of the long mirrors to admire her new persona. Without reconfirming their existence, she liked the new shape of her hair and the new extent of her makeup. Her clothes suited her. Her suitcase was the only reminder of the life she had left behind.

'Alicia Kent' had cleared her first hurdle in this new land and in her new identity. Her lips broke into a smile of triumph.

*

Abdul Rashid, who before his conversion to Islam was called Adam Russell, made no stir as he entered the lobby. Inside he was trembling, filled with a sense of duty but feeling less than confident that he would carry out his assignment faithfully.

Rashid was a young man, slight in stature, olive skinned and angular in appearance. His nose was hooked and his hair black and straight. He prided himself on looking like his father, whom he considered a magnificent person. Rashid's hair had been fashionably cut in London and he wore a new beard. It itched but he was proud of it as a badge of his new religion. His father insisted that he be well dressed, and he was enjoying wearing the well-cut jacket and trousers that he had been told were appropriate for a rich young Arab visiting a posh hotel in the Mediterranean. He looked into one of the long mirrors. He was surprised but pleased at what he saw. "God is Great," he whispered to himself.

As his eyes got used to the subdued light of the lobby, he saw the reception desk. He had never stayed at an expensive hotel before; in fact, he had never stayed at any hotel at all. He had not told them that in London. He tried to remember his instructions. He was to be unobtrusive. He hadn't known what that word meant and had to look it up in his Collins student dictionary. He was not to be noticed, that was it. He could do this, he thought, because he had done it so many times growing up as a poor Arab boy called Adam Russell in Peckham in southeast London. There he tried to hide from the rest because he was different. He wondered what the taunting boys at his comprehensive would think of him now, all dressed up and with two suitcases filled with expensive clothes from the best shops in the West End.

Abdul walked across the lobby soundlessly. The deep rugs on the marble floors felt soft under the soles of the tan moccasins that Achmed, his brother, had insisted he buy in one of Harrods' men's shops.

No one watched as Abdul crossed the lobby to the big counter. An unoccupied receptionist was at her computer and must not have been aware of him. Abdul cleared his throat quietly. She looked up, startled.

"Oh, I am sorry, sir, I didn't hear you."

Abdul felt he had passed his first test at being unobtrusive.

"May I have your passport, please," she requested in English and then said, 'your passport' in Arabic.

Rashid gave her his British passport in the name of Adam Russell. It was genuine but indicated that he had been born in Beirut not the United Kingdom.

"Mr Russell," the receptionist said, reading his name. "Your room is booked for a week. Is that correct?"

"Yeah, that's right. One week. From today 'til next Saturday, May first."

The receptionist looked up at the young man in a way that made him feel uneasy. Did she recognise his Peckham accent?

She asked him to fill out the registration card. He wrote carefully, in typical British schoolboy script, spelling out his English name and an address in London, just as he had been instructed to do.

"I will need to make a copy of your passport," she said. She disappeared for a moment and then returned, his passport in hand.

"And what credit card will you be using?"

Abdul Rashid took out a platinum card that bore Adam Russell's name and had a limit of twenty-five thousand pounds. The amount staggered him when

Achmed handed it to him weeks before. "Try not to exceed that amount," his brother had told him. "Before you do, let us know."

"You are in room 406, sir. I will have Giorgio take up your cases."

"I would like to buy some Maltese money, please." At that moment he could not remember the word 'exchange'.

"Yes, sir."

Abdul liked being called sir. No one had ever called Adam Russell sir before, not even at Harrods, where he had been eyed with suspicion because of his youth and working class accent.

He bought one thousand Maltese lira, a large sum for him, put the money next to the sheaf of pound notes in his new Hermès wallet, and proceeded to his room.

*

One of the porters led Loren Axt also known as Alicia Kent, through a beautiful courtyard filled with flowering trees and colourful plants and dotted with small landscaped nooks with benches and tables. She assumed that a person could retire there for a private tête-à-tête or a good novel, and rued the fact that she would not have time for this during the next week.

Loren was satisfied with her room as she entered it. She noticed that the outside door had a small, hand painted porcelain placard telling her that this was the "Hyacinth Room." A student of languages, Loren speculated that the room might have been named after a gem, a flower, or a colour. Whichever the case, the decorator of the room had used the purple colour sparingly and with comforting effect.

For the last few years she had spent so much time in dingy apartments, hovels and drafty country outposts in dank woodlands, that the pure luxury of the room startled her. She had changed during those times. She had endured hardships she could not have imagined when she graduated from Georgetown University. Now she was here.

Her room was decked with flowers in vases near the bed and in the living area. The porter put her suitcases on racks near the large armoire, which she discovered contained ample room to hang her clothing and abundant drawer space for her personal things. Off the main room there was a small recess where she found the breakfast bar, the refrigerator and a small table set for a meal for two.

Loren put down her bag and sat down at a writing table set in a corner that overlooked the garden. She opened the leather portfolio that lay there and again was surprised. It contained not only the usual room service menu and list of guest services but also a delicate appeal to first-time guests to fill out a Kennington hotel preference list. Alicia Kent was urged to note if she wanted a room with an outside view with a balcony or one on the ground floor opening on to the garden. Did she prefer one or two beds and what softness? She was given a selection of eight types of pillows and asked if she wanted sheets and blankets or a duvet or both. Other choices included the preference for a television or not, which language or languages for her satellite service, any other electronic devices such as a DVD or VCR, what kind of films she would like to see and in what language, what sort of drinks she wanted in her mini-bar, did she want pre-breakfast coffee or tea delivered to her room and at what time, which morning newspaper or newspapers she wanted at her door in the morning and any special valet requirements. The Kennington hotels, with the permission of the guest, would log this information into their computer banks so that a return guest would not have to ask for any of these items. The form stated that guest's preferences, if not changed, were honoured on every visit.

Too bad, thought Loren, that Alicia Kent would exist no more in a week's time and Loren Axt would become a piece of history. Idly she filled out the lists. Later that evening she was surprised to see that all her requested items had been provided.

*

Arriving at his room on the fourth floor, Adam Russell undid one of his new cases and took out his Qur'an and prayer rug. It was time for afternoon prayers. The imam had taught him to be strict about the formal act of prayer, one of the five major Pillars of Islam. Adam liked the structure of his new religion and its simplicity. His mother had tried to teach him the ways of her own Christianity, but he found its tenets confusing and conflicting. When his mother died, he had left his great-aunt and great-uncle's home in Peckham, where he and his mother had lived. He felt, with his olive skin, black hair and Middle Eastern looks, he was no longer wanted there. He also abandoned their English religion. In a makeshift mosque above a Lebanese greengrocer's shop on Old Kent Road he had found a religion that matched his skin, hair, and eyes.

"There is no God but God, and Muhammad is the Prophet of God," he intoned in English and then carefully repeated it in Arabic. The latter words came slowly but held more feeling for him.

*

Despite his colourful appearance, Conan FitzRoy was meticulous in his personal habits. Because he was travelling by car, he brought four cases with him. Two contained his European wardrobe, one his lighter wardrobe for the next part of the trip, which was to Egypt, and the fourth his personal effects.

FitzRoy always returned to suite 411. It had a magnificent view of Grand Harbour and a spacious bathroom that filled with caressing steam when he poured his bath. The tub was so large and deep that he could hedonistically abandon all the chills of a British winter. FitzRoy found the bathroom in his suite at the Kennington Valletta a clever innovation. Perhaps the Romans had invented the idea of modern plumbing, but neither the Knights of St. John nor the British had perfected it. The door to the bathroom gave one the feeling of entry into a secret space that was the future where the main rooms echoed the magnificence of the past. The plumbing fixtures were ultra-modern. The bathroom was a place to escape into. The architect, FitzRoy assumed, had been clever in not trying to replicate the past but rather to repudiate it. The only bow to Malta's history was the blue and white accent tile pattern, which FitzRoy had once seen in the ruins of one of the auberges of the Order of St. John here in Valletta.

Conan entered this special place. He laid out his shaving kit and brushes beside one of the two marble sinks. A navy blue terrycloth robe hung on its appointed hook.

The first time Conan had stayed at a Kennington hotel he had indicated that he preferred a dark robe; he felt it hid some of his girth.

Waiting for his tub to fill, he surveyed his luggage. He hunted out a trendy bag intended to be hung on the back of a bathroom door with pockets where his numerous chemist's bottles were neatly lined up like bullets in a rifle belt and boxes of medications tucked neatly below. He found the bag disgusting because he did not want to admit the reason for its existence. He had been shocked when his doctor told him that his heart was in danger. His heart! FitzRoy did not remember heart trouble in his family. He refused to attribute any coronary trouble to his lifestyle. Overeating and over drinking were a part of his life, not a cause for his death. He hated the medications. He took them only on the insistence of his niece Bridget.

Bridget Mary Martha O'Connell was the only person alive whom Conan FitzRoy really loved. From her birth he had felt a special bond with her, a closeness that had no limits. It was Bridget who had bought the wretched bag. "Uncle Kevin," she had said when she gave it to him, "people live with heart disease for ages and ages. Take the medicine your Harley Street doctor has given you. You have paid him dearly for his advice." It was Bridget who made sure he had packed the nasty bag with all its required contents. She had labelled each medication with the date it should be taken. Although Conan no longer practiced the staunch Calvinist faith of his family, he thanked God for Bridget's existence and her care of him.

Every morning and every evening he drew out the appropriately labelled bottles and packets, dispensed the doses, thought fondly of Bridget and swallowed the contemptible tablets. They made him feel nauseous so he washed them down with strong coffee laced with cream and a liberal amount of raw brown sugar in the morning and the best single malt whiskey he could find in the evening. The poison that caused the disease eased the taking of the antidote that was meant to cure it.

Returning to Malta had been an exquisite idea. A greater joy had been seeing Elspeth Duff. In her presence he did not always have to be as pretentious as he knew he had become.

And that other alluring young woman in the lobby, who was she? He must invite her to his table this evening and find out. Yes, Malta would prove to be a salvation. His heart already beat more steadily.

4

By some internal clock that never has been explained by science, Elspeth awoke before the wakeup call from René LeGrand. Her hand brushed her pillow and her tactile senses reacted with pleasure. How intelligent of Eric to buy Egyptian cotton for his bed linens. Less perceptive people might not have recognised the origin of the sheets and pillowcases, but their fineness would register in their unconscious minds and translate it as sleeping well at a Kennington hotel.

Her gratification was short lived. Today was the twenty-fourth of April, and tomorrow Saieda, whoever that might be, would contact whomever was the addressee of the email to begin an operation for an unidentified exchange to take place probably at the Kennington Valletta hotel. Worse, Pericles might already be staying at the hotel. Elspeth railed at the vagueness of the email message and its elusive threat. She had grown up in the Scottish Highlands and had inherited a ferocity of spirit, which to date had been useful in handling real situations not electronic suppositions. She had dealt with crime ever since the bitter and still unsolved the murder of her fiancé, Malcolm Buchanan, but her professional investigations were of offences already committed and not crimes that were intended but not yet carried out.

How could one fight an unknown future event? And

what was to be exchanged? Arms, personnel, drugs, money, false identity papers, fake credit cards, computer disks or information too sensitive to convey in any other way? Any, some, or all of the above? She groaned and rose from her bed.

When René's call came at six, she had already finished her shower and was getting dressed for the evening. From her armoire she pulled black silk trousers, a moss-coloured silk blouse and a jade green jacket. When accented with gold jewellery her costume could pass at any non-formal occasion. She combed her light brown hair and applied a hint of makeup. She looked at her jaw, which was too strong, and her nose, which was too chiselled, and determined that she would pass muster. She took a deep breath and prepared herself for duty.

Elspeth crossed through the gardens, which were filled with the evening scent of gardenias and orange blossoms, and approached René and another man at the end of the lobby. Local guests who had come for their evening meal were strolling in through the front doors and waiting by the lift to go to the dining room on the top floor of the hotel. René greeted most of them by name, as the local clientele provided an important part of the hotel's profitability. As Elspeth watched Eric Kennington's newly appointed manager, she realised that he had a quality of graciousness that no guest, local or foreign, could resist. She nodded at him approvingly and his eyes acknowledged the compliment.

The affable young man at his side had the characteristically long and dignified face of the Maltese. He also was welcoming each guest and, when suitable, speaking in Malti. He looked up at Elspeth and obviously knew who she was. His smile was infectious and she smiled back.

"*Bonsoir*, Elspeth," said René, again giving a French inflection to her name. "You have not made the acquaintance of Pietru Parra, my night manager. He has been at the hotel since the Kennington Organisation took control, and it is true that he knows more of what happens here than any other person on my staff."

Elspeth extended her hand to Pietru in greeting. His grip was firm, and then he turned her hand over and gave it a small, old-fashioned kiss. Elspeth delighted in this gesture.

"*Bonasira*," she said in barely passable Malti. "Good evening."

"*Bonasira, sinjura*," he said. "Good evening, madam."

"Pietru will continue on here," René said. "At this time I usually withdraw behind the desk, and watch to see if my guests are safely registered and to be of assistance if I am needed. Come with me."

"Of course," Elspeth agreed. "Thank you, Pietru."

"The pleasure is mine," he responded. Despite his Maltese countenance, his English accent was impeccably Mayfair.

"Pietru is a great asset to me," René said when they were out of earshot. "He is from Valletta, so when local people come here in the evening they feel welcome. But he also was trained in London at the Savoy, and consequently understands the needs of our international visitors. I rely on him completely, as I do on all my staff."

Elspeth understood. When she had come to the hotel as a child with her aunt, Magdelena Cassar, at the very end of Malta's days as a British colony, all of the guests were colonials—matrons, retired majors, those of a venerable age who were living in genteel poverty and an occasional Maltese such as her aunt, who was renowned as a pianist in the music world in Europe and therefore acceptable. Throughout recorded history Malta had been the colonial fodder of many nations, lastly the British, and each was as imperious as the one before. Now Malta was independent and prosperous in its own right, and in a few days' time would gain full membership of the European Union. Unlike the former owners of the hotel, the Kennington Organisation now catered to its Maltese guests with great pleasure.

René led Elspeth to a niche behind the reception desk where the whole lobby and front doors were visible.

"We can speak here without being heard," he said. "I find this convenient if a guest has a problem."

He took a paper from a portfolio he was carrying. "Here is the roster of our guests, their room numbers, and their home addresses."

Elspeth quickly ran down the fifty plus names. She handed the list back to him.

"Tell me what you know about them, René. Do you suspect any of them is Pericles?"

René dodged her question. "Our most distinguished guests are Sir William Gaunt of the British Foreign and Commonwealth Office, Lady Gaunt and their entourage, which includes five other people including two sergeants from Scotland Yard in charge of their personal security.

They arrived yesterday as representatives of the British government for the accession of Malta into the EU and were accompanied here by the British high commissioner, Sir Richard Munro, whom I have met on various occasions."

"Did you say Sir Richard Munro?" Elspeth was thankful that she did not bleat out "Do you mean Dickie Munro?" In London Tony Ketcham had told her she would be working with the British high commissioner to Malta, but had not given her his name. Elspeth knew that a high commissioner in the Commonwealth of Nations held a post equivalent to an ambassador elsewhere and therefore was important.

Learning the identity of the high commissioner suddenly brought her assignment too close to her personal life. This disconcerted her.

René watched her with a curious expression. "Do you know the high commissioner?"

Elspeth nodded. "Since my schooldays in Scotland."

"He has been high commissioner here for the last six months and comes here to dinner on occasion," René said. "The high commissioner's official residence is currently under reconstruction so the Foreign and Commonwealth Office appealed to us to allow the British delegation to stay here. I have put them on the third floor, and no other guests will be allowed there. We have staff posted by the lift and stairs to see that the delegation's privacy is not broken. We have been informed that they will not be here often other than to sleep and change their clothes, as most of their functions are either at the British high commission or at various government buildings here in Valletta. The

Scotland Yard sergeants with the Gaunts have set up their own security measures to make sure no unintended incident occurs here in the hotel. I assume you will want to coordinate your mission with theirs."

Elspeth bristled silently at his use of the words 'your mission' rather than 'our mission'. She thought that she and René had formed an alliance.

"Yes, of course, although I'm sure Detective Superintendent Ketcham has already taken care to do so," she said.

René did not seem to notice the coolness of her reply. Her mind flew on. Could Sir William Gaunt be Pericles? How could she find out? Elspeth was grateful that the Gaunts, as representatives of Her Majesty, were being so well taken care of by both the Kennington Organisation and the British government, but could they be involved knowingly or inadvertently in the exchange mentioned in the email? Was there the threat of kidnapping and prisoner exchange? It seemed unlikely but acts of terror at any scale at a Kennington hotel had seemed unlikely too, until now.

René LeGrand touched Elspeth's arm, interrupting her thoughts. "Do you see the couple just coming in? They are Monsieur et Madame Dumont of Tours and Gigi. Gigi is allowed to stay in the Dumont's room only because of her impeccable manners."

Elspeth knew that all Kennington hotels had kennels, and smiled at René's exception for Gigi, a beautifully clipped standard poodle.

"I have put the Dumonts on the second floor with a view to the gardens and the city. They visit several times a year. Madame Dumont's daughter and her husband live in

Sliema with their five children. The Dumonts prefer to stay with us and make day visits only to their family. Monsieur Dumont is a retired mayor of Tours, and Madame is the owner of a house of fashion there. They are always happy to be here—and perhaps not in Sliema," he said with only a hint of a smile.

They watched a middle-aged British woman demand that her numerous cases be carefully loaded on a trolley at the front doors. Her companion fussed beside her. The concierge greeted them by name and obliged them.

René shook his head with a kind look. "Miss Frances Knoll and Miss Joanne Fanshaw, also on the second floor, come every April from the Isle of Wight. They are interested in archaeology and spend their days at digs at one or another of the various temples. They are always welcomed by the archaeologists as they contribute generously to their endeavours."

The next guests to arrive were more reserved and were dressed in the conservative manner of wealthy New Englanders. They nodded to René with familiarity as they approached the reception desk.

"Mr and Mrs Michael Davenport from Connecticut have a suite on the first floor with a view to the harbour, and are on their third visit. They are known to us," René said. "He is in some sort of finance and spends several hours a day on the internet corresponding with his brokers. She prefers lounging in the garden with a book and sightseeing with a private driver."

René frowned briefly at the next guests, an ageing man with slick black hair accompanied by a much younger and unnaturally blonde woman who was taller than he. He was excessively attentive as he bowed to her when they came through the doors.

"That must be *il signor* Gianni Lugano from Rome. He has listed his companion as his wife, but I suspect otherwise. They are on the fourth floor."

Elspeth smiled and made no comment. Hotels, even Kennington ones, frequently saw these sorts of guests. They did not look like members of the Red Brigade.

Shortly afterwards, a large coach pulled under the porte-cochère, and began disgorging its numerous occupants, all of whom looked tired.

"This is a tour led by the Smithsonian Institution in Washington, DC. They are all on the first floor and second floor. I understand that these tours are very dear and only attract those who can afford such things. They fill fifteen rooms I have all their names and addresses. We have found that the members of these tours before have been quietly enthusiastic about Malta and Gozo. We welcome them back each year."

The reception desk was inundated with new arrivals. René suggested that Elspeth and he move back to his offices in order to allow the receptionists to do their work. He left word that he could be called if needed.

René led Elspeth down the hallway into his office, where neatly spaced piles of paper littered his glass-topped desk. He tapped one of them as if to reassure her that he had been diligently at work while she had slept.

After they were seated, Elspeth asked, "And the guests who have already checked in?"

"Mr FitzRoy, whom you know."

Elspeth silently acknowledged the acquaintance.

"Seamus Riley, Mr FitzRoy's driver, who is staying in one of the rooms reserved for servants in the basement near the kitchens. Sir William's sergeants occupy the other rooms there when they are off duty."

These rooms, a holdover from earlier days when people did travel with servants, were less expensive than normal rooms, and were still favoured by the few guests who wanted their staff nearby. Elspeth suspected they appealed to both FitzRoy's and the British government's attempts at economy.

"And the stray ducks?" she asked.

"Stray ducks? Ah, *oui*, the new people?"

"Yes."

"Dr Kahlil Hammud, on the second floor, is a professor of Arabic Studies from the University of Durham in the UK, but he has an American passport. Mr Adam Russell, of London, who is on the fourth floor and looks Arabic, lists his profession as greengrocer and speaks with an uneducated accent. He is nineteen years old and, although he has a British passport, he was born in Beirut. Finally a Mademoiselle Alicia Kent of New York, who lists no occupation, but is so well dressed one can only assume she is of independent means. Her room is next to yours off the garden."

"No dowagers?"

René laughed, sharing the joke. Mediterranean resorts were infested with wealthy dowagers. "No, not today." Then he became serious again. "I have faxed this list to Detective Superintendent Ketcham, and noted that you would ring him."

"Thank you, René. You're very efficient. What's your impression of tonight's guests?"

"There is no one who stands out except perhaps Mr Adam Russell. He arouses my interest not only because of his Arabic heritage but also his age, accent and profession and because he is anxious and trying so hard to be unnoticed. He tips on the toes. I do not know why he came here. Otherwise the guests are of the type we are accustomed to at the hotel."

Elspeth ran over the list once more and agreed with René's assessment of the guests, although Pericles had to be hidden somewhere among them. "May I use your conference room to call Detective Superintendent Ketcham?"

"It is ready for you. The line on the white phone is secure."

Elspeth went into the small room, and settled in one of the uncomfortable-looking comfortable chairs that matched the ones in René's office. As her call was put through to London, she thought of Richard Munro, now the British high commissioner to Malta.

In the five years she had worked for the Kennington Organisation, she had lost all touch with him as she felt he might disapprove of her divorce from her husband in California and her taking up the full-time pursuit of bringing the few miscreants at the Kennington hotels to justice.

Originally he had appeared in her life in the tow of her cousin, Johnnie, the current Earl of Tay. Johnnie had invited Richard to the rambling farm on Loch Tay, from whose name Elspeth's many-times-great-grandfather had taken the title of Tay for his earldom, which was granted when the Hanoverians defeated the Jacobites in the mid-eighteenth century. Elspeth hated the title, her loyalty always being with the brave soldiers fighting for the freedom of the clans, but Johnnie was a favourite cousin and she forgave him for not renouncing his birthright, as if it had been possible. Approaching her sixteenth birthday, she was seldom involved with anything but her romps on the braes and along the burns surrounding her home beside Loch Rannoch and her studies at Blair School for Girls. She had set her sights on Girton College at the University of Cambridge and spent much of her time with her books.

Elspeth looked back with amusement at the image she must have presented to Richard the first time they met. Her father had dropped her at Kenmore at the bottom of Loch Tay that morning, and she had hiked several miles to Tay Farm on the south side of the loch, her family's two black labs bounding ahead of her. She still remembered that she wore a hand-me-down kilt and a moth-eaten jumper. She expected she had forgotten to comb her hair that morning. Her concern for her appearance had only come when her Aunt Magdelena took her to Paris the summer before she entered Girton, and paid a French countess to teach Elspeth the arts of deportment and dressing with classic French style. Before that, she, Johnnie and Richard had driven around in an old Austin mini, played cards well into the night and regaled each other with the most preposterous tales. Then Richard took his degree at Oxford and joined the Foreign and Commonwealth Office, and Elspeth entered Girton and fell in love with Malcolm Buchanan.

Malcolm had awakened in Elspeth her sense of being a woman, of feeling passion and of loving life and Malcolm equally. They had spent five months in that halcyon world where nothing matters but the person you are with. Then on the night of their engagement, he had been shot to death outside the walls of Girton College. Richard had come to her the day after the murder and had escorted her to her home in Scotland. For that she had always kept a special place for him in her heart. But Richard's gentle care and concern and even his shy attempts at telling her that he loved her could not bring Malcolm back.

Tony Ketcham's voice on the other end of the line broke her reverie. As she greeted him, Elspeth pulled the list of registered guests out of its folder and ran her eye down it. She suspected Tony might be doing the same thing.

"Do you see any difficulties with our guests from your end?" she asked.

"It sounds as if most of them are regulars or well-spoken for and probably above suspicion. These days we are always wary of people with Middle Eastern backgrounds although we can leave no one out. You have two guests with Arabic connections, and of course we will investigate them further. I will contact Interpol about Gianni Lugano, although I suspect that the reason for his visit is romantic in nature." Tony's voice changed and he chuckled. "We will of course check Alicia Kent of New York, but she hardly seems the terrorist sort. She probably is a rich girl recovering from a failed romance."

Elspeth bit her lower lip. "Hardly illuminating, is it? Perhaps Pericles, Saieda and Phoenician chose the Kennington Valletta because we are so sedate, a quiet place for them to do their dirty work under the guise of respectability. Tony, in London you mentioned that Scotland Yard has assigned a detective inspector here. Has he arrived in Valletta?"

"Yes. DI Evan Davies-Jones. He's in residence a few metres down from the hotel in a safe house on Triq San Pawl, Saint Paul Street."

"I know the street," Elspeth said.

"I'm also making arrangements for the high commissioner to introduce you to the rest of the team in our investigation. I set up an appointment for you to meet Sir Richard at the British high commission in Ta'Xbiex at ten tomorrow morning. He'll introduce you to the Interpol undercover agent from Lyon who has been assigned to cover this case and is also finding a way for you both to meet DI Davies-Jones."

"That's excellent. Tony, why didn't you tell me Richard Munro was high commissioner here?"

"I thought you would be surprised. He said you have remained friends."

Next, Elspeth rang the number Tony had given her for Richard Munro at the high commission. He had not yet left for the evening and answered the phone formally.

"It's delightful to hear from you, Elspeth. How long has it been since I have seen you? Seven years or more? I've been expecting your call. Tony Ketcham told me that Lord Kennington was sending you to Valletta. How Lord

Kennington must hate all this. Terrorism is not the sort of thing one expects at a Kennington hotel, unlike your usual hotel thieves and that sort of thing."

Elspeth suppressed a smile. "Eric Kennington would not be pleased if he heard you imply that we have our usual thieves. But, yes, you are right, he does dislike any disruption to the perceived perfection of his guests' hotel stay. At the prices he charges, that doesn't seem unreasonable."

Richard laughed. His baritone voice was richer and deeper now than it had been in his youth, and it still held a sense of great gravitas. "Elspeth, we have an official appointment at ten in the morning. Come earlier and share breakfast and news of you. I'm staying at the home of one of Marjorie's cousins in Sliema. The house has a lovely fourth floor terrace garden open to the Mediterranean, and is sufficiently protected from the wind to be comfortable in the mornings. I promise a good cup of very special tea sent to me from Sri Lanka."

They set the time and she rang off. Dear Dickie, she thought. He never seemed to change. In his mind the colonies still existed but as a sort of Eden where one could feel the security of the British Empire as it was a hundred years ago. His wife, Lady Marjorie, had always enhanced the vision. Elspeth wondered how Richard was coping now that Marjorie was dead.

René was waiting for Elspeth as she emerged from the conference room.

"It should be a quiet night here tonight. The Smithsonian tour is having their meal on a harbour cruise, the Dumonts have gone to see their children and the Misses Knoll and Fanshaw have retired to their room for dinner. I don't know the plans of the other guests, but many have left the hotel already."

Elspeth welcomed this calm. It might be her last. "Conan FitzRoy has asked me to join him for dinner," she said. "I suppose I ought to go, although a cup of broth, some chewy Maltese bread, cheese and fruit in my room sounds more appealing."

"As usual, Giuseppe is preparing sea bass for Mr FitzRoy, and a delicate lemon torte that is his new *specialité*. You will not be disappointed," René said.

"I expect I won't be."

"Pietru sent me a message that Mr FitzRoy will be in the bar before dinner and has asked you to join him."

Elspeth sighed from both fatigue and a sense of duty.

5

Conan FitzRoy loved to talk, particularly to women. He admired women as much for their intelligence as for their beauty. Age didn't matter; brains did. When he could, he surrounded himself with women. If no attractive one were available, he would sit quietly by himself in a public setting, cross his hands across the expanse of his stomach and grin. His eyes sometimes offered a welcoming invitation. At other times he simply half-closed his eyes and waited for suitable prey. Tonight was no exception.

FitzRoy, sitting in the bar facing the interior courtyard, watched the young woman he had seen earlier enter the garden as the sun was setting. In the glowing light she looked ravishing. The red sequins of her evening jacket picked up the final rays of the sun that found their way through the garden, and small flecks of light showered her face with a spray of sparkling red reflections.

Effulgent, thought FitzRoy. He loved obscure words and this one perfectly described her. He invited her to sit next to him, and she, no doubt seeing a large and probably harmless older man, accepted with amusement.

FitzRoy liked being the centre of attention, and when he enticed the young woman to his side, he nodded to her as a king would to a courtier.

He could talk for hours and often did. He knew what he said was clever and well-informed. Often his ideas were outrageous but they were never dull. If a hostess thought her party might lag, she invited FitzRoy, ordered three more bottles of good wine and knew her success was assured.

*

By the time Elspeth entered the bar, Conan and Alicia Kent were in the midst of a spirited conversation. As Elspeth approached, they were discussing the influence of the Phoenicians on the explorers of the fifteenth century, an apt conversation for visitors to Malta.

Elspeth accepted a glass of white Bordeaux that she knew came from the private stock FitzRoy kept at the hotel. She savoured its coolness and complexity. Conan introduced her to Alicia, but Alicia was fully engaged in her conversation with Conan and gave Elspeth only a slight nod. Elspeth decided to sit back and enjoy the repartee without getting involved. She soon realised that Alicia was a woman of hidden intelligence, who responded to FitzRoy with exuberance. During any conversation with FitzRoy, however, no one could stay quiet for long. He would say the most outlandish things as bait. Soon the three of them had progressed from the topic of world trade in the ancient world to the requirements imposed on Malta for entrance into the European Union. When the waiter came to tell FitzRoy that his table in the dining room was ready, they were debating the effects of capitalism and the role of the Mafia in the former Soviet republics.

Elspeth would have liked to excuse herself and retire to her room but she could not let go of the last remark FitzRoy had made, that the Russian Mafia was better than the threat of the gulag. She knew she would not sleep well because she would be thinking of a stinging but brilliant reply. Better to take him on now than lose the momentum of the conversation or the precision of her retort. FitzRoy had trapped her and she knew it. Elspeth tacitly admired FitzRoy's skill. He gleamed with possessiveness.

*

The Kennington Valletta's dining room was on the top floor and overlooked the harbour and the city. FitzRoy escorted his guests from the bar to the lifts on the ground floor. Elspeth, by courtesy, took the lead. She joined arms with FitzRoy and entered the lift with anticipation of the conversation to come. The dining room at the Kennington Valletta always delighted Conan FitzRoy. It was ornate, almost gaudily adorned, and recreated an atmosphere that recalled the greatness of the knights of Malta. The lights in the cut glass chandeliers were dimmed as the last stages of twilight filled the floor-to-ceiling windows to the south and west. The harbour now lay calm below. FitzRoy could see the brightly lit deck on a cruise ship and the occasional running lights of passing small craft. The vehicular traffic below had died down so that only a few headlights and taillights traversed the square at the front of the hotel and streets leading down and out of Valletta.

FitzRoy escorted his guests to a corner table that was always reserved for him when he was in residence. He lowered his bulk into a gilt chair from another era. Two waiters, dressed in formal evening dress, drew back similar chairs for Alicia and Elspeth.

He breathed a sigh of contentment. "This is one of my most cherished moments each year," he said. "And this year I'm doubly blessed by the company of two beautiful ladies to share dinner with me."

Happiness filled him.

FitzRoy liked a production made of his meals. Therefore, before he had dressed for the evening, he had gone to the kitchen to confer with Giuseppe to make sure all arrangements for the dinner were just as he wanted.

This year Giuseppe informed FitzRoy that he had chosen a first course of Bosc pears imported from France that he had found in the market early that morning. Slices of pear would be overlaid with braised walnuts, Gorgonzola cheese and a raspberry vinaigrette sauce. Next would come a partridge terrine inserted into the lightest of pastry crusts.

FitzRoy was delighted when these delicacies arrived at the table, and were served by the waiters, one for each diner. But the triumph of the meal came when Giuseppe flung open the doors of the kitchen and held aloft a silver platter carrying the sea bass à la FitzRoy. The waiters followed with heated plates, serving trays and carefully chosen bottles of wine. FitzRoy smiled benevolently and Alicia and Elspeth made appreciative remarks.

FitzRoy knew that the fish had been caught that morning, and kept alive until the moment of preparation. Giuseppe assured FitzRoy earlier that the ingredients for the sauce followed his secret recipe exactly, and the preparation of the courgettes, aubergines, green and yellow beans and tomatoes, would be under his personal supervision. The resultant aroma evoked the exoticism of Arabic cooking, the freshness of Maltese vegetables, Mediterranean fish and the pungency of Sicilian oils.

Giuseppe personally arranged the plates for FitzRoy and his guests. Each item was put in its precise place, and the food was steaming hot. The wine was poured as the fish was served.

"Please, eat. *Mangiate*," Giuseppe commanded.

Their initial bites were taken in reverent silence. Giuseppe bowed regally before returning to the kitchen, and FitzRoy thought he would add more to his usual high gratuity.

"Have you guessed what makes this sea bass so incredibly delicious?" FitzRoy challenged his guests. Neither Elspeth nor Loren could answer. FitzRoy laughed. "Nor have I, except for the garlic. Giuseppe has promised to leave the recipe to me in his will, and at that time will give me permission to publish it. He assures me no one will be able to prepare it as he does, which is probably true."

*

As the meal progressed, Elspeth watched the other diners carefully. In the section of the restaurant reserved for hotel guests, Gianni Lugano occupied a secluded table, and was attacking an antipasto with gusto. The blonde woman with him looked bored, and was picking at her food. At a table by the window, Mr and Mrs Davenport were speaking softly to each other. And in the middle of the space a young Arabic-looking man sat uncomfortably by himself. Elspeth had not seen him before but he was certainly Adam Russell.

Gianni Lugano and 'wife' took little notice of what was happening around them. The Davenports seemed quietly amused, obviously having seen this FitzRoy ritual during their previous visits to the hotel. Elspeth wondered what Adam Russell was thinking. He sat and ate his roast chicken, his fork and knife grasped in an upward position and his eyes lowered to his plate, but his ears seemed to pick up on all that was going on around him. His troubled look made Elspeth curious.

Elspeth turned her attention back to her dinner companions. She marvelled at Conan FitzRoy. The more he ate and drank the more florid his speech and ideas became. Soon he was expostulating on the wonders of the islands of Malta and its people, the excellence of their cuisine and the nobility of their oenology.

*

FitzRoy had not made his mark with London literary hostesses without being sensitive to lack of attention. Perhaps he was going on too long, he thought.

"Alicia, my dear," he said, changing his focus from the food and himself to his young guest, whose mind seemed to be wandering, "I have a brilliant suggestion. Tomorrow you will accompany me on my annual visit to one of my dearest friends in Malta who owns my favourite vineyard on the island. Our trip there will be along the historic roads that have crossed this island for many thousands of years. You can't match that longevity in America, can you? Even in the British Isles, we find Malta's history most august. I suggest we leave at noon, as we will be fêted at the vineyard and undoubtedly offered lunch."

Alicia paused and finally smiled. "I'd love to go," she said.

FitzRoy was pleased. "My niece has set up the appointment for me, and I confirmed it shortly after I arrived. Elspeth, although you are invited too, I know you'll be immersed in hotel business, since you probably wouldn't be here if that were not the case. I don't envy you your job. Here we are in one of the most delightful places on earth, and you must work!"

Elspeth nodded graciously. "I don't find that a tragedy, Conan, when one of the benefits of my job is that I'm able to share delightful times such as these with you and Alicia."

"Ah, yes, I represent decadent decay and she the freshness of youth. What a perfect combination. I must include that in my next book."

"I read your book before coming here," said Alicia. "For Americans, Malta is a bit of an unknown. I had no idea that this was such an embattled fortress during World War Two."

FitzRoy lifted his glass and saluted one of the Grand Masters of the Knights of St. John whose portrait was on the wall near at hand. "The resistance to the Axis siege here exemplifies the bravest and most courageous actions of humankind. My first visit here was in nineteen seventy-five, but even then there were hundreds of people who told stories of tenacity that you would not believe. The Maltese are an old people. As with people who have so much history, they believe in their own destiny. There are fire and dignity in the Maltese. One must admire an island group this small, which has been overrun by almost every Mediterranean power, Phoenicians, Greeks, Romans,

Arabs, Spanish, French and finally British, and who have not only survived but kept their own language and culture."

Alicia cocked an eyebrow and challenged FitzRoy. He loved it. "Do you do all your own research?" she asked.

"Not all, no. I leave delving into the dusty tombs to a group of doctoral students at Cambridge, who delight in meagre pay to pull the plums from the ashes. What is more I have an adoring secretary in London, who ensures the accuracy of modern-day things. Still I always interview the important sources myself. You cannot get the essence of how people feel or react if you do not talk to them individually. The three months I spent here in Malta talking to the survivors of nineteen forty-two gave me more of the feeling of the times than any amount of research. That is when I came to love Malta, and why I come back every year."

Elspeth broke in. "And what are you working on now, Conan? Malta's struggles from colonialism to its accession into the EU?"

"Ah, no. Malta, I think, has come to terms with itself, despite its local politics. No author of historical fiction can ignore the bigger struggle today—radical Islamic terrorism. Of course, terrorism has always existed and always will, but we focus more attention on it now. No terrorists before have brought down two major skyscrapers nor has so much money been spent in hunting them down. My latest idea is to penetrate the mind of people who finance this terrorism. We can try to understand the fanaticism of the terrorists themselves, but one would think the financiers would be more level-headed. Apparently this is not so."

He took the last bite of his fish and continued. "I come from Northern Ireland, where terrorism is a way of life. Irish ultra-nationalists are caught up in it. There is generational memory that for them is consuming to a point of irrationality. Force or bombs cannot negate it, only re-education can. I think terrorists are neither intellectually focused nor inclined to alter their viewpoint, and they always seem to be able to find people who are willing to finance their dreams."

FitzRoy felt he had a captive audience. Alicia seemed spellbound and Elspeth, as always, looked amused.

"And so my next effort is going to be about the history of money and extreme Islamic terrorism. We all have read about the way Al Qaeda uses a financial network without banks. My ideas are still preliminary. I have just begun my research in earnest."

FitzRoy took a deep breath and crossed his hands across his stomach. He spotted the waiters coming from the kitchen, each bearing a plate of Giuseppe's new lemon confection. The tart but sugary flavour was a perfect antidote to the succulence of the fish, and gave FitzRoy a chance to send his compliments to the chef.

"And now," said FitzRoy, "let's arrange for our excursion tomorrow. I'm to be at the vineyard at one in the afternoon. Shall we meet in the lobby, Alicia? Is twelve still agreeable to you?"

"Yes, that's fine. I'm meeting someone at ten, but I'm sure I'll be back by twelve," Alicia said.

*

When Elspeth returned to her room after dinner, she checked her email to see if any other information had come in from London. A message just in from Pamela Crumm asked Elspeth to contact Lord Kennington first thing in the morning. Pamela was, as always, working late. An email from Detective Superintendent Tony Ketcham said he had his staff pursuing the leads they had talked about earlier. He reiterated that the high commissioner would have more information for her in the morning, which would be conveyed over encrypted diplomatic channels.

The climate in Malta in the spring is almost perfect. It reminded Elspeth of the twenty-plus years she had lived in California. Before retiring, she stepped out of her room into the enclosed garden and looked up at the crescent moon. A star, or perhaps the planet Venus, shone brightly nearby. The scent of jasmine, lemon blossoms and boxwood abounded. It seemed impossible that there was terror in the world and that it had invaded this hotel. The garden was designed to make one forget, but Elspeth could not.

Who was Adam Russell? He was obviously Arabic but with an English name and working class accent. Dr Hammud? Was he originally from the Near East? Alicia Kent? Was she just a charming, rich young woman or something else? Tony Ketcham said he could not trace her. Had Elspeth dismissed the group from the Smithsonian out of hand? Was there someone in that group who might be Pericles? Gianni Lugano hardly seemed dangerous, nor did his lady friend. Then there was Sir William Gaunt, with his own security detachment. Was his presence the greatest threat? Unable to still her thoughts, she turned from the garden and entered her room.

The infusion of cool sea air through her window promised the freshness of the next day, yet fatigue overtook her after the events of the last thirty-six hours. She slept fitfully. She dreamed that all the people in the hotel came to breakfast with masks held up to their faces. One person lowered his mask so that he could eat. He had no face. His head was like one in a De Chirico painting or one on a milliner's form. Suddenly everyone lowered their masks and they too had no faces. Too much rich food, said Elspeth's practical Scottish mind, and too much of a tendency not to let go of her work after retiring to bed. Elspeth rang room service for a cup of cocoa and finally settled into a dreamless sleep at three a.m.

6

The Honourable Sir Richard Alexander Hamish Munro, Knight Commander of the Order of St. Michael and St. George, Her Majesty Queen Elizabeth's High Commissioner to the Republic of Malta, was waiting for Elspeth when she arrived at his quarters near St. Julian's Point. He felt an uplifting sense of anticipation that for the last thirty-eight years had always come over him when he knew he would see Elspeth.

He watched from the fourth floor as Elspeth paid the taxi driver and came up the stairs of the house. She looked at the piece of paper in her hand, and seemed to be checking to see if she had the right address. The house, he knew, looked almost abandoned among the newer buildings that lined Triq It-Torri and the Mediterranean seafront beyond. The peeling pink paint on the building's Rococo façade suggested dereliction, and the broken shutters hanging crookedly on its barred windows shouted neglect. All this hid the many treasures inside. Elspeth looked at the number again, shook her head and pressed the doorbell, which hung haphazardly out from the wall.

Now that the moment had come, he took a deep breath and wondered again what he should say or if he should tell her how he felt. He had loved her from the first time he had seen her when she was approaching sixteen. She was a lanky, unkempt, devilish young woman, who had a swift wit and keen intelligence and seemed not to care about him other than he was a diverting friend of her cousin, Johnnie.

Then she went to Girton College and fell in love with Malcolm Buchanan, whom Richard considered totally unfit for Elspeth's affections, and whose family was unknown to anyone in Richard's acquaintance. But he knew Elspeth's love was genuine, and after Malcolm was murdered Richard could see the devastating effect on Elspeth. She had buried herself in her books, finished a law tripos and left Cambridge with a first. Richard assumed Elspeth would return to Perthshire, as she always said she would, to enter her father's law practice. Instead she joined Scotland Yard to pursue a career in righting criminal wrongdoings.

Richard had made overtures to her about deepening their relationship but knew his suit was hopeless. So he had married Lady Marjorie Staunton, daughter of the Earl of Glenborough, who had been the British high commissioner to India when Marjorie was growing up. Their marriage was celebrated at St. Margaret's Church, Westminster, with minor royalty attending. Richard's family was of the aristocracy but he was a second son. The Glenboroughs were clear that they considered the match acceptable but not brilliant for their youngest daughter. She was approaching her thirtieth year so they did not object. Wags in the Foreign and Commonwealth Office whispered that Richard had advanced more quickly in the diplomatic service than some others because of his marriage.

Shortly before Richard's wedding, Elspeth had impetuously run off to Hollywood with Alistair Craig, a lowland Scot of little breeding who was said to be extraordinarily talented and was making a name for himself as one of the best coaches in swordsmanship and gun fighting in the film industry. Elspeth and Alistair had met when he was directing a gun battle filmed on Tower Bridge in London and needed Scotland Yard to step in to avert the crowds. Richard had been horrified when she eloped four weeks later.

He knew that Elspeth had changed over the years. The tragedy of Malcolm Buchanan's murder had sobered her, and her years married to Alistair in Southern California had matured and softened her. He had always been puzzled at what Elspeth found in these two men. He thought both of them to be egocentric and self-absorbed, certainly not worthy of Elspeth's intelligence or radiance. As a young man, Richard could not have fathomed Elspeth's metamorphosis. He had imagined her at middle age with a brood of boys, perhaps his and hers, all just down from Fettes, Eton, or Oxbridge, tumbling all over each other. She would be living in a large rambling house on a loch in the Highlands, with dogs and horses and fêtes and good works to attend to. Instead she had raised two children in the shadow of her husband's Hollywood career, divorced him five years ago and taken up a high-pressure career with the Kennington Organisation.

What odd twists and turns life allotted to each person. Every one of Richard's old friends had found ways to lead lives that their childhood personae would have found unimaginable, Elspeth's chosen path being the most unexpected of all.

Over the years, Richard and Marjorie exchanged Christmas cards with Elspeth and Alistair, and whenever

Richard and Marjorie passed through Los Angeles, perhaps once every three or four years, they would have tea or dinner together. Often Alistair was on set or off working at some distant location, and then only the three of them would meet. Each time Elspeth seemed to arrange things so that she was never alone with Richard. Richard wondered why. As the years passed, Richard began to feel concern for Elspeth who he suspected was finding her arrangement with Alistair less than she had hoped for. But what could he say to her and when?

Everyone said his marriage to Marjorie had everything a career man could ask for, a wife who fit perfectly into the diplomatic community, provided him with close companionship and never gave him cause to worry or doubt her. They had sustained thirty years of marriage in a comfortable but chaste relationship that had ended when she had died the year before. But through it all he had always loved Elspeth.

He had not seen Elspeth since her divorce. The Christmas cards had ceased. Hearing Elspeth and Alistair had gone separate ways, Marjorie assured him it was inappropriate to contact Elspeth until she indicated that she wished to stay in touch. Richard learned Elspeth worked for the Kennington hotel chain only when he had met her cousin Johnnie three years previously in Edinburgh. Elspeth sent him a note of condolence when Marjorie died, which was addressed to him at the Foreign and Commonwealth Office in London but gave no return address. She enclosed an inner envelope marked personal, although in the current world climate the FCO security office had opened it. Inside her salutation was 'My dear

Dickie' and in closing she had penned 'As ever'. The note was warm but slightly impersonal. But even in his sorrow over Marjorie's death, he traced his finger slowly and lovingly over Elspeth's signature, which she always wrote boldly. Until Detective Superintendent Ketcham rang him from London the Thursday before, he heard no more from her. He had considered writing to her at the Kennington Organisation, but he did not know how to approach her, suspecting that if she wanted to hear from him she would have put a return address on her letter.

Now as he watched Elspeth puzzle over the address and the appearance of the door below, his heart filled with what he had felt for her all these years. Richard Munro, he thought in mock introduction, you who always took the safest possible road, it is my pleasure to present Elspeth Duff, the impetuous, unpredictable woman who you have never been able to get out of your heart.

He had instructed the housekeeper to bring Elspeth to the fourth floor terrace. He waited, staring out to the sea as he heard the rickety Art Deco lift make its way up to the terrace. Would she look older? Women at her point in life did begin to show their age. Certainly Marjorie had, but by then the cancer had already begun.

The gates drew open, and he turned and saw her standing there, looking about, slightly disoriented by the sun off the sea and the jumble of furniture on the terrace. His heart thumped. She had become handsome.

Then she saw him and a smile covered her face. Richard watched with nostalgia as Elspeth approached him. He saw her the way she had been when he had first seen her at fifteen, striding across the hills with two black labs chasing around her. She had arrived breathlessly at the spot where he had been standing, poured out a line from Shakespeare, and explained she was memorising lines for a play that her mother was directing at her school. In those days Elspeth brought a spirit of freshness into his life that he could not find in the drawing rooms in London or at his college at Oxford. She had a vitality and beauty that cold, damp air brings to those who shun the hearth for the rigours of the wind and the mist of the moors.

His reverie was broken when she said, "Dickie, how are you?"

Her delight at seeing him was obviously real. She crossed the terrace, hands extended towards his. As she came closer, he saw her eyes, always disturbingly dark cobalt blue, and felt the intense complexity in them. She greeted him with a slight shyness he did not understand and only the smallest hint of sadness that had been there since Malcolm Buchanan had died. She was dressed to perfection in a stylish business suit and moved with worldly grace, but he only saw the girl with whom he had first fallen in love. He took her hands and smiled back into her eyes.

"So we meet again," he said. "It has been too long."

*

After looking for a long time at Richard—his tall, slender stature, short cut hair, greying at the temples, and long, thin face—Elspeth finally lowered her eyes and withdrew her hands.

"I haven't stayed in touch, have I?" she said. Despite her anticipation at seeing him, she suddenly felt awkward in his presence. "I am sorry about Marjorie. I wrote to you. I hope you got the letter."

"Yes," he said. "Thank you. The FCO passed it on."

She smiled and swallowed. "Well then, Dickie, here we are thrown together after all this time."

"Yes," he said, but she could not read his thoughts.

"I haven't been in touch because I thought you would disapprove once again," she blurted out, which were not the words she had intended to say. Richard's disdain for her life choices had always unsettled her.

"Disapprove?" He looked puzzled.

"About my leaving Alistair. Divorce. That sort of thing. But it was the right thing, although it was hard on Peter and Elizabeth. Children always care, even if they are adults. They both have their own lives now, so it was time for me to have mine." She thought she had said it badly, but wanted to tell him what she was feeling if they were to work together over the next few days.

"Yes, of course," he said, his voice stiff.

"I shouldn't have brought it up, should I? I never quite do it right for you, do I?"

She meant her voice to be light hearted but it was not. She remembered how reproachful he had been when she had told him about loving Malcolm and how shocked he was when she had eloped with Alistair.

"I was perhaps too severe when we were younger," he said.

"You've always set too high a standard for me, Dickie," Elspeth said, "as if I were more than a mere mortal. But in the last five years I've pulled my life together, and needed to do it my own way without admonishment from anyone. But come, this is getting us nowhere. Since we seem to be involved over the next week in this terrorist thing, we should be friends again. Let's have some breakfast. It looks marvellous."

Breakfast was laid out on a tea trolley, from which they served themselves. Elspeth took a large slab of Maltese bread, buttered it ferociously and laid a thick layer of marmalade on it. She accepted a cup of tea although she had already drunk two cups of strong black coffee at the hotel.

The tension of their greeting passed.

"I came to Malta after Marjorie died because I needed to forget the slow agony of her last months," he said as they settled into their breakfast. "Some said I was being put out to pasture, that the posting was less important than my previous ones, but I needed a place to put my life back together. It was I who requested a small and quiet place like Malta. I needed somewhere to come to face being alone and find some peace with that."

"But I've now come with my threats of terrorism and mayhem. I've been known to bring things like this into your life before, haven't I. The mayhem, I mean."

"At least you have made my life a bit more interesting. You always have," he said, laughing.

They ate and retold old memories and in the process Elspeth relaxed.

"You must wonder at this place," he said.

"I do," she said, looking around the terrace.

"Hardly a conventional house for the high commissioner's residence, but I make do while the official residence is being redecorated. Come downstairs and see."

He led Elspeth into the treasure box of the house below, brimming with ornate objects of every international style.

"Marjorie's cousin," Richard explained, "was a world traveller and collector who kept the exterior of his home in a state of shabby disrepair in order to discourage would-be thieves. I'm sure you saw the high modern towers on each side."

She nodded.

"Having bought his home shortly after the Second World War, he refused to concede to the intrusion of contemporary life in Malta. He filled his home with a clutter of beautiful things, as you can see."

After showing her the rooms below, he finally said, "But we must move on. The car is waiting downstairs."

"I've enjoyed myself immensely," she said.

He touched his hand to her cheek. "Let's not let this current problem keep us from doing this again."

"No, let's not," she said, flattered by his tender gesture and relieved that she had been courageous enough to be honest with him.

7

As they left the building, Elspeth watched Richard's posture straighten, as if he was assuming his official role. He guided her out to the narrow pavement and between two tightly packed cars, and helped her into the waiting car. After they were seated, he turned to business.

"In London Tony Ketcham undoubtedly told you about the Interpol agent they are sending out," he said formally.

"He did mention it but didn't give me any details. He said you would," Elspeth responded in a professional tone as if nothing had happened between them earlier.

"She'll be arriving in Ta'Xbiex almost immediately. So shall we proceed to that pompous office of mine?"

Elspeth caught the edge of a smile on his face but did not respond.

The official car, an ageing black Rover saloon car, wound through the narrow streets of Sliema, which eventually opened out to Triq Marina. They proceeded down the edge of the waterfront, and finally arrived at the imposing five-story British High Commission building. It overlooked hundreds of boats docked at a marina busy with weekend sailors. Richard and Elspeth entered through a back entry and took a private lift up to the top floor where the high commissioner's office was located.

As Richard escorted Elspeth into his office, she

looked up curiously, seeing why he had described his office as pompous. Indeed, the office bore all the trappings of past imperial might. Despite the modernity of the recent renovation of the building, his official space had high, coffered ceilings, Victorian paintings depicting unnamed battles and heavily carved furniture all jumbled together in homage to the past greatness of the British Empire. The only nod to the twenty-first century was the computer that occupied a corner of his desk. Not sure if the interior decoration was Richard's idea or something he had inherited from a predecessor, she said politely, "So this is where you spend your days."

Richard rang for his personal assistant Margaret, a fusty, grey-haired woman in an unfashionable frock, who bustled into the room as if glad to be occupied on a Sunday. Elspeth considered that Margaret could not be much older than she but what a different life Margaret must have had from her own. She was glad when Richard introduced her simply as "Elspeth Duff from the Kennington Valletta hotel."

Margaret simpered, "There's someone waiting for you in my office."

"Please show her in, Margaret."

As they waited for their guest, Richard took a seat behind the ornate mahogany desk and said, "Her name is Loren Axt. You will know her."

Elspeth frowned. "I don't think so."

"I understand that you and Conan FitzRoy had dinner with her yesterday evening. Of course, she was using a different name."

As Loren came in the room, Elspeth was aware that

Alicia Kent of the evening before was an able actress. Loren walked with a confidence that Elspeth had not seen the night before. Loren half winked at the high commissioner and gave Elspeth a mischievous grin.

"Did I pass the test, Ms Duff?" Her trans-Atlantic accent was less broad than the one she had affected at dinner. Elspeth assumed that Loren had been in Europe a long time as she spoke with the soft voice American expatriates often acquired when living abroad.

"With highest marks," laughed Elspeth. She had found Alicia witty but lightweight. Loren Axt gave off an impression of competence and efficiency.

As they settled around the high commissioner's pretentious desk, Loren explained, "There's an advantage I have found working undercover. An unattached twenty-something woman isn't taken seriously. Men tend to flirt and preen. Older women are dismissive and secretly jealous. You can sit and listen to conversations while others don't think you are capable of being interested. Men will tell you things to impress you without realising that they may be revealing more than is appropriate. No one remembers to be discreet. That's an incredible asset for someone who does listen and has a good memory."

Elspeth recalled her early days at Scotland Yard and acknowledged the truth in what Loren had said.

Richard turned to Elspeth and arched his eyebrows. "London has told me not to cross Ms Axt. Reportedly she's an excellent marksman, has a brown belt in judo and can speak five languages, as well as a smattering of Arabic and Italian. I think we're absolutely delighted to have her on our side."

"Of course." Elspeth turned to Loren, admiringly. "I was in doubt, I must admit, when Detective Superintendent Ketcham told me Alicia Kent was untraceable. I already had put you at the top of my suspect list."

Loren laughed, seemingly pleased at her deception. "I did fool you!"

"You did indeed," Elspeth said.

"Good, my assignment is to blend in so that I can be watchful. If I fooled you, I can fool anyone."

Elspeth smiled in amusement, and then turned to business. "When I met Detective Superintendent Ketcham in London, he mentioned an undercover branch of the Public Safety and Terrorism Sub-Directorate of Interpol. You must work for that forbidding-sounding organisation. Perhaps you can fill me in more completely. I'm still a bit puzzled as to why both you and the Yard have become involved in what on the surface would seem a benign exchange at the Kennington Valletta."

"Have you ever heard the expression 'Need to Know'?" Loren asked.

Elspeth nodded. "One only is told what one needs to know in case one is captured and tortured."

Loren seemed amused at the direness of Elspeth's description. "Ms Duff—Elspeth—I think we both are currently circumscribed by a need to know, whether or not we will be tortured. My handler, yes I have one, has given me the bare facts, but I presume we're mixed up in something much bigger than the email they showed us. Our roles may be small but I expect vital."

"Why is Interpol involved?" Elspeth asked.

"Sir Richard can tell you more, perhaps. The Maltese

government, of course, knows I'm here."

"Richard?"

"Interpol cannot act on its own, only with permission of a host government, but since the Kennington Organisation, a British enterprise, is most threatened, the Maltese Commonwealth and Foreign Office has asked for my intervention," he said, and added, "rather as a favour to them."

"Are you used to operating this way?" Elspeth asked Loren.

"Under cover? All the time. It keeps life from being dull."

"What an interesting life you must lead!"

"Not always," Loren said with a twisted smile. "Some of my assignments have bordered on tedium and necessitated extremely unpleasant living conditions. My job usually is to extract as much information as I can while staying unsuspected. I have scars from bedbug bites to attest to my tenacity."

"This assignment must be a relief then. At least you must find your accommodations comfortable with no bedbugs allowed," Elspeth said, instantly liking Loren.

"They are magnificent—my accommodations, not the bugs. Not the usual venue for terrorist activity, believe me."

Elspeth watched Loren as she spoke, and wondered why a young American woman would have chosen the lifestyle she had just described. Loren had the kind of beauty that many healthy and athletically fit young women had nowadays, leanness in her face and figure which accentuated a strong bone structure and muscular tautness.

Her trendy haircut, expertly applied makeup and fashionably cut clothes accentuated her attractiveness. What motivated Loren to be involved in such deadly work?

Richard cleared his throat and interrupted the two women. "The detective superintendent has asked me to make certain arrangements to connect all the players who will be working together this week. Ms Axt, or rather 'Alicia Kent', would not usually make contact with a Scotland Yard detective inspector seconded to the Maltese police. I'm to make that possible. Detective Inspector Evan Davies-Jones from Scotland Yard flew in day before yesterday, ostensibly as a liaison with the Valletta police force. Actually DI Davies-Jones is a member of Tony Ketcham's team, and has been asked to keep close contact with you, Elspeth, as a member of the Kennington Organisation security staff, and you, Ms Axt, representing Interpol."

"Richard," Elspeth said, still puzzled, "can you shed any more light on why Scotland Yard is so concerned with this intercepted email? In London Tony mentioned that he thought the situation serious, but how can an exchange at the hotel set off such a drastic reaction? Under normal circumstances wouldn't all of this go unnoticed? In the hotel business we turn a blind eye to a great deal that happens under our roofs. Unless the security or wellbeing of the guests is impacted, we assume a very laissez-faire attitude."

"My assumption is that the email is part of a major operation and we are small pawns in it," he said.

"Then tell me, Richard, what do you have in mind as to where we all might meet? At the hotel?"

As she addressed Richard, Elspeth became aware that she had never seen him at work before. He had always been stiffly reserved in her presence when visiting California with Marjorie, but in his own milieu he was relaxed and charming and very much in charge. His eyes caught hers but she could not interpret his expression.

"I understand, Elspeth, that your aunt, Magdelena Cassar, still lives in her farmhouse on Gozo," he said.

She wondered how he knew the connection. She did not remember ever mentioning it to him.

Elspeth replied, "Yes, I visited her there about a year ago on my way back to London from Kenya. She hardly leaves home these days. She's as grand as ever, but her health and eyesight are beginning to fail. She seems to fear going beyond areas where she can get about with familiarity. I phoned her last night after I arrived to tell her I was here, and she begged me to come out to see her."

"Does she still hold soirées at her home on Gozo?" Richard held Elspeth's eyes steadily She suspected he had already planned the nature of the meeting.

"Are you suggesting DI Davies-Jones and Loren could meet by chance at such a gathering? What a good idea." Elspeth did not break his look. "I'll ring her and find out. Aunt Mag will surely be able to dig up a crowd of artistic people who live near her in San Lawrenz. Loren can come as my guest, and she and DI Davies-Jones can meet casually there. Richard, you must have a reason to explain why he should be invited. He is Welsh; does he sing? I'll ask Aunt Mag to invite Conan FitzRoy as well. She and Conan have met several times before." Elspeth's mind flew to the possibilities. "Brilliant, Dickie!" she said forgetting to address him formally.

Loren looked up at Elspeth with a raised eyebrow but said nothing.

Slightly embarrassed, Elspeth picked up her mobile and called her aunt, who had just returned from Sunday Mass. Magdelena Cassar declared that she was free that evening, and she would be overjoyed to see her niece, Sir Richard, whom she had met on several previous occasions, and their friends. Elspeth knew that her aunt would mobilise the Italian couple who took care of her into a frenzy of activity. Finding other guests would present no problem. Elspeth had visited the village of San Lawrenz often enough to know that any social activity by the artistic and literary community there involving Magdelena Cassar was always an event, even on short notice.

Elspeth turned to Loren. "You have a treat coming, believe me. My aunt is one of a kind."

Arrangements made, Loren rose to take her leave. Richard explained he had official functions until half past five that evening but would meet them later in Gozo. His wife's cousin had given him the use of a motor yacht, conveniently docked at the marina across the street, and he could make a fast voyage to Gozo, arriving at the time the other guests were expected. He promised Elspeth and Loren a leisurely sail back to Valletta when the soirée was over.

"Before I leave, may we speak a moment in private, Richard, about this assignment?" Elspeth asked. They were standing in the reception area outside his private office, where they had just said goodbye to Loren.

"Of course, my dear."

Elspeth noted the endearment but let it pass.

Richard spoke to his personal assistant, indicating that he no longer needed her, and led Elspeth into his private office and closed the door.

Elspeth did not sit down, but instead walked over to the window and looked out over the yacht basin below, and then up to the cliffs surrounding Valletta above. She was acutely aware of his standing behind her, so near to her that his body might have touched hers, but it did not. Suddenly she wished in her heart that it had, but then her mind scolded her for her foolishness.

"It's about William Gaunt," she said without mentioning her reaction to his closeness. "Does he pose a danger to the Kennington Valletta? I cannot imagine that Eric Kennington would have agreed to his stay there if a threat existed, but Eric can be optimistic about his staff's ability to handle high profile guests. His attitude has caused me difficulty in the past."

Richard turned away from her and invited her to resume her seat. She chose to stay by the window instead. His face showed no emotion, and Elspeth had no indication that the feeling of a wish for closeness between them that had just passed through her was apparent to him.

"I have known Will Gaunt for years," he said. "We served together in New Zealand, and I always found him quite solid. No worries there. He's rather a 'podgedog'."

Elspeth let the moment at the window go, but she knew something had happened between them. She grinned at his term instead, one they had used in their teenage years, meaning someone who was both pudgy and dogged.

"But how then did he get his title?" she asked.

"Connections in the Labour Party," Richard said with some contempt.

"And Lady Gaunt? Is she a 'podgedog' too?" Elspeth lowered her head and, not blinking, stared at Richard from under her eyebrows, a look she had used many times in their youth.

He laughed, obviously remembering the gesture. "I don't know whether she is or not, although I doubt it," he admitted. "Marjorie and Will's first wife were friends in Wellington. Will's wife died several years ago, and he married again soon afterwards. Although his new wife is much younger than he is, I never heard of any scandal associated with their marriage, despite their age difference. Just the usual thing, his finding someone younger to fill his life." His voice remained noncommittal.

Elspeth wondered if Richard had ever had similar feelings for younger women and felt a small stab of jealousy, although she pushed away the reason for it.

"And the new Lady Gaunt? Could she be involved in the exchange?" Elspeth asked.

Richard shook his head. "I shouldn't think so. Their visit here is so tightly scripted, as official visits always are, that I doubt an occasion would arise. Just between the two of us, she doesn't appear to have the wit to be involved in anything as clandestine as the email would suggest."

Elspeth smiled inwardly at Richard's assessment of his colleague's young wife, but experience had taught her that any member of the human race, intelligent or not, could become entangled in nefarious affairs without knowing so. The Gaunts would bear watching.

"You will be with them over the next few days, Dickie. Let me know if you have any suspicions they are involved, 'podgedog' and trophy bride or not. One never knows."

"Your wish is my command," he said, rising and bowing like an actor in one of the melodramas that Elspeth's mother was fond of producing for the Blair School for Girls. Sometimes, Elspeth remembered, her mother had coerced a reluctant Richard into taking a part in the plays.

They both laughed. Elspeth was glad the tension had passed.

Richard offered his car to Elspeth but she refused. "I'll walk back to Valletta. I need time to think and I won't get it at the hotel." He took her down to street level and past the security guard. Elspeth shook his hand formally and thanked him for breakfast and his help.

Without looking back, she crossed the road and walked along the yacht slips. The morning had turned sunny after an earlier cloudiness and there was only a slight wind off the sea. She rounded the end of the marina and made her way towards Valletta along the deserted pavements.

Elspeth had always loved walking in Malta on Sundays. Everything came to a standstill on the morning of the Sabbath. The streets were empty and shops closed, their wooden or roll-down metal doors secured with large locks. The occasional cars moving along the roads seemed to slow their pace in deference to the day of rest. The few people she passed were either adventurous German or

French tourists or families strolling in the sunshine on their way to church. She heard church bells in the distance.

Trying hard to push any personal feelings for Richard aside, Elspeth thought of her task ahead. The email intercepted by GCHQ nagged at her. Who were the real players? Tony Ketcham had implied that the participants in the exchange had chosen the Kennington Valletta because of its quietness and gentility. Therefore they would probably be guarded in what they did, but she knew that something could go awry.

Elspeth had worked for the Kennington Organisation for five years, and this was her hardest challenge to date. She was aware that she served at Eric Kennington's pleasure, and to keep her job he must always be placated.

Elspeth Duff's decision to take a job working for Lord Kennington was a surprise to her friends, to her mother and father in Scotland and to her two adult children. Her announcement that she was tearing up all past ties and entering the service of Lord Kennington as a roving security advisor, defied reasonable explanation to those closest to her. Most were unaware that her relationship with her ex-husband had slowly disintegrated into the morass of Hollywood culture in which they had lived for more than twenty years, but that she should—at the age of forty-eight—uproot her life for the pursuit of a well-paid and seemingly luxurious but single life was puzzling to all of them. Elspeth never had given reasons nor told her friends and family that her professional choice involved more hardship, skill and intelligence than they could imagine. She simply smiled and said it was time for a change. Elspeth's choice was not merely hormonal. For too many years she had lived in the shadows of her past and the sham of her marriage to Alistair Craig. Then on the thirtieth anniversary of Malcolm Buchanan's murder, which had occurred on the eighteenth of May, nineteen sixty-nine, she walked away from the restrictions of her life. She had never regretted her choice.

She had dabbled in crime in Hollywood, but when she finally decided to make her split from Alistair Craig permanent, she had decided to re-focus her attention on the pursuit of criminal justice. She presumed, however, that re-entering the law enforcement profession at her age was probably impossible. Furthermore she could not decide on which side of the Atlantic Ocean she wanted to live. Her son lived in San Francisco and her daughter and family in East Sussex, south of London.

One of her outrageously wealthy friends in Hollywood, whom Elspeth had saved from certain conviction for theft, had convinced her that the best way to make any of life's major decisions was to pamper oneself. Suspecting that Elspeth, as a Scotswoman, had natural proclivities towards parsimony, the friend gave her an all-expenses-paid four-day stay at the Kennington Beverly Hills. During her many years on the fringes of filmdom, Elspeth had been in and out of most of the famous hotels around Los Angeles, but had never experienced the level of luxury the Kennington hotel offered. At first it offended her liberal views on the distribution of wealth, but she was seduced into its understated richness. Not one to spend an idle few days and bored at pure indulgence during her stay she came across a crime being committed and helped apprehend the perpetrator. Her cleverness came to the

Kennington Organisation's attention. A fortnight later, Lord Kennington flew her to London and offered her a job and a solution to her trans-Atlantic dilemma.

Elspeth looked up to the high limestone bulwarks that had protected Valletta over the centuries and saw the hotel on the skyline. Elspeth said a private prayer, more a hope than supplication to whoever might be listening, for the hotel's safety. Could she satisfy Eric Kennington this time? She was not sure.

She made her way along the public gardens and past the Hotel Saint John, which stood outside the old walls of Valletta. She crossed the maze of the bus terminal, which even on Sunday morning was filled with the gaudily painted buses waiting to take tourists and Maltese pleasure seekers to the beaches and other holiday spots on the island. She passed under the high city gates and climbed the hill past the ruins of the Opera House, which had been badly damaged in the bombings during the Second World War and never restored to its former glory, and walked quietly by St. Catherine's Church whose doors were open beckoning passers-by to the mass that was underway. Except for the few shopkeepers catering to small crowds of tourists looking for souvenirs and the American fast food restaurants at the entrance to Triq Ir-Repubblika, Valletta continued to enjoy its day off. Elspeth only half-saw these sights, wondering what it would be like to be a care-free tourist, but her mind dwelt on the hidden terror to come.

As she approached the hotel, the group from the Smithsonian was gathered around a waiting bus. Silently, Elspeth wished them Godspeed on their travels and a safe stay at the hotel. What had René told her? The group would be staying for three more days. That gave her time to review the list of forthcoming bookings with René and Tony, but she suspected that this detail would have been already taken care of.

Spurred on by a sudden passing shower, Elspeth entered the hotel and sought out René. She once again was aware of the precise hand of Comfort and Service. Why would anyone want to disturb them? Someone obviously did.

8

Elspeth came into the lobby of the Kennington Valletta with the familiarity of a long-time member of Lord Kennington's personal security staff. Every Kennington hotel was different, but the security within them followed a similar pattern.

In the public areas of the hotel, the reception area was laid out cleverly. Here in Valletta, the lobby with its Baroque opulence allowed hidden areas where unseen staff could perform state of the art functions such as connecting to the internet and linking up to operations in London and around the world. The concierges' desk concealed multi-functioning telephones and computer screens. The uniforms of the lobby staff were designed so that mobile phones did not produce angry bulges. Earphones were almost imperceptible. Lord Kennington had directed that any guest or visitor who looked mildly lost would receive immediate but non-invasive assistance. This also allowed the staff to ferret out those who did not belong and escort them politely to destinations other than the hotel.

Operations on the upper floors were equally well planned. At each lift area, a house telephone and brochures with the hotel floor plan and emergency exits were displayed on ornate tables with vases of fresh flowers. A hall porter was always in attendance but seated in an unobtrusive alcove. Security cameras along the wide corridors were tucked in coved light wells or in the ceiling decoration, and were visible only to those who knew they were there. The cameras were monitored twenty-four hours a day from screens in the security room as well as René LeGrand's office. Whenever an unknown or questionable activity was observed, a member of the hotel security staff would be immediately dispatched to the area. This had been a controversial innovation. Eric Kennington had weighed the camera's installation carefully, but felt that a single guest's privacy was counterbalanced by the wellbeing of all the guests at the hotel. The videotapes were routinely destroyed after it was ascertained that they showed no security problem. Patrons who might be committing indiscreet but legal acts did not need to fear that the Kennington Organisation would forward these tapes to the police, private investigators or files of record. The guest's security was paramount, not the guest's morality. Gianni Lugano and *la signorina* who was not his wife need have no fear that their blatant secret would be saved for posterity.

When Elspeth retreated into the back offices where she waited for René LeGrand, she knew that she would not have to breach these strict rules set by Eric Kennington. If guests felt spied upon, they would not return, even if all of their activities were innocent. It was a tender balance, and Eric was intractable about this balance being assiduously kept.

Elspeth had promised Pamela Crumm that she would telephone Eric Kennington that morning at his country home in Essex. She performed this task immediately on entering René's private conference room, now her office.

Eric answered his mobile after multiple rings, which suggested to Elspeth that he might be otherwise occupied. She had never been privy to his home life, despite her lightly veiled questioning of Pamela about it, but from the sounds in the background he seemed to be at a family breakfast. He soon moved to a quieter space. Elspeth wished she had more dramatic news to justify breaking into his weekend rest.

"There is very little to report at this point, Eric. I met the high commissioner this morning. He is assuming the role of coordinator of operations, and I think is secretly enjoying being a part of something other than his normal duties. The Interpol agent is in place and seems highly competent. I'll meet the Scotland Yard inspector this evening. Now we begin the hardest part—waiting."

Eric audibly took a large swallow of some liquid. "How is René LeGrand taking this? Since he is relatively new as a manager, I want to make sure that he is giving you sufficient backup."

Elspeth imagined Eric Kennington's ever-expanding midriff encased in striped pyjamas and a terrycloth robe inscribed with 'Comfort and Service'. She tried to bring her mind back to the business at hand.

"At first René was nervous about my being here, perhaps because I work directly for you or because having this sort of issue to deal with may reflect badly on his management, but we are working on forming a partnership of sorts. I'm relying on him to rally the hotel staff, not scaring them but making them more observant. When I spoke to him last night, he said he would be organising meetings between small groups of the staff and the two of us. As you know, the staff here are highly seasoned and well remunerated. Do I have your authority to offer a bonus to any staff member who provides me with information?"

Eric did not respond for a minute. Elspeth imagined him leaning back and staring at the ceiling in a habitual gesture of thought. Instead, she heard him cry, "Hell and damnation!" and what sounded like his blowing across the top of his cup. Tea was always served hot at the Kennington hotels, and Elspeth guessed this was also true at the Kennington residence.

Finally he spoke. "No, only imply that there might be some recognition. I think if we offer a reward, we will be flooded with information that will be confusing. Here is what I suggest. Assign each member of the room staff to be more vigilant than usual of any items left in the rooms. You need not be specific as to what type of thing. They should make a list for each room every day. If the exchange is of an object, watching the ebb and flow of the objects in each room may give us some vital information. We might find that one object found in B's room one day may be found in A's room the next day. If this happens when A doesn't know B, we are on to something.

"The cleaning staff should make a list of items left in the public areas," he continued. "They shouldn't take these items to lost property right away, as we've taught them. They should leave them in place and see if anyone else picks them up."

Elspeth thought she could hear the gears of his mind working.

"The reception staff should make note of any items left in the room after guests check out or boxes left behind the reception desk at any time," he continued. "Have reception write down who leaves keys at the desk and who doesn't. They should make note of what each guest is wearing and if they add or lose clothing other than at times they have just come from their rooms."

Eric Kennington took another noisy drink from his cup.

"The car park staff should jot down the time of arrival of each car, its make and model and its number plate. Also if the condition of the car has altered, a dirty car is clean, a clean car is dirty, a headlamp is out and then is repaired. That sort of thing."

Another swallow.

"The wait staff should watch guests who are eating or drinking, and also see if any items are exchanged or left behind. The fitness room and shop staff should do the same."

Elspeth was amazed by his mental inventory of the hotel spaces.

"The doormen should watch every arrival and departure, and record, if they can, the destination of each car and taxi. Also they should be aware of any packages left in taxis or taken out of them. Even the kitchen staff should be alert. They should report if any guest is using the back doors as a way to leave the hotel or to come back in. They should also watch the deliveries, and see if anything unusual passes in and out of the hotel or if any guest makes contact with any of the delivery people."

Elspeth was taking rapid notes, although she had considered most of these things already.

"And keep the tapes from the security cameras. I want you to secure these and not let any of the rest of the staff know you are doing so, except René. I can't have the guests think that we keep any lasting record of their activities, although in this case we may need a permanent record."

Elspeth drew another bullet point on her list.

"But most of all remind the staff that any reporting should be unobserved, and no guest, not even a guilty one, should feel any inconvenience or disruption."

Elspeth had heard this mantra many times before.

"We can compensate the staff at the end of this business in a way that is appropriate. I'll think about what form that might take," he said.

Elspeth was amazed once again at the quickness of Eric's organisational mind. For someone whom she considered a big picture person rather than a detail person, he outlined a credible plan, almost without thinking. Elspeth doffed an imaginary hat to her employer. It was he, not anyone else, not even Pamela Crumm, who had made his hotel empire a success.

"Most of all, Elspeth, the very minute anything breaks, I want you to be in touch with Detective Superintendent Ketcham first and me and Pamela second. The sooner we get rid of this awful threat, the better!"

"Of course, Eric," she said dutifully. She rolled her eyes and sighed inwardly.

"I'll have Pamela type up a plan and send it to you within the hour, so keep your email open and check frequently."

Elspeth was not sure how Eric Kennington communicated with Pamela when he was at home. The next time she saw Pamela, she would ask. Pamela would probably not answer her.

9

After a leisurely morning at the hotel and a stroll down Triq Ir-Repubblika to make sure his book was still stocked in the local bookshop, Conan FitzRoy entered the lobby with his usual flourish just before noon. He was still filled with the glow of the indulgence of last night's dinner. His doctor was too pessimistic. How could the contractions of a muscle, albeit the heart, interfere with the pleasures of life? After all that young, beautiful thing known as Alicia Kent found him attractive. All women felt his magnetism; the events of his life vouched for that. He breathed a sigh of contentment. Life was truly wonderful.

As he waited for Alicia to join him, FitzRoy watched Elspeth cross the lobby and go into the offices behind the reception desk. He admired her from afar. Other guests came in and went out. Many appeared to be local families here to have Sunday dinner. Some were tourists but he did not recognise any from the night before. The Arab-looking young man came out of the lift and settled into an easy chair in a quiet corner near the reception area. He did not seem to be waiting for anyone but simply was passing time watching the comings and goings of the guests and staff.

Elspeth came out of the back rooms and went to the reception desk. She then looked up. Eyeing FitzRoy she smiled and came out to where he was standing.

"Dear Conan, I did so enjoy last evening. What is

more, I was speaking to my aunt Magdelena Cassar not long ago and mentioned that you were staying here. She sent her regards and also an invitation. She is having a small soirée this evening in Gozo and asked that you join us. Alicia Kent will be there and so will Sir Richard Munro, the British high commissioner."

FitzRoy beamed and accepted with as much of a bow as he could manage. He had been to Magdalena's soirées before, one when Elspeth was there as well. The select company always appealed to FitzRoy.

Elspeth told him that she and Alicia Kent were travelling together and would catch the six o'clock ferry to Gozo. FitzRoy opted out from joining them for their voyage. He said would come later, as he had both five o'clock and six o'clock appointments that were too important to miss, even for Magdelena Cassar.

Alicia Kent arrived in the lobby ten minutes after FitzRoy and Elspeth had parted. His anticipation of Alicia's arrival had not been in vain. She had dressed with magnificent casualness. Her tan trousers, short orange jacket and yellow tee picked up the colours of a multi-coloured heavy silk scarf that FitzRoy assumed must have been purchased on the Rue Faubourg St. Honoré. Her radiant smile, however, could not have been bought in Paris or Milan, but was instead the product of American youth and health. FitzRoy, had he been a lesser man, would have felt jealous of her svelte figure.

FitzRoy drew his arm through Alicia's and ushered her outside, just as the hotel valet pulled FitzRoy's Mercedes up to the entrance. FitzRoy made sure she was settled in the passenger seat and went around to the driver's side. Today he would drive, showing Alicia his skills on the road, and consequently he had given Riley the afternoon off. He touched the steering wheel and felt the grandeur of the car at his fingertips.

Under his skilled hands, the great car moved slowly through the narrow streets outside the hotel and was soon beyond the bastions of the city. Heads turned as he drove because the Mercedes was larger and more expensive than the cars normally seen on the roads in Malta.

"We're making quite a stir," Alicia said.

"Indeed," he answered.

As they drove into the countryside, FitzRoy found that his passenger had an attentive ear. He told her about his life or at least the fiction of it, and she seemed to be quite dazzled.

"Your book on Malta strikes such a great chord of authenticity. Last night you said you do the interviews yourself. Is that true?" she asked.

"Not all of them. I pick the people I want interviewed or at least the type of people. If my research students find individuals who have important stories that will enhance the book, I interview them and keep extensive notes not only on what they say but also on how they act."

"Will you use me?" Alicia asked.

He chuckled. "The main characters in my books are always fictitious, but they are almost always a composite of people I know, people I have interviewed and my own imagining of what it would be like to be that character. I like to get inside my characters. I can only do that if I understand how someone in their space in the universe would feel or say or look; where they would love and work and play; how they would treat their spouse and friends and lovers."

"I haven't told you about my life," she said, her eyes challenging.

"No, worse luck."

"I probably won't," she said. "It's been very usual."

"I always spend time writing on location," he continued without responding to her, "because the location as much as the people stimulate my imagination. Normally I conceive my plots first and make the location fit the story. Most stories could take place in a variety of places, so I always choose a place I would like to know more about."

FitzRoy slowed the car to allow a farmer to herd his goats past it.

"Now I'm resting for several weeks before beginning the new book we talked about last evening," he said after the road ahead was clear. "One cannot avoid the Islamic extremists these days, so that will be my focus. That has interested me ever since September the eleventh."

Although the roads were rough, the Mercedes surged ahead and flowed smoothly over them. The car's width caused some problems. The roads were laid in Roman times and were bordered by stonewalls, some built two millennia before.

As they proceeded, Alicia said, "I would think your research would be dangerous."

FitzRoy overtook a small battered Fiat ahead of them. The road was barely wide enough for them both. He muttered a disparaging remark about obstructions on Malta's roads.

"I never put myself in any danger if I can help it," he said. "There are many Arabs these days, particularly the Arab intelligentsia, who are extremely knowledgeable about what happens in Arab cultures. That is that type of person I shall contact initially. In fact, although I promised my niece I would get complete rest this next three weeks, I've already made a contact here in Malta, who has indicated that he can provide some interesting sources in order to begin my research."

FitzRoy swerved the car to avoid a pothole. "Here we are at Roberto's vineyard," he said. "I've been promised that last year's picking has produced some of his best wine yet. You should not be put off by the guidebooks' disparaging remarks about Maltese wines or the fact that many of them are made using Sicilian grapes. There are secret caches hidden here from all but the knowing few."

FitzRoy made his way down the treeless drive and headed towards a large limestone building surrounded by oleander bushes and several clumps of palms. He pulled into a large car park that had instructions posted in Malti, English, Italian, German, French, Spanish and Japanese. Obviously others had discovered this vineyard, but today there were no other cars there. FitzRoy pulled the Mercedes into a small patch of shade, threw his keys on the dashboard and cracked the sunroof open.

"I doubt opening this will help much," he said. "Even at this time of year the sun is strong at midday. Come meet Roberto Guerrero, one of Malta's best vineyard owners. He's not famous because he only provides the grapes for wines that never leave Malta. These wines are excellent and must be tried. When my niece set up my appointment with Roberto, he told her that he had a special wine for me to try this year. I'm filled with anticipation!"

FitzRoy came round the car and held open the door for his guest. She was applying a bit of lipstick as he flung open the door, and in a startled moment dropped her lipstick case on the floor beside her seat. FitzRoy waited for her as she fumbled for it under the seat. She did not find the case, but instead smiled at him and took his proffered hand.

"It's my lipstick," she said. "I'll get it when we get back. I hope it doesn't melt."

They walked along a path that bisected the rows of gnarled grapevines dusted with the small yellow-green leaves freshly awoken by the spring weather. The early afternoon sun accented the freshness of these tender beginnings of next year's wine.

"Ah," said FitzRoy, content.

*

Loren had expected Roberto to be Maltese, so she was surprised when a tall Spaniard with a farmer's hands but a gentleman's politeness greeted them at the door of the large farmhouse. Roberto had set out a table filled with two pots of red and pink geraniums, fresh loaves of bread, several kinds of cheese, and a bowl of fresh fruit. In the middle of the table were eight bottles of wine, each bearing a hand-drawn label. Roberto grinned as he motioned to the bottles.

"I will not tell you which is my favourite, but instead let you pick yours, *Señor* Conan and *Señorita* Alicia." He used the Castilian pronunciation of her name.

He drew back two rustic wooden chairs and invited them to sit down at the table. As they were doing so, he brought a tray of wine goblets from a nearby sideboard.

The ceremony began, obviously to the delight of both Conan and *Señor* Guerrero. One made a flourish of offering a fresh glass and delicately pouring the wine; the other went through the ritual of savouring the wine's aroma, taking small sips and making appropriate noises before pronouncing judgement. Loren watched them with amusement. She tasted the first and second of the wines and then cried off, saying she did not have the head for such things. She found the wine more potent than she had expected. She nibbled some bread, took a small piece of the cheese and sections of an orange.

The solemnity of the occasion was interrupted half an hour after it had begun by a knock at the door. Roberto rose steadily, although he had matched taste for taste with FitzRoy, and went to the front of the house. There was some conversation in what sounded from a distance like Italian, a language she knew only slightly. She could not hear all of what was being said, but she caught the words truck, puncture and no problem.

Roberto returned to his guests. "The road is rough, and we get many people who have a flat tyre. Poor man, he has just arrived from Italy with a large delivery, and had to change a tyre on his lorry. I do not envy him the task. I have contacted the public works again and again and written to the papers, but no good has come of it. *Señorita*, I apologise for my adopted country. Having one of the oldest civilizations in the world does not relieve us of modern-day responsibilities. I am thankful it was not one of the lorries that carry my wine."

Loren smiled. She had read of the rocky roads in Malta. As she settled back into her chair, she speculated on what life would be like for her were she an ordinary holidaymaker rather than a special operative. The old world quality here appealed to her. She felt she would like to come back to Malta when her assignment was finished.

FitzRoy and Roberto tried several more wines before the truck driver returned with thanks for being able to use the car park for repairs. The mood of the wine tasters, however, seemed to have been broken. Now the time had come for FitzRoy to make his selections. He decided immediately on one of the reds, but debated over two of the whites.

Then he announced, "I shall buy a case of all three!"

"Do you want to take them with you, *amigo*?"

"No, I think not. It sounds as if the road I had planned to take is too bumpy. I don't want to bruise them. Will you have them delivered to the hotel by the main roads, please?"

As the two men negotiated payment, Loren strolled out into the sun. The farmhouse was surrounded by patches of daisies and the whole afternoon took on an unreal flavour. Loren felt flooded with happiness. "Harden yourself, Loren," she said to herself. "Now isn't the time to go soft."

Loren wandered down a path through the budding vineyards behind the house and sat in the warm sunshine looking over the sea. She could hear the waves below and smell the acrid salty air. Idly she brushed away a fly as she sat reflecting on the last four years of her life—the times when she had posed as a dedicated, unattractive and fanatical female, dressed in odd bits of clothing bought at thrift shops, spouting doggerel to earnest but misled young terrorists from different parts of the world when she had played the widow of an underground communist leader and when she was the young and innocent American tourist who could be seduced, kidnapped and robbed of her money. She smiled and wondered what her new acquaintances in Malta would have thought had they seen her during some of her previous assignments.

Her reverie was interrupted by the sound of laboured breathing behind her. She turned to see Conan stumbling down the path. She sprang up and hurried up to him.

"My dear, we are ready to move on," he said, obviously gratified that he did not have to walk all the way down the hill.

They made their way along the dusty path towards the car, which now had become an oven. FitzRoy slipped behind the wheel, took his keys from the dashboard and turned on the ignition. Soon the air conditioning cooled the car. Conan turned out on the road, which indeed was as bad as the truck driver had indicated.

"I am delighted with Roberto's new wines, quite superior this year! Although I think they'll not hold their flavour. He doesn't use any sulphites, you know, which make wines harsh, so while the flavour is superb, the longevity is questionable."

Conan glanced down at the dashboard and let out a sigh. "This clock has always been a bit dodgy. You can't know the number of times I have complained about it. It runs fast continuously. What time do you have, my dear?"

"Just about ten of four," said Loren.

"I'm afraid we must immediately return to the hotel. I have an appointment at five, and must clean up a bit before then. We still have enough time to take the long route around so you can take in some wonderful vistas of the cliffs and sea. You'll find Malta as spectacular as I do after you see some more of the countryside."

FitzRoy accelerated the large car and settled in to more storytelling. Loren relaxed against the now-cool leather seat, ran her finger up and down a small scar that marred the seat's perfection, and hoped that the detour would keep them longer before they returned to the hotel. The day had become radiant and the sea had an intensity of blue she had never seen before. She wanted to have Conan stop the car and to walk along the cliffs, but she felt his impatience. He drove with a steady hand despite the amount of wine he had consumed.

Forty-five minutes later they slipped under the porte-cochère of the hotel. Just as the doorman opened the door, Alicia remembered her lipstick. She ran her hand along the seat's edges and under the seat. Bother, she thought, I must have dropped it in the parking lot at the vineyard. The case was one of her favourites during one of her rare moments of rest and recreation in Paris, when she felt money was no object. She must remember to ask FitzRoy about it tomorrow.

10

Sunday, 25 April 2004 – Day 2 Evening

Loren was tired when she returned from her outing with Conan FitzRoy. He was not an easy person to be with. Despite his effusive charm and unending enthusiasm, he demanded that he be paid attention to and that the questions he asked be answered in the way he wanted them answered. As the afternoon passed, she had wearied of this.

She retired to her room, grateful for the cool interior and the view of the garden. She lay on her bed and contemplated the evening ahead. In Lyon, her handler had briefed her on her responsibilities and those of the police. Hers was covert, so as to identify any suspicious activity; the police were to take the active role of apprehending any suspects or seizing any property. She had been told that as Malta was still a member of the British Commonwealth, London was sending an inspector specialising in terrorist activity, particularly any enterprise that might involve the illicit transport of any persons or goods into Commonwealth nations. She had his name. Detective Inspector Evan Davies-Jones.

She punched her pillows and stretched her long legs. She imagined what he might look like. He was probably balding with a comb-over, tending to overweight. He undoubtedly smoked. Definitely his clothes would be rumpled. He would be wearing something right off the rack from Marks and Spencer that would be far too heavy for

Malta's spring climate, and it would make him sweat. Already she was cooling on meeting him. The high commissioner had suggested that she take a romantic interest in him as a cover so that they would have a reason to meet together later. Would Alicia Kent really form an attachment to such a sloppy looking man?

Acknowledging her ill humour, she went into the bathroom and poured herself a hot bath, adding one of the hotel's bath oils. She sank into the jasmine-scented water and sighed. She washed the dust from her hair, wrapped it in a towel and enjoyed the luxury of a long soak.

Loren dressed slowly and reapplied her makeup. Looking in the mirror, she questioned whether she really would like to be Alicia Kent. Probably not. Alicia's existence was too idle. Loren had chosen her life because of her love of action and the necessity of rapid decision making that action required. She thrived on the unexpected. Loren suspected that Alicia Kent only had rushes of adrenalin during tennis matches. And she probably had never shot anyone except with a camera.

Elspeth had warned her that the ride on the ferry over to Gozo might be cool so Loren dressed accordingly, choosing a light woollen dress and jacket from her new wardrobe. She wiped the steam from the bathroom mirror and surveyed her image once again, surprised by her own elegance. Probably she would look too chic for Evan Davies-Jones. Such speculation would do her no good. This evening was business, and she had to conduct herself accordingly.

She picked up her handbag and coat and headed for the lobby.

*

Conan FitzRoy returned to his room, emptied his pockets of their change, handkerchief and keys. His niece Bridget always chided him for ruining the lines of his trousers by carrying so much in them. He would retort that he would not be reduced to carrying a bag filled with far more things than he had in his pockets. They had shared this joke for many years.

He admitted to himself that he was a bit tired and thought of cancelling his trip to Gozo despite his liking for Magdelena Cassar, a woman who he felt had a stature similar to his own. He would take a dose of those horrid pills and then have a bit of a lie-down before his appointment at five and his meeting with Dr Hammud at six. He wondered what Hammud had to say to him. Would he be able to give Conan the leads he needed in Cairo? Could he have important information himself? Yes, interviews were exhilarating, although his doctors in London had warned him to get three weeks of rest before beginning work again.

Blast it, he thought, why should this wretched heart bother me? I come from strong stock. But his intelligence overcame his emotion, and he went to the bathroom, took out one of Bridget's neat vials and swallowed the medications.

*

Elspeth's afternoon had been a long one, and she was looking forward to finishing putting Eric Kennington's security plans in place. René had been with her all afternoon and had been invaluable in judging the mood of the staff and their reaction to Lord Kennington's requests.

Eric had directed her not to alert them to the immediate danger. Elspeth had told the staff that the procedures were part of a new programme, in case there was a terrorist attack, and that his lordship particularly admired the loyalty and efficiency of the personnel at the Kennington Valletta. He had chosen this hotel as the test site. Some of the staff seemed bothered by the extra work, but most were excited to be part of something that would alleviate some of the daily repetition of their jobs.

Elspeth looked up and saw that it was approaching five. She was to meet Loren at quarter-past so she went to her room to freshen up. She surveyed the clothes she had brought with her, and remembered that she had packed a beautifully hand-embroidered shawl that her son had brought her from India. It was warm and decorative and was woven in several bright hues that she knew complimented her light brown hair, cobalt blue eyes and clear skin. She shook her head and laughed at herself for thinking that Richard Munro might like it too. You are getting to be a bit silly from jet lag, she said archly to the mirror by the door as she left her room, but knowing it was more than that went out to meet Loren.

*

Because the normal boat service from Valletta to Gozo was out of commission, Elspeth had ordered a hotel car to take them to the north of the island to get the ferry from there. The doormen opened both doors of the car for them, and the two women settled comfortably into the back seat.

"Elspeth," Loren asked, "do you know Sir Richard? I noticed he always called you by your first name, although he called me Ms Axt, and you once called him Dickie."

Elspeth bit the corner of her lip. "I suppose I was transparent, wasn't I? A slip that I believe the high commissioner did not appreciate. Richard Munro was my cousin's closest friend when they were at Oxford, and he spent several summers in Perthshire where I lived as a girl. Please forgive my ineptitude. I've known Richard for a long time and am used to calling him by his Oxford moniker. But now I should tell you about my aunt, who will be our hostess tonight. She is truly unique and her story is a magical one."

Loren was not looking forward to the party, so she was pleased to be entertained on the way there. Elspeth's story might provide the only diverting part of the evening.

Elspeth launched into her narrative with the gusto of one who enjoyed a good tale. "My Uncle Frederick and Aunt Mag, whose name is Magdelena Cassar, met here in Malta, where he was stationed in the army during the Second World War. They fell in love amid the bombings and deprivation that afflicted Malta during the war. Unfortunately Aunt Mag was married. Being a good Roman Catholic she would not divorce her husband and marry my uncle, although her husband was suspected of being an Axis collaborator and had disappeared from Malta. I have never heard the full story, but after the war Magdelena Cassar became one of the most famous concert pianists in Europe."

The story caught Loren's interest and she said so.

"Uncle Frederick's wife, my real aunt, died after the war was over and he became a free man, but Aunt Mag held fast to her religious convictions," Elspeth said. "After the war Uncle Frederick helped Aunt Mag establish her musical career and became a permanent part of her life."

"What happened then?" Loren asked.

"They travelled a great deal, but when in Malta they lived in the Gozitan farmhouse we will be visiting tonight. When I was very young, my parents whispered the word 'mistress' whenever Aunt Mag's name came up. But, as she had firmly established herself in my heart as well as my uncle's, I always assumed the term mistress meant a kind of secret fairy godmother. When I became older, I fled to her whenever things in my life became too difficult to bear, a habit I continue unrepentantly to this day. My own parents, who I know love me in a different sort of way, expect me to be hearty and brave; Aunt Mag even now wraps me in a blanket of love in a way that, I think, mere Scots could never comprehend."

"Nor American suburbanites," said Loren with more passion than she had expected to express.

Elspeth glanced at Loren curiously. "Aunt Mag saw me through romances and their demises, academic pressures and glories and adolescent fights with my parents," Elspeth said. "She held me in her arms for hours after my fiancé died and let me weep. Most of all, she taught me that love was a real commodity. I have always thought that she defrosted the frigid Scottish girl inside me, and persuaded me that the world was a wonderful place to explore and relish beyond all the hardships of growing up."

Suddenly Elspeth seemed to become embarrassed. "But then perhaps I have said too much," she said.

"I wish," Loren said almost inaudibly, "that I had had a 'fairy god-mistress' in my life."

111

"Few girls do," Elspeth said. "I always am thankful I did. When we get to Gozo you'll see what a treasure she is. But now tell me about your trip to the vineyard."

It was nearing sunset when they reached the ferry terminal, and they could see the ferry as it entered the jetty. Its great jaws opened as it approached the dock and devoured the waiting cars and passengers as well. Abandoning the hotel car, Elspeth explained that they could take a taxi when they reached Mgarr on the other side of the channel between Malta and Gozo.

Elspeth and Loren found chairs in the enclosed area of the upper deck, which protected them from the wind, and they sipped the Perrier they had brought from the bar below.

As they settled in, Elspeth pointed to the island of Gozo ahead and said, "My aunt's home is unique, as you will see. Her family is both Maltese and Gozitan, and the Gozitan side has lived in Gozo for centuries. Their home is just outside the small village of San Lawrenz and within view of the sea."

Elspeth went on, "The home is small in comparison with many of the farmhouses on Gozo, but it is beautifully situated on a high cliff overlooking the sea and is surrounded by a high stucco fence, which is entangled with a rare golden bougainvillea. When I was a child, I felt that entering through the high iron gates made me invisible to the rest of the world, and I had a secret place where my wonderful Aunt Mag lived with her prince Uncle Frederick, and no one knew about them but me. The house was originally built—one can hardly say designed—as a farm building with the lower floor being for the carts, horses, and hay, and probably chickens, pigs and goats as well. The upper floor was the family's living space."

"Is that typical?" Loren asked.

"The layout? Yes. When Aunt Mag took possession of the house, she, with a stroke of individuality, adapted it to her own lifestyle. On one side the lower floor is now the garage for the cars and an apartment for Teresa and Giulio, the Italian couple who have taken care of her as long as I remember. Teresa is an excellent housekeeper and cook, and Giulio a fastidious gardener, caretaker and handyman. On the other side are the guest quarters, which open out to an enclosed garden that is Giulio and Aunt Mag's pride and joy. Although she fancies herself a gardener, he does most of the planting design as well as the daily labour."

Elspeth waved beyond the glass barrier of the ferry's windows at the last of the sunlight, which canted across the stark hills of the island. "Gardens are a necessity in this harsh landscape, and you'll find few houses that don't have them. To bring your attention to the main space above, Aunt Mag commissioned a semi-circular covered staircase, lined with terra cotta pots filled with hibiscus of every colour. Actually, my Uncle Frederick began this collection when he brought Aunt Mag a rare peach-coloured hibiscus he had found in Trinidad. Giulio keeps these plants blooming all year long, even in the winter when the winds are high. As I go up the staircase, I always feel I am mounting the stairs to a royal ball, even now. When Aunt Mag retired, she completely redid the upper floor. I've decided not to describe it to you but wait for you to be surprised when you enter it."

Loren by this time was as charmed as any child drawn

in by a fantasy. But with twenty-first century cynicism she said, "Do you guarantee I'll be surprised?" She flushed slightly, remembering her reaction to the lobby of the Kennington Valletta.

"I promise. Let me only say that Magdelena Cassar spent decades playing the piano in the grand Baroque concert halls of Europe. When she came back to Gozo, she combined that influence with the simplicity of a Gozitan farmhouse. In her exuberant and eclectic fashion, the farmhouse was transformed into the home of the grande dame, splendidly simple, simply grand. I'll be interested to see your reaction."

"I can hardly wait," Loren said, wishing she were coming to the party under different circumstances.

Their taxi from Mgarr arrived before the iron gates shortly after seven. Although it was still spring, when other flowers were only budding, the bougainvillea that climbed the perimeter wall was in full bloom. In contrast, the ancient vines of the wisteria that draped the gate were just beginning to show signs of their future lavender splendour. The gates were opened by an ageing Italian man whom Elspeth introduced as Giulio. He greeted Elspeth with a burst of Italian charm, "Ah, *Signorina Elspetta, Signorina Elspetta*, I wait for you all day long, and *la signora* Magdelena said you should bring this *bellissima* guest. Come in. *Entrate*."

The final rays of the setting sun painted the walls orange and gold and threw indigo in the shadows. The scent of the flowers offered a bouquet of new smells for Loren. She had already fallen under the spell.

Small candles in glass containers along the walkway ushered Loren and Elspeth up the flower-lined stairs, luring one to the rooms above. They climbed slowly up the grand staircase. At the top of the stairs, Elspeth drew open the tall wooden doors with an ease of motion that she explained was testament to Giulio's constant attention and consideration of his employer's advancing age.

Loren drew in her breath. Magdelena's great room was indeed great, being five metres tall and encompassing much of the building's footprint. Exposed rafters, carved in a tracery of ancient wood in a fashion no longer attainable by today's craftsmen, held the vast space with a strength and beauty Loren had seldom seen. French doors opened to a large balcony populated with a jungle of potted plants and boasting a view of the sea beyond. The walls were plastered and painted a yellow that reminded Loren of the colour of daffodils. The glow of the paint and the soft lighting filled the room with the warmth of wellbeing.

One wall held a large gilt-framed mirror that reflected the two concert-grand pianos snuggled together in the middle of the room. A mediaeval tapestry filled the opposite wall. Loren later studied the tapestry, a beautiful work depicting a maiden with a lute entwined with a unicorn, and a plethora of medieval flowers and musical instruments stitched into its background and border. The fourth wall, broken by several high wooden doors leading to unknown places, was more personal, decorated with several colourful paintings by Maltese artists who painted in the school of Matisse and a whole section of photographs that dared the viewer to recognise people ranging from Magdelena's family to the musical grandees of Europe, royals, presidents and premiers of the last half century. Loren squinted and could see an American film star or two as well. Most of the photographs were inscribed to the great Magdelena Cassar.

Wooden chairs stood around the pianos. Several rococo settees were already occupied with the evening's guests. Magdelena, despite the short notice, had gathered fifteen of her friends for the party, perhaps luring them by the promise that the British high commissioner would be attending. Loren guessed a few had met him and that most would be happy in the future to count him among their acquaintances.

Magdelena's home was filled with flowers. The tall doors to the balcony were open, and the sounds of the waves could be heard over the murmur of the voices in the room.

Richard Munro stood by Magdelena, who was making introductions. Loren surveyed the room for her policeman but could not find him. Most of the men seemed attached to women who most likely were their wives. Elspeth had said that Evan was a rising star in the police. Wouldn't that imply some degree of youth despite Loren's earlier misgivings about his appearance?

Magdelena broke away and rushed to greet the new arrivals, her loose-fitting caftan and several scarves flowing round her in a multi-coloured display. "Elspeth, *cara*, you are here at last," she gushed, embracing her niece, kissing her on both cheeks and then warmly grasping Loren's hand with a hand heavily laden with rings and speckled with age.

Richard came up behind them and gave Elspeth a chaste peck on the cheek as if they had not met for a long time and their acquaintance was slight. He allowed himself to be introduced to Alicia Kent and expressed delight at meeting her.

"Let me introduce you to someone who's just arrived from London. Evan Davies-Jones," Richard said. He gestured to a young man who had come up to his side.

With dread Loren turned to face her policeman and, seeing him, she drew in a breath. He was one of the most handsome men she had ever met. He was tall, his face angular, and his clothes fitted in a style that only a good London tailor could manage. She held out her hand.

He smiled, turning partially towards her and gave a boyish grin. "Unfortunately, I no longer have a hand to shake," he said. Then she noticed that one sleeve had been tucked artfully up and fastened with an invisible pin.

Richard said, "You may ask. He lost his arm but the Minister did not lose his life. It seemed a bargain price to pay."

Evan turned full face towards her, and she saw a long scar down the right side of his cheek and neck. The severity of the mutilation was obvious.

Evan and Loren fell into easy conversation, and soon all the other voices in the room faded into oblivion. They walked out on to the balcony together. Loren did not notice that Magdelena had agreed to play or that the others had gathered around one of the two grand pianos, but soon the music that had delighted concertgoers for years flowed into the Mediterranean night. The rhythm of the waves, the scent of the sea and Magdelena's garden and the fluid notes of Chopin mingled and rose and filled Loren's soul.

Evan Davies-Jones leaned on the balcony rail and looked out into the night. Loren was acutely aware of him as she stood beside him. Neither spoke as they watched the night sky. Her eyes searched out in the darkness to find the sea.

He finally broke the silence. "Have you been to Malta before?"

"No," she said, "but I'll come again when I can. For pleasure, not for work."

"Do you mind your work?" he asked.

She shook her head. "No...well perhaps only in moments like this, but...but this doesn't seem real." She hoped he did not see her jaw tighten.

"It doesn't seem real, does it? Shall I call you Alicia?"

"Yes, I think that would be best, although I am just getting used to the name myself. I've only had it for two days. Do you like the name Evan?"

"Yes. I've had it since I was born so it doesn't take getting used to."

Loren turned towards him and was struck once again by his handsomeness. She wondered if he always arranged to stand with his ravishing rather than ravaged side visible to his companions. If she ever got to know him better she must ask him.

"Evan." She paused. "You obviously know about my mission and where I come from."

"Yes, I've worked with several of your colleagues before but never such a beautiful one." He grinned widely.

His comment both annoyed and pleased her.

"They've given me rather nice rags, don't you think?

You should'er seen me last time out," she said in a poor imitation of a Cockney accent.

"Dowdy?" he asked.

"No, complete grunge. I still feel dirty just thinking about those clothes, although I did wash them regularly."

They both laughed. "I shouldn't have liked being instructed to show interest in someone dressed in grunge," he said. "I appreciate Superintendent Ketcham's sensitivity towards your role in this assignment. Do you know him?"

"No, the high commissioner has told me about him and his role in our operation. Lyon always tells us to stay away from the police. In fact, when Sir Richard told me what role Detective Superintendent Ketcham expected me to play, I was amazed. My grunge associates wouldn't know me again, but I guess they wouldn't stay at a Kennington Hotel. I think I'm safe from recognition."

"Do you mind playing the romantic role?" Evan asked.

"It is a breath of fresh air. Do you mind?"

Evan chuckled at her question.

She wondered if he knew enough about her sub-directorate to know that most of its members led hazardous existences when they were working. Interpol's undercover operatives were known for their toughness, hardness, deadly skills and their dedication to the eradication of crime and terrorism. She knew 'Alicia Kent' did not look the part.

The last chords of the nocturne flowed through the windows and the sound of soft applause followed.

"No," he said. "I'm delighted by your cover."

He might never know who the person was beneath the

disguise of Alicia Kent, she thought. He had undoubtedly been told her name was Loren Axt, but he did not know that was also not her real name. Her handler always insisted on a double cover name.

*

Elspeth seemed distracted throughout the evening and finally Richard drew her apart. "Elspeth," he said, taking her hands in his, "I feel you are not here with us this evening."

She did not let his hands go but gave no response to his touch. "Dickie, I'm concerned that Conan FitzRoy isn't here. Something is definitely wrong. I feel I should go back to the hotel. Will you look after Loren and Evan? They seem to have hit it off, haven't they?"

He looked at her eyes, which were troubled. His heart missed a beat, and he wished he could hold her tightly to him. Instead he said, "They do and genuinely."

"I'll make my own way, Dickie. I'll say goodbye to Aunt Mag before I go."

"Yes, of course," he said, wanting to smooth the worry from her face.

She broke away and hurriedly left the room.

Magdelena's parties always ended promptly at half past nine. Her insistence on this, Richard had heard, was sacrosanct and was never violated if one wanted an invitation in the future. As the last guest from San Lawrenz left, he watched Loren and Evan come in from the balcony.

"Ah, darlings," said their hostess, "my excessively-responsible niece says she needed to return to the hotel and has already left. I retire at ten and so shall not see you again this evening. I have done my duty to the high commissioner and my niece as promised, but even for them will not change my schedule. Good night, my dears, and fare you well over the next week. Elspeth mentioned that you have much to achieve. Good night, good night."

Richard came forward as she left and said, "May I speak to the two of you in the morning room?"

Magdelena's morning room faced east. Like the rest of the house it was sparsely furnished under high ceilings. Each piece of furniture was magnificently baroque but there was no clutter. The only crowdedness was the multitude of additional photographs that lined the walls.

Richard motioned them to take a seat. "I had wanted to talk to you briefly before we go back to Malta. I think we may trust that this is as secure a location for your instructions as one could hope. Evan, I want you to come to the high commission tomorrow. Detective Superintendent Ketcham has arranged for a secure conference call, and needs to give us the latest information they have in London.

"In the meanwhile, Loren, you will return to the Kennington Valletta. We want you to go out jogging with Evan in the morning, pretending you had set this date up tonight, but mainly to get any new instructions. Anyone at tonight's party can attest that you two hit it off. I congratulate you two on such a convincing show. We want you, Loren, at the hotel all day tomorrow awaiting any instructions. Since we have no idea when anything will happen, we want you to be as observant and flexible as possible. You can write letters, have a leisurely breakfast and lunch, sit and read in the garden and do any number of idle things. You can complain of fatigue after tonight's outing."

Loren acknowledged her orders with a resigned nod.

11

Despite the beauty of the evening and the pleasure of Richard Munro's presence, Elspeth felt uneasy. Her mind kept going back to the hotel. She wondered if the night staff under René's instruction had been as receptive to Lord Kennington's plan as the day staff had been under hers. Most of all where was Conan FitzRoy?

Before leaving Gozo she promised Aunt Magdelena she would return when she was free of her obligations at the hotel.

On the taxi ride to the hotel Elspeth worried that FitzRoy had not appeared at the party. On the trip to Gozo, Loren had relayed her conversation with FitzRoy earlier that afternoon, particularly about his forthcoming appointments. Elspeth wished she had listened more attentively. Elspeth wondered whom FitzRoy was meeting at five o'clock. Was the meeting to take place at the hotel? Would it be prudent to ask FitzRoy to interview his sources elsewhere if there was any chance of danger? Would this request be offensive to someone who so frequently stayed at the hotel? She did not know. She would call Eric Kennington in the morning for his advice.

It was well after ten when she reached the hotel, and she asked for the night manager, Pietru Parra. She made her way into the back rooms. Pietru found her in the small conference room that she had made her own.

She wanted to reconstruct FitzRoy's movements after he returned to the hotel from the vineyard, hoping to find out why he had not gone to Gozo.

"Pietru, have you seen Mr FitzRoy this evening?" she asked.

"Yes, he left the hotel just before five and returned about an hour later. He had coffee with Dr Hammud in the garden after that. Dr Hammud left the hotel just before seven for the airport."

"I see. When Dr Hammud left, what did Mr FitzRoy do?"

"He came into the lobby and used the house phone to ring his driver, telling him to bring the car around in half an hour for a trip to Gozo. Mr FitzRoy then went up in the lift and came down about ten minutes later. He had on his outdoor cape and had his big stick and fedora. He ordered a double whiskey soda and went out into the garden again. When Fernardu took him his whiskey, Mr FitzRoy said he was not feeling well and would not require his car after all. I have not seen him since then. I have been busy working with the night staff to instruct them on the new security measures," he added as if to assure her that they had taken Lord Kennington's directives seriously.

"Did anyone see Mr FitzRoy return to his room?"

"Not that I am aware of. Let me call Fernardu, the head waiter, in the bar and ask him. I have briefed him on Lord Kennington's new security measures."

Fernardu appeared promptly. He was eager to tell what he knew.

"I served Mr FitzRoy a whiskey in the garden. I

glanced at the clock in the bar when I went out to serve him. It was just seven ten. He did not look well. His face was red and twisted. I thought he had had too much drink or that he was wearing too much clothing. He asked me to make arrangements to cancel his trip to Gozo. I left him sitting where he was. Because of the cool temperatures in the evening, people don't usually sit outside, but he had on his cape. I know big people do not get cold the way little ones do." Fernardu was a small man. "Then I went back to the bar. I didn't see him come in from the garden, but things were busy after the big group of Americans came back from dinner so I didn't pay much attention."

She asked, "Did you serve him any drinks when he was with Dr Hammud?"

"No, not alcohol. Dr Hammud ordered coffee. Mr FitzRoy had the same."

Elspeth turned back to the night manager. "Pietru, did any of the desk staff make contact with Mr FitzRoy after that?"

"I'll make enquiries and let you know immediately." He then gave directions to the waiter. "Fernardu, please go outside and see if Mr FitzRoy is still in the garden. If he drank a double whiskey, he may have fallen asleep."

Fernardu did as bidden. He quickly reappeared. "Yes, yes. He's still on the bench, but he has fallen on his side."

"Let me take care of this," Elspeth said. She had never seen FitzRoy affected by drink before. Discretion was indeed called for. "Pietru and Fernardu, can you manage if we have to carry him to bed?"

Elspeth went straight into the garden. The night chill had subdued the scent of the flowers. The low-level garden lights cast large shadows and played tricks on her perception.

She found the slumped figure of FitzRoy filling a bench in a secluded place near the middle of the garden. He would not have been seen from the interior of the hotel.

Elspeth leaned over the silent form. "Conan, wake up. We'll take you up to bed. Help is coming."

She took his hand, hoping to rouse him. The hand was cold. So cold that she knew FitzRoy would never feel any touch again. He was dead.

Part 2

Message intercepted at GCHQ, Monday, 26 April 2004, 0300 GMT

Congratulations on success of exchange. Saieda's plan accomplished. Phase Three to begin immediately. Haste is extremely important. Contact Helios at hotel for Saieda's latest instructions. —Phoenician

12

The phone gave off those blaring noises that those devices always emit when one is awakened from deep sleep. Richard Munro answered it sleepily, and received the chilling news as he stared into the blackness of his bedroom.

"Yes, send it along immediately. I'll be downstairs and take delivery myself. Don't let anyone else know for now."

Richard pulled on the shirt and trousers that he had worn to Magdelena Cassar's party the night before, and was at the door when the courier arrived. Closing and locking the door after him, Richard unbuckled the leather pouch the courier had handed him, and took out an envelope marked 'Confidential'. Inside was a single sheet of paper. He read it quickly and then again carefully.

Congratulations on success of exchange. Saieda's plan accomplished. Phase Three to begin immediately. Haste is extremely important. Contact Helios at hotel for Saieda's latest instructions. — Phoenician.

The code decipher had scrawled a note at the bottom of the page. "Message received by GCHQ at Cheltenham at 0300 GMT today. Sent for your and ED's eyes only at the request of Detective Superintendent Ketcham."

129

Richard looked at his watch, which read a quarter to seven. With the time zone difference between the UK and Malta it was now only a few hours since the message had been intercepted. Fast work, Tony, Richard thought. Tony Ketcham must have been informed as soon as the message came in. Richard wanted to contact Elspeth immediately, but, considering the early hour, he waited until after he had showered and dressed in fresh clothing before ringing her.

Her voice was hoarse with fatigue when she took his call, but she seemed to come to full attention when told a second message had come from Phoenician.

"Where are you, Dickie? Can you come here?"

"I think we will be more private if you come here to Triq It-Torri. I gave my housekeeper the night off last night so we shall have the house to ourselves."

*

Elspeth dressed hurriedly, finding cotton trousers, a brightly coloured tee, a large over shirt and flat shoes in her armoire. She hoped the quality of the cut of her clothes and hair would compensate for the dishevelment she was feeling inside. She did not take the time to address the darkness under her eyes.

A doorman found her a taxi, and she arrived at Triq It-Torri forty-five minutes later. Richard came out to greet her. He smiled but his eyes looked distressed. He hugged her perfunctorily.

They took the ancient lift up to the terrace. The small cab forced their bodies to touch, but she did not withdraw, finding pleasure in the inadvertent act. The ride was short but rattling, and they came out on to the terrace where the tea trolley stood among the jumble of furniture.

He had laid out a simple meal of toast, jam, tea, and a basket of fruit.

"Will you have a cup of tea?" he said.

"Do you have coffee?" she asked, and then realised she was being impolite. "Sorry," she said. "That was rude. Tea will be lovely."

He poured it out, and she accepted the cup with as much grace as her embarrassment over her blurted-out words would allow.

"Please Dickie, show me the message."

He opened a pouch lying on the table and handed her a piece of paper. "Tony sent this for your and my eyes only. Although Loren and Evan should know too."

She was aware he watched her as she read.

"How can this be possible?" she said looking up at him. "We were so diligent all day yesterday at the hotel. And who is 'Helios'?" She did not expect him to answer. "Dickie, this can't be happening, not this and FitzRoy too." She shook her head trying to shake away the ugliness of the truth.

"FitzRoy?" he asked.

"Conan FitzRoy died at the hotel last night," she said quietly, still feeling the horror of touching his cold body. "We found him in the garden when I returned from Gozo."

"How terribly ghastly for you, dearest Elspeth."

She put her head in her hands. "Death's not an easy thing," she whispered.

"Do you want to tell me about it?" His voice was soft.

"I was concerned he hadn't come to the party in Gozo, so I enquired about him when I got back to the hotel. They told me he was in the garden, where we found him. He apparently suffered some sort of heart attack. But…"

Richard reached out for her hand. "Who, Elspeth, is we?'

She looked up, smiling weakly. "The waiter from the lounge bar, whose name is Fernardu, and I."

"How dreadful," he said, sorrow in his face.

She grimaced. "Yes, it was…very dreadful."

"Tell me what happened," he said.

Elspeth rose, abandoning her tea, and walked to the glass at the edge of the terrace. She was aware Richard followed her, although she did not turn to face him.

"We found him apparently asleep in the garden shortly after I arrived back from Gozo. He'd been drinking, according to Fernardu. At first I thought he had passed out, which would have been unusual. Normally he took his drink quite well, although he always drank heavily."

"I'm sorry I wasn't there to help you." His words were tender-hearted. "I wish I'd come back with you to the hotel after the party."

She did not respond to his concern but continued, "When I was certain he was dead, I called the night manager, Pietru Parra, and begged his assistance. Fernardu and Pietru picked up Conan's body. They pretended he was drunk and dragged him out of the garden into the back offices. Thank goodness this took place late enough in the evening when few people were around. No guest and few of the staff actually saw what happened, except perhaps Adam Russell who sat tucked away in a dark corner of the bar. I let Fernardu leave for the evening, gave him today off and swore him to secrecy. He crossed himself as he left the back entry, obviously thankful to be gone. But I assume the whole staff will know everything this morning."

Richard listened quietly, standing close behind her. He paused and then said, "But you couldn't have left FitzRoy's body in the back rooms?"

"No, of course not, Dickie. Luckily DI Davies-Jones and Loren Axt came into the hotel last night soon after we had removed the body from the garden, and asked at the reception desk if I had returned. The receptionist showed them to the back rooms. I can't think why I wanted to protect Loren, I'm sure she is tougher than I am, but I sent her off to bed. Evan helped me call an ambulance and made arrangements for Conan's body to be carried off to the police morgue."

Elspeth felt the muscles in her throat contract with revulsion at remembering handling FitzRoy's body. She wondered if Richard noticed her shudder. Finally she wrestled her feelings under control and said, "Does this tie in with the message we just received from Tony Ketcham? What worries me most is the phrase '*Helios at hotel*'. Who could Helios be? We all missed the first two phases of Saieda's plan and the exchange. Now what?"

Richard gently took Elspeth's arm and led her back to the breakfast table. He poured out fresh tea for them both and offered Elspeth the toast rack. She took a slightly charred piece of bread and spread jam over it. She absently took a large bite and chewed it slowly.

"I don't want to think that Conan FitzRoy is involved in the exchange, but can't disregard it," she said. "On the way over to Gozo last night Loren told me about her trip with Conan to the vineyard. They discussed his research

133

for his new book, but I didn't really listen to what she said. Now I am sorry I didn't."

Elspeth was aware that Richard had stopped sipping his tea.

"Will you see her this morning?" he asked.

Elspeth nodded. "I'll ask her again. Dickie, I'm dealing with ghosts and demons here—with my own dislike of death, with Eric Kennington's aversion to any disturbance at his hotels and with my own feelings of inadequacy. We've now reached Phrase Three without knowing what Phases One and Two were. And we have a whole cast of shadow figures mentioned in the emails, one of whom is lurking at the hotel. I must act quickly, but I've no idea in what direction to go." Elspeth put her fingers to her temples and rubbed them.

"Do you think FitzRoy might be connected somehow to these shadowy figures?" Richard asked.

"Knowing FitzRoy, I think if he were that it would be unknowingly. He is—was—too open. I never knew him to be secretive. He enjoyed being, as Peter would say, 'out there'." Peter, Elspeth's son in San Francisco, favoured the California vernacular.

Richard thought a moment before he spoke. "Do you think his death was from natural causes?"

Elspeth sat back, surprised at his words. "I never assumed otherwise. Oh, Dickie, you're right. We should find out for sure."

Her thoughts turned back to the night before. Although in her career she had brushed with death occasionally, she had always had an abhorrence of it after Malcolm's murder at Cambridge. Conan's death was no exception. The immediate activity of removing the body from the public areas of the hotel had numbed her feelings in the moment. But in the end she couldn't avoid facing what death meant. It was not only the end of someone being physically alive but also the end of any future relationship with that person. The person could live on in one's memory and fill one with sorrow, or be remembered with love or hatred, but there would be no more sharing, nothing more to look forward to. Everything within one's relationship with that human being had been defined. There would be no further mystery, no anticipation and no hope. A relationship that held an infinite variety of possibilities became frozen. Memories would fill one but soon only the strongest of these would survive. Other memories of other people would slowly take their place. She knew this would happen with Conan, who was an amusing and occasional acquaintance, just as it had happened with Malcolm, who had been the person she had loved the most in her lifetime. She would not cry for Conan the way she had for Malcolm, but she would miss Conan. In the end, she wondered, would anyone cry for FitzRoy?

"Elspeth, can you help us find FitzRoy's next of kin? It would seem natural that the hotel would do so."

"I'll do what I can. Pamela Crumm is a great resource for this sort of thing. I'll let you know."

A church bell in the distance struck nine. Elspeth begged off another piece of toast, and said that her presence in the hotel was needed.

The insistence of the sun on breaking through the haze seemed to emphasise the pressing need for action. But what action? Who were the real players? The exchange was complete. What had been exchanged? Phase Three was ready to begin. And Saieda, who ever she/he was, seemed to be fully in charge.

With these thoughts Elspeth decided to forgo the luxury of the long walk back to Valletta, and had Richard phone for a taxi.

*

As the lift clattered its way down from the terrace, Richard put his arms about Elspeth, and she rested her head against his shoulder.

"Thank you, Dickie," she whispered, "for listening and offering sympathy but not advice." He knew her response to him was more from gratitude than love.

After she left, the memory of the softness of her body lingered against his. He went back to the terrace and took the tea trolley down to the kitchen.

13

Loren Axt woke just before seven when she sensed there was activity in Elspeth's room next door. She heard Elspeth leave her room a few minutes later. Loren knew that Elspeth had been up late dealing with FitzRoy's death, and wondered why the early departure. Had something happened?

Shortly before nine, Loren emerged into the street. Already, weekday morning traffic was bustling through the plaza in front of the hotel and along the narrow streets that crisscrossed the centre of Valletta. She had tucked her mobile phone in the pocket of her jogging suit, and as soon as she was out of sight of the hotel, she removed it and punched in Evan's stored number. Evan answered immediately.

"Good morning, Alicia," he said. "I can see you from here. Turn right on Triq San Pawl. I'll join you there."

She was amazed at how bright he seemed. He must have gone to bed long after she had because Elspeth had asked him to help with the arrangements for Conan FitzRoy's body.

Loren turned the corner into the narrow street, she and saw Evan jogging in place. He smiled radiantly.

"Fairest of mornings to thee, Mistress Kent," he said. "May the sunrise bring thee sustenance for thy day." A haze obscured the early sun, but this did not seem to dampen Evan's enthusiasm.

"Did you have any rest?" she asked, surprised by his merriment.

"Hardly any. But let's keep moving. I've a great deal to tell you."

The cracked, uneven concrete pavements, punctuated with short flights of low steps, made her concentrate on her feet as they jogged. They moved along the narrow passage between the illegally parked cars, half on the pavement and half on the road. Cars sidled down the street, scarcely scraping by those lining the pavement. Still, Loren and Evan kept up a quick pace. Evan spoke to her whenever they could jog together.

"Superintendent Ketcham rang me a short while ago, and said GCHQ has intercepted another message. It seems the exchange, whatever it may have been, has already happened," he said.

Loren moved ahead for a moment in order to circumvent a small van whose driver was unloading a truckload of cardboard boxes and taking them into a lace-curtained shop. Evan soon caught up with her. His breathing came steadily—the way the breath does of a seasoned runner. "The email indicated that there is someone staying at the hotel, code named Helios, and this Helios seems to be privy to 'Saieda's latest instructions', whatever they may be. What's more, haste is stressed."

Evan was forced behind Loren once more. When he came abreast, Loren matched her stride to his. They reached the lowest part of Triq San Pawl, and began to ascend the hill towards Fort St. Elmo. The storekeepers along the way were opening the large wooden doors that protected their shops at night, exposing the diversity of items they sold—from fine lace to tins of baked beans. As Evan avoided a scrawny dog and came up alongside Loren again, she asked, "Is there any more information about these people—Saieda and gang?"

"Not yet. But now we know definitely that someone in the hotel is involved."

Loren raised her head to look at him, and stumbled on a large crack on the pavement. Her recovery was automatic, but she did not pull away from the hand Evan extended to her.

"Everyone at the hotel is so upper middle class, so wealthy and so non-threatening," she said.

"Like you?" Evan asked.

She grinned. "Like Alicia. But there is this one young man who is always creeping around. On my way to bed last night I saw him sitting among the shadows at the edge of the bar and watching me. He looks Arabic, so I have instinctively typecast him as one of the ones we are looking for. He just doesn't fit. His discomfort is palpable. I keep asking myself why, if he is one of them, would they put him at the hotel where his whole demeanour makes him seem a misfit?"

Evan stopped briefly to avoid kicking a pigeon pecking a piece of fruit squashed by a passing car. Then he picked up his pace. "I don't know, Loren. But we can't let it go. What do your instincts tell you?"

Loren noted that he called her Loren rather than Alicia. She did not know if this was to show that he was addressing her as a fellow professional or if he wanted to differentiate his conversations with Alicia Kent from those with Loren Axt.

"When terrorists venture out of their own element, they often make obvious mistakes. I've seen this many times, and I'm sure you have too," she said. "Because these mistakes seem so obvious to us, we view them as…" she groped for the word, "stupid. Like when before nine-eleven the intelligence agencies in the US didn't pick up that there were people who wanted to know how to fly a plane but not land it, a definitely stupid thing. I guess if they had, the disaster might've been averted. Am I being too simplistic?"

"No, I don't think so. That happened in northern Spain last year. A terrorist posing as a Spanish policeman hit his head accidentally and swore in Basque. He seemed unaware that he had done so, but it was the first indication that he might be working against the Spanish authorities."

They jogged on for a moment in silence. Guests at the hotel might have been surprised that the beautiful Ms Kent would have chosen such strenuous exercise so early in the morning, she thought.

Evan broke off the run as they rounded a corner and the fortified walls and portcullis of Fort St. Elmo came into view. They slowed to a cooling walk. Loren was saddened that the moment had to end but Evan brought them back to reality.

"I've got to leave you soon. I'm due at police headquarters by ten, and need to look respectable. I promised Elspeth I'd help sort out the problems caused by FitzRoy's death so I'll have to rely on you to monitor the uncomfortable guest. I'd suggest that you get in touch with

Elspeth as soon as you get back to the hotel to tell her we've talked."

She smiled at him and said, "Evan, thanks for the run. Elspeth can fill me in on the rest."

They finished their run at a calming pace. As they came closer to the gates into Fort Elmo, Evan turned to her.

"Loren, I wanted you to know that last evening wasn't all play acting." Then he raised his hand in goodbye and left her behind. Deep in thought, she turned and retraced her steps back to the Kennington Valletta.

As Loren arrived at the main entrance, she saw Elspeth alighting from a taxi. Elspeth saw her and waved. Loren noticed her casual dress and fatigued eyes, but Elspeth did not give any explanation.

"Alicia, I hadn't expected you up so early this morning," Elspeth said.

Loren laughed, trying to sound frivolous. "Just a short morning jog. Last evening was so delightful. I adore your aunt! And of course, Evan Davies-Jones was so…" She paused. "We went out running together this morning. There is no better way to start a day. I feel…" She let the emotion float into the air.

"Oh to be young again," said Elspeth. "What are you up to today?"

Loren improvised, remembering Sir Richard's instructions the night before. "I'm rather tired after last night. I thought I might stay at the hotel this morning and write a few postcards." Loren wondered what false addresses to use for the recipients of postcards from 'Alicia' and if the worker in the dead letter offices would enjoy greetings from Malta. Postcards demanded no return address.

"Come and have a bit of breakfast with me before you settle in," Elspeth said.

"Let me shower first," Loren said.

Half an hour later, Loren found Elspeth sitting at a table nestled in a quiet corner of the breakfast room and now dressed in her professional clothes. No other guests were in sight.

Alicia Kent dropped into a chair. Her makeup was perfect; her clothes draped across her body with ease. She had dressed in a low cut tee shirt, tailored trousers, and a fashionable clinging cardigan. She also carried a popular novel.

Elspeth poured coffee for them both, and offered a croissant to Loren, who shook her head but instead took a piece of fruit. "You talked to Evan this morning, I take it," Elspeth said.

"Yes, when we were jogging up Triq San Pawl to the fortress."

The waiter had moved near the door and struck up a conversation with the concierge, which left the two women to their confidences.

"Did he tell you about the new email?" Elspeth asked.

"Yes, partly. He said you would fill me in," Loren said, sipping the coffee Elspeth had given her.

"Come with me to my office when we have finished eating. I've spoken to Tony Ketcham in London and he agreed I should show you the whole message. In the meantime, tell me, did you and Evan have any insights that might be useful to us here at the hotel?"

Loren detected tension in Elspeth's voice, and realised that terrorism is not something a senior security advisor to the Kennington hotels would deal with every day.

"We both wondered why the hotel is involved," Loren said. "Logically it makes no sense. But I think this anomaly is for a good reason." Loren repeated her conversation with Evan. "I've dealt with terrorists many times before," she shared. "They aren't Kennington Hotel guests or at least not typical ones."

Loren, visually keeping up her role of Alicia Kent, continued to sip her steaming cup of coffee and cut a dainty bite of the perfectly ripe pear she had chosen. A casual observer would not have guessed the topic of their conversation from a distance.

"Everyone here seems to fit in except for the young Arabic man who seems to creep around. Do you know any more about him?" Loren asked.

Elspeth confessed she knew only that his name was Adam Russell, and he has a British passport and a London address. "I don't know why he is here," Elspeth said. "You're right. He doesn't fit. Scotland Yard is tracing him. I'll let you know what they discover."

They finished their breakfast in a leisurely fashion. As they emerged from the breakfast room, Elspeth turned to Loren and said in a tone that other guests might be able to hear, "Come with me, and let me see if the staff did pick up your jacket, Ms Kent."

She escorted Loren into the back offices and into the small conference room. Elspeth unlocked a file drawer in the desk in the corner and took out a strong box. Twisting the lock, she opened the box and drew out a sheet of paper.

"I asked Sir Richard to write out the message for me. Helios is clearly identified as being at the hotel, but we still know nothing about Saieda."

Loren read the note quickly and looked up at Elspeth, who was rubbing her forehead with two well-manicured fingers.

"Could Helios be Adam Russell?" Loren asked.

"Possibly. When I spoke to Tony Ketcham, he said he'd send out a detective constable to find out Adam's London roots. I thought you'd follow up here at the hotel. Linger about the lobby, watch Adam and follow him if necessary."

As Elspeth spoke, Loren picked up a note of authority in Elspeth's voice that had not been there before. She's more in charge than she looks, Loren thought, and less calm. Elspeth repeated the orders Sir Richard had given Loren the night before.

"I'm to assume the role of an idle tourist who has little to do," Loren reiterated. "I'm not sure I can be as grey a presence as our lad from London, despite the fact that I've been trained in the art of being inconspicuous."

"Oh, another thing, Loren. Did Conan FitzRoy tell you who he was going to meet at five o'clock?"

Loren shook her head. "No, I wish he had. I'm sorry about his death."

Elspeth smiled sadly. "So am I. Report back as soon as you can, particularly if you find out anything that may be useful." Elspeth's words were commanding although spoken softly. "I keep my mobile with me and can be reached at any time. Or you can ring Evan."

"Will do," Loren said.

As she emerged from the hotel offices, she called back rather loudly so others could hear. "You'll let me know if anyone finds it later."

*

Adam Russell was sitting near the concierge's desk and saw the person he had discovered was called Alicia Kent come out from the back area of the hotel. He decided that American women like this would be better off if they knew more about the teachings of the Qur'an regarding the modesty of women. No Muslim woman would expose herself outside of her home the way Alicia was doing as she walked into the writing room and flounced into a chair at one of the desks. He tried not to remember the girls at his comprehensive.

14

After Elspeth led Loren back to the lobby and returned to her office, she found a message asking her to contact the Kennington Organisation offices in London, which she did promptly. Pamela Crumm took the call, which she then put through to Eric Kennington's home in Essex. Elspeth assumed he had not yet left for the City.

When he answered, Elspeth heard him dismiss someone, whom she assumed was his valet. Eric came back on the line. "Damned fellow always wants to poke his nose into my business. Elspeth, the British high commissioner in Malta rang me just moments ago in response to my call to him, and I asked him to cooperate with you in every way possible in the difficulties surrounding Conan FitzRoy's death. I want you to make sure that our other guests are not disturbed in any way. You know the routine."

Elspeth silently groaned at his endless mantra. But Eric Kennington's rise into the stratosphere of international boutique hotel owners depended on pleasing and protecting guests, and Elspeth knew it was her job to see this was done. With rare exception, this assignment being one, Elspeth enjoyed her job, and admitted it gave her a style of living that she could not otherwise afford. Consequently, she answered him with polite deference.

"Yes, of course," she said, as if hearing his request for the first time. "As far as I know, no guests saw us when we removed the body from the garden last night. DI Davies-Jones was incredibly useful, and I'm certain the high commissioner will assist us. He's an old family friend from Scotland. Did I tell you that we had breakfast this morning?"

"No, we didn't exchange niceties," his lordship said irritably. "Although the high commissioner may be used to having British nationals die in Malta, I am not."

His imperiousness always exasperated Elspeth.

"I want you to make every effort to see that the name of the hotel is not associated with Conan FitzRoy's death. Arrange it with your high commissioner. There are to be no implications in the press that anything happened at the Kennington Valletta that might cause discomfort to present or future guests."

"Yes, of course, Eric," she said, hoping she was hiding her forbearance. "I've already discussed this with René LeGrand, and certainly I will do so with Sir Richard."

"And what else are you going to do about Conan FitzRoy's death?" he demanded.

Elspeth was glad she had formed the embryo of a plan. "We'll need to be in touch with his next of kin. The high commissioner said he'd see if they have anything on record about FitzRoy's family, but he asked me to intervene. Actually I think Pamela can find this person more efficiently than the FCO. Will you have her look into this? I need to know who will be in charge of receiving his personal effects."

Eric Kennington softened his tone. "If, Elspeth, you didn't have a job that always had you trotting all over the world and instead stayed at home and read the scandal rags the way Pamela does, you'd know that FitzRoy acquired and shed a number of wives over the course of his career. I don't know his current marital status, but obviously he wasn't travelling with a wife in tow. I'll make sure that Pamela gets the name of FitzRoy's solicitors, and will have her ring you back. Keep your mobile with you."

I always do, she thought.

"Then I'll leave the details to you and Pamela," he said. "I expect that FitzRoy, with all of his flamboyance, was not necessarily a man of business. His lifestyle would lead one to think he allowed less grand people take care of these mere details of daily life."

Elspeth laughed, glad that Lord Kennington had stopped ranting. Pamela Crumm, she knew, relished reading the latest gossip in the popular press especially when many of the featured people had stayed at the Kennington hotels and might well do so again.

Eric barked a final order into the phone. "And extend every courtesy to the heir. We want the heir to feel proper gratitude to the hotel management for an accommodating stay."

After she settled the handset into its cradle, Elspeth stood still for a moment, and considered FitzRoy's life and death. His death seemed anticlimactic after the grand presentation of his life. She had known him for almost five years and yet strangely she knew nothing of his personal life. Had he set up his public life this way for a reason?

Now she would never find out.

She went in search of René LeGrand and found him in his office. René had a copy of the Kennington Organisation's operations manual on his desk and together they discussed the procedures normally employed in the event of a guest's death. Usually people who died at a hotel were elderly and had suffered a heart attack or stroke in their beds. Removal of the body by local paramedics through the rear entrance was the standard course of action. If anyone did see the ambulance, whose drivers were instructed not to use flashing lights, the casual observer would conclude that the guest in question was ill. If people enquired about what happened, they would be told the guest died in hospital. Deaths did not occur at Kennington hotels.

No one had asked about FitzRoy's death in the garden the night before. Both Elspeth and René were reasonably confident that the removal of the body had gone undetected, except for perhaps by Adam Russell burrowed in the corner of the bar.

Elspeth saw that René had a schedule for the day lying on his desk. No events were planned at the hotel except the regular weekday routine. The restaurant on the top floor would be open from noon until four and then later from seven until closing. The bar in the lounge would be open until the last guest had left, which considering the sedate clientele of the hotel was usually before midnight.

The group from the Smithsonian was to gather in the lobby at eleven. They were scheduled for an excursion to the picturesque fishing village of Marsaxlokk on the south side of the island, where they would have a catered lunch and a guided walk, and would not be returning until teatime. René and Elspeth agreed that the concierge would escort the group into the tearoom on their return and that the tea would be a little more lavish than the already opulent teas routinely served at the hotel. That way they would be well filled and hopefully less likely to wander out into the lobby where they might hear rumours about FitzRoy's death.

Sir Michael and Lady Gaunt and his party, accompanied by several members of the Maltese Commonwealth and Foreign Office, were spending the day on Gozo and had already left the hotel. This left the staff to their morning duties.

Just after half past ten, Rene and Elspeth called the weekday staff together. Apparently they all had heard of the death, and Elspeth wanted to make sure they knew what had actually happened. She also wanted to instruct them on what was expected of them in the next few days.

All looked up at her expectantly. She cleared her throat before speaking. "Mr FitzRoy died last night in the garden," she began. "He was alone at the time. We had his body removed when his death was discovered. He had recently had heart trouble, and we assume that he died of a heart attack. Unless you particularly enjoy historical fiction, you may never have heard of Mr FitzRoy, but he is well known by many readers, particularly in Britain, Canada, Australia and America. Mr LeGrand and I want to make sure that as few of the guests as possible know about what happened. We've sent messages through the British high commissioner's office to the British, Canadian, Australian and American press stating that Mr Conan

FitzRoy, the historical novelist, was found dead in his sleep last night in Malta. The Kennington Valletta was not mentioned in the release, and we hope that the name of the hotel will remain unpublished. If the press does find out that Mr FitzRoy died here, I am sure that they'll ask about the circumstances. Lord Kennington personally told me this morning he wanted to avoid publicity of this sort at all costs. Therefore it is essential that none of you say anything to the press. If questioned, simply say you know nothing. Do the same if any of the guests here asks you about Mr FitzRoy's death."

Elspeth looked over the room and watched the staff's heads nodding in agreement.

René added his own directive. "Mr FitzRoy's rooms will be kept locked, and nothing is to be removed. We do not want any of the room attendants to enter the suite. Because the death was sudden, there may be an investigation by the police. We will request that this be carried out by plain clothes inspectors, and either Ms Duff or I will show them to the rooms."

René then repeated the instructions in French, Italian, Spanish and Malti. Although all of the staff were required to speak English, he told Elspeth that he did not wish that there be any misunderstanding.

The staff went back to their work. Some murmured comments to each other as they left the staff room, but, when they reached the public areas of the hotel, they resumed their tasks without the slightest sign that anything unusual had happened.

Elspeth returned to her office and rang Eric Kennington, who would now be in his office. She assured him that all procedures had been put in place. Then she sat back in her chair and felt curiously deflated. When she had arrived in Valletta, she had been charged with finding and defusing an imminent but amorphous threat at the hotel. Now, instead, she was dealing with the ever-so-real death of a friend, who only yesterday had embraced her with the fullness of his life. She knew she would miss Conan FitzRoy in the years to come. Who else could enter a lobby with such extravagant flamboyance? Who else could host such sumptuous dinner parties?

"Goodbye, Conan," she whispered into the air. If there were a heaven, she thought, would his entrance into it be outrageous?

15

Evan finished his run shortly after Loren left him at the bottom of Triq San Pawl. He returned to his flat, bathed and dressed. Although usually a fastidious dresser, today he took special care, knowing he might see Loren during the day. He chose a dark grey suit he had purchased in Spain the year before, the style more European than British and hand-tailored. He chose a dark tie, which befit a police officer on duty.

Evan made sure the unoccupied arm of his jacket was neatly pinned up. When he had lost his arm, he had been offered a prosthetic limb. He worked with the police surgeons and physical therapists for months, but always found the device intrusive. Since he was naturally left handed, the loss of his right arm was less of a problem than it might otherwise have been. He still had a good portion of his upper right arm, which he had learned to use skilfully, so skilfully in fact that many of his friends and colleagues soon forgot his infirmity. Evan still played rugby, rode, played one-handed tennis and ran half marathons.

The facial scar was another thing. He had discussed this with the police psychologists at length. Why should he be so shattered by the scar? Three bouts of plastic surgery had only helped somewhat. He still remained handsome,

153

but every time he shaved or combed his hair, he saw the flaw. He had spent hours trying to figure out why the facial scar was so much worse than the loss of the arm. Both of his parents had been physically beautiful. His mother at age fifty-five still turned heads on the street, and his father's advancing years had only increased his handsomeness. All the mothers of the boys at the small boys' boarding school where Evan's father taught fell secretly in love with him. The boys called him Mr George Clooney the Elder. Evan idolised his father, who was witty, scholarly and filled with old world charm. Both Evan and his sister had inherited their parents' good looks, and learned to enjoy what that brought to their lives.

Then there had been the bomb. Evan had received numerous citations for his sacrifice that had saved the minister's life. The Prime Minister had personally asked that he come to Ten Downing Street. He had received a Queen's Police Medal, and been recognised at Buckingham Palace. The Queen thanked him for his bravery.

Evan was not prepared for what he might see when the bandages were removed. Nor was he prepared after each corrective surgery. He hated his new face, no matter how often he looked at it. When women looked at him, he heard their slight intake of breath and then felt their pity. Again and again and again he told himself it did not matter, but it did.

Last night he met Alicia Kent a.k.a. Loren Axt. He had not expected her. He knew he was to meet an Interpol undercover operative and she would be a woman. He was told she would be posing as an unattached, wealthy

American, and he should look as if he was attracted to her and make a sufficient show that he wanted to continue his relationship with her. He imagined what she would be like, tough, short, and with an unattractive twang in her voice. But she appeared tall, fit and outwardly gentle, and spoke with only the trace of an American accent. He was instantly enthralled.

When he had turned to her the evening before, she did not take in her breath. He felt she had looked not at the scar, which covered much of the right side of his face, but at him. Later she had acknowledged the scar when she gently put her fingers up to it and asked how it had happened. Her eyes were kind and caring and without revulsion. She was the only person he had ever met to whom the scar seemed a symbol of courage, not the invention of a mad monster. At that moment he fell in love with her.

No, Evan, he said to himself, you are here on duty. Your mission is critical and this woman is as trained a professional as you are. She has the skills to kill without a weapon. She would sacrifice her life or a limb, as he had, in the service of international peace and justice. She, as he, could not have a private life that in any way would interfere with the cause of eradicating terrorism. Yet he wanted her to become part of his life.

Suddenly, he understood the power his family's beauty had over other people. It was so easy to accept the fawning as a natural part of his family's being, fawning that was a constant reminder that they were a special breed, a little above ordinary beings. Evan began to see why the loss of his special face had been so difficult. The loss of the arm made him a hero. The loss of the face had made him less than perfect; it had made him ugly.

Last night on the balcony at Magdelena Cassar's farmhouse Loren had caressed the scar with the slightest touch, and he had been made beautiful again.

As he finished his grooming, Evan looked at himself again and saw the scar. Her touch had made it different, an honour to bear. He wanted to shout 'touch it again'. Then he felt foolish.

FitzRoy's death had complicated things. When Evan was growing up, he had read all of FitzRoy's books. FitzRoy's heroes became Evan's heroes and he imagined being in their place. The books had a major impact on his future career.

Now Evan had to deal with the corpse of this giant man. Without life there was no personality. Evan understood from Loren that FitzRoy's effusiveness, knowledge and intelligence had made him an excellent if somewhat verbose companion. The large dead body that now lay in the coroner's morgue had none of these qualities, and Evan was responsible for what was left.

With the help of the Maltese police and the coroner, Evan had seen to the removal of the body from the hotel the night before. Throughout the process, he watched the smooth efficiency of Elspeth Duff. She showed no sign of repugnance at the task, only concern that none of the other hotel guests would learn what had happened. If she had feelings of sorrow, he was not privy to them.

DI Evan Davies-Jones smoothed his suit jacket as he scaled the steps up to the police station. He waved to the round-cheeked constable at the desk who was smartly outfitted in the dark blue uniform of Maltese policewomen and who seemed to have taken a fancy to him, and made his way to the desk that had been assigned to him in a back room. The sergeant on duty handed him the daily roster, an envelope from the coroner and instructions to proceed to the superintendent's office as soon as possible.

Evan ripped the envelope open and skimmed the coroner's words, which noted it was too early to determine the exact cause of Conan FitzRoy's death and an autopsy would be needed to provide conclusive results. Evan knew the police had the right to perform an autopsy in the case of sudden death from an unknown cause, so permission of the next of kin was not needed. But he suspected that the exercise would prove to be a moot one. The night before on the terrace Loren had mentioned FitzRoy's dismissal of his heart ailments. Evan picked up his phone but did not find anyone at the coroner's office. He left his mobile number on the answerphone with instructions that he be called when the autopsy was finished.

Next he went to see the superintendent, a large man with the long patrician face characteristic of many Maltese, who greeted Evan warmly and gestured for him to sit down.

"I spoke to Detective Superintendent Ketcham at the Yard this morning," the superintendent said, "and he shared the latest developments at the Kennington Valletta with me. We agreed that the best course of action would be for me to assign you to the FitzRoy case since that will give you an excuse to be at the Kennington Valletta. You will be working with DI Dominick Lapira, my best

157

forensic investigator. I have instructed him to make a thorough search of Conan FitzRoy's room in case there is any evidence that FitzRoy is…was involved somehow in the other operation at the hotel, although both the Yard and I don't think so. You will find that Inspector Dom is a force unto himself. If there is anything wrong, he will find it."

During his orientation at the Valletta police station, Evan had met Lapira briefly. Inspector Dom, as everyone in the station called him, had greeted Evan with excitement, glad, he said, to be working under the shadow of Scotland Yard, where he had taken several training courses. Inspector Dom was a small and dapper man with thinning hair combed back and fixed with gel. His charcoal double-breasted suit fit immaculately over his tight frame, and his black eyes shone with intelligence. Inspector Dom's colleagues assured DI Davies-Jones that little escaped his eyes.

Shortly after half past ten Evan and Inspector Dom were shown into the manager's office of the Kennington Valletta. Elspeth and René LeGrand were waiting for them. René offered a brief tour of the security arrangements at the hotel, explained the security monitors and re-ran the videotape of the removal of Conan FitzRoy's body the night before. Inspector Dom viewed the arrangements and tape without expression, nodding at this and nodding at that. At the end of the tour he finally spoke.

"When I was a child," he said, "this building was in near ruins. It was hit many times by the Axis bombs during the Siege of Malta in the Second World War. After the war many people in Malta and in the UK gave money to have the building restored because it was once an auberge of the Knights of St. John and so important to our history. I have not been inside since I was in my twenties when my fiancée asked me to bring her here to tea. I was a 'rookie cop', as the American television programmes say, and the extravagance, even faded, overwhelmed me. I felt very uncomfortable, as we Maltese were not openly welcome here in those days, although my fiancée said we were as good as any of the patrons of the hotel. I think, however, that the hotel suffered from the malaise that accompanied the breakup of the British Empire and the end of the British occupation of the island. I am glad that the building has now been restored by the Kennington hotels and can show off the true magnificence of Malta. And," he said with a delicate cough, "I understand that the tacit exclusionary policy at the hotel no longer is in effect."

Elspeth, who knew the hotel's history, expressed her welcome to the inspector on behalf of Lord Kennington and an invitation to him and to his wife to return to the hotel as her personal guest when the investigation was over. He beamed at the prospect.

"Inspector Lapira, I hope…" Elspeth said, returning to the reason for his visit.

"No, no, *sinjura* Duff, you must call me Dom!"

"Inspector Dom then. I hope that you will feel free to ask for anything you need to help with your investigation. Mr FitzRoy's death comes at a time when our security staff is involved in another…" Elspeth seemed to hunt for a diplomatic word, "exercise. Your help and discretion in investigating Mr FitzRoy's death will be very much appreciated by all of us here."

Inspector Dom dipped his head and smiled at her. "The pleasure is mine, *sinjura*. Please understand that this is a formality we must perform when a foreigner dies unexpectedly in our country. I will try to be in and out as quickly as possible."

Evan was not sure if Inspector Dom was aware of the other threat to the hotel. Elspeth had suggested it and Dom had not reacted.

"Let me take you up to Mr FitzRoy's suite," Elspeth said. "We've alerted our staff to make sure the rooms have been left undisturbed. I hope that you'll understand when we take the service lift to the fourth floor that we need you, even in plain clothes, to stay out of the public eye."

"Yes, *sinjura*, I know. The Kennington hotel is not a place for the police."

"Thank you for your understanding," Elspeth said.

After Elspeth left FitzRoy's suite, Inspector Dom laid out his kit and began his investigation with a professionalism that Evan found reassuring. First Dom photographed the rooms' walls and floor and then the furniture. He paid particular attention to FitzRoy's personal items, his clothing, his fold down shaving kit that hung from the bathroom door, his jewellery case, his whisky flask, the papers on the desk, a small gift box that contained a pair of gold earrings and his briefcase. The inspector took extensive photographs of FitzRoy's travel documents, his laptop computer, the handwritten sheets in the folder next to computer and the small digital camera that lay next to them. He handed these last things to Evan.

Evan was disconcerted when Inspector Dom, who had been collegial up to this point, addressed him by his title, "Inspector, I have finished with these. Please take charge of them." Then he waved his hand at Evan in dismissal. Putting me in my place, Evan thought, since I have no direct authority in Malta to investigate a sudden death, only to handle the terrorist threat.

The minutes were ticking by towards the first of May before which Saieda's operation was scheduled to end. Today was April twenty-sixth, and there were three and a half days left in Malta's independent status outside the EU. Did the exchange or 'Phase Three' have anything to do with this? Or could it have?

Evan's mind raced. Who was Helios at the hotel mentioned in the second message? Loren told him as they jogged up Triq San Pawl that she was leery of the young Arab man who was so out of place at the hotel. No one else staying at the hotel fit the profile of a terrorist. Part of Loren's job would be to track him in the next few days, which distressed Evan. He had no real cause for concern other than his growing attachment to Loren. She was in the trade and had surely been in many situations more dangerous than this. Following Adam Russell would be as common for her as it would have been for him. Still he fretted. Better to get the investigation of FitzRoy's death over with quickly and leave any of the mopping up in the capable hands of Inspector Dominick Lapira.

After being dismissed by Inspector Dom, Evan took the service lift down to the private hotel offices out of respect for Elspeth's plea for insulating the guests from the police. She responded immediately to his knock on the door of the conference room where she said she would be working.

"How is Inspector Dom proceeding upstairs?" she asked.

"Slowly but thoroughly. I'm not sure what he hopes to find. Whatever it is, his methods are meticulous, and I'll not be missed. In the meantime he has entrusted me with FitzRoy's computer, his camera, his travel documents and what looks like his notes. These should be secured for his next of kin and passed on along to them. Do you have a place to store them here at the hotel that is more secure than the safe at the front desk?"

"Yes, we have a vault back here, but don't you think the police should keep them instead?"

He considered her request. "I see no need; both Inspector Dom and I have looked them over and he photographed them. FitzRoy's personal papers seem to be in order. You will find his passport and tickets on to Cairo and his scheduled return to London. He planned to fly from here to Cairo and send his car back from here to the UK. I looked briefly at his notes. His handwriting is scrawling and he seems to use some sort of shorthand, so they are largely indecipherable. I tried to boot up his computer but it's password protected. There's no chip in his camera. In fact we couldn't find any chip in his room at all. I assume that he was so well acquainted with Malta that he didn't need to take photographs here, or he had forgotten his chip but planned to buy one in Cairo. No, I think these things are quite safe in the hotel vault."

Elspeth took the items, made a written inventory of

them and handed the receipt to Evan. "Just in case there's any issue over these things."

Evan approved of her thoroughness but he expected her actions were as routine as Dom's.

"Have you heard anything more from London?" he asked.

"No. I've been trying to find FitzRoy's next of kin. I just finished talking to our office in London and they're trying to get the information for me. We need to know where to send his effects. We're assuming that the high commission will handle the details for the transportation of the body."

"In the meantime, have you had any further word about the exchange or Helios?" he asked.

"No, none. We've alerted the staff. Beyond that, I hope that Loren and I can discover more. FitzRoy's death has been an unpleasant diversion."

"It has," Evan said with heartfelt annoyance. "I'll stay in touch. Inspector Dom should have completed his checks shortly, and I'm sure he will let you know when he is finished. I plan to get back to the main event as soon as I get back to the police station. Detective Superintendent Ketcham sent word that he wants me to find out more about FitzRoy's movements after he got back from the vineyard."

"Thank you, Evan. You're always welcome here, both officially and as a guest."

Evan took his leave shortly afterwards. As he emerged from the back entrance to the hotel, his mobile phone rang. The coroner was on the other end of the line.

"Inspector, our autopsy on Conan FitzRoy's body has

uncovered some unexpected results. I won't go into the details on the phone, but I think both you and Inspector Lapira should return to the station as soon as possible."

"What results?"

"His body shows every sign of his being poisoned."

16

Elspeth's mobile rang after Evan left the conference room. Pamela's deep, distinguished tones came through from London. Elspeth was always amazed by Pamela's delivery, and secretly suspected she had studied elocution, although Pamela had never admitted it.

Elspeth did know a great deal about Pamela's background, which Pamela had told her all about over cups of tea, glasses of wine, and late night dinners. Pamela had devoted her life to the hotel chain. She had not done this out of blind devotion to Eric Kennington but because of the opportunities her position afforded her. She had left secretarial college with the highest marks for efficiency, but the principal of the school had recommended that she seek a job out of the eyes of public commerce because of her small size, twisted back, large facial features and poor eyesight, which necessitated thick spectacles. Pamela knew she was not a beauty but she knew she was quick and good. Too many of Eric Kennington's secretarial staff had flirted with him. He did not like flirting. He had no intention of being diverted from his only goal—extremely fine hotels with extremely fine reputations in extremely fine buildings and with extremely fine service at extremely high prices. Pamela had made it her goal in life to see that she shared that ambition. Eric knew this. He had made her

165

a partner in the firm many years before, letting her buy a large share of the privately held stock. As he became rich and famous, she too became wealthy. Theirs was a partnership that became essential to the hotel chain's success. He had the genius, vision and the exquisite taste; she had the organisational skills and mastery of detail. Outside the business domain they had no social contact, but the business usually consumed ten to sixteen hours a day, which they shared together.

Most employees who entered Eric's office dismissed the ugly woman who was in the room with his lordship, and Pamela preferred it that way. In the days before computers, people assumed Pamela was a stenographer, and, when computers appeared on all desks, people presumed she was a vestige of the past. They were wrong.

When Elspeth first met Pamela, there was a spark between them. Elspeth knew instantly Pamela's importance to the Kennington Organisation, and Pamela knew she knew. They exchanged a knowing smile at the interview where Elspeth was offered a job. After Elspeth agreed to become a part of the Kennington Organisation, Pamela invited Elspeth to a gourmet meal and a tête-à-tête. Pamela and Elspeth became friends.

They had another bond. They were two of the few people who felt comfortable standing up to Eric Kennington. In the course of his success, he had acquired an imperious tone with his employees and most were slightly frightened by him, but neither Pamela nor Elspeth was. Had he been conscious of this, they suspected he would have admired them for it, but would probably also have railed against them for conspiring against him.

Today Pamela dismissed all formalities and got straight to the point. "His lordship asked me to give you the following information," she said with a twinkle in her voice.

"Has he come into the office in one of those moods?" Elspeth asked.

Pamela let out a loud chuckle but did not respond, her answer clear by her tone. "Conan FitzRoy's solicitors are White and Edgewood. They're an established firm with offices in London, Edinburgh, and Belfast. His particular solicitor is Brian Edgewood, grandson of one of the founders. I telephoned the firm as soon as their offices were open. I took the liberty of giving this information to Sir Richard Munro before ringing you so that the high commissioner would be the first to notify Mr Edgewood of Conan FitzRoy's death. I then informed Mr Edgewood that you would be telephoning him from Malta to discuss the arrangements at the hotel. He will be expecting your call."

Since Pamela made no attempt at small talk, Elspeth assumed that the door connecting Pamela's office to Lord Kennington's was open and he was in earshot.

"I'll phone them directly. Thanks and ta-ta, my friend. Put an extra lump of sugar in his tea for me," Elspeth said.

Elspeth could hear Pamela's muffled laugh at the other end of the line. "Good luck, ducks," she whispered with less than perfect vowels.

Elspeth's father headed a firm of solicitors in Perthshire, and she was aware of the ranks of personnel one had to appease before being put through to a partner in a legal office. White and Edgewood Solicitors was no exception. Elspeth was appropriately vetted and finally Brian Edgewood came on the line.

Elspeth put on her most self-important voice. "Mr Edgewood, the Kennington Organisation has asked me to contact you directly. My name is Elspeth Duff. I am one of Lord Kennington's special security advisors and have been given the responsibility of making arrangements to facilitate the return of Conan FitzRoy's effects to the United Kingdom. I understand that Sir Richard Munro had already contacted you and given you the details of Mr FitzRoy's death." She thought she might have overdone her tone, but from the lawyer's response she obviously had not.

"Yes, Mrs Duff. I have spoken to Sir Richard," a haughty voice said. Elspeth noted that the solicitor's old-fashioned way of addressing a businesswoman. She let it pass.

"As Sir Richard already told you, Mr FitzRoy apparently died from a heart attack at our hotel in Valletta last night. We made arrangements to have his body removed to a local mortuary, but we do not know what his wishes were regarding burial. We also do not know his next of kin, if it is his wife or another relative. We would like to invite him or her to stay here at the Kennington Valletta while the arrangements are being made for the disposition of Mr FitzRoy's remains and property." Yuck, she thought, how pompous can I get?

"Thank you, Mrs Duff. I will need permission from the next of kin, of course, to discuss this with you."

Elspeth imagined his nostrils flaring and his mouth turning down as he spoke. She mimicked this gesture mockingly and was glad the call was not being videoed. Lord Kennington would have not been amused.

"I would appreciate it if you could let me know as quickly as possible," she said, stressing the word quickly. "I can be reached on my mobile, which I keep with me at all times. As you may have assumed, Mr Edgewood, the hotel has an established procedure when someone dies. We use the utmost care to see that we do not disturb other guests. We have notified the local police because of the suddenness of the death. They have just completed their investigation of Mr FitzRoy's suite. We do not suspect any foul play, but we don't want to remove Mr FitzRoy's effects from the hotel until the police are satisfied that his death resulted from natural causes."

"I quite understand that, Mrs Duff. It may take me some time to contact the next of kin. She is abroad, although she left us her address because of Mr FitzRoy's ill health. As soon as I have her permission to work more fully with you, I will ring you directly."

Elspeth had dealt with lawyers all of her life. She had considered joining her father's practice at a time when she was young and had frequented his office as a teenager under the indulgent eye of his senior clerk. In her time at Scotland Yard, she had dealt with the best of London's solicitors and barristers, as the crimes she investigated were mainly white-collar ones and the perpetrators were often business and government officials who wanted to stay out of the news. Their lawyers were often aloof but always respectful. American lawyers were different, as she had found out during her days dabbling in private investigation in California. They wanted to be involved in every detail, to stretch every law and boundary, and they were usually critical of the opposing lawyer. She had dealt with lawyers in Australia, Kenya, Hong Kong, Egypt and Indonesia, among other countries, and in each place lawyers had their individual way of dealing with the law and their client's interests. But of all these lawyers she had dealt with, she found Mr Brian Edgewood the most instantly irritating.

Ringing off, Elspeth put fingers to her temples and then shook her head violently. Get the cobwebs out, Elspeth. Mr Brian Edgewood was not worthy of the feelings he conjured up in her. She knew she was tired, but there was little she could do about her fatigue until FitzRoy's affairs were concluded and they had solved the puzzle of the exchange and Phase Three of Saieda's plan.

17

Once Loren had discussed the plans for the day with Elspeth, she began to feel dissatisfied with them without knowing why. She took herself into one of the small writing rooms that lay alongside the lobby and sat down at the desk. She drew out a sheet of the heavy engraved stationery watermarked with the Kennington Organisation crest. She began to doodle on it, not only to seem busy but also to organise her thoughts, by making boxes with arrows that to anyone else would be meaningless.

She drew three columns for the phases indicated in the second email. She thought of the wording of both email messages which were now etched on her memory. The two emails were the only concrete items that they had. She reviewed them in her mind.

22 April: Confirming Pericles staying at Kennington Valletta. Put plans for exchange in place. Saieda will contact you morning 25th April with time to begin operation. All activity must be completed in Malta before 1st May. Timing and precision essential. —Phoenician

26 April: Congratulations on success of exchange. Saieda's plan accomplished. Phase Three to begin immediately. Haste is extremely important. Contact Helios at hotel for Saieda's latest instructions. —Phoenician

Who were the players—Pericles, Saieda, Phoenician,

Helios and the recipient of the emails? She suspected that Phoenician was and would remain off site—the messenger. Saieda, man or woman, was obviously the mastermind. Where was he or she? The intended recipient was obviously not at the hotel but Pericles and Helios probably were.

She was not convinced that Adam Russell was the whole or even a part of Saieda's plan, although he might be Pericles or more likely Helios. If he were, it would be important to find out more about him. Loren hoped he would appear today and take up the post somewhere in the public areas just as he had the day before. She would watch him more closely, although she hated the inactivity of doing so.

*

Adam Russell sat up in bed. He had missed morning prayers. He wanted to turn over and forget, but he heard the distant voice of the imam who had taught him in London. Adam asked Allah's forgiveness. He was not quite sure if asking forgiveness was something from his mother's Christian religion or from Islam, but in any case it would not hurt. As he came to greater consciousness, he remembered the night before.

From his seat in the lobby the afternoon before he had watched as the clown-like English writer addressed as Mr FitzRoy rushed to greet a distinguished Arabic gentleman who called himself Dr Hammud. Dr Hammud had earlier addressed Adam in the very politest of Arabic terms, assuming that he, Adam, was a fellow Arab. Adam had replied carefully in his best Arabic. Dr Hammud had smiled at him.

He watched this FitzRoy leave the hotel and then return to have coffee with Dr Hammud. Shortly afterwards Dr Hammud had checked out of the hotel, asked that his bags be sent to the airport separately and departed by taxi. He saw FitzRoy go up on the lift, come back down and go back into the garden.

Adam had his tea in the bar. He ordered a variety of snacks from the menu and a Pepsi-Cola. As he was finishing his meal, he saw the waiter take a large whiskey out into the garden.

Afterwards Adam found a seat in the main lounge where he could see the front desk and, by looking in the large mirror, the front door as well. He watched the tour group assemble and leave for dinner and various people take the lift up to the dining room and down again. He counted their numbers and later carefully recorded it in his report. There was little other activity after that until the group returned about nine.

He moved to a quiet corner of the bar and ordered another Pepsi. Just after ten he saw the confident woman who seemed to work for the hotel come in through the main door. She reminded him of the head teacher at school, although Adam thought that she was better dressed than the head had ever been. The woman consulted the person at the reception desk and quickly went to the back. There seemed to be some activity in the garden, but he could not see exactly what it was.

Adam looked at the clock beside his bed and noted that it was now half past eight in the morning. He quickly arose and paid his respects to Mecca even though he had missed the first prayers of the day. There were no calls from minarets in Valletta to remind him of the appointed hours, only the striking of the quarter hours from the church bells.

He thought of his tasks for the day. Achmed had told him to record the activities in the hotel at all times of the day. What type of guests frequented the lobby? What kind of and how many people were at the desk? What times of day was the desk busiest? How many people ate in the restaurants—for breakfast, for lunch, for tea, for dinner? What were the daily activities in the bar, in the lounge and in the garden? What kind of service was there later in the evening?

After eating breakfast, Adam resumed his post in the lobby. Achmed had told him that even though he was now a Saudi citizen, while he was staying at the Kennington Valletta, he was to stay British. Adam was aware that other guests in the hotel might recognise his Peckham accent, so he decided to speak as little as possible. He sat patiently watching the activities of the other guests before returning to his room to record them in his awkward schoolboy letters. He wished he could write them in Arabic. He practiced the pretty script of his new language in the quiet moments when he was in his room.

Adam had been told to meet Achmed every day. They varied their appointed time depending on the activity that Adam had been asked to watch. If lunchtime activity was important, then they met afterwards. Today Achmed had asked him to meet at noon in the Knight's Café at the Hotel Saint John outside the city gate.

Adam was in awe of Achmed, his brother. There was twenty years difference in their ages. Achmed had grown up in the luxury of the homes of a Saudi sheik; Adam had grown up in Peckham. Achmed had spent many hours with Adam, who now wanted to be called Abdul, teaching him Saudi etiquette and the manners that rich Saudis observed while abroad. Achmed had spent two years at an expensive English public school and had been coached by instructors from the Royal Academy of Dramatic Arts in speaking the Queen's English. Adam had listened carefully to all Achmed tried to teach him. He hoped to show Achmed he had learned well. Adam was still aware that he did not speak like an Arab sheik or an English gentleman. Achmed told Adam that, as a Saudi businessman, Sheik Abdullah Rashid was intent on giving his sons the advantages he had not had when growing up in the tents of his grandfather's family. Achmed had told Adam that Adam's mother's conversion back to Christianity and her divorce had caused the sheik great anger, but that by proving himself Adam would go far to remove that anger. The rewards seemed so high for Adam that he had never asked why he had been sent to Malta and the Kennington Valletta, and Achmed had not told him.

At eleven, Adam returned to his room. He saw his reflection in the mirror on the door and admired his new beard. Beards were not acceptable at his relative's home in Peckham but his brother and father both had beards—and in the world of Islam beards were preferred.

Half an hour later, Adam Russell left the hotel carrying the leather portfolio Achmed had given him under his arm. He clutched it anxiously, feeling its importance.

As soon as he was out of sight of the doorman, Adam stood taller. In his mind he became the son of his wealthy father. His quiet step became confident as he headed for the square. He raised his head up and looked at the cloudless sky above the buildings along the narrow street. Yes, now, he thought, my brother and my father will see how good I am at observing things. I will give them the information they want. Those people at the hotel look down on me because they think I am inferior, but they do not know. Let them look down their long white noses. My father and brother are strong and rich. In the end they will be in charge.

Adam Russell, now thinking himself as Abdul Rashid, son of Sheik Abdullah Rashid, continued along past the ruins of the opera house and mingled among the tourists coming out from Triq Ir-Repubblika. Walking among the crowds, he passed under the city gates and crossed the bus station yards. At noon he approached the Hotel Saint John.

Achmed had been very clear in his directions to Adam. I am staying at the Hotel Saint John in room 516. "When you arrive, have the concierge ring me. We will have lunch in the Knight's Café. I think you will enjoy it. The café has one of the best lunches in Malta."

Adam approached the concierge's desk. His new clothes fit him smartly and made him feel important. His family had sent him on a mission and he had much to report to them. He was proud to be Abdul Rashid, not the schoolboy Adam Russell. God is Great.

*

Loren had been trained to watch her subject's sense of concentration. As she followed Adam out of the hotel, he seemed absorbed in his own thoughts. He fingered his portfolio as if reassuring himself that it was still with him.

Loren could see his nervousness.

Staying well behind Adam, Loren entered the Hotel Saint John a moment or two after he did and watched him. Because his back was turned and the foyer empty, she was able to escape his notice. Adam did not look around. He told the concierge that he wanted to speak to Achmed Rashid in room 516. He was handed the house phone, nodded several times and then said, "I will meet you at the Knight's Café in five minutes."

Adam Russell left the reception desk and passed Loren without looking at her. Improvising, she told the concierge that she had wanted lunch and had heard how good the food was at the hotel. He informed her that the restaurant was not open at noon but lunch was served at the café, which was down the hall to the right.

Loren had been taught the art of taking on a variety of personalities to fit her operational needs. Being the glamorous Alicia Kent might play well at the Kennington Valletta, but she could become unremarkable with a slight change in her body carriage, the removal of lipstick and a hat to cover her hair. Few people looked at a nondescript person and, even if they did, the face was soon forgotten. Loren found the ladies' room and made the appropriate adjustments before proceeding to the café, where she saw Adam seated with a middle-aged Arab man dressed in a well-tailored suit. This must be Achmed Rashid.

Loren tipped the waitress who approached her five Maltese liras, which was far too generous by design, and asked for a table behind the screen that divided the smoking from the non-smoking area but from where she could see Adam and Achmed. Loren pulled a paperback novel from her bag and propped it up on the table. She asked for a glass of Delicata white wine, a local speciality Conan FitzRoy had recommended. Poor Conan.

The two men ignored her and ate lavishly. She ordered a vegetarian panino and trusted that it would be served quickly. She hoped the waitress would think that she was travelling alone and that the table she had specifically requested had some sentimental significance, perhaps from an earlier and happier visit to Malta, or perhaps a broken love affair.

The thought of being the object of pity amused Loren. No, she was from Interpol out for vengeance against the unjust and no one there knew it. She wondered what would happen if she admitted it. She suppressed a giggle. She seldom thought of her days before she was recruited into Interpol's secret net. The last humiliating months in Washington were ones she wished to forget. After she had broken her engagement with Mitch, her mother had accused her of being heartless while Loren wanted to scream out, "Can't you see it is all wrong! Can't you see I won't be happy fulfilling *your* life's dream?"

Then she found a way out, a way to disappear from her old life. She had snapped it up hurriedly, and for the last four years had no regrets, not even in the most boring of moments during her less glamorous undercover assignments. Her handler continually had her change her appearance. She learned different speech patterns, so that soon no one could place her point of origin.

In those rare moments when she had time off, she relished being in Europe. She explored the major cities, learned about art and architecture and music. She studied

European history and visited many of the spots where historic events had taken place. Often they were just a deserted farmer's field, devoid of a marker, found only after careful historical research.

She had learned to delight in her own intelligence and curiosity, and cherished the diversity of what she found. Each place she visited gave her a present of something new, a new fact, a new thought, a new point of view. Was she lovelorn? Hardly. She was a person highly skilled in the art of discovery and self-defence. Had the waitress only suspected, she might have paid more attention. Now, Loren thought, there was the complication of DI Davies-Jones and her growing feelings towards him.

Loren suddenly became alert as Achmed Rashid asked Adam if he wished to practice his 'native language'. Achmed spoke slowly, to Loren's relief. She had spent a year studying Arabic after nine-eleven. She had a facility with languages, but she had not used Arabic frequently enough to follow a hurried conversation. To her relief, her Arabic proved a match for Adam's.

"I write out a report for you," Adam told Achmed in halting Arabic. "I give you answers to the questions that you give me. Some things I do not know but try to see the answers. I want to find out everything you ask for. I see a lot but want to see more. Please tell me the things you want to me to get."

"Abdul, you have done well. Our father will be pleased with your work," Achmed said condescendingly.

Loren puzzled a moment about the name Abdul and then quickly guessed this was Adam's Arabic name. She did not understand the word father; perhaps she had misinterpreted it.

Suddenly Achmed looked up in her direction. She quickly averted her eyes to the stylised line drawing of a knight on horseback that hung on the wall just beyond Adam and Achmed's table.

Achmed's eyes slipped past Loren and went back to concentrating on Adam's halting speech. Whether in a gesture of pity or frustration, Achmed switched to English.

"Abdul, please keep watching every part of the operation at the hotel. Every piece of information you get will help. Tomorrow we want you to find out how people arrive at the hotel. We know that the hotel has a car that goes to the airport, and do people who come by sea bring their own cars to Malta? Do they park at the hotel? Does the hotel have a shuttle for passengers on ferries who choose to leave their cars in Sicily? What do people who come by ferry bring with them, and particularly what do they take away? Go to the ferry terminal and get this information. Ring me when you find out."

"Yes, my brother. I'll do all I can."

Looking at Adam the way one would at an under-achieving child, Achmed suddenly changed the subject. "How do you like Malta, Abdul?"

"There is still British colonialism here," Adam said, stumbling over the long word, "and a class society. At the hotel, the people are rich and they are European. Most are British and American. There are some French and Italians too. There was one guest named Dr Hammud. He spoke to me in Arabic and I was able to tell him God is Great. There are signs in Japanese, I think it is Japanese, so there may be

Japanese guests sometimes but there are no Japanese there now," he said.

"Have you seen any of the members of the official British delegation to the EU ceremonies to take place this week? Do you know which floor they are staying on?"

Loren almost choked on her panino.

"The third floor is blocked off, so I think they are staying there," Adam said. "But I haven't seen the officials."

Achmed nodded at Adam and looked encouragingly, and then he shifted the subject of his inquiry. "I am told that the Kennington Hotel chain welcomes any person who has high status and sufficient wealth to pay their high room rates. They say Lord Kennington came from a humble background but became who he is today because he understood that the rich always want to pay high prices to keep the others out. Much is to be said for that philosophy if one *is* rich."

"There's wonderful things in the hotel," Adam said ungrammatically. "I like the soap and shampoo and shaving things in the bathroom. The towels is heated on a hot bar. At night someone puts chocolates on my pillow, and every day they put new flowers in my room. My mother loved flowers. She bought them even when we had no money."

"When one pays eight hundred pounds a night for a room, one gets flowers and chocolate. What do those small chocolates cost? Fifty pence apiece? The flowers are sent in from the Kennington nurseries outside Casablanca. Can you imagine the price tag?" Achmed said.

"Flowers is everywhere. When I sit downstairs, I

watch the servants put them in the pots. They take every dead flower away. Each morning there's new flowers."

"Yes. Lord Kennington insists that every one of his hotels have fresh flowers daily. In Malta that is not a problem. In St. Petersburg, he puts the room rates just a bit higher to pay for a fresh delivery of flowers from Morocco every day."

"Does the lord have business with Arab countries?"

"His lordship promotes business with any country where he can buy cheaply commodities that make his guests happy. It's a quality worthy of a Saudi." Achmed laughed and Adam joined in, although he looked a trifle confused.

Loren followed the content of the conversation closely. A casual listener might have assumed that Achmed was an indulgent master and Adam an eager student, but was there any hidden meaning in what they said? It sounded as if Adam were the innocent. Was Achmed involved in Phase Three or could he even be Saieda? From what he said he might be trying to find a way to smuggle whatever had been exchanged off the island by using a guest at the Kennington Valletta who might board the ferry. Loren had been told many times in training to examine her first impressions. Often they had the truth in them but that the truth could be cleverly disguised. She found no insight in what Adam and Achmed had said, however.

Achmed soon finished his lunch and his business with Adam. Loren had already calculated her bill and left a generous amount to cover it. She slipped out of the café and ducked into the ladies' room in order to avoid meeting

Adam as he left the restaurant. She washed her hands, brushed out her hair and rummaged in her bag for her lipstick. Then she remembered she had dropped it at the vineyard. What a bother. Luckily she had a spare.

Looking once again like Alicia Kent, she re-emerged into the lobby as Achmed was leading Adam through the revolving doors out of the hotel. Achmed reassured Adam that he was a worthy son and wished him a safe trip back to the Kennington Valletta with Allah as his companion. Loren noticed that the portfolio Adam had carried earlier was nowhere to be seen. Where was it? And what was in it?

Achmed hailed a waiting taxi for Adam.

Loren waited until Achmed came back into the hotel. Then she went outside and summoned her own taxi, the next in the line.

"Follow the taxi that just left," she said.

"Are you a detective from America?" her Maltese driver asked. "I have seen on TV that many women are detectives in America."

Loren smiled. Why not, she thought.

"Yes. This is very important. There's a great deal of money involved."

"Is it the wife who is having the affair?" the driver asked.

Loren wondered about the question. Then she realised that Adam's youth, dark looks and good clothes might make him look at first glance like a young man who would be attractive to older rich women.

"Yes," she said, playing along.

"And you work for the husband?"

"Mmm."

"Have no fear. I am Anthony. Pawl, the driver of the other car, is my brother. I will call him to slow down and tell me in Malti where he is going. This gigolo will not get away with it. It is not good to break up a marriage."

Loren could not have wished for a more cooperative taxi driver. Malta was a small island and she guessed the Catholic sense of family and the sanctity of marriage were strongly felt.

Loren became conspiratorial. "Tell your brother that you and he will save a very important American family from a very great tragedy. Particularly for three children."

"Ah, children." The driver began telling her about his wife and five children, their joys and sorrows. Loren continued to say "mmm" which kept his monologue running for the entire trip. After they had pulled out into traffic, he called his brother, Pawl, who, Anthony said, told him that the ultimate destination was the Kennington hotel but that his fare had asked to go by way of Paolo.

"Why would he want to go to Paolo? What's there?" Loren asked, wishing she had spent more time touring the island.

"The very fine Tarxien Temples. They are very ancient, many years before even the Phoenicians."

"I can't imagine why he would want to go there," Loren said more to herself than Anthony.

"Pawl said he wanted to see the mosque. It is the only mosque in Malta. We are a Catholic country and have many fine churches but only this mosque. It is new and not very beautiful. I have seen pictures of the mosques in…."

Loren listened to Anthony with only slight attention and asked him to keep following Pawl's taxi. The surveillance lasted almost a half an hour. As Pawl's taxi passed the mosque, which was both new and not very beautiful, the brothers arranged it so that Loren would get back to the hotel and be out of sight when Pawl's taxi arrived there. Anthony assured her that if she wished, he would be her driver on all her 'detective trips' and handed her his card. She could not suppress her smile. She tipped him generously and added something for Pawl.

Loren returned to her room and picked up her mobile to contact Evan at the police station. She realised how much she was looking forward to speaking to him and not strictly for professional reasons either.

Evan had not yet arrived when Loren called him. She hesitated to call his mobile which, she knew, he used while in the field, and could not justify her call to him as an urgent one.

She tried his flat but got his answerphone. She left a message, washed away the dust of the day from her face and hands and called room service for tea.

As she stretched out to enjoy her tea, her mind went back again to the past. She had not thought about Mitch for months, but suddenly there in the café he had been in her thoughts. She wondered what her life might have been had she not broken off the engagement. The breakup had hurt at first, but she knew then and continued to believe that marriage to him would not have worked. He was not able to cope with competition from her. He always needed the edge. He had to win at games or he silently pouted. At first she had not minded that she had to dampen her intelligence and her athletic abilities. Then she began to realise that was who she was. A pattern in her life had been to give in to those around her. If only I had been born rich, beautiful and stupid, she had often thought. How easy life would have been then. But she did not believe that. She could not make her life a pretence and in the end she had not compromised.

At first the loneliness was terrifying. She threw herself into her training and then into her work with Interpol. The hours of excitement and sense of importance of her job had sustained her over the harder, earlier days. But her thrill on finally cutting ties with her home life, which for so many years were strained, had left her joyous. Now her sense of purpose filled her. Being on assignment was exhausting but exhilarating. Times in Lyon between assignments gave her time to plunge into her studies of languages and new cultures. When she had moments of unbearable aloneness, she would go running.

She drew out her breath and took another sip of tea. She still had that little girl inside her, so well nurtured by her mother, who whispered that she was not quite perfect because she was not attached to a man. Why was she thinking this now? She had been disappointed when Evan was neither at the police station nor at his flat. Why should that matter? Was her mother telling her that now she had another chance? Go away, Mother! Stay away! You messed up your life; don't mess up mine!

"Damn!" Loren said out loud. She took the last swallow from her teacup and decided to seek out Elspeth.

Loren found Elspeth behind the reception desk.

"Ah, Ms Kent. I trust you had an enjoyable day

touring."

"Yes, Valletta is a lovely city, so old and charming. Ms Duff, is there somewhere I could speak to you privately? There seems to be a problem in my room."

"Yes, certainly. Please come into my office."

Elspeth led Loren past the official back rooms of the hotel into the operations centre. Banks of television monitors lined one wall and one of the security staff was watching the screen focused on the lobby, restaurant, lounge, bar, bookstore, car park and front entrance. Cameras were also trained on the back entry to the kitchen and the main lobby to the lift. The lift lobbies on each floor were monitored, and there were cameras pointing down the guestroom hallways on every floor. She noticed that five people were exercising in the fitness room.

Elspeth explained. "We don't keep permanent recordings of anything in order to protect the privacy of our guests. But we have had unwanted visitors in the hotel on occasion."

"Does every hotel do this?"

"The good ones all do. It's a service to the guests who expect safety if they are paying high room rates. Lord Kennington requires that only highly trained personnel be allowed to watch these monitors. We pay the staff handsomely so they will be silent about what they see."

They proceeded down the hallway past the working areas of a well-managed hotel. Elspeth opened the door into a small conference room and invited Loren in.

Loren related her experiences of the day. "Adam Russell seems such an innocent. He acted as if he were…a puppy trying to please a new master."

"An innocent entangled in a web of deceit that he does not understand?"

"Exactly."

"Could he be assuming that role?"

"I don't know. Today there were so many conflicting things going on. He seemed bashful when he came out of the lift this morning. Yet when he left the hotel, he seemed suddenly puffed up, almost cocky, but at the same time a bit nervous. When he met his brother, however, he became shy and almost obsequious. When his brother smiled at him, he beamed. When his brother said he was pleased, I had this feeling that Adam would either melt or wet his pants. Then most curious of all, he took a taxi back here and asked that it take a long route around, going to the town of Paolo to see a mosque."

"What do you make of that?" Elspeth asked.

"He may be a dupe."

"Meaning?"

"Adam may be being used by Achmed, who might be Saieda."

"I wonder, but, as you spoke, I did consider the possibility," she said. "Tony Ketcham sent some more information about Adam to Richard Munro. Adam appears to be a British citizen, born in Beirut of a half-British half-Lebanese mother and a Saudi father. Adam and his mother immigrated to London fifteen years ago and he grew up in Peckham. His mother moved in with her aunt and her aunt's husband, who were not delighted to have relatives 'from Arabia' staying with them."

"Peckham?" Loren asked.

"Peckham is a working class neighbourhood in the

southeast of London. Recently it has become the home of many Africans. Most are Christians. There are some African Muslims there but they are looked down on. Tony's staff interviewed Adam's great-aunt today who said that Adam's mother had died a year ago. Adam left home shortly afterwards and the great-aunt has not heard from him since. The message was 'good riddance'."

"Did Detective Superintendent Ketcham find out where Adam has been for the last year?"

"Tony is following that up. He will let Richard know as soon as possible."

"And in the meantime?"

"And in the meantime, keep your eyes on Mr Adam Russell and his connection with Mr Achmed Rashid."

18

When she had met Evan Davies-Jones at Magdelena Cassar's party, Elspeth could not ignore the scar across his face. She wondered what effect it had on him professionally. He showed no signs that it mattered, but she sensed that his inner wound might be greater than the outer one. She had also noticed Loren's attraction to him, and hoped it would not affect either Loren's or Evan's judgement over the next few days. Elspeth recognised everyone's flaws, particularly her own, but she did not want personal shortcomings or complications to overburden the resolution to the problem at the hotel. She trusted Tony Ketcham's judgement in his choice of personnel, and with doubt she hoped for the best.

When Evan had entered her makeshift office after leaving Conan FitzRoy's room earlier that morning, she felt his eagerness but also his edginess. She put this down to his frustration over having to deal with Conan FitzRoy's death rather than the problem of the exchange. She felt tugged in the wrong direction by Conan's death as well, but felt relief when she was left to her own devices after Evan left the hotel. Her need to take control of events in the hotel had been nagging at her all day.

A small possibility existed that Conan was unwittingly involved in the exchange, considering the topic of his newly planned book, but Elspeth doubted it. She looked at the pile of items that Evan had left her. Perhaps FitzRoy's effects would provide some clues.

She laid FitzRoy's belongings out on the conference table one by one, sorting through them. She took up a stack of papers that seemed to be notes citing a variety of books on the Arabic monetary system. Elspeth leafed through the handwritten papers, trying to make sense of them. They appeared to be organised by date. The listings ranged from eighth-century documents to several articles that had appeared in the international press only days before.

She also found a sheaf of computer printouts, probably generated by a research assistant. Conan had made marginal notes in his large, scrawling script: "Confirm this!!" "Check with Hammud." "Not according to Jacques Renald!"

Elspeth looked for any notes FitzRoy might have made regarding his conversation with Dr Hammud the night before, but she found none. She also could find no mention of the appointment he had scheduled outside the hotel at five o'clock.

Abandoning the papers, she pulled over his laptop and tried to access its files, but she, like the police, did not have Conan's password.

Among his belongings, she found his plane ticket and travel itinerary. He was booked on a flight to Cairo leaving Valletta in two weeks' time and had a return ticket back to London three weeks after that. He had booked a room at the Kennington Cairo, which made Elspeth pleased by his loyalty to the Kennington chain.

In his passport wallet she found another piece of information, one she had been looking for. A card simply

stated: "In case of emergency, contact Bridget O'Connell."
Two addresses were listed: one in Belfast and one in
Rome. There were telephone numbers for both places and a
mobile number. She also found the name and telephone
numbers for White and Edgewood, Solicitors, in London
and Belfast.

Who was Bridget O'Connell? Why was she listed
before White and Edgewood? Elspeth seldom read the
tabloids, as she no longer had to linger in supermarket
queues, but she doubted that Bridget O'Connell was
FitzRoy's current wife.

Should she ring the mobile number? What would she
say if Bridget O'Connell answered? Hello, I am Elspeth
Duff and Conan FitzRoy has just died. Who are you? That
was not quite the Kennington standard.

She had read the hotel procedures for informing the
relatives of a deceased guest several times before but
wanted to again. René had given her the manual that
Pamela Crumm had written many years ago. Still, Elspeth
hesitated before picking up the phone. She could simply
call Brian Edgewood at White and Edgewood and ask who
Bridget O'Connell was.

Before making her decision, Elspeth rang room
service and ordered a small lunch of local cheeses and
tomatoes with crostini on the side, favourites of hers when
staying at the Kennington hotels around the Mediterranean.
A satisfied stomach might alleviate her indecisiveness.

No sooner had she put down the house phone than her
mobile rang.

"Mrs Duff?" She recognised the solicitor's voice.

"Speaking."

"I have been in touch with Miss Bridget O'Connell, who has given me permission to impart information to you regarding Mr FitzRoy. Miss O'Connell is Mr FitzRoy's next of kin." Elspeth decided that perhaps the old system of identifying a woman by her marital status had some benefit. 'Miss' Bridget O'Connell was not 'Mrs' which confirmed Elspeth's supposition that the woman was not FitzRoy's current wife.

"Yes, after reading through Mr FitzRoy's papers I had assumed she must be. You should know that the police gave me his personal effects for safe keeping."

Mr Edgewood did not clarify Bridget O'Connell's relationship to Conan. "Miss O'Connell holds Mr FitzRoy's power of attorney," he said. "Since Mr FitzRoy often travelled in many distant parts of the world in pursuit of information for his novels, Miss O'Connell assumed charge of his affairs when he was away. Miss O'Connell is presently residing in Rome, where Mr FitzRoy often visited her. When I informed her of Mr FitzRoy's death, she was greatly saddened but on my urging consented to travel to Malta to facilitate the return of Mr FitzRoy's remains to the United Kingdom."

Despite her dislike of Brian Edgewood's manner, Elspeth bowed to his efficiency. Barely three hours had passed since he had first been informed of Conan's demise. "Thank you, Mr Edgewood, for letting me know. When can we expect Ms O'Connell in Valletta?"

"She said she would be ringing me later today to let me know her travel plans, and I shall let you know them as soon as I do, Mrs Duff. Of course this sort of thing is not easy for a young person."

Elspeth was bemused at the solicitor's remark. He sounded young himself, but a voice could be deceptive.

"Yes, of course. Rest assured, Mr Edgewood, that the Kennington Organisation will do everything we can to help Ms O'Connell, including buying her a first class plane ticket if one is available on her flight and having a car meet her at the airport. If she is a British citizen, I'm sure the British high commission will also do all they can to facilitate her arrival and her departure from here."

"Miss O'Connell has a British passport, and the high commission most certainly should help."

Good manners and hotel policy did not allow Elspeth to ask for more information about Bridget O'Connell. Why had Mr Edgewood referred to her as a young person? What age made one a 'young person' to the stuffy Mr Edgewood, third generation of White and Edgewood, Solicitors? Elspeth conjured up a picture of the solicitor in a high, starched collar and morning coat straight out of Galsworthy. She knew she would find out more about 'Miss' Bridget O'Connell when she arrived at the hotel.

The Kennington Organisation would under normal circumstances handle the details of returning FitzRoy's body and belongings to the UK. Elspeth would have made arrangements through the Maltese Foreign Office and the British High Commission as a matter of course. The British high commissioner would not normally become involved in such a routine matter. The uncertainty of the last two days had been harrowing enough, however, that Elspeth suddenly wanted to talk to Richard. Although they had parted just hours ago, it seemed like days to Elspeth. She dug in her handbag for the paper on which Richard had written out his direct number and dialled him.

"Dickie, I hadn't realised," she said after she related the contents of her conversation with Brian Edgewood "that there still were such archaic firms left in the twenty-first century. Why did I suppose that all of the world had been Americanised by films and television?"

Richard chuckled. "Elspeth, my dear, you have changed and are impatient that others haven't changed with you. Impatience, you know, is an American trait. Bigger, faster, better, louder. Do you ever long for the days when we all were civil to each other, took time to be polite, guarded each other's privacy and communicated by handwritten letters?"

Elspeth suspected that Richard longed for those days more than she did, and wondered if he minded her impatience. Then she was bothered that she cared. "Not when I am dealing with a possible act of terrorism in one of our hotels and the death of a prominent figure to compound the situation. Dickie, it is good to talk to you. I hope I'm not being a pest."

"Far from it. I'm delighted you rang." Elspeth knew he was speaking the truth. She thought of the comfort of his caress in the lift that morning.

Elspeth leaned back in her chair, glad to have someone with whom she could talk and whom she knew and trusted. "I don't know what to expect of Bridget O'Connell. Hopefully she'll be less formidable than Brian Edgewood, Solicitor," she said.

"You realise that FitzRoy's real name was Kevin O'Connell, don't you?" Richard said.

Elspeth sat up quickly. "What?"

"His first novel about the partition of Ireland was first published under that name. The book was notable because it dealt with the Irish problem in the early nineteen twenties from the Loyalist point of view. How long have you—did you—know Conan FitzRoy? I'm amazed you never read any of his books. They are steeped in history."

"I tried once but found the book long and wordy. Aren't they all about war?"

A reverential tone crept into Richard's voice. "Yes, superficially, but he dealt with war from a personal point of view. Often his main characters were people affected by the war and not soldiers. He always conveyed the idea that war was not about battles but about all the people involved directly and indirectly in a war arena. His books were so well researched that, as a reader, one felt there. The books are truly a good read. He wrote terribly well."

"So you are a fan."

"As long as I can remember. When each new book was published, I had it sent out to me wherever I was. I'd sink into it and forget the heat or the cold or the insects or the latest diplomatic flurry."

Elspeth imagined him sitting on the veranda of a British hill station in the rain forest, stretched out in a planter's chair and opening the covers of FitzRoy's latest novel that had just arrived from Blackwell's book shop and been delivered in a dust-covered Land Rover by special post.

"Then Bridget O'Connell must be someone from his family," she suggested.

"Undoubtedly she is."

"I feel sorry about Conan. He was so terribly full of

life, and I feel a real force has been extinguished. I'll take your suggestion and read his books."

"It's a pity there'll be no more of them. You mentioned that he was going on to Cairo. He must have found leads there for his new book. I'll miss being able to read his story. He had such a fertile mind."

"Dickie, what are the British government's procedures for transporting a British citizen's remains back to the UK?"

"Oh yes, that must be tended to," he said with a sigh. "Normally I'd have the consular office look into this, but this time I'll take personal charge. I never really knew FitzRoy, although through his books he was a friend for many years. I certainly owe his family some comfort after his death."

Then Richard cleared his throat. "Elspeth, for old times' sake, shall we have dinner this evening? The Gaunt party is dining with friends in the Maltese diplomatic service and is in good hands. I won't be needed until the morning."

Elspeth knew how much of a relief a break would be. "I'd like that very much. I've been so absorbed in all the events of the last three days that an hour or two away would be wonderfully refreshing."

"I know a small Maltese restaurant, totally unassuming, off Triq Ir-Repubblika. Let me fetch you at half seven and we can walk there."

"Thank you, Dickie. You are a godsend. I'll be ready."

Elspeth then contacted Pamela Crumm. Knowing Pamela followed the lives of the rich and famous, Elspeth probed Pamela's mind for information.

"Was Conan FitzRoy married? Funny I shouldn't know after all the times I have met him."

Pamela thought for a moment. "Yes, wife number…mmm…five. Someone with a French name. I think it may be Angelique. Let me go to my computer."

"You'd make a good snoop, Pamela."

Pamela snickered. As well as indulging a personal pleasure in following the popular press, she kept extensive files of all frequent guests. "Here it is. Angelique Benoit is her name. Conan FitzRoy was sixty-two. She's definitely younger, platinum hair, heavily-made up eyes, tight clothing and a bit too much cleavage."

"I should have guessed," Elspeth said.

"The gossip rags say she was after his money, but I think she soon may have discovered he had more fame and bravado than cash. Recently she's been seen with the much younger crowd in the West End and in Chelsea with men, or rather boys, in tow."

"Do your files give any clue who Bridget O'Connell might be?" Elspeth asked.

"FitzRoy's real name was Kevin O'Connell." Pamela said, confirming Richard's information. "His first novel, called *A Border Drawn*, was about the partition of Ireland. Afterwards he came to London and changed his name. He devoted the next twenty-five years to writing. He became more famous with each successive novel, but he never again wrote about Ireland. That seems strange doesn't it? Let me see here."

"What?" Elspeth asked.

"In 1978 his brother, his brother's wife and a friend

were killed in an explosion in Belfast. No one was ever caught but the IRA was blamed. The press photos show FitzRoy at the funeral, looking totally devastated. He was married when he came to London, but shortly afterwards his wife returned to Ireland and divorced him. Soon he assumed his flamboyant personality and multiple wives. Every time he married, the wife got younger. Every time a wife strayed, which they all did over time, he'd head off to exotic parts of the world to pursue a new book. The wife would sue for divorce. He was always one step ahead of his creditors and she would get nothing. But his new book would be a hit and he would inflict his need for youthful matrimony on someone new."

Elspeth chuckled. "Now, tell me, Pamela, where in the scheme of things is there a Bridget O'Connell?"

"I'll find out," Pamela said with a tone of absolute certainty.

19

Monday, 26 April 2004 – Day 3 Afternoon/Evening

After the coroner's call, DI Evan Davies-Jones gave up hope of lunch and returned to the police station and went directly to the police morgue. Like most police officers, Evan considered death a part of his job and had faced his own near demise on several occasions. For him, the emotional rush that came when he confronted his own death was so acute that actually dying seemed a secondary consideration. The task of examining the dead after the fact, however, held none of the tension of the moment. Viewing a body after an autopsy still sickened him, although he had learned to control his physical queasiness. Consequently he entered the coroner's office in the morgue without enthusiasm.

Inside, Evan found the coroner, a small, elderly Maltese dressed in a black coat and vintage bowtie, bent over a police file. He looked up from his papers, and appeared to be pleased at the arrival of the police officer from London.

"DI Davies-Jones, thank you for coming. I want to tell you my findings regarding the death of Mr Conan FitzRoy. Because everyone thought that he had died of a heart attack, I looked for all the usual signs of this. Instead I came up with the surprising results I told you about earlier. I will spare you the details of my methods," the coroner said. Evan was relieved.

"There was no sign of a heart attack having caused his death, but he had suffered heart damage before. I found evidence of heart medication that he must have taken several hours before his death. In his system also was a fatal amount of sodium cyanide."

"Sodium cyanide?"

The coroner drew his half-glasses down his thin nose. "It appears that the poison was administered in a time-release capsule as there were traces of the capsule left. Because of the capsule, he would not have immediately felt the effect of the poison. When the capsule disintegrated, he would have suffered convulsions and subsequent death. I speculate that he was poisoned sometime yesterday afternoon or during the early evening, but did not die until later."

"Suicide?" Evan asked.

The coroner tapped the papers in front of him. "Probably not. I've never known a suicide to delay his own death with a slowly dissolving capsule."

Evan's thoughts raced back to his conversation with Loren the evening before, when she had told him about her trip with FitzRoy. At the vineyard, FitzRoy had drunk heavily and eaten things that Loren refused. Was this where FitzRoy swallowed the capsule? FitzRoy disappeared from the hotel at five o'clock, before he had returned and drunk coffee with Dr Hammud. Fernardu served FitzRoy a whiskey in the garden at about seven.

"How long did it take for the capsule to dissolve?" Evan asked.

"I would say no more than three hours depending on

what the victim had eaten."

"Do you know what time FitzRoy died?"

The coroner nodded. "Yes, probably between seven and nine o'clock, no earlier than that. His body was still slightly warm when you brought him to the morgue; rigor was just beginning to set in. His body temperature indicated death occurred about three to five hours before I saw the body just after midnight."

Evan calculated quickly. The capsule probably had been administered no earlier than four o'clock. When had Loren returned to the hotel? Just before five, as he remembered.

"Have you let Inspector Dom know?" Evan asked.

"Yes, a short while ago."

Hoping he could push the investigation of FitzRoy's death onto Inspector Dom, Evan said, "Keep me informed, will you?"

"I will, Inspector. You need have no concerns about that." The coroner turned back to his files.

When Evan returned to his office, he picked up his phone and rang Elspeth.

"Poison!" was her startled response. "Not a heart attack."

"So it seems."

"Why? I mean, why would someone poison him?"

"I'm sure that's a question that Inspector Dom will be trying to answer," said Evan, his voice on the edge of peevishness. The lack of lunch was beginning to tell. He decided to return to his flat to microwave something rather than endure the protracted ritual of a Maltese lunch or the uncertain taste of a hot meat tart bought at a stand in the arcade along Triq Ir-Repubblika.

Climbing up the stairs to his flat on Triq San Pawl, his irritation continued, this time focused on the finicky Inspector Dom, although there was little doubt that Inspector Dom was good at his job. Evan was also annoyed about his attraction to Loren Axt. He had other plans for his life. Perhaps he was only tempted by her physically. He found her beautiful and his own family history had taught him the power of beauty. He ground his teeth in frustration. Why was she so distracting?

He dreamed of an evening alone. He could have a glass of dry Maltese red wine at the café around the corner, then take a walk along the harbour wall or up to the fort on the hill. He could dine at the small trattoria he had found near his flat, and listen to the Maltese patrons speak their strange language. Then he would go to bed early and listen to the street sounds until he fell asleep, the way he had when first arriving in Malta, enjoying the sensation of being in a strange and exotic place. But this was April the twenty-sixth and May the first would soon follow.

The flashing light on his answer phone greeted him as he opened the door. Few people had the number at his flat. His heart jumped when he heard Loren's voice.

"Hi Evan, this is Alicia." The voice gushed a little and Evan grinned. He preferred Loren Axt to Alicia Kent, but admired Loren's ability to modify her personality just enough to play the role of a rich, idle tourist. "I've spent the day traipsing around old buildings, having a long and boring lunch and riding in taxis on crazy traffic-filled roads. I'm now luxuriating in the serenity of the

Kennington Valletta, and I don't want to move a step. Do come and join me for dinner. It would be so lovely."

Evan cursed. Not because his dream for the evening had been shattered, but because he suddenly wanted to go to the hotel, wanted to see Loren and wanted to do so more than any other thing in the world.

Later Evan stood in the lobby waiting for Loren. He watched the guests move in and out of the space. Most spoke in quiet tones as the space seemed to dictate that they should. They moved fluidly between the lobby, the lounge, the entrance and the alcove for the lift up to the restaurant. Evan reflected on how the wealthy insisted that their comfort be attended to silently.

Loren did not keep Evan waiting long. She came in through the doors from the garden and smiled as she saw him. It was a genuine smile.

Evan took in his breath on seeing the simple red dress and her delicate woollen jacket that sheathed her lithe body. The clothes suited Alicia more than her jogging togs of the morning, and filled Evan with an embarrassing warmth. He returned her smile like an awkward teenager.

"I hear some delightful music coming from the piano in the bar. Shall we go in and see who's playing?" he said.

They sat close to each other without touching, listening to classic dance tunes. They ordered glasses of wine, and then drifted out into the garden. The night was cool, and they found themselves alone at the far edge of the garden along the balustrade overlooking Grand Harbour. Neither mentioned that this was where FitzRoy had died the night before.

Loren set aside Alicia Kent's persona and recounted her day and her pursuit of Adam Russell.

"Tell me again who Adam met at the Hotel Saint John," Evan said, trying to resist taking her hand.

Loren held his eyes steadily, her voice now professional. "An Arab named Achmed Rashid. When he arrived, I heard Adam ask the concierge to ring Achmed in Room 516. Achmed, who met Adam in the café, called Adam his brother, and also called him Abdul. Both spoke of their father. Their father seems to be directing some sort of operation that requires intimate knowledge of the Kennington Valletta and the activities of Sir Michael Gaunt and his party. What puzzles me is that Achmed's questions were mundane. Why wouldn't Adam's brother stay here himself? An Arab guest of some wealth and apparent breeding surely would be less out of place here than Adam Russell, wouldn't he?"

Wishing he found Loren's eyes less alluring, Evan swallowed and nodded. "We need to discover why the Arab brother or father cannot come here and would send Adam in his place. If we can find that out, we are halfway there. I'll go to the Hotel Saint John tomorrow and find out who the mysterious Achmed is. It will be gratifying to follow a real lead rather than being so entangled in the FitzRoy matter."

Loren asked, "Was all your time today taken up with Conan's death?"

Evan put back his head and appealed to the stars that were beginning to appear above the garden. He wanted to say that he had thought of her all day, but instead said, "It was an exercise in frustration. I've been assigned to a dedicated and meticulous inspector from the Maltese police force who has analysed and photographed every dust mote in FitzRoy's room. I was finally able to escape and have a few words with Elspeth Duff, a lady I like enormously by the way."

Loren looked up at him and his heart bumped. "Elspeth told me that Adam's last year was mysterious," she said. "London reports that his relatives didn't know where he was and are amazed that he is the subject of questioning by the police. A Scotland Yard constable visited the relatives in Peckham, a place in southeast London that is, how should I say it, economically challenged."

Evan grinned at Loren's attempt at political correctness. He too knew of Peckham.

She continued, "His great-aunt and great-uncle seemed suspicious when the police officer asked them if they knew that Adam had come into some money recently. They disavowed having any connection with him after March of last year. But all day, as I was following him, I wondered if we are chasing shadows."

Evan shook his head. "I don't think so."

Loren knit her beautifully shaped eyebrows. "But are we profiling?"

Evan thought every terrorist investigator in the world was asking the same question, trying to balance fairness with necessity. He tried to focus on her words not her eyes. "We probably have to. What other evidence do we have?"

Loren turned from him and faced out towards the harbour. A speedboat cutting through the water below seemed to catch her attention. She looked back at him.

"Elspeth showed me some of the hotel security earlier. I'd no idea that luxury hotels had such sophisticated ways of watching what goes on. You can't sneeze in a public space without someone in the tombs of the hotel giving you a blessing for better health—and the health of all the other guests. But I'm concerned," she continued. "Adam Russell may seem an innocent, but I don't believe that his purpose here is innocent. What type of guest snoops the way he does? I heard him giving information to his brother about the minutiae of the hotel. What was that about? Why information about toothpaste and shampoo and about flowers? What was in that portfolio Adam no longer had when he left the café? Could it contain maps or marked-up hotel brochures? Did it contain something innocent like room rates or something else altogether? What would a rich Arab staying at the Hotel Saint John need to know about the Kennington Valletta that is not available on the internet? And why was Achmed so interested in Sir Michael Gaunt? It doesn't make sense. I know I may be profiling, but we may also be following something that should be investigated."

Evan looked about the garden behind them to make sure no person could hear their voices. "Loren, there is one other piece of information I have not yet told you. When the coroner examined FitzRoy's body, he found that FitzRoy had died of an overdose of sodium cyanide administered in capsule form. The coroner estimated that the capsule was swallowed several hours before FitzRoy died; the earliest time then would be four o'clock when you were still with him. Did he eat or drink anything between four o'clock and the time you returned to the hotel?"

"No, not after four. We left the vineyard at ten of four. Conan noted the time on the car's clock as we started back because he said he had an appointment at five."

"Did he say anything more about the appointment?"

"No, just that he needed to 'clean up' beforehand. I assumed he meant dressing for Magdelena Cassar's party."

"Did he mention Dr Hammud?"

"No, he didn't."

"Did you get any sense of what the five o'clock appointment was about?"

"No, he changed the subject immediately after saying he had the appointment," Loren said. "At the time it seemed unimportant."

"I see," Evan said. "Of course it didn't but now it may be. Tomorrow I'll try to find out what happened between five o'clock and FitzRoy's return to the hotel. There's always the disturbing thought that FitzRoy became involved in something more dangerous that he thought. But, Loren, it's been an exhausting day." Evan remembered the small amount of sleep he had the night before. "Come, Ms Kent, let us dine lavishly and make an early night of it."

20

When Elspeth emerged from the hotel's garden, Richard was waiting for her in the lobby. He looked up as she entered and his eyes were filled with admiration. He smiled and Elspeth was glad she had taken so much care deciding on her clothes and jewellery. She had chosen a long, fawn-coloured suede coat that hid all but the edges of a claret-coloured Thai silk frock, which she knew became her, and she wore a wide gold choker and earrings, which she had commissioned in Florence in the style of Nefertiti.

It had been a long time since she had gone to dinner alone with a man, but because Richard was a friend of such long acquaintance, she felt she need not worry that he would get the wrong impression of her intentions, despite the foolish feelings she had had the day before in his office. Still, she was pleased by his approving smile. She accepted the dry kiss on her cheek and welcomed the offer of his arm.

On the way to dinner, they chatted casually as they walked. Sighing, she let herself enjoy the smell of the sea and the gentle fading light that fell on Valletta's quiet back streets.

Richard led her into a small restaurant tucked down an alley off of Triq Ir-Repubblika that was so narrow that two people could hardly walk abreast. Mounting three crooked stone steps, he opened an old wooden door and motioned Elspeth to enter the space beyond. She was drawn in by the pungent smells of Mediterranean cooking, garlic, spices and oils, and the aroma of freshly baked bread. She had eaten fitfully during the day and hunger overtook her.

A large, effusive woman greeted Richard in rapid Malti but she did not use his title. She called him *Sinjur* Richard, Mister Richard. She chattered delightedly at his return. Elspeth tried to pick up the words. She only recognised words like happy, nice woman, romance, we welcome her. As she led them into the dining room, filled with tables covered in red and white checked tablecloths and sturdy wooden chairs, the woman's slight nudge spoke visibly of her matchmaking tendencies.

Elspeth grinned and said to the woman in her halting and probably incorrect Malti, "He has been my friend for almost forty years."

"*Namrat*? Sweetheart?"

Elspeth chuckled, and hoped the blush she was feeling did not show. "*Le*. No."

The woman switched to English. "What a pity. He comes here often, alone. Now you come with him. He needs a sweetheart."

She rattled the many bracelets on her arms as she waved them on. The room was filled with the heat of an open wood burning oven and the chatter of the many patrons, mostly Maltese. The woman said something in rapid Malti that Elspeth did not understand. Richard, who seemed to have gained some fluency in the language, flushed slightly. He did not tell Elspeth what the woman had said. Instead he asked the woman in English to lead them to 'his' table.

"OK but how come she speaks Malti?" she said, flinging her head up at Elspeth.

"Her aunt is Magdelena Cassar."

"The famous pianist?"

"*Îva*. Yes, Magdelena Cassar is my aunt."

"Then I greet your lady." She took Elspeth's hand in her large one and shook it up and down. Elspeth smiled in amusement.

"Marija, you are shameless!" Richard laughed. "Now I expect your best meal."

Marija hugged the menus she was carrying to her ample breast. She obviously was not intending to give them to her new guests. "Then let me choose and you can be surprised. I have a special meal only for my best customers."

"That would be splendid," Richard responded with a smile. "You have never disappointed me."

"Now I will leave you alone to talk about being children together and maybe more." She swished her large body around and hustled among the other tables.

Elspeth laughed out loud for the first time in days and let herself relax. Since her divorce, she had sworn off any social life apart from the acquaintances she had made at the hotels, such as Conan FitzRoy, and particularly avoided any closeness to men. She did not trust her own judgement in forming relationships that might develop into something more than friendship. She found enough diversion in the social functions at the hotels to keep her from being lonely. But tonight she was enjoying herself, and allowed herself to give way to the charm of her hostess and Richard's caring attention. The restaurant surprised her. She had expected something grander, but fell immediately under the spell of its warmth and welcome. She was amused by the patter between Marija and Richard. Elspeth had never before known that he had a flirtatious side.

He took the chair across from her. The table was small, and after they were settled, he reached for her hand, laying his gently over it. She did not draw hers away as she might have with another man. Instead she enjoyed the lightness of his touch.

They sat quietly but she did not mind. Finally he said, "I know you have longer acquaintance with the Maltese than I do, but in the few months I have been here I feel so embraced by the Maltese people and their zest for life, which Marija so completely personifies. I stumbled on this restaurant one evening when loneliness came crashing down on me, as it sometimes does. The mistral was blowing, I had been in deadly dry meetings at the Foreign and Commonwealth Office all day and I was hungry but really didn't care if I ever ate again. I just wanted the pain inside me to go away. I came through the door to get away from the wind, not to eat. I think Marija picked up on my sorrow. She led me to this table and, like this evening, didn't give me a menu. A glass of wine appeared and then a meal that I only remember as being hot and soothing."

Elspeth turned her hand and took his in hers. "I am sorry, Dickie, I truly am," she said instinctively. She imagined that after thirty years of marriage to Lady Marjorie, he had been devastated by her death, although he did not say so directly. Elspeth remembered the merriment that she had shared with Richard when they were young, and wondered if Richard had been happy with Marjorie. She was not sure. Could Richard regain the light-heartedness he had with Elspeth and Johnnie in those halcyon summer days on Loch Tay? Or could she for that matter?

As if reliving the scene of his first night at Marija's, Richard continued, "When I went to pay the bill, she said, 'What you owe is a promise that you will come back many times and each time we will make you happy again.' I've come back on many occasions and always found the same welcome."

"I think Marija has half captured your heart, Dickie," Elspeth said with a grin, hoping to break the mood he had just set.

He did not seem to hear her. "I truly hope Marija never finds out my official capacity here in Malta. Although I fear that one day she may pick up a newspaper with my picture in it. Especially this week when I'll be attending so many ceremonial functions not far from here."

Elspeth looked up at Richard, realising how important this small place was to him and feeling touched that he would share it with her.

"I have an idea," she said.

"What's that?" he asked.

"Invite her to the high commission and have her photograph taken with you in full regalia. She could hang it at the door with your signed message in Malti complimenting her on her excellent cooking and hospitality."

Richard looked down his long aristocratic nose, the

way he had in his youth when feigning haughtiness. "Don't you think that might ruin the simplicity of this place?"

She screwed up her face, trying not to laugh, but could not help grinning. "Perhaps you are right. Let her be surprised one day."

"Exactly," he said. His self-satisfied manner reminded Elspeth of the way he used to show her and Johnnie that they had indeed gone too far and only he, Richard, could get them out of the fix in which they found themselves. Elspeth chuckled openly, and from Richard's sideways look at her assumed that he could probably read her thoughts. She took in a deep breath and wished that they were back in Scotland without any of the intervening years of triumph and tragedy between them. If they could go back, what would they have changed? Elspeth could not decide.

A waiter who seemed to know Richard asked if they wished wine, and Richard ordered a pinot grigio without consulting a menu. Marija brought the bottle, encased in a terra cotta sleeve wrapped in a simple cloth, and two large wine glasses. She stood behind Richard where he could not see her. As she poured out the wine, she winked at Elspeth and left them to their private conversation.

Elspeth held her glass up to the light of the candle flickering between them on the table. "Thank you for this respite from the storm."

"The pleasure is indeed mine," he replied, raising his glass to her. His eyes had lost their sorrow.

He touched the back of her hand, this time more intimately. She drew back almost imperceptibly. Her reaction surprised her, not because she found the caress of his fingers offensive but because she found it unsettled her. She was convinced she was no longer susceptible to a man's touch, but this new acquaintance with Richard had shaken her. She had chosen a life of work without emotional complications and was happy in her choice, but the gentleness of Richard's gesture moved something dormant in her in the same way that his standing next to her in the window of his office had earlier. She had forced herself to disregard the first instance but she could not deny this one.

As they sipped their wine, they talked of Scotland, recalling the two summers that they had romped through Perthshire jammed in Johnnie's disreputable Austin Mini. Elspeth felt a deep sense of pleasure creep over her.

"You cheated at cards, didn't you? I always thought so," he said.

"Unfair," she said. "I only switched decks when I saw you and Johnnie had marked them."

"Having marked the new decks, of course."

"Of course," she admitted, her memory brimming with laughter.

"How much has happened since then," he said.

She lowered her eyes from his. "Yes," she said.

His mood suddenly sobered, and he hesitated as if trying to formulate his words. "Do you ever think of Malcolm?" he asked gently.

Elspeth swallowed and coughed. A roller coaster of emotions swept through her. The question was an obvious one, since they both were aware that their lives had altered when Elspeth had gone to Cambridge and fallen in love with Malcolm Buchanan.

"I'm sorry. I should never have asked," he said hurriedly.

"No, it's all right," she said, clearing her throat. "We've never really talked about it, have we? Not in thirty-five years." She grimaced.

He did not speak but she felt his tenderness.

"Truthfully, there is seldom a day in my life when I don't think of Malcolm, and wonder what might have been. It's a wound that time hasn't healed, the unknowing, the mystery and, yes, most of all the loss. You would have thought after all this time it wouldn't matter, wouldn't you?"

"I can see that it still does," he said.

The sadness that had left her when they entered the restaurant filled her once again. She blinked back tears and set her jaw.

"I've often thought of revisiting the whole thing, going back now and trying to find out why Malcolm was killed and by whom. It would open all the pain of those first days after his murder, but it might resolve things for me finally."

"I expect it might," he said.

"I still appreciate all you did for me then. Have I ever told you that?"

It had been Richard who came to Cambridge shortly after Malcolm's murder and took her back to her family home on Loch Rannoch. She remembered little of the long train journey except that Richard had been beside her and had let her grieve.

"If I do decide to go back to find out what did happen, will you help me, Dickie? You are one of the few people I still know who was there."

"Yes, of course. Of course you may," he said softly.

Suddenly she felt uncomfortable that she had made her request. She gently withdrew her hand from his and busied herself with her knife and fork, straightening them out along the pattern of the tablecloth although they were perfectly straight to begin with.

He remained silent, perhaps because he knew he had touched a nerve too tender for her to discuss further. The moment lingered. Finally he said, "Do you enjoy working for Lord Kennington? Not the luxury but the job."

She was relieved he had changed the subject and could return to a bland topic.

"He pays well and I can't ignore that. Most of my cases are much less frightening than the one here. They often involve protecting dignitaries, but there also are the cases of fraudulent credit card use, sometimes vandalism, often financial juggling by guests or hotel suppliers, and recently a swindler preying on hotel guests and his lordship as well. I like discovering the schemes behind the crimes. Many of them are terribly clever. But I have never dealt with possible terrorism before. Suddenly my work has become a reflection of the new world order rather than the ageless world of the wealthy. I haven't decided whether I like this or not."

Richard left his hand resting near hers, but did not try to take possession of it again. "Do you ever see Alistair? Do you mind my asking?" he asked.

She became confused. Why was he asking her such personal questions? She responded more out of courtesy than alacrity. "No, you are too old a friend not to wonder.

217

We meet at the occasional family gathering and sometimes at Christmas. Our separation happened mainly because we lost interest in being together, and therefore I have no hard feelings. I am usually amused rather than annoyed by his pretentiousness when I see him but no longer feel any attraction."

"Is that difficult for you?"

She bit her lower lip. "No, it isn't because it's honest."

An expression of relief crossed his face. "You always surprise me, and you have for all the time I have known you."

"Don't you think that at all odd, Dickie? Often I surprise myself."

He laughed. "Elspeth," he said and then paused, "During all these years have I really hidden what I feel for you? You must have known."

She lowered her gaze and looked back up into his eyes, which sometimes were hazel and sometimes green and which held hers intently. "I often suspected," she said with a flick of her eyes and a suppressed grin. His earlier penetrating questions obviously had a purpose behind them other than simple empathy for her.

"Is that why you never allowed yourself to be alone with me when Marjorie and I were in California?" he asked.

She did not answer immediately. She gave him a wry smile. "As I remember, you and I were both married—and not to each other."

"Neither one of us is married now. Do you think we might become more than childhood friends?"

"Let's wait and see," she said, nonplussed. "We'll be working together all week, and by the end of it you will undoubtedly find me irritating and stubborn. You always said I was."

"Only in jest. Have I offended you by speaking?"

She shook her head. "No, it's me that's the problem. I expect I'm quite different from what you envision me to be."

"Are you happy with your life?"

"I'm satisfied," she said.

"Then I'll reserve my right to speak to you again at the end of the week," he said. His voice was tight.

"You may if you like, but probably you will wish otherwise. I won't hold you to it." She gave him another grin but her heart was not behind it.

Blessedly their conversation was interrupted by the arrival of dinner. The presentation reminded Elspeth of Giuseppe's two nights before. The fanfare and visual preparation were humbler, but the bouquet of garlic and spices was the same, although tonight's foods were pasta and sausage in a fragrant tomato and olive sauce rather than sea bass extraordinaire. Marija, like Giuseppe, acknowledged her triumph.

They ate for several moments without speaking, enjoying the simple, spicy food and cold wine. The awkwardness of Richard's questions passed and the silence pacified her. The problem at the hotel, however, crept insidiously back into her mind.

Elspeth took a mouthful of the sausage, chewing appreciatively. After swallowing, she said, "Who do you suppose Saieda is? And who at the hotel could be Helios?"

"There's no way of knowing."

Elspeth nodded. "That's what is so perplexing. Why our hotel? Eric Kennington can be exasperating even in the best of situations. If it weren't for Pamela Crumm's calming influence, I would have strangled him long ago. He has this infernal habit of expecting me to find a brilliant answer to every problem he gives me. Of course, I'll have to admit, he does treat me well when I do so."

"And so he should," he said in a silly falsetto. Elspeth was relieved by his humour.

"Yes, you're right," she admitted and laughed, "but the situation here is more perplexing. Terrorism is frightening when it penetrates the world of the very rich. Now not even Eric Kennington can protect his hotels, much as he would insist on it. We live in a terrible time."

"Because money can no longer buy security?"

"Yes, and because none of us can feel safe, not even if we have all the money it takes to stay in a Kennington hotel. Unfortunately Eric believes my presence at one of his hotels will provide him instant peace of mind."

With a sigh, she rolled the pasta on to her fork and examined it for a brief moment. She wished she were at Marija's with Richard Munro under different circumstances.

21

Tuesday, 27 April 2004 – Day 4 Morning

The night attendant was dozing when Adam Russell reached the reception desk. During two days hovering in different spots in the public areas, Adam had watched the guests hand in their keys when leaving the hotel, and he was beginning to understand the routine. The receptionist jerked to attention when Adam laid the key on the counter.

"Good morning, sir," the receptionist said.

Adam liked being called sir by this older man, whose olive complexion matched his own. Adam knew it was not necessary to say where he was going, the man was not his schoolmaster, but Adam had learned from the Qur'an that elders are to be honoured. In any case, Adam liked the man's open manner.

"Good morning," Adam responded.

The receptionist smiled. "You are up early, sir." It was just before six.

"I'm going to morning prayers that are held at the home of Imam Muhammad al Mustafa on Triq San Kristofer." Adam read the street's name carefully and gave the receptionist the number, which had been given to him by his imam at the mosque on Old Kent Road in London, with whom he covertly continued lessons after meeting the Rashids. Doing this required secrecy, as he felt guilty about avoiding the greengrocer's shop where he had lived after leaving Peckham. Adam knew the greengrocer wanted Adam to marry his daughter. When Adam revealed his impending trip to Malta, the imam had told him that there were few Muslims in Malta, but that prayers were held daily in small groups at the homes of several imams on the island.

"Can you tell me how to get there?" Adam asked of the receptionist, who gave him a map of Valletta.

Adam had not strayed far from the hotel, but in his few excursions had noticed the preponderance of churches. When passing each one, he thought of his mother with sadness, knowing that she had not discovered the true faith.

"Thank you, and Allah be with you," Adam said.

He left the lobby, and following the map he turned down Triq San Pawl. Valletta was a small city, based on a grid, and the streets were clearly marked on the stone plates engraved in the sides of limestone walls of the buildings. As it was close to sunrise, the early light brought out the texture of the rough stones of the walls of the buildings, Adam had no trouble seeing the signs and finding his way.

Adam walked along the narrow streets, watching his steps across the uneven pavement, and pondered the lack of mosques in Malta. While passing time the day before, Adam had read a booklet in the lobby that told Malta's history. A thousand years ago, Islamic forces had ruled Malta. He wondered why Valletta had so few reminders today of a culture that had been so rich and so powerful in Malta centuries before.

Only losing his way once, Adam found the building where the imam lived. He was joined by several other men made their way into the dim interior and up the stairs to the imam's rooms. Adam felt a sense of pride he had not known before when he entered the house. He took off his shoes, washed his feet and was ready to worship his new God.

After prayers, the few worshippers left the room slowly. Adam was the last to linger. He stayed and talked to the imam, who was from Saudi Arabia. In Peckham, as a refugee from Beirut, Adam was an embarrassment to his English family. In the imam's presence, he loved being a part of his Saudi family in a place where their traditions were sanctified in a small space filled with beautiful paintings of Arabic script taken from the Qur'an. When he finally emerged from the imam's house, he was deep in thought about what the imam had said to him.

Adam turned up the street towards the hotel. The cool April weather reminded him of spring days in London when he had spent time sitting in his family's back garden dreaming of being something better than the outcast at his comprehensive. He had wanted respect, but in those days as a teenager with Arabic features in a neighbourhood with the prejudices of both the English working classes and African immigrants, he found none. His mother had loved him, that he always knew, but her skin was fairer than his and people hardly noticed that she was half Lebanese. Adam had always felt the unfairness of it.

Now things were different. Adam had money for the first time in his life. He was staying in one of the posh hotels on the island, where important people stayed, like that fat old man who drank too much and who had disappeared. Adam was called 'sir' by the staff of the hotel, whereas a year ago shopkeepers in the West End of London would have told him to move along. Here in Malta he felt he was part of a Muslim community, even if a small one.

He was worried that his brother Achmed did not fully embrace Islam. Achmed seemed determined to be westernised, down to the precise upper class English accent. Adam was aware of his own accent, but the people at the hotel did not seem to notice it, at least not openly. While following his newly found father's instructions as carefully as he knew how, Adam preferred to spend his free time in his studies of the Qur'an than in the pursuit of a snooty English public school manner.

As he walked, Adam thought about the things Achmed had asked him to do at the Knight's Café yesterday. He was so in awe of his family that he never thought to ask Achmed why his family wished to know the things that he asked Adam to find out. Adam was intent on giving accurate information in order to impress his brother. Growing up being acutely aware of those around him, he had developed a keen faculty of observation in order to stay clear of bullying by his schoolmates, and this skill was serving him well in his present assignment for the Rashid family. The notes he had given Achmed yesterday were carefully written in English in his schoolboy hand. He wished he could have written them in Arabic, but he knew it would be many years before he could master that language.

Achmed had asked him to get information on the ways guests got to the Kennington Valletta once they were in Malta. In his room Adam had found a pamphlet called *Arriving in Malta and Getting Around*. Malta was a small island but had over a quarter of a million cars. Hotel residents were advised not to hire a self-drive car because of treacherous traffic conditions, but instead get around the island by public taxi or in a private car with a local driver. There were instructions on how to get a fair price for either. All this seemed to be general information, so Adam decided he needed to find out information specific to the Kennington Valletta.

He had already visited the hotel's underground car park. Most of the cars had Maltese number plates. He had noted that the hotel had no scheduled shuttle service to the airport. Private cars were sent to greet arriving guests. The large group of Americans had their own coach. Others arrived by taxi. The French grandparents had brought their own car, and had talked to the receptionist about how the ferry from Sicily had become more crowded and less reliable each year.

Achmed had suggested he investigate the ferry. Adam could consult the pamphlet when he got back to the hotel. He wondered why Achmed had asked him to find out about such obvious things, but surely Achmed had a reason other than merely testing him.

*

Frustrated by her inactivity the day before, Loren was looking forward to her morning run and had plans to join Evan at six. But when she entered the lobby, René Le Grand was at the front door speaking to the doorman.

"*Mademoiselle* Kent," the manager called out. "May I have a word with you before you are off on your morning exercise." He took her aside and told her about Adam Russell's destination.

"Does the night attendant know exactly when Adam left and how long the prayers will take?" Loren asked.

"Let us ask him," René said. The attendant knew both answers.

Loren checked her pocket for her mobile phone and headed for the hotel doors. Once outside she hit the button that she had programmed for Evan's mobile number.

She told him her location. The imam's quarters were within walking distance. Loren and Evan, posing as lovers engaged in the twenty-first century form of courtship known as early-morning jogging, could easily circle by it several times without becoming conspicuous.

The street outside the imam's house was steep and narrow, its sidewalk uneven and at the steepest parts became stairs. Evan and Loren negotiated the pavement and stairs several times before the prayers were finished.

They watched several men come out of from the imam's house and then waited for Adam. He came through the door fifteen minutes later and apparently did not notice them.

Loren and Evan talked as they jogged. Although Loren relished Evan's company, she reverted to their professional roles as they ran.

They turned a corner and Loren noticed that Evan carefully manoeuvred his position so that the good side of his face stayed on the side near her.

"I plan to go to the Hotel Saint John this morning to follow up on Russell's brother. He seems to be a good lead. I thought I would talk to the manager directly," Evan said. "Inspector Dom has given me his name."

Loren looked down and skilfully avoided a crumbled

part of the pavement. "Yesterday Elspeth told me that Sir Richard will be contacting London again this morning to see if Detective Superintendent Ketcham has discovered more about our pigeon down the street. Evan, Adam Russell seems so innocent."

A real pigeon waddled in front of them, eyed them with a hostile look and fluttered off.

"Could his brother be directing him?" Evan asked.

"I couldn't tell from the conversation yesterday. Achmed was asking Adam for information mainly about the hotel. My concern is that Adam may be a pawn. Elspeth said he and his mother had gone to London from Beirut when Adam was young. He grew up in Peckham."

"That would explain his accent."

"I don't understand, she said." They jogged around a woman clad in black who was sweeping the pavement in front of a shop.

"I know you have regional accents in America so I knew without asking that you are not from Texas."

"I can fake a Texas accent if you like."

"No thanks," he said chuckling. "But seriously, at Scotland Yard, particularly those of us dealing with terrorists, are taught to recognise the finest nuances of accents, almost to the point where we can recognise which neighbourhood a person comes from. I have dealt with suspects who claim to be Whitechapel born and bred but with a hint of an Italian accent that made me wary. Others who said they were from a certain part of Manchester spoke with a trace of Algerian French or Russian, and they were immediately suspicious. Several suspects betrayed themselves by not understanding that a keen ear can detect

227

their origin. Rather like Professor Henry Higgins."

"Did you pick up Adam's Lebanese connection?" Loren challenged.

"No, but Adam probably arrived in London when he was young enough that he would have lost his earlier accent."

"I couldn't pick one up but I've not been trained to do so. I'll have to see about that when I return to Lyon."

They jogged on in comfort, pacing each other and Loren felt disappointed when Adam arrived back at the hotel.

"Loren, be careful," Evan said in parting.

Loren laughed and gently touched his scarred cheek. "You, too."

*

Richard Munro sat in the back of his official car and instructed his driver to take him to the Kennington Valletta. He had asked Elspeth to have breakfast with him at Triq It-Torri but she had declined. He suspected she was unsure about being alone with him again after he had told her his feelings the night before. He was relieved that he had brought up the subject but he could not read her response. In one way it was self-deprecating and standoffish, but in another hinted at some reciprocity of feeling. He thought of the turn of her head, the flecks of light in her light brown hair, the intensity of her cobalt blue eyes and her sometimes quick and sometimes deep responses to his questions. Last night he had gone to bed with a smile and a full heart and dreamed of his youthful summers on Loch Tay.

He chastised himself for his thoughts. This morning

they must devote themselves to business. The email message Tony Ketcham had sent yesterday had been disturbing. The exchange had been successful but now Phase Three was underway. But the most Elspeth and Tony's team had discovered were the awkward actions of a young Anglo-Arab man, whose main crime to date had been skulking about the public rooms of the Kennington Valletta and meeting his brother who called himself Achmed Rashid. Why would Adam Russell do that so openly if the two were involved in covert terrorist activity? On the other hand, could Achmed Rashid be the intended recipient of the two intercepted emails and Adam Russell be Helios? Or was the hotel mentioned in the second email the Hotel Saint John and not the Kennington Valletta? Richard couldn't make sense of it. He wanted to ask Elspeth if Adam Russell had internet access, expecting that all rooms in the Kennington Valletta were wired for DSL, but that would do Adam little good if he did not have a laptop computer.

Richard was now sorry he had never served in an Arab country. Malaysia, where he was high commissioner for four years, was largely Muslim, but the Malaysians were not Arabs. He doubted comparisons should be made between the Arabs and the Muslims of Southeast Asia.

*

Elspeth had mixed feelings as she waited for Richard to arrive at the hotel for their breakfast meeting. Their dinner together the night before had disconcerted her. Her life became easier when she had decided five years ago to focus on her career. Pamela Crumm had questioned this emotional withdrawal more than once, but Elspeth was always quick to change the subject.

When the receptionist called to say Sir Richard had arrived, she was still in conflict with her emotions. Would this meeting have more appropriately taken place at the high commission? Why had she asked him to come to the hotel instead? She knew it had just as much to do with her wanting to see him again in private as it had to do with business, but she did not trust herself to be alone with him at his home on Triq It-Torri.

Elspeth had requested that breakfast be brought into her temporary office. After Richard was shown in, she accepted his light embrace and his kiss on her cheek but did not return them. Instead she said, "I'd like to be like Loren and go jogging every morning but quite frankly, Dickie, I much prefer having breakfast with you, even if we are going to talk only about terrorism and murder."

Suddenly she felt embarrassed. Would her forwardness be accepted as courtesy rather than boldness?

He grinned more fully at her remark than simple good manners would warrant. "The pleasure is mine, my dear," he said.

She poured tea for him and coffee for herself. The table had been set with Kennington exactness, the napkins complementing the tablecloth, a small vase of fresh flowers gracing its centre and cutlery set out for a full breakfast. Elspeth hoped Richard would not misread the elaborateness of even a simple Kennington hotel breakfast as a snub to the homely repasts he had offered on his terrace on the two previous days. He served himself generously from the sideboard; she restricted herself to her coffee and took a bowl of yogurt and fruit.

As he finished his meal, Richard turned to an attaché case, which he had set on one of the chairs. From it he withdrew a brown paper folder that bore the words 'On Her Majesty's Service'. He ruffled through several sheets of paper and handed one of them to Elspeth.

"This morning one of my staff brought around this communiqué from Tony Ketcham's office regarding Adam Russell," he said. "As we already know, he left Peckham months ago. Tony's office tracked him shortly afterwards to a job as an assistant at a Middle Eastern greengrocery on Old Kent Road in London. The proprietor told Tony's people that Adam had worked there, and he had started attending prayer services at a local mosque soon after his arrival. The mosque was one of those small affairs that are scattered throughout southeast London, mainly serving the immigrant population."

"But how did that lead to the Kennington Valletta?" Elspeth said.

"One day about three months ago Adam suddenly resigned from his job, wished his mentor, the greengrocer, well and left abruptly, saying he had discovered he was the son of a sheik. His employer was quite upset as he had a daughter a year younger than Adam, and had begun to make hints that both he and his family had hoped they might involve Adam more completely in both the business and in their domestic affairs."

Elspeth skimmed over the paper Richard handed her. "Now here Adam is in Malta, with well-cut clothes, an excellent haircut, a neatly trimmed but obviously new beard, a handful of valid credit cards and money to spare, which I suppose we can attribute to this mysterious sheik."

"Not exactly mysterious," Richard said, taking back the paper. "The address Adam is using here in Malta as his residence is the address of Sheik Abdullah Rashid's business offices in the City and as you know, Adam had lunch with Mr Achmed Rashid at the Hotel Saint John quite openly yesterday. But how did Adam connect with the Rashid family? I must ask Tony to follow up on this, although, knowing him, I suspect he is probably already doing so."

Elspeth poured herself another cup of coffee but he declined more tea. She took a swallow of her coffee and looked up at Richard watching her. She responded to his smile rather more warmly than she wished she had.

"Most certainly," she said, sipping her coffee. "Did Tony say anything about Dr Hammud?"

"It appears that he is a legitimate professor at Durham University. One of Scotland Yard's staff spoke to him and he confirmed the meeting with FitzRoy. Dr Hammud said he provided FitzRoy with several contacts in Cairo but nothing more."

"Was Tony satisfied with that?"

"He seemed to be."

"We'll have to accept that, I suppose," Elspeth said, and changed the topic. "Bridget O'Connell, who I discovered is Conan's niece, is due in on the afternoon Air Malta flight from Rome. I talked to Pamela Crumm, and it is Lord Kennington's desire that everything to do with the removal of Conan's remains be handled as quietly as possible. You can imagine what it's like, Dickie. A death at a hotel makes future guests wonder if they are 'in the room' or 'in the space' where the death happened. Even the staff, particularly the long-term staff, can feel the same way. We have had incidences where we have had to assign only new employees to clean a room where a death occurred. Of course, Conan died in the garden. Now we hope the gardeners are not spooked. I'm sure, for all the love Conan had for display, he wouldn't have liked turning people away from our hotels. To help matters along, Lord Kennington asked that we give every accommodation to Bridget O'Connell. I want to thank you for your help with the exit documents. I know this isn't your normal duty at the high commission."

Richard continued to look at Elspeth but she could not read his expression. Finally he said, "No, it isn't, but I'll do what I can to help. I've already telephoned my colleagues at the Maltese Foreign and Commonwealth Office, and they are preparing suitable papers. Ms O'Connell should have no difficulty. I've instructed my staff to ask Air Malta and British Airways about the shipment of the remains to London or Belfast, whichever place Ms O'Connell desires."

Elspeth smiled at him, this time limiting her feelings to admiration. She knew of his reputation for smoothing things along. In that moment, Elspeth envied Lady Marjorie. This sort of sordid detail must have always been taken care of so graciously by her husband. Elspeth compared this with her own life and her own husband's inattention to her. Her life had taken so many unexpected turns. She did not imagine that had been so for Marjorie.

After Richard left for the high commission, Elspeth went back into her office filled with hope that the encounter with Bridget O'Connell would be an easy one. She sent the staff to prepare one of the better rooms on the fourth floor, which had a view of Grand Harbour facing west. Sunsets filled that room with a warm glow that even a grieving relative would find beautiful. She had the staff supply appropriately sombre flowers and a basket of fruit, chocolates, local wine and Irish teas and biscuits. She made the final inspection of the room herself and was satisfied. Then she instructed the staff not to disturb the room until Ms O'Connell's arrival.

She ordered a hotel car to be at the airport well before the arrival of the flight from Rome. She called the Air Malta office and requested that Ms O'Connell be given every accommodation on the flight at the expense of the Kennington Organisation. Whoever this Bridget O'Connell might prove to be, she would not be neglected by his lordship's staff.

With preparations made, Elspeth sank back into her chair in the conference room and drew out her breath. Having long since given up the Episcopalian faith of her parents, she said in whispered prayer to some unknown force: Please, let this all go smoothly so that I can get back to more important things.

22

Tuesday, 27 April 2004 – Day 4 Morning

Returning to his flat after his run with Loren, Evan Davies-Jones took off his jogging clothes, threw them into the laundry basket, showered and shaved. Evan put on the suit he had worn the day before, along with a white shirt and conservative tie, and was ready to go to the Hotel Saint John. He checked himself in the mirror, the best side of his face forward, and acknowledged that he had chosen his clothes well.

Evan walked to the police station and commandeered a car from the police department pool and a driver who was familiar with the island. Although the Maltese drove on the left, their idea of courtesy on the roads, or lack thereof, differed sharply from the driving habits in the UK. The distance between the police station and the hotel was short, but the intricacies of the morning traffic slowed the journey and consumed enough time for Evan to work out how to approach the manager of the hotel without using any form of subterfuge.

The Hotel Saint John was less historical than the Kennington Valletta, but it gave the same feeling of providing comfort to its guests. The large glass doors under the porte-cochère led into a high-ceilinged hallway with a view into the large main lounge.

Evan approached the concierge's desk and waited

until a middle-aged American woman, as flamboyant in dress as she was in speech, discussed all the options one had to visit the 'goddess caves', as she called them, booked one of the tours, changed her mind, chose another, then finally decided to hire a private car. The concierge was patient in a way Evan could not fathom. Evan was at first amused and then irritated by the delay, but shortly got a well-rehearsed apology and the concierge's full attention.

"I am Detective Inspector Evan Davies-Jones and would like to speak to the manager," he said, pulling out his Maltese warrant card.

Evan watched the look of dismay cross the concierge's face but offered no explanation. The concierge picked up a phone and with polished tones summoned the manager from an inner office.

When the manager approached, Evan identified himself, but this time added that he was from Scotland Yard on assignment to the Maltese police.

"What may I do for you, inspector? Perhaps you would prefer to talk in private."

The manager of the hotel directed him away from the concierge's desk and into a small office at the edge of the lobby. Evan now knew Elspeth Duff well enough to understand that a hotel's main concern was the sense of wellbeing perceived by the guests. A visit from a policeman, plain clothes or not, was not something any hotel management wanted known to the public.

The manager made a short phone call summoning tea and biscuits. Having been taught that the most efficient way to get information from someone was to cut through formalities, Evan came to the point without waiting for the arrival of the refreshment.

"I trust you can help me," Evan said. "As a member of the Counter-Terrorist Bureau of Scotland Yard, I've been sent to Valletta because the Yard believes that a crime with international repercussions is in process here in Malta. I'm sure that you are aware that since the attack on September the eleventh and the wars in Iraq and Afghanistan we have been particularly vigilant in following all leads that would allow us to avert any tragedy to innocent people around the world because of Islamic extremism. We are aware that areas where tourists from the UK and America gather might be targets for hostage situations, as has been too painfully demonstrated even before the tragedy in New York."

Worry showing on his face, the manager nodded at Evan's words. "We have already added more security at the hotel," he said.

Feeling he had set the right tone, Evan continued. "We're trying to get information on people we suspect may know something about the plotting of a crime here in Malta." Evan was careful not to define the nature of the crime.

The manager nodded. "In today's world we all fear what the terrorists might do next. Our hotel chain has some of the best hotels in the world. It's most unlikely that we would harbour terrorists here."

"Please be assured," Evan said with calculated sincerity, "that we don't think that you've done so, but we're trying to find out more information about a person who has connections with one of your current guests."

"It is not the hotel's policy to give out information on

our guests."

Evan could hear the tightness in the manager's tone and decided to take advantage of it. "Scotland Yard does not, of course, have authority here in Malta, but I am working closely with the Maltese Police. Perhaps if I called..." He let the sentence dangle.

"That won't be necessary."

A quiet tap came at the door and a waiter brought in the tea tray bearing a teapot, two china teacups, milk and sugar and a plate of sweet biscuits. The waiter poured out tea for both of them. The manager thanked the waiter and dismissed him before continuing. "Which guest did you have in mind?"

"A man named Achmed Rashid who is staying in Room 516. Do you know him?"

The manager gulped his tea and coughed. He put down his cup before answering. "Mr Rashid stays here frequently, as do many other members of his family. But how do you know his room number?"

"What can you tell me about him?" Evan asked, ignoring the manager's question.

The manager paused before answering. "Mr Rashid's father is Sheik Abdullah Rashid. Sheik Abdullah is a very rich businessman with commercial interests all over the Mediterranean. I'm sure you can find information about him on the internet."

"Do you know anything about his past?"

"The sheik or Achmed Rashid?"

"Either one or both," Evan said, hoping to find out information that might not be in the public domain.

The manager gazed at his teacup. After a pause where

he seemed to consider how much he wished to tell, he answered. "Their origins are well known in the Arabic world and certainly to any of the members of the current jet set."

The manager frowned. Evan knew he would need to prompt him. "What are the Rashids' origins?"

"Sheik Abdullah's forbears were nomads. His grandfather led one of the larger tribes in Saudi Arabia. His sons succeeded him."

"How? You just said this is common knowledge."

"I suppose it is," the manager said. "The grandfather was murdered and his sons came under suspicion and were cast out from their tribe. The eldest son, the current sheik's father, Sheik Muhammad settled in a small city near the coast, learned some English and started working in a British bank, which was on the verge of bankruptcy. He was bright and soon took over the bank and turned it around. After the war, the Americans built an air force base nearby and Sheik Muhammad took the small profits from the bank and opened a so-called American hotel. He was clever enough to ignore the taboos of Islam within the confines of the hotel. He also established a shuttle service to and from the gates of the air base, so that airmen who had drunk too much did not pose a threat outside the base. Soon the sheik founded a bigger bank in Jeddah. This one prospered as well. He sold the hotel near the airbase and bought a fruit and vegetable importing business. With each new venture he made more money."

Evan watched the manager, who seemed to relax as he warmed to his narrative.

"It is, however, Sheik Abdullah, his oldest son, who

has the real touch," the manager said. "The importing business needed reliable shipping. Sheik Abdullah bought one ship and soon owned a fleet of them. He imported goods not found in Saudi Arabia but that the rich oil moguls there were demanding. His businesses grew exponentially. Soon he had businesses in Syria, Egypt, Lebanon, Tunisia, Turkey and Morocco. His interests range from the food industry, to restaurants, to hotels and to transport. Sheik Abdullah began running cruises for his fellow Saudis, Egyptians and other Arabs, always catering to Islamic tastes. His empire has spread internationally but mainly in the Arabic regions. I've heard he now wishes to expand into Europe."

I could have found all this on the internet now that I know Abdullah Rashid's name, Evan thought. "To your knowledge has the Rashid family been linked at all to the most recent radical Islamist movement?"

The manager started reflexively. "Not that I know of. The Rashid family, like all prosperous Arabic families, is large, of course. Sheik Abdullah has had six or seven wives I believe, although never more than four at a time as is the custom of Islam. Several died, and one he divorced, a half-Lebanese half-British wife who ran away from him."

"Does he have many children?"

"About twenty I think but I can't be sure. Our current guest is one of the oldest, I believe."

"Has Achmed Rashid stayed here often?" Evan knew his question demanded the manager address personal information about Rashid that breached hotel policy. Evan was not sure he would answer.

After a pause the manager said, "Quite often. Achmed

is very fond of the nightlife on Malta. He lives in London but visits us once or twice a year. Unlike his father, he has adopted British dress and mannerisms. He was trained at the London School of Economics but seems to prefer spending money to making it." The manager smiled weakly. "He is very outgoing and treats my staff well. He is always welcome here."

"Why does he stay here when he comes to Malta rather than the casino hotel in St. Julian's?"

"He seems to prefer us. His family has always stayed here and we give him every luxury. We wouldn't like to have his father take his custom elsewhere or even try to buy us out."

"How long has Rashid been here on this visit?"

"Three days. He arrived from London on Saturday."

Evan noted mentally that Saturday had been a busy time for arrivals in Malta—Elspeth, Loren, FitzRoy and Adam Russell as well as Achmed Rashid.

Evan used his most official voice. "What does Mr Rashid do to occupy his day?"

"He rises late," the manager said. "He uses the athletic facilities and the pool and eats lunch, usually after the midday rush. He goes out in the afternoon and seldom returns until well into the evening or early morning. Otherwise, I know nothing of his activities."

Evan knew he could have Rashid followed if it became necessary to learn more. "Did you see Achmed Rashid at lunch yesterday?" he asked.

"I was not here when lunch was served, but I can call the head waiter if you wish."

"That will not be necessary." Evan did not tell the

manager he knew this information.

Evan modified his tone. "We do not suspect Achmed Rashid of any wrongdoing, but feel he may have made contact here at your hotel with someone who is involved in the crime I'm investigating. The man in question is British, born in Lebanon, who had lunch with Rashid here yesterday." Evan went on to describe Adam Russell. "He called Rashid 'brother' but this probably was only a term of respect. If he comes to the Hotel Saint John again, I'd appreciate it if you would ring me on my mobile. Here's the number."

The manager looked disquieted. "I do not wish to disturb my guests, Inspector Davies-Jones."

"You don't need to. Please, just ring me. Also if you have a copy of Mr Rashid's passport I would like a copy of it. If not, will you please provide me with his address in London."

The manager picked up the house phone and asked that a copy of Rashid's passport be brought to him as well as Achmed Rashid's addresses both in Mayfair and in Jeddah.

Evan rose and thanked the manager for the tea, although his cup remained full. Even Evan was surprised by his next question that was the product of the spur-of-the-moment inspiration. "One other thing," Evan said before leaving the room. "Do you know the author Conan FitzRoy by sight?"

The manager relaxed on the change in topic. "Yes, Mr FitzRoy, poor soul, often dined here, although we never could convince him to be a guest in our rooms. We almost persuaded him this spring but, after consideration, he went back to the Kennington Valletta. He was devoutly loyal to the Kennington hotels."

Evan assumed the manager's past tense meant he had heard the news. "Did he visit here two evenings ago?"

"I do not know, inspector but I can call in the concierge. Why do you ask?"

Instead of answering the question, Evan put his hand on the back of his chair and let silence build. As if to fill the uncomfortable void, the manager said hurriedly, "Mr FitzRoy was a great celebrity here in Malta. He would occasionally consent to do a book signing as long as we kept his books in stock in our gift shop."

The manager picked up his phone and summoned the concierge. Evan let the silence linger.

The manager seemed relieved when the concierge appeared. He instructed him to answer the inspector's questions.

"Did you know Conan FitzRoy?" Evan asked.

"Yes, when he was in Malta he frequently visited here," the concierge said. "I have always enjoyed his books and looked forward to his coming. I'm sorry about his death."

"Did you see him on Sunday evening?"

"Yes," the man recalled, "he was here. He is—was—a hard person to miss. He came in just as I was finishing my shift. He acknowledged me, as we have met many times before, and went into the gift shop."

"Do you know why?"

"No, not exactly. The manager of the gift shop said he had called ahead to make sure the gift shop was open. He made a grand entrance, strode to the gift shop, transacted his business and then strode out of the lobby with quite a flourish." The concierge's face gave no hint on his opinion of FitzRoy's actions.

"Did you see him carrying anything when he left?"

"He wasn't carrying anything, but I could ask the assistant in the gift shop, who unfortunately won't be on duty again until Thursday. I can ring her at home."

"No, but please give me her number."

Now we know where FitzRoy was during the missing moments, Evan thought. But had FitzRoy taken anything from the gift shop? And then passed it on knowingly or otherwise to Saieda's cohorts?

As soon as Evan was in the police car again, he made a note in his Blackberry about the gift shop, picked up his mobile and rang Tony Ketcham in London. He read Rashid's passport number off to the detective superintendent, and promised to get in touch again after he reached the high commission, where he was headed. Then he rang Sir Richard.

As the police car sped through the streets towards Ta'Xbiex, Evan thought of contacting Loren. She had promised to leave her mobile on vibrate, but he decided it was best to let her stalk her prey without disturbance.

What was FitzRoy's business in the gift shop? Was it important? Evan was not sure.

When Evan arrived at the British High Commission, he found Richard in his office working on his computer.

"These things don't have the friendliness of those pretty young things they used to send out to us from the FCO. I miss them," Richard mused.

"Computers are faster and probably more accurate,"

Evan said.

"Young women in those days came out to the ex-colonies to find a husband or get away from overbearing parents. They were fun and always made one feel younger. My wife used to laugh at me every time a new secretary would arrive. 'If they make a terrible hash of things,' she would say, 'give them to me and I will make them right.' And she did. She loved computers, although she was quite old-fashioned in most other things. And now, Evan, what are you here about?"

Evan filled the high commissioner in on his trip to the Hotel Saint John, and then asked, "Can you put me through to Detective Superintendent Ketcham on a secure line?"

"Of course." Richard picked up the grey telephone on his desk and gave instructions. When Tony Ketcham came on the line, Evan recounted his morning activities in more detail. The detective superintendent listened and promised to get back to them as soon as he could follow up the lead.

Tony Ketcham told Evan that he had never heard of a connection between Sheik Abdullah Rashid and any terrorist group. "The sheik is well known in Mayfair. He spends freely. He often brings one or two of his wives to London on a shopping spree. He is well treated by the shop assistants, as you can imagine. Still I'll get my staff to dig deeper."

When the call ended, Evan sat back in his chair.

"Loren thinks we may be profiling Adam Russell," he said. "Or that he is being set up unwittingly."

"I would agree with the former but we have no choice but to assume his involvement. There's no one else at the hotel even vaguely suspicious. Every other guest is accounted for whereas Russell isn't."

"Does that condemn him?" Evan asked.

"It only suggests him."

"Do you mind if I ring Loren on my mobile? She promised to leave her 'cell' —as she calls it —on vibrate as she follows Adam Russell."

"Please do, Sir Richard said.

23

As she came into the hotel after her jog with Evan, Loren saw Adam at the reception desk and heard him ordering breakfast in his room. He was apparently unaware that meals could be ordered directly from room service. Loren therefore knew that she had perhaps half hour or more to set up her surveillance of Adam that day.

Returning to her room, she dressed in jeans, a grey sweatshirt and a cheap pair of running shoes. She wore sunglasses and pulled her beautifully coiffed hair back so tightly that it would have brought tears to her hair stylist. In her bag she put an unassuming crushable straw hat that would cover her face if required, and she scrubbed off her makeup. Her tote bag from the local store where she had bought the running shoes also held a supply of her Parisian makeup in case she quickly needed to restore her identity as Alicia Kent.

Loren went to a quiet corner of the garden where she could see the lift and waited for Adam. He appeared a half-hour later and asked for a taxi in fifteen minutes. He was referred to the concierge.

Remembering the taxi driver from the Hotel Saint John, she dug into her purse and found his card. Anthony, that was his name. She reached him on his car phone and asked him if he would like to come to the Kennington

247

Valletta and continue the chase. The prospect of driving with the 'American detective' obviously filled him with delight.

"I will be waiting for you outside, *sinjura*, in five minutes."

Loren found his battered Toyota parked precariously on the street next to the Kennington Valletta. She slid into the slick plastic-covered backseat complete with lace antimacassars.

Anthony winked conspiratorially at her, and he pulled the taxi into the street and slightly down the hill from the hotel to a spot where Loren could see the entrance but the doorman could not see her. She sat patiently while Anthony, who appeared more edgy than he had been the afternoon before, told her for the second time about his family. Loren only half listened. She got the impression that to Anthony, and other Maltese, family was life. As he rambled on, Loren thought of her own pitiful family, who understood neither relationship building nor familial loyalty. Was the difference because of the newness of American culture and that Malta had one of the oldest extant civilisations in Europe? Or was it the influence of the Catholic Church? She could not be sure.

Loren watched the group from the Smithsonian climb into their bus, and she admired the tour leader's skill at loading the people quickly. The bus pulled out from the hotel, revealing Adam Russell, who was just getting into a taxi. In her musings she had almost missed him. She chastised herself and brought her mind to attention.

At Loren's instruction, Anthony ground the old Toyota into gear, grinned and eased in behind Adam's taxi.

They cruised down the hill from the hotel and turned towards the shipyards.

Loren judged that Anthony's skilled driving and familiarity with the spider web of Malta's roads would keep him close to the taxi ahead. She let her mind slip back to Evan Davies-Jones and knew she found him singularly attractive. She wondered if she would ever know him well enough to ask him about his feelings about his scar and missing arm. That was unlikely, as both Loren Axt and Alicia Kent would cease to exist at the end of the week. Before this, she had never regretted leaving an assignment behind or having her identities lost in the ether.

Anthony broke into Loren's thoughts. "I think they are going to the ferry."

"The ferry? Which one?"

"The one from Sicily. People who come to Malta by car take the ferry from Catania or Pozzallo. The ride is very rough if the sea is angry, so many people are seasick when they arrive."

Loren pulled out a map from her bag and took note of the location of the ferry docks under the cliffs along Grand Harbour.

The traffic on the road as they headed towards the docks consisted of ramshackle lorries and vintage vehicles that the Maltese are more likely to drive than tourists from abroad.

"Do many people use the ferry?" she asked.

"In the summertime, yes. Many people come on holiday. In April the sea is too rough and most people prefer to fly."

"Pull over here." Loren pointed to a barrier that

surrounded a construction site across from the dock. She shrank back into her seat and watched Adam Russell leave his taxi. The taxi drove away.

Panic filled Loren. What if Adam was going to take the ferry? She did not know the ferry schedule and had not thought to bring a passport with her.

"How long does it take the ferry to get to Sicily?"

"Three hours to Catania, less to Pozzallo, but the ferry going there is very small and most people go to Catania," Anthony said.

If Russell did leave, she would have to find a way to get a message to Sicily to have him followed there. She could call her handler in Lyon if necessary and admit her folly, although she was loath to do so. Interpol operatives were expected to be both prepared and resourceful and not to whine.

Her frustration over following Adam Russell took a turn. To date nothing indicated that he was the eyes and ears for the terrorists at the Kennington Valletta, but perhaps that was what they wanted people to think. What had the second email message said? *Contact Helios at hotel for Saieda's latest instructions*. But if the hotel was the Hotel Saint John not the Kennington Valletta, Helios very well might be Achmed Rashid.

There must be a good reason why Adam had chosen to come to the ferry dock. Perhaps the real explanation was that Saieda was arriving by ferry, and Adam had been dispatched to see to her or his safe arrival. When Adam and Achmed Rashid had talked at lunch the day before, they made no mention of Saieda or anyone else arriving in Malta. Had they used an open code that she had missed? If

Saieda did arrive, how would Loren know who he or she was? Would Adam contact her or him or would he merely report the arrival to Achmed Rashid? The ramifications of these scenarios were mind-boggling.

Another possibility was that Adam had slipped whatever was exchanged to Achmed the day before and Adam would quietly board the ferry and disappear.

Loren's mind went into high gear. She needed to have a plan and then a backup plan.

"What time does the ferry go to Sicily?" she asked Anthony.

"In the early mornings to Catania, the afternoons to Pozzallo. Both return in the evening, if the weather allows it."

Thinking rapidly, she elicited Anthony's help. "Do you have a pencil and paper?" she asked, hoping that he was fully literate.

"Yes, Ms Detective. While I wait in the taxi queue, I write poetry. In Malti. Then I translate it into English."

Loren was ashamed to have doubted him.

"Anthony, I want to follow our man inside the building and have you wait outside. I'll go in behind him. If he leaves before I do, follow him—on foot if necessary. If he talks to anyone, get close to him and write down what he says."

Loren leapt from the car, entered the ferry building and looked for Adam Russell.

She saw him approaching the ticket counter, which was staffed by a young and attractive Maltese woman.

He took a brochure from a steel rack on the counter. "How much does a single ticket cost and also return?" he asked.

The woman at the counter recited the passenger fares and that for cars for both destinations, giving the price in Maltese lira and in euros.

"And is there more than one trip a day?" Adam asked.

"To where? Catania? Pozzallo? Not before June," she said, "I will give you an up-to-date brochure." This puzzled Loren. Why would the brochures in a rack at the counter be out of date?

The woman turned to a copier behind the desk. She made a copy of something and handed it to Adam. He did not look at it but simply folded it and put it inside the brochure he had already taken.

"Do many people come to Malta from Europe on the ferry?"

The woman bristled slightly but corrected him gently. "Do you mean from Sicily? Malta is a part of Europe. In fact," she said proudly, "we are joining the EU on Saturday."

Adam's face flushed. "No, I mean, do people use the ferry to come here on holiday?"

"Yes, some do, particularly in the summer. Only a few cars come at this time of year. Mainly they are cars that have been driven to Sicily for the day or two and are returning to Malta. We have more ferries in the summer."

Adam persisted. "Do tourists come with their cars? Is it difficult?"

"Most tourists fly. It is hard to get through customs, and therefore easier to hire a car and driver when one gets here."

Adam ran his finger around his collar and plodded on.

"What about the officials—the customs?" he asked. The doggedness of his question made it appear that he was trying to word it in the right way.

"You'll have to ask them. Their office is around the corner and up the stairs," the ticket agent said. She seemed bored with Adam's persistence.

Loren, who was now wearing her hat and dark glasses waited patiently behind Adam. He turned from the desk and nearly ran into her. He gave apologies but did not look up.

Loren watched him leave the building and hoped Anthony would be in pursuit. She asked for a brochure. The agent gave her one from the rack.

"Is this updated?" Loren asked.

"Yes, only the ones in Italian are not."

Loren wondered if this were true. After all Adam had spoken in English. Did the copy given to Adam contain something?

Leaving the building, Loren saw no sign of Adam or Anthony. She quickly rounded the corner and found a small door. This must be the door for customs, as there were no doors immediately beyond it. When she entered, there was only a miniscule winding stairway up to the second floor. Could Adam and Anthony have disappeared up this stairway? Removing her straw hat and sunglasses, she shook out her hair and took a windbreaker from her bag. She put it on and pulled up the hood. She put on the expression of a lost tourist. She mounted the stairs, hoping no one, particularly Adam and Anthony, would try to come down them, as they were too narrow and winding for anyone to pass unnoticed.

At the top of the stairs, she found herself in a hallway with blank walls. She was concerned that she could be trapped in close quarters with Adam, who might then recognise her. A door stood ajar at the end of the hall. A small sign indicated it was the customs office. Seeing Anthony's back and his scribbling in his notebook, she made a hasty retreat back to the street. The construction on both sides of the street made crossing dangerous, but she saw a duty-free shop in the distance and headed in that direction. She ducked under the shop's portico just as Adam, with Anthony close behind, came out of the building.

Loren did a quick surveillance of her surroundings. The duty free shop was closed so she could not hide inside. Instead, she took her camera out and walked to the large chain link gates that appeared to be the gates used by cars arriving on the ferry. With a show of intent, she started taking photographs of the limestone cliffs above the ferry terminal. In the distance she saw Adam hail a passing taxi and head in her direction. Anthony jumped in his taxi and made a precarious U-turn. As he passed the duty free shop, he flung the passenger side door open. Loren jumped in the car and slammed the door.

"Have we lost him?" she asked.

Anthony held up his car radiotelephone. "Only for the moment. My friend Henry is driving the taxi. I radioed him and asked him to slow down so I can catch up."

Loren grinned at Anthony's resourcefulness. "Do you know where they are going?"

"Henry said to Paolo, to the mosque."

"Again?"

Anthony looked at his watch. "I think they will be there in time for noonday prayers."

Loren sat back trying to think. Was Adam taking the copy of the brochure to someone meeting him at the mosque? What could be in the brochure?

"Keep back a bit. Tell me what happened at customs."

Anthony spoke into his car radiotelephone again and got a crackled response in Malti. Ignoring traffic, he turned towards her and said, "When we get to the mosque, I will read you the conversation. My wife, who trained in secretarial school, taught me shorthand, because sometimes I am in the middle of a poem when I get a fare, and cannot write out all my thoughts in long hand." Loren wondered if there was special shorthand for the Maltese language.

They wound recklessly through the narrow streets towards Paolo. The lunch hour was nearing and traffic had picked up considerably. Anthony's conversation turned to his opinion of Maltese drivers. Loren hardly listened, deep in her own thoughts.

Henry's taxi left Adam at the mosque. Anthony found a spot in the shade of a tree at a nearby parking lot. Loren could tell that he was uncomfortable being there and asked why.

"We do not like Arabs here," he told her. "They come illegally from Tunisia and Algeria, trying to get to Italy. Often they are shipwrecked and we have to take care of them. They are ignorant and unclean."

Loren, knowing what she did about Islam, was amazed by this prejudice.

"Our man is not very intelligent," Anthony continued. "He went to the customs officer and asked dumb questions.

Here, let me read this to you."

Man: Do many cars come here from Europe, I mean from other parts of Europe like France and England?

Customs: Sometimes; sometimes not.

Man: I mean, do tourists come here often by car?

Customs: Not at this time of year.

Man: In the summer?

Customs: More often.

Man: Is it hard to go through customs? The ticket seller downstairs said it was.

Customs: Used to be. We always look for smugglers. People coming here like to smuggle in car parts. They come in with a new car and then change all the parts and leave with old parts. Until now, we keep a close eye on them, keep engine numbers and make notes on the condition of the car. Then we check them as they go out.

Man: Used to be hard? What now?

Customs: Who knows? Nobody has told me what happens when we join the EU on Saturday. Anything could happen.

Loren had Anthony read through the conversation again. Anthony added his commentary this time. He said that the customs officer, who was old and fat and probably accustomed to an occasional gift to let things through for his friends and possibly feared that with the changing rules he would lose that advantage.

"Of what interest could this be to Adam...to our man?"

"I think he was trying to get information, but not to ask for it directly. The customs official seemed angry with him for taking up so much time, and he finally turned his back and went back to his desk."

"Was there anything passed between the customs agent and our man, any papers?"

"Nothing I could see."

"Let's wait until he's through his prayers and see where he takes us next."

"He is not an intelligent man," Anthony said again.

Maybe so or maybe not, thought Loren. She was beginning to believe that Adam was devious not stupid. Why would he come to the ferry terminal and ask seemingly inane questions? Questions with which apparently even he seemed uncomfortable. What was he really up to? What was on the Xeroxed piece of paper? She would have to ask Elspeth to have the room staff check to see if Adam had brought the photocopy of the brochure back to his room, although she knew Adam could easily give it to someone in the mosque or simply leave it behind for someone to pick up after he had left. Adam may not have been as innocent as she once thought. *Contact Helios at the hotel.* Was Adam Helios?

24

Elspeth wished the arrangements for the arrival of Bridget O'Connell had taken less time. Normally such preparation would have been assigned to the booking staff or at least the person on that staff who handled important visitors, but Elspeth had known Conan FitzRoy and did not want to end her relationship with him by leaving the formalities to an impersonal member of staff. The balance between staying connected with Evan, Loren, Tony and Richard Munro and their activities and dealing with the FitzRoy crisis, as she labelled it in her mind, was a difficult one. Perhaps, she thought, she could quickly dispense with Bridget O'Connell and then devote herself full time to Saieda's planned Phase Three. She always found it easier to complete one task before going on to another, but at the back of her mind she knew she might not be able to afford this luxury.

At two o'clock feeling hungry and giving in to her fatigue, she left her desk and ordered a light salad, which she decided to eat in the comfort of her room. Room service left a brimming tray filled with an opulent array of cutlery, linens, flowers, and food. She would have not judged the chef's creation as a light salad.

As she ate, Elspeth thought about Conan FitzRoy. She had not been fooled by his preposterousness but she had been seduced by his charm. She was not looking forward to meeting his next of kin. Several times in the course of her employment for the Kennington Organisation she had handled deaths that occurred in the hotels and even one that involved foul play. Up until now, the person who had died was unknown to her. This time was different. Conan FitzRoy was not a faceless being whose body had been removed before she had been called. She had known him as a guest at the Kennington Hotels across the world, she had shared drinks and ardent conversation with him on many occasions and only two nights ago she had celebrated Giuseppe's triumphant presentation of a dish called à la FitzRoy. She admitted that she had liked him and been amused by him. And in the final moment when she had found him, she had been the first to touch the coldness of his death.

How had the cyanide been given to him? Elspeth had reviewed his travel documents and tickets and found that he had planned to be away from London for two months. Despite Conan's outer flair, he had been a methodical man. Elspeth had seen his way of packing his medications, the small neatly labelled bottles and packets, filled with an assortment of varicoloured tablets and capsules, each with a date and time. The pockets in his medicine bag held sixty-five days of medication, presumably to allow for any travel difficulties. According to his papers, FitzRoy had left Rome nine days before his death and nine days of medicine were gone.

Among Conan's things, the police had found his prescriptions, another precaution if he were delayed. Evan told Elspeth that Inspector Dom had consulted a local chemist to confirm which of the multi-coloured pills was which. He also had examined the remaining bottles and packets and confirmed that each held the exact amount of medication prescribed. This seemed to indicate that poison was administered some other way. But how?

The coroner had suggested that the cyanide was in a time-delayed capsule that could have been taken up to three hours before it dissolved. Conan and Loren had returned to the hotel before five. Conan had left the hotel close to five and been gone for almost an hour. He had been seen entering the hotel a few minutes before six o'clock, after returning from his outing. There he had met Dr Hammud and then had gone to his room. He came back down about ten minutes later to have a solitary drink in the garden. The coroner said he had died between seven and nine. Therefore the poison could have been given to him anytime from the time he left the vineyard and returned to the hotel with Loren until the time he was given his final drink in the garden by Fernardu.

This puzzled Elspeth. It was infuriating in circumstances such as this that Eric was so insistent that the gardens in his hotels should offer private alcoves where guests could be unobserved. Had anyone joined FitzRoy in the garden after Fernardu had left? Lord Kennington would be vexed by her implications that the design of his hotel had contributed to Conan's death. Elspeth smiled at this. She had known Eric so long and so well.

Of course there was the faint possibility that Conan had a supply of the drug that had killed him and that he had staged his own death. It would have been a dramatic gesture but did not accord with Conan's love of life. In any case, Evan had said that the coroner had specifically ruled out suicide.

Elspeth's thoughts turned to Richard Munro. She was acutely aware of his attention over the last two days and her own unintended reaction to it. She recalled the look in Richard's eyes the night before, heard his words again and felt his hand on hers. Abruptly she pushed these images from her mind, knowing she wanted no place for them in her life.

Elspeth finished her meal and pushed the tray away. She was annoyed with herself that she had resorted to an old habit of emptying her plate when her thoughts were preoccupied.

Bridget's plane was not due until five so Elspeth took advantage of the hiatus. Getting her mind off the forthcoming meeting with Bridget probably would do her more good than sitting and rehearsing what she would say, and certainly dwelling on Richard Munro had no future. She called room service to remove the tray and indulged herself with two hours of dreamless, deep sleep.

25

Bridget O'Connell sat on the flight from Rome to Malta and considered her uncle. When she was growing up in Belfast, he was the father figure that she did not have in her own father, who had been dedicated to the Unionist Cause and not his own family. That was before the bombing.

Later her uncle had become—or rather was—a mockery to the Cause. He had abrogated his Ulster roots for the role of a successful 'British' historian and author. In doing so he had shed his Belfast accent and made at least some inroads into being accepted by the Establishment, if not as one of their own, at least someone who knew the rules well enough not to be an embarrassment. His fame and eccentricity covered any gaffes. His attentiveness to women charmed them, although he quickly tired of them. But the final straw, as far as Bridget was concerned, was that when he took his *nom de plume*, he had the hubris to pick a name that connected him with the English monarchy—FitzRoy, *fils roi*— son of the king.

Then Bridget discovered her uncle's betrayal. On the night Bridget's parents died, Kevin O'Connell had disappeared before the IRA bombing that killed them. He had claimed that he did not know beforehand what was going to happen. Bridget learned three years ago that he had been told of the bombing but warned neither his close friend nor his brother and sister-in-law. Bridget could never forgive him for that, but despite this he was the only family member with whom she kept in touch.

Bridget had left Ireland as soon as she was financially able, finding the Troubles intolerable. She felt the deep anger that a child does towards her parents' IRA murderers, an anger that had grown with time. Why the hell couldn't the bloody Catholics go back to their side of the border? Why did they want to rule the land that was populated mainly by Protestants? Bridget had no sympathy with the unification of Ireland and when she was a teenager decided to fight the injustice of the union. After six years of activism in Northern Ireland, she chose to emigrate and now lived in Rome.

Bridget's relationship with her uncle was closer on his side than hers. She often felt that he was trying to atone for hiding his knowledge of the bombing that killed her parents. She also knew that she was the only close blood relative he had left. Her uncle's relationships with multiple women were legendary, but he was too boastful, perhaps as a cover for his own self-deception, to attract men friends. By default, she alone had become the entirety of his family, although she trusted him not at all and saw the ultimate hypocrisy of his life.

He had developed heart problems several years ago, which was not surprising considering his lifestyle, and in his denial, most of all to himself, he hid his growing illness from everyone except from her. She could see the impact it had on him. Angelique, his fifth wife, had been too busy partying to notice the change or even perhaps to care.

Although her uncle had been acknowledged by the

Crown for his contribution to the promotion of British literature, he had never achieved the thing he wanted most—a knighthood. "Sir Conan FitzRoy," he would say, "Now that has a most sonorous ring." Bridget suspected that he had chosen the first name because the title would have sounded so well with it. "Sir Kevin" didn't work for him. But the knighthood had never come and Kevin O'Connell never got his 'Sir' with or without his name change.

Bridget had last seen her uncle when he left Rome on his way to Malta. Just under two weeks ago, he had driven into the courtyard of her complex of flats in a long, black Mercedes. He had been greeted by a bevy of chattering Italian boys, excited by the arrival of the car that was fit for a *signore* of great importance and from which emerged a vast man with cloak and stick. He hardly could walk through them and decided instead to shower them with the small change in his pocket. Scattering it away from the car, he had hobbled into the building while the boys were scurrying to collect the small rewards.

Uncle Kevin had stayed with Bridget for three days, allowing time to get his Mercedes serviced. He had spent his days visiting parts of the Vatican that he imagined could become critical to a future novel. To his delight, his private guide, an English-speaking priest, had read his books and had showed him areas that were normally closed to the public.

Uncle Kevin had insisted that, when he left Rome, he would leave in splendour. Consequently Bridget arranged for his car to be taken into the garage of a friend to be polished and cleaned until it shone like new. She had noted a small blemish in the paint and had it buffed as much as possible, although a slight scar still remained. It was a relief when he left, again scattering coins to distract the boys, although this time he used coins of smaller value.

Bridget wondered how she would feel about her uncle's death after all the details of his death were attended to. Would she grieve? Would she still feel angry? Would she in the end miss him? She wasn't sure but she thought not.

He had asked his solicitors to call Bridget, not his wife, if he died. He had designated her his heir and not Angelique. Angelique had been given a very mean settlement. She was to keep her clothing, which was extensive and expensive, but FitzRoy had always kept the precious jewellery in his own name. The will specified that it should be sold and that the proceeds given to the War Museum in Valletta.

He had requested that Angelique not be present at the reading of the will, in the same way she had been present for FitzRoy neither in life nor death. She dropped hints, or sometimes slurred them at drinks parties, that she was Conan FitzRoy's wife, but she preferred the company of her toy boys. The toy boys were impressed by her wardrobe, jewellery and connections and enjoyed her indulgence towards them. Bridget knew they would disappear as soon as the contents of the will were made known. Bridget was left the copyrights and royalties from all her uncle's books as well as his personal effects. His other possessions were heavily encumbered, and what was left of his property would need to be sold to pay the debts of his indulgent lifestyle.

Bridget gathered up her book and handbag as the descent to Valletta was announced. Now there was the business at hand. Her uncle's body would need to be prepared for burial and returned to Northern Ireland, where he asked to be interred under a large headstone in a conspicuous spot in the most prominent of cemeteries in Belfast. His hired car was already scheduled to be returned to London. Earlier, she had arranged the car's shipment from Valletta to Marseille, and hired Seamus Riley to take the car to London by road. She would accompany Uncle Kevin's remains back to Belfast.

These organisational details came easily to her. She had been in charge of her uncle's affairs for the last few years. He had trusted her that much, although she wondered if he would have continued to do so if he had known her true feelings towards him. It all started when she discovered the betrayal. Now it would soon be over. Her emotions were mixed but she did not feel sorry.

She was not looking forward to the next few days. Fatigue overcame her, and she wished there was time to ask the flight attendant for another cup of tea.

*

Elspeth had the front desk ring her in her office when Bridget O'Connell arrived. As Elspeth emerged into the lobby, she surveyed the various people standing there and was surprised when she picked out the person who must be Bridget. She was fair rather than dark or redheaded and was dressed in jeans and a tight-fitting jersey. Her coat, which hung open, was an elegantly cut, full-length Irish tweed. Bridget's Italian leather boots had excessively high heels and very pointed toes, which was the current fashion.

What most caught Elspeth's attention even from a distance was the intensity of feeling that Bridget seemed to carry. It looked like anger. Could Bridget be this angry because of FitzRoy's sudden death? Did she resent that the smoothness of her life had been upset by her uncle's demise? Murder might have caused such a reaction in Bridget, but to Elspeth's knowledge no one had mentioned murder to FitzRoy's solicitors or to anyone else who might have known Bridget. Elspeth had expected distress or sadness but certainly not anger.

Bridget turned her face fully towards Elspeth as she approached her. Her eyes were inky in contrast to her otherwise pale colouring. She used little makeup but her thick, dark lashes ringed her dark brown eyes. What exact grief or anger or depth of feeling was behind those eyes? Elspeth could not be sure.

"Ms O'Connell, of course you have my condolences. I am Elspeth Duff. Welcome to the Kennington Valletta, although I know the reason for your coming is painful."

She put out her hand to shake Bridget's but Bridget did not reciprocate. Elspeth put down her hand and said, "We have taken what steps we could at the instruction of Mr FitzRoy's solicitors. Thank you for coming to help with the final arrangements. We have a room for you for as long as you wish to stay. It's always sad for us when our guests are here for such sombre reasons."

Bridget brushed aside Elspeth's sentiments with a flick of her hand.

"Ms Duff, you must understand my urgent need to conclude the business of my uncle's death. Grieving must take its own time. I appreciate your attention to the matter.

I wish to return his body to Belfast with all due haste. I've arranged for his driver to take my uncle's car back to London on a ship leaving tomorrow. I don't wish to continue paying the outrageous leasing fees. Can you tell me where my uncle's body is now?"

Elspeth drew back at Bridget's curtness.

"At a local mortuary. I have all the information for you in my office, but first let me show you to your room."

Bridget acceded to the offer with a raised eyebrow and followed Elspeth to the lift. Elspeth contrasted this to Conan's regal entrance only days before. Those few days had changed so many lives.

After she returned to her office from showing Bridget her room, Elspeth suddenly had an intense feeling that Conan's death, which had until now seemed such an irritating diversion, may not have been a side issue at all but part of the main event. Conan was Pericles of the first email. Elspeth was sure of it. Therefore he was central to Saieda's plot. There was no immediate reason for her idea. Was it her Scottish sensibility, maybe a long forgotten touch of the fairies that stirred this reaction? Richard and her cousin Johnnie had often teased her about this when they were young, particularly when she was able to catch them out.

Conan's presence at the Kennington Valletta had inflamed a violent reaction—his death. Had his actions in Valletta somehow compromised Saieda's operation? Why would his arrival at the Kennington Valletta have been a prelude to his murder?

Conan had died from cyanide from an unknown source. Elspeth again recalled the well-ordered vials of medications that hung from the door of Conan's bathroom. Any member of the staff or anyone who might have gained access to his room would have been able to alter any of his tablets. These medications would have been available to anyone if they considered that Conan was impeding their undercover activities. She would ask the security staff to go back over the tapes to see if any unauthorised person had entered FitzRoy's rooms during his visit. Elspeth's mind raced. Adam Russell's room had been closely monitored, but no one had thought to watch FitzRoy's before his death.

Elspeth wanted to talk to someone about her deduction. She thought for a long time before she decided to ring Richard. Finally, she picked up the handset and dialled his direct number. What had made her feel so strongly that FitzRoy's murder might be involved in the main event at the hotel? Certainly not the touch of the "wee fowks," as they were called in Scots. At an early age, her father taught her to interpret information in multiple ways, and insisted she should always question the obvious. This was compounded by her training in law at Cambridge and in the fundamentals of police investigation at Scotland Yard. Whatever the reason, real or paranormal, Elspeth was certain that her assumptions about Conan FitzRoy were true.

Richard answered immediately, splintering her thoughts.

"Oh, Dickie, I'm glad I reached you," she said. "I rang to let you know that Bridget O'Connell has arrived. She is settling in to her room now. As soon as she comes back downstairs, I'm going talk to her about the arrangements being made for Conan's body and effects. I thought I would call you in the meantime to see if there is any progress on your side. Bridget seems in a terrible rush, as if the sooner she is out of Malta the better."

"You sound a bit rattled, if I may say so, my dear, and that's unlike you. I am making arrangements on this end," he explained. "Now tell me, what do you think has caused Ms O'Connell's impatience?"

Elspeth paused at his question. "She was horribly brusque, and I can't understand why. Perhaps she is still in shock and simply wants to get the difficult parts over with. But there's something else. After I talked to Bridget, I had this feeling," she hesitated at the word, "that Conan's death is somehow central to this whole mess and that he was murdered for something he said or learned or did here. I'm certain he was Pericles. Does that make any sense to you?"

Richard did not answer for a moment. Then he said, "Not quite. Can you tell me how you got this idea?"

Since Elspeth's idea had been intuitive rather than rational, she tried to find a more persuasive way to explain it.

Clearing her throat, she said, "Basically it's an intuition; no, it's more than that. A strong premonition." Elspeth now wishing she had kept her thoughts to herself.

"A Scottish sensibility?" he said.

She stuck out her jaw and felt her face redden, glad that Richard could see neither reaction. "Perhaps," she said with dignity, "or perhaps years of experience dealing with the less seemly side of the human race."

He chuckled.

She continued. "I'm troubled by Conan's activities

during his stay this year. I'm trying to remember the exact conversation that Loren, he and I had at dinner on Saturday night," she said. "Conan said he was starting work on a book about the financial networks in the terrorist world outside of the usual banking systems. You know that. He gave the specific example of the system that Al Qaeda uses to move their funds. Adam Russell was in the room at the time having dinner by himself. Our party was boisterous, at least by Kennington hotel standards anyway. I'm sure Adam could have overheard anything we said."

"I don't see how that makes FitzRoy Pericles or links him with Adam, if Adam is implicated at all."

Momentarily Elspeth thought his statement sounded a bit condescending, but she chose to accept it as rhetorical instead.

"He must be," Elspeth said.

"Perhaps, just perhaps," he said with so little inflection that Elspeth thought he might be teasing her. "Have you asked Loren how she feels about this?"

Elspeth was glad he had changed the tenor of the conversation. "No, she's out this afternoon following Adam. I expect her back later."

"Good. Why not ask her what she thinks? Loren, has, as I remember, an almost instant recall of conversations. Tell her to be in touch with me when she returns. I'll have her over here and take down everything she remembers about her conversations with FitzRoy. After all, in the last two days of his life she, more than any of us, spent time with him. Elspeth, when you have a moment, write down your recollections too and why you think them important. Also how Adam reacted during the dinner. Ring me if anything else comes within your 'sight'. He chuckled again.

"Dickie, I find you quite wicked and always have." She rang off before getting his reaction but she could not help smiling. He had not, it seemed, lost all of his sense of humour.

Next she called Eric Kennington, conveying the same information but not mentioning a Scottish sensibility. He gave her no new instructions, and asked her to stay diligent, keep a close eye on Bridget's safety and keep him posted.

After Elspeth rang off, René knocked at her door. He informed her that Adam Russell had returned to the hotel and retired to his room. He had asked room service for tea and some biscuits. When they were delivered, he had put the Do Not Disturb sign on his door.

"Thanks René. Please ask Ms Kent to come back here when she returns. Here's a note for her."

"I will see she gets it."

"Thank you. Right now a pot of tea and some food, cucumber sandwiches if you have them, does sound like a splendid idea. As long as I lived in America, I never could schedule my inner clock to omit a cup of tea and small bite to eat at this time of day."

After René left, she pulled out a piece of Kennington Valletta stationery and began to make notes to see if she could rationalise her sudden revelation.

Elspeth's note taking was interrupted by another knock at the door.

"Come in," she called. Bridget entered the room. She had shed her tweed coat but not her hostility or high heeled boots. She twisted down in one of the leather chairs and sat without relaxing.

Elspeth did not relish the interview and decided to stay as business-like as possible. "Ms O'Connell, we will do everything we can to make your arrangements as easy as possible. I've notified the British high commission and they're taking the necessary steps to have your uncle's body prepared for shipment. They've asked if you want to accompany his body back to the UK."

Bridget glared at her. "I instructed Mr Edgewood that that my uncle's body is to be cremated. He didn't practice any religion and therefore no rites are necessary."

Elspeth pursed her lips and wondered if Conan would have liked so little fuss. "Mr Edgewood told me you had requested cremation, but Malta, as you know, is heavily Roman Catholic, and I believe cremation here is generally discouraged. It would be better if you arrange for that in the UK. I just spoke with the British high commissioner. He has called British Airways, which will make space for you and your uncle's coffin on the flight to London and on to Belfast on the day after tomorrow."

Bridget pulled a packet of cigarettes from her pocket. She drew out a cigarette out and lit it without requesting if this was acceptable. "I plan to leave tomorrow," Bridget said after inhaling and blowing out a long stream of smoke. "As I told you, I have already made arrangements to have his car shipped to Marseille and driven back to London. I would prefer to accompany my uncle's remains, cremated or otherwise, on the same vessel, which goes on to Belfast. There's no need to have them shipped by air. He would have liked the fanfare but I don't, and his estate probably cannot afford the expense."

"I see," said Elspeth, feeling provoked by Bridget's pre-emption. "There is one more thing, Ms O'Connell. When your uncle arrived here, he said he came for his yearly rest, but also told us that he was beginning a new book involving terrorists and their transfer of funds outside of the banking system. I'm sure you are aware that your uncle enjoyed intellectual and historical discussions, particularly with people who could help him in the research of his books. Before his mur...death, he contacted several people inside and outside the hotel. One of these contacts may have been responsible directly or indirectly for his demise."

Elspeth cleared her throat in order to stop coughing from the cigarette smoke.

"That brings me to a delicate point," she continued. "Last week Scotland Yard warned us of the possibility of terrorist activity here at the hotel. We have not pinpointed any suspects who might be involved nor do we know if any guest here might be implicated."

Bridget sat silently smoking, expressionless, so Elspeth went on. "Your uncle's death at first appeared to be a heart attack but when the autopsy was done, cyanide was found in his system. The local police have concluded that he was murdered."

Bridget said nothing. She uncrossed her long legs and looked around for an ashtray. Elspeth retrieved a plate from her tea things, which were still on a sideboard. As she handed Bridget the plate, Elspeth was perplexed by Bridget's detachment.

"Your uncle's curiosity about terrorism," Elspeth

continued, "may have led him to discover some piece of information that made his knowledge a dangerous thing and eventually led to his death. It also may be that your uncle put this information into his computer before he died. No one has the password so the police could not open it. The police now have his notes, medications and computer, but did not keep his passport and travel papers which they gave to me, as they seemed unimportant in the police enquiries. As a precaution we have placed the documents in our vault and the police have made copies."

Bridget said simply, "I'm sure you have taken all the precautions you feel necessary." Was she being sarcastic?

"We will be releasing these papers into your custody now that you have arrived. However I would like you to be aware that you may be in danger here in Malta. We fear there might be an attempt made to retrieve something your uncle found, and you might possibly be harmed in that attempt."

Bridget's ground out her cigarette. "Ms Duff, I assure you that as a person who grew up in Belfast during the time of the Troubles, I am not frightened or even apprehensive of a might-possibly-be-chance of terrorists attacking me. They have no possible reason to do so."

Inwardly Elspeth ground her teeth. She affected her most professional voice. "We at the Kennington hotels are always concerned with our guests' personal safety. If your uncle was murdered, we've failed in our task. If beyond that, you are placed in danger, then we are doubly remiss."

"Is it just for the hotel's reputation?"

Elspeth could feel herself becoming increasingly annoyed by Bridget's discourtesy. As accommodating as

Elspeth was trying to be, the young woman was unnecessarily rude. Outwardly keeping her calm, Elspeth plunged forward, "With your concurrence, we've decided to take security precautions around your visit."

"No, I don't want that. There is no danger!" This was the first strong emotion Elspeth had seen in Bridget since she had entered the room.

"We can't be sure of that. It's only for your protection."

"I don't need protection. Can't you understand? Spending two bloody days in a bloody posh hotel on a resort island is not a threat to those of us who have survived troubles far worse. It would be like telling a holocaust survivor you are providing them protection from the village idiot."

Such an intense expression of feeling puzzled Elspeth. In fact, Bridget's whole demeanour and style seemed out of place. Conan had been a flamboyant man but he had manners; this young woman did not. Elspeth was now fully exasperated. Her job was to assure the safety of the hotel and its guests, but now she also had to deal with a hostile young woman who in all likelihood was in danger of being killed.

"Ms Duff, I've had a long and unpleasant trip here. I wish to leave Malta as soon as I can. That's all I have to say." Bridget stood up and trod out of the room, leaving her cigarette end behind.

26

After reconnoitring the mosque, Loren returned to Anthony's taxi and took a seat beside him. He was gnawing at his pencil and looking at his notepad.

"A poem?" Loren asked.

He nodded and showed it to her but she could not understand the Maltese words.

"After watching that old and fat customs official, I know Malta must change," he said. "We cannot keep our old ways and must become more modern. Therefore I am composing a poem to the arrival of the new and ways of combining the best that we have with the best of the twenty-first century."

"An honourable theme but I like the old Malta. You shouldn't lose what is Maltese in order to become a part of the greater Europe."

He was unmoved. "We will become a part of the greater Europe. To remain completely in Malta's past will not be a good thing."

Loren did not pursue the argument.

They waited without speaking again until prayers were over. Men emerged from the mosque one by one. She saw Adam putting on his shoes. He shyly approached an older man, perhaps an imam, dressed in traditional Arabic dress. The older man listened to Adam, gently put his arm on the younger man's shoulder and guided him back into the building. They disappeared along a corridor that led into what appeared to be a school building beyond.

Loren could not decide what to do next. Had Adam slipped out by an unseen exit? Perhaps. Or he simply might have joined an activity taking place at the school. Loren and Anthony continued to wait throughout the afternoon. The street was quiet and no one seemed interested in them. There was a call for afternoon prayers but Adam was not to be seen. Finally Loren instructed Anthony to return to the hotel.

Loren felt tired and unfulfilled by her day's work. When they reached the hotel, she paid Anthony his due and a large tip, although he protested that helping the cause of the American family made tipping unnecessary. As she approached the door into the lobby, she noticed a fair-haired woman in front of the hotel. The woman was wearing a long tweed coat, which struck Loren as odd considering the warmth of the evening. The woman was looking out over the harbour and smoking agitatedly. She looked at her watch several times, threw her cigarette on to the pavement as if in disgust and turned back into the hotel. Behind her one of the doormen fetched a dustpan and broom and swept up the remnants of the cigarette, thus returning the entrance to its earlier pristine condition.

Just after Loren entered the hotel, she was approached by a member of the concierge's staff and was given a message concealed in a heavy envelope similar to the ones she had seen at the writing desk that morning. She opened it and found it was from Elspeth Duff asking her to come to the office or to Elspeth's guestroom if she returned after five. Following instructions, she crossed the garden and rapped on Elspeth's door. Elspeth greeted her with a refreshing smile. They settled into the chintz-covered chairs in the room's sitting area. The room reminded Loren of the British country homes she had seen on BBC Television.

"Who is our new arrival in the long tweed coat?" Loren asked as she accepted Elspeth's offer of a glass of wine.

"Bridget O'Connell. Conan's niece."

"Is she meeting someone here?"

"What makes you say that?"

"I just saw her outside. She kept checking her watch as if she were waiting for someone. As I was coming in, she gave up in disgust and came back inside."

"Ms O'Connell is a woman who seems to have cornered the market in unpleasantness. She could have learned civility from her uncle, but she apparently did not."

"Has she upset you?" Loren asked.

Elspeth shook her head. "No. Certainly I've encountered much worse in the course of my job. As much as I don't like her manner, I'm concerned. If one member of a family dies in a hotel, it's considered an unavoidable tragedy, but when two die, it's a disaster. Loren, with your training in observing people and as you go about the hotel, I want you to watch her. Not obviously as that will only irk her further. I don't think you will be able to strike up an acquaintance with her. She's far too hostile. However, her life may be at stake, and I don't want that possibility to become a fulfilled promise. I think her uncle was more involved in the terrorist threat than we had thought before.

He may have discovered what was being exchanged, where the exchange was to take place or, even worse, he may have been directly involved in the exchange, knowingly or otherwise. I think he may have died because of where he was or what he heard or what he knew. I don't want Bridget to die as well, particularly as she may be the unwitting carrier of that information which may be among Conan's things."

"Why do you think that?" Loren asked.

"A sixth sense? I keep coming back to the second email message, which confirmed that the exchange had taken place and Saieda's plan, whoever Saieda may be, had been accomplished. It was sent approximately six hours after Conan's death and about three hours after I discovered the body." An involuntary shudder ran through her.

"Are you all right?" Loren asked.

"Like most people, I dislike violent death. I saw to it that his body was carried to the back hallway and the ambulance came to the car park when no one was about."

"Adam Russell was in the bar," Loren said.

"Yes. True. I saw him as well."

"Which means he may have seen you with Conan's body."

"Do you think he's Helios?" Elspeth asked.

"I'm not sure. His actions seem innocent enough but he may be."

"Conan made a number of contacts on Monday. Roberto at the vineyard or someone in the gift shop at the Hotel Saint John could have been involved in the exchange. Loren, I think your recollection of your time with Conan will be critical because Conan may have told you something that is important to our understanding of what happened the evening Conan died. Sir Richard has asked that you go to the high commission in Ta'Xbiex and set down everything you remember. He has great faith in your powers of recall."

"I'll go first thing in the morning. But how could Conan's niece be involved in this?" Loren asked. "And what do you think the danger is?"

"Therein lie certain sensibilities," Elspeth said somewhat cryptically with the hint of a twinkle in her eye. "But, seriously, Inspector Dom has Conan's notes, medications and computer, but I'll be turning all the rest of Conan's personal belongings over to Bridget either later this evening or in the morning. She wants to leave tomorrow, and there's no reasonable excuse for us to delay her. I'm concerned, however, that she has expressed complete contempt of the notion of any danger."

"Is there anything other than watching that I can do to help?"

"I'm developing a plan but I haven't worked it out completely," Elspeth said. "René put Bridget in a room within full view of a security camera that we have angled to record anyone coming or going near her room. There doesn't appear to be any need to monitor her room because the threat is from without not within. I need to keep out of her way so I won't enrage her further, but as Alicia Kent you can be a disinterested guest who has no direct connection to her. I may ask you to do more this evening."

Loren's face twisted in a pained smile. "That will be a relief after today."

Loren told her story and expressed her frustration over the inconclusive activity of her day.

"What do you think Adam was doing today?" Elspeth asked.

Loren pursed her lips. "I can't be sure. And what's more I've a sense even he wasn't sure. I've always felt uneasy about our targeting Adam. He appears to be such a babe, so incredibly gullible. Coming back in Anthony's cab I kept thinking if Adam could have been set up as a decoy, the obvious person to follow in order to divert us from other things taking place, or that he's very clever and has been instructed to act the fool."

Elspeth stopped with her wine glass in mid-air and stared at Loren, and then nodded slowly.

"Yes, both are real possibilities. Let's talk to Richard, Evan and Tony Ketcham and see what they think."

"I mentioned this to Evan this morning. He's coming for dinner this evening. Both business and pleasure," Loren said, grinning broadly. "I'll bring it up with him again."

"And I'll ring Richard. Let's meet in my office after dinner."

After Loren left her, Elspeth picked up the portfolio she brought from the office, pulled out the heavy Kennington Valletta stationery covered with the notes she promised Richard and resumed writing. If her assumption was correct that Conan was Pericles, then there could be a connection between Adam and Conan. Adam might have been in contact with Conan, but she had no knowledge that the two of them had spoken. She must ask the staff. So far Adam had not posed any overt threat to any of the guests, but if faced with the possibility that his connections to the exchange could he be a danger to Bridget O'Connell?

Elspeth shoved aside her notes, and hastened from her room, her plan suddenly swirling through her head. She must find René LeGrand.

*

Adam Russell left the mosque shortly after afternoon prayers and caught a taxi back to Valletta. He needed to get some exercise after a long session of intense study. He had the taxi drop him at the bus terminus. He decided to walk along the long curved wall of Triq Girolamo Cassar looking out over the cliffs and the view of Grand Harbour. He felt more at ease than he had since arriving in Valletta, and was eager to tell Achmed the things he had learned at the ferry and the mosque. He entered the Kennington Valletta with a new confidence.

He crossed the lobby, trying to ignore the picture of the big Christian general on the ceiling, because he considered the painting an attack on Islam. Entering the lift, he mistakenly pressed the button for three instead of four. The doors of the lift opened, and Adam was confronted by two armed and hostile guards who told him to move on. This must be the floor where the English nabob was staying. Adam's confidence faded, and he made apologies using a schoolboy's terms.

Shaken, he got off at his floor. He avoided a ladder in the middle of the hallway where the maintenance staff was adjusting the lights in the ceiling. One of the men politely showed him around the ladder, but Adam glanced up and saw a camera in the light fixture.

Once he had closed his room door and regained his

breath, he took out his mobile, a state-of-the-art satellite model that pleased him greatly. He dialled a number he had memorised, and spoke rapidly into the phone. As he did so he wondered how he could be so taken by both a religion that was centuries old and a technology that was leading the way to the future. He put these complex thoughts out of his head, and chose instead to concentrate on Achmed's voice coming through the earphone.

"God is Great, my brother," Adam intoned into the phone. He still struggled to get the idiom correct. "I've spent today finding out about the way people and cars come to Malta by ferry. It's not like the airport. They check carefully for smugglers coming into the country and going out."

"Was there anything in particular?" Achmed asked.

"I saw a woman at the ferry station who I saw in the hotel before. She was trying to find out the schedule of the ferries."

"Anything about the ferry, not the woman."

"No, I didn't find out anything else except that taking the ferry's very hard if you have a car."

"OK," his brother said. "What else have you learned?"

"There's something I just saw. They have security cameras in the corridor. I saw one being repaired today."

"That's usual," Achmed snapped.

Adam choked out loud at Achmed's impatience.

Achmed must have heard him because he said, "OK, my brother. You're doing fine. Continue to be as observant as possible but do not call attention to yourself. They must suspect nothing."

As Adam rang off, he wondered what it was that Achmed thought the hotel might suspect. He didn't think he had done anything wrong. He had always been slow to doubt but doubt had begun to fill him.

His thoughts were interrupted by a tap at his door.

The hall porter, with whom Adam had spoken several times, greeted him in Arabic.

"*Salaam*," the porter said and then switched to English. "Today when you were out there was trouble with the plumbing in your room. We fixed it but since there was an inconvenience the manager has asked me to give you this voucher for dinner at eight. There will be no charge."

Adam remembered the days in Peckham, where an offer of a free meal in such a grand dining room never occurred. He decided to accept the kind offer from someone who spoke Arabic, who must be a true follower of Islam and undoubtedly could be trusted. Tomorrow he could tell Achmed another good thing about the management of this hotel.

27

Elspeth knew rabbit was a favourite meal in Malta and Giuseppe had created one of the most famous rabbit dinners in the Mediterranean. The main dining room at the Kennington Valletta served this succulent concoction every Tuesday evening and both local Maltese and tourists flooded the rooftop restaurant to share in this coveted repast. Fifteen tables were reserved for hotel guests and there was always a waiting list for all the others.

Putting her plan into place, Elspeth consulted René and the maître d' about the availability of tables. Loren and Evan would be dining at the hotel, and Elspeth expected both Adam Russell and Bridget O'Connell would also be there because both had been given vouchers for dinner. René produced a seating chart of the restaurant, and together he and Elspeth finalised the arrangements for the second seating. The maître d' was told to hold two carefully chosen tables, one for Bridget and one for Alicia Kent. Elspeth designated a smaller table for Adam Russell.

In actions that first puzzled the dining room staff and then amused them, René and Elspeth moved among the three tables, sitting in one chair and then another until they both seemed satisfied with their choice. Then René selected a table in the rear corner of the room and instructed a waiter to put his personal reservation card on it after the first diners had left.

"*C'est bien ça, mais oui*?" he asked Elspeth. "That's good, isn't it?"

"I think it will do very well," she replied, pleased by the result of their work.

Elspeth returned to her guestroom, where she rang Richard and told him about her plan. Elspeth detected his genuine regret when he said he had an official function that evening with Sir William Gaunt and the British delegation, but Richard urged that she stay out of harm's way. He asked her to call him later and tell him the events of the evening and the success of her plan.

At seven forty-five Elspeth arrived in the dining room, took her seat at the manager's table in the corner and ordered a Perrier with lime. Just after eight Bridget O'Connell came in. She was still dressed in jeans, but, with a nod to the dinner hour, had donned a dusky orange-coloured Italian silk blouse, several buttons opened to reveal a bony chest, and two chains of green and gold beads, which complemented her light hair. Per Elspeth's plan the maître d' led Bridget to her table. Elspeth had positioned Bridget so that she could not see Elspeth but would be within her hearing range. Bridget took her place before the waiter had time to hold her chair for her and picked up the menu without glancing at the opulence of the room or view.

Evan and Loren were next to arrive. He was dressed in a dark, woollen jacket, suitable for the cool Maltese evening and a black shirt with a Nehru collar. Although his dress shoes appeared to be conventional, Elspeth suspected they had been designed to allow him to run as swiftly as if he were wearing a pair of trainers. Loren had assumed her Alicia Kent persona to perfection. The black silk skirt fit perfectly without clinging and the dark red of her blouse heightened her clear complexion and dark hair, which she had swept up on one side with an intricately enamelled comb that reminded Elspeth of one she had seen in a small shop in the suq in Marrakech. The maître d' showed Alicia and Evan to a table in the middle of the room behind Bridget.

Ten minutes later, Adam Russell came in shyly and was placed at the table near Evan and Alicia but with his back to them. Without waiting for the waiter, Adam yanked the sides of the chair in order to pull himself to the table.

After reading the menu, Bridget motioned the waiter who stood to attention nearby.

"I have invited someone to have dinner with me," she told him. "My uncle's driver. When he arrives, show him to my table." The waiter bowed slightly and conveyed her instructions to the maître d'.

As Elspeth had hoped, the arrangements went seamlessly when the newcomers arrived, despite the wild card of Seamus Riley.

From her chair, Elspeth could see Bridget's back in the mirrors that lined the gilt-edged cornice at the top of the restaurant wall. Elspeth watched Bridget's dinner guest arrive. Elspeth had not paid much attention to Seamus Riley before, although she knew who he was. He was tall and muscular and seemed ill at ease. Although he was dressed appropriately for the meal in suit and tie, they did not fit him well. He reminded Elspeth of an Irish gamekeeper who had been at Blair Castle when she was young. Riley looked as if he would have been more comfortable in a hunting jacket and Wellingtons than in a suit with shoes that were not quite the right colour. Now you are being a snob, Elspeth thought, remembering the odd assortment of clothes she had worn as a girl.

Bridget greeted Riley gruffly. Obviously Bridget's ill manners were not limited to her discussions with Elspeth. Riley did not seem to notice. Bridget asked the whereabouts of her uncle's car. He stated flatly that it was in the hotel car park. She asked if there was damage to the car that would require any payment to the leasing company in London. He said there was none. Neither ordered the rabbit. She opted for pasta and he chose the roast beef. Bridget ordered an expensive bottle of burgundy. They ate in silence.

René and Elspeth were served chicken, as prearranged, but neither ate more than was necessary to preserve their pretence as diners.

When Bridget and her guest finished their main course, she leaned over to him and began to discuss in almost imperceptible tones her plans for the removal of FitzRoy's remains from Malta. Elspeth strained to hear.

"The hotel had ideas about flying him back to the UK. I didn't accept," Bridget told him. "I made other arrangements before coming here."

The man nodded and used a piece of bread to soak up the last drops of his jus.

They both declined any confection or savoury. Bridget ordered tea and he ordered an Irish whiskey. He drank his quickly, said he would meet her in the morning so she could inspect the car and left the room. She remained for several minutes at the table and watched her tea grow cold. Finally, she summoned the waiter and instructed him to put the extra meal on her room bill, which made Elspeth suspect Bridget expected the Kennington Organisation to pay for it.

Just as Bridget started to rise from her chair, Adam Russell pushed back his chair and fled from the room. Bridget turned to watch him. Her whole body tensed. She spun around on her heel and dashed from the restaurant. Only Elspeth seemed to notice, as most diners seemed intent on finishing the last morsels on their plates.

*

Adam Russell ate alone. As had become his habit, he watched the people in the restaurant, but he did not recognise the new blond woman. Adam did not order rabbit. Reading the menu, he was not sure if rabbit would be allowed under Islamic dietary laws. In any event, his upbringing in Peckham made him distrustful of food that was called *lapin*. He reviewed the choices offered carefully, and finally ordered roast chicken. He asked for apple juice, although secretly he would have preferred a pint of lager.

As he sipped his juice, he sank into thought. He had considered eating somewhere else this evening. He had reported to Achmed all he could learn about the restaurant and taken sample menus to him the day before. Adam was tiring of his role and the hotel was getting on his nerves. He longed for one evening out, perhaps at the British pub he had seen just off Ir-Repubblika Street, with good English ale and chips like the ones they served at the Gull in Peckham. He might even be able to cheer over the latest football match on a large screen telly he had noticed when passing. But the hall porter was so kind about the free dinner and the problem in his room earlier, and Adam did not want to offend his new Muslim friend by refusing the generous gift. Adam felt uncomfortable in the quietness of the dining room. People spoke too softly to each other. It was hard to hear conversation from any other table, although he was not really interested in what they were saying. All too bloody posh, he thought.

How much longer did Achmed want him to stay? Today was a useless day, except for his trip to the mosque. When Achmed invited him to join in this 'business trip' to Malta, Adam had been filled with importance and excitement, but now he had spent four senseless days watching the operations of the hotel and going to the ferry terminal. What bloody good was it? Why hadn't Achmed done these things himself? Adam had never questioned his mission before. All at once he became nervous. What if he was being set up? He had not done anything illegal. Yet when he was at the comprehensive, he'd watched some of the boys rigging up ways to get others in trouble. The scapegoats were sent to places they should not have been and to do things they should not have done. Then they were ratted on. This whole scene at the hotel smacked of the same thing.

Stop being stupid, he said to himself. The Rashids are not hooligans. They're a great merchant family, known throughout the Mediterranean as keen businessmen. Adam remembered an article he had seen in *The Sun* about the bin Laden family. They too were well known, as builders not as businessmen. But then there had been the terrorist Osama. The older bin Ladens were friends with presidents and prime ministers, while the son plotted to blow up skyscrapers.

Adam began to sweat. Was he doing something that would involve a terrorist attack? Would the Rashid family send him here to find out information that would prove useful in a suicide bombing? Why else did they have him describe everything in such detail? Why had Achmed warned him not to attract suspicion? Adam had heard that terrorists took years to set up their operations. Could he be part of an extremist Muslim plot? No, Islam was a good faith, a loving faith, a faith where charity was a core tenet. The imam in London had taught him that, and they had said it again at the mosque this afternoon. The Rashids were good Muslims. Achmed was too westernised to be involved with radicals. Yes, yes, that was right. There could be no trouble.

Adam's stomach twisted. He tried the chips he had ordered and then pushed them away. If Achmed was involved in a plot, then Adam was too. Adam wished he were back at the greengrocers. He remembered reading what happened to those who were caught in the attacks on the towers in New York. They were sent to Cuba with no trial at all. Would that happen to him? Why had he been so taken in by the clothes, the travel and the luxuries? He had enjoyed working at the greengrocers. He remembered his first days of discovering Islam and his acceptance into the group at the mosque in London. The teachings were gentle and kind if one accepted the true faith. He remembered the shy smiles of his employer's daughter and the kindness she had shown as he learned the ways of a Middle Eastern family. And then Achmed had come to find him.

Adam pushed back his chair and staggered up. Had his own family set him up? He must get out of this place. He looked around confusedly. Where could he go? He ran from the room.

*

Elspeth had been watching Adam's reflection in the mirrors along the top of the dining room walls. She could see the contortions on his face and could sense the disturbing thoughts were going through his mind. As Adam fled from the dining room, Evan spoke quickly to Loren and slid out of the room behind him. Elspeth saw Loren beckoned the waiter. "Inspector Davies-Jones just got paged," she said. "Please hold his dessert. I'll go on with mine."

Elspeth placed her napkin on the table, nodded to René, rose and went over to Loren's table.

"May I join you? I see that Inspector Davies-Jones has been called away."

"Oh, Ms Duff. How kind," Loren said in Alicia's simpering voice. "I had no idea that policemen could be called so suddenly. Won't you sit down? I would rather not eat alone."

Elspeth motioned to the waiter and ordered decaffeinated coffee. The waiter brought it with Alicia's dessert.

"What happened?" Elspeth whispered.

"Evan said he was watching Adam. When Adam sat down he seemed quite normal but a trifle bored and a bit brooding. Then he looked puzzled and suddenly his face turned to panic, as if he had realised something dreadful. The way you do when you remember you have left a boiling pot on the stove an hour before. That's how Evan described it, only he said 'hob'. I noticed it too."

Elspeth nodded. "I saw it as well."

"Evan said when he left to tell you it wasn't a bomb."

Elspeth smiled despite her concern. "What could he possibly have meant by that?"

"He meant, I think, that Adam reacted very differently from someone who was about to set off a bomb," Loren said, as if she were saying something quite ordinary.

"Do you people get training in reading faces?" Elspeth asked.

"Definitely. Particularly in the expression in the face of someone about to blow himself to pieces in a public place. Fanatics about to annihilate themselves for their cause secrete a distinct smell and get either an ecstatic or avenging look that is unmistakable. I've seen it several times. Sometimes we were able to stop the attack but several times we were not."

Elspeth lowered her voice even more. "I want you to join me as quickly as possible downstairs. We need to give Evan every bit of support. I'll make a bit of light conversation with you and then leave."

Loren cocked her head. "And I'll look annoyed; eat a few more bites of this scrumptious mousse, which deserves much more attention than I'm giving it, and join you as quickly as I can."

28

Evan was close behind Adam as he bolted from the dining room. Adam was tearing at his collar as if choking. He dashed for the lift down to the lobby. The doors closed before Evan got there. Evan looked frantically around for the emergency stairs, and took them two at a time down to the ground floor. He came into the lobby just in time to see Adam outside disappear into the night behind some parked cars.

"Did you see where he went?" Evan gasped.

"Sir?" The doorman's tone was stiff.

"A young Arabic-looking man."

"Mr Russell, sir?"

Evan was annoyed by the doorman's correctness as no other person was about.

"Yes. I'm Inspector Davies-Jones from the police. I need to know where he went." Evan pulled his warrant card from his pocket and flashed it at the doorman.

The doorman came to attention. "Yes, sir. Mr Russell ran across the square and turned down Triq Sant'Ursula." The doorman pointed the way. "He was in a great hurry, sir."

"Thank you," Evan said and fled out the door.

Darkness obscured the buildings that clutched to the narrow streets and hid Adam from Evan's view, but Evan could hear the sound of Adam's steps echoing off the limestone walls. Evan remembered that the first part of the street morphed into stairs. There was little street illumination. The lamps through the lace curtains of the overhanging enclosed balconies gave little help. Fearing turning his ankle, Evan slowed down until he finally became adjusted to the low level of light. The street descended steeply and then rose again up in the direction of the silent walls of the tourist exhibition centre.

Adam ran more slowly than Evan, who soon drew near him. Adam did not seem to hear footsteps behind him, although the street was deserted. Adam's pace faltered as he got to the spot where the hill began to rise. His breathing was laboured, and he coughed several times. He started to run again when he neared the exhibition centre. He pivoted and zigzagged towards the plaza in front of Fort St. Elmo. He turned back to the street that ran to the top of Triq Ir-Repubblika. Reaching a wall with a signpost above, he grabbed the rail. He did not move for a long time. As his gasps calmed and his breathing resumed its normal rate, he slowly looked up at the fort beyond silhouetted by the night sky.

Evan stood in the shadows and watched him. Any policeman in pursuit had to decide if his suspect was dangerous. Adam had never shown any signs of violence, and Evan was almost certain he did not have a gun. Evan had to make a hasty judgement. Should he approach Adam and confront him? Should he continue to dog him and try to find out why he had acted so peculiarly in the dining room? Or should he return to the hotel? Evan had followed many guilty suspects before. Adam's reactions did not fit the mould. Most suspects looked furtive. Adam looked confused. He seemed to be dealing with a puzzle he could not piece together.

Evan crossed the wide street and approached Adam.

"Mr Russell," he said with authority. Evan's intention had been to speak to Adam as a stranger, but Adam's look of fear had changed Evan's words.

Adam cowered, looking like a rat cornered in a kitchen.

Evan reached out and caught Adam's arm. "Don't panic. I saw you leave the hotel, and I thought you might be in some sort of trouble. I'm a policeman. I wanted to make sure you were OK."

"I haven't done nothing wrong," Adam stammered. "They just asked me to come here and watch. There's no harm in that, is there? It's no crime."

Evan could smell Adam's fear. "No, you've done nothing wrong that I know of. I'm trying to help you," Evan said.

"They just asked me to watch everything and then report to them everything I saw. No bloody harm in that!"

Evan considered his best response and said, "No harm if they meant no harm." He assumed "they" were the Rashids.

Adam eyes slid from one side to the other as if trying to see if they were in earshot of anyone else. "I don't know what they meant. I mean they didn't tell me. They just said watch."

"What were you to watch?"

"Everything."

"What's everything?"

Adam swallowed hard. "What kind of people came

and went. How you got in the hotel. Was there one bloke or two to open the door? Did they watch you when you came in? Could the people at the desk see the people coming in and out? Was there a 'conserge'?" Adam could not get around that word.

Evan helped. "Concierge?"

Adam blew out his breath and nodded. "Yeah. You know the blokes who snoop around the lobby and stand behind a desk to answer stupid questions. They asked me how you got to the lift and what happened when you got to your floor. They wanted to know about all the people who were in the halls and who came to clean the rooms. Watch the service is what they said."

"Who are 'they,' Adam?" Evan asked in what he hoped was an avuncular voice.

Adam drew himself up unexpectedly. "My father and brother." His voice was suddenly filled with pride. "They're very important people."

"Is Achmed Rashid your brother?"

"Yes, and my father's Sheik Abdullah Rashid. He's a very big man."

"When did you find out that your father was Sheik Abdullah, Adam?"

"My name is Abdul, not Adam," the young man said. "Abdul Rashid, like my father."

"Abdul, yes, OK."

Adam's manner changed again. "Why're you asking me this? How do you know who I am?"

Before Evan could answer, a feral cat dashed out from the darkness and hissed at them. Adam leapt up onto the parapet that lined the street and jumped over the wall. Evan ran to the edge but it was too dark to see where Adam had landed or if he was hurt. Knowing that many parts of the bastions dropped precipitously, Evan tore open his mobile and punched the key programmed for the police station.

*

Elspeth checked her watch. It was now approaching half past nine and Loren had not appeared in the back office. Elspeth realised that she had grown fond of the young American woman and was getting anxious. While waiting, she thought of ringing Richard Munro, but decided against it. Instead, she pulled out a sheet of stationery and continued scratching down her reasoning about Pericles.

Half an hour later, Elspeth was close to finishing her scribblings when Pietru Parra showed Loren in. Elspeth's concern at the delay must have shown in her face.

"Sorry I took so long," Loren said. "First I got cornered by a very drunk Englishman who was out to save the empire from the European Union. Then I thought it best to change into something which could hold up better than what I was wearing if anything happens later."

Elspeth remembered that at dinner Loren had been dressed fashionably in dark red silk. This suited Alicia Kent dining with her debonair British policeman but certainly would not stand up to anything more strenuous.

"Wise choice," Elspeth said and relaxed. "Will you have a cup of tea, some Grand Marnier or a brandy? We should relax before hearing from Evan."

"Do you have herbal? Much as I would like a brandy, I don't want to dull my senses until we know what's happening with Evan. He rang me on his cell phone as I

299

was changing and said Adam Russell had jumped over a wall near the fort and disappeared."

Loren recounted Evan's recent encounter with Adam as Elspeth filled and plugged in the kettle she had found in a side cupboard.

Elspeth held up a box of tea bags. "Raspberry apple with a touch of chamomile straight from California."

"Wonderful," said Loren.

They settled into their chairs, their tea mugs cradled in their hands.

"Tell me more about why Evan told you not to fear a bomb?" Elspeth asked, leaning back but not relaxing.

"Sure. There are several types of terrorists. One very distinct type is the often-unwitting person sent out to check out a site, deposit money for an unknown purpose and carry information between knowing parties—that sort of work. In some ways they're the zealous minions, driven to help those they would like to emulate but too slow or unqualified to be a part of the actual attack."

"You sound as if you think Adam Russell is this type."

"Don't you think Evan's conversation with Adam just now seems to have confirmed that?"

Elspeth nodded. "Probably. Still why did Evan mention a bomb? Even the thought makes me shudder."

"The Kennington Valletta is a small, beautifully appointed hotel in an historic building but hardly an internationally significant landmark except to the pampered traveller. Blowing it up wouldn't achieve much. The only target might be Sir Michael Gaunt, but he doesn't sound very significant in world events. Besides, he does have his own tight security. No, I think whoever has decided to operate within the Kennington Valletta has done so because it is so unlikely a target. Therefore no bomb."

"Mmm. Yes, I reached the same conclusion and I'm glad you concur," Elspeth said as she rose and poured out more hot water into their cups. "Your theory would suggest that now that the exchange has taken place, the Kennington Valletta is no longer useful to Saieda and his or her cronies. I keep remembering that the second email mentioned Helios at the hotel. If I am right and Conan FitzRoy is key here, he must be connected somehow to Helios. It's a pity that Bridget O'Connell has made it quite clear that she wants nothing to do with us. Her sole purpose seems to be to finish all the affairs surrounding Conan's death and return his body to Belfast, the car to London and herself to Rome. If only she were more cooperative, she might be able to steer us to other people whom Conan contacted in his latest research, people who might give us some insight as to who Helios might be. But we don't really have time for that I suppose."

Loren tucked her long, slender legs up under her body and considered her mug. "I've thought a lot about what you said earlier, and just said again, that Conan's death was a part of a larger scheme."

Elspeth wished she were young enough and lithe enough to twist her body in the same posture Loren had just assumed.

"I keep being nagged by the thought that Conan being in Malta when the exchange was to take place is too coincidental," Elspeth said. "True coincidences are rare. Suppose this wasn't a coincidence. Then, you see, one thing led to another. Conan being here, the exchange and then his murder. I think Phase Two was the exchange and Phase Three the murder. I don't know what Phase One was."

Loren simply nodded.

"Loren, are you worried about Evan?" Elspeth asked, changing the topic.

Loren flushed slightly. "We're trained to be concerned with every member of the team."

"You two seem to be hitting it off. I'm glad. Evan is very attractive despite the scar and the lack of an arm. In fact, I think the scar makes him human rather than godlike. Without it, he probably would be a less nice person. Oh to be several decades younger."

Loren looked up at Elspeth, puzzled. Then Loren laughed, and asked straightforwardly, "Surely there is a Mr Duff?"

"Once there was an Alistair Craig. We were married for more than twenty years, but it's over now."

"Do you have children?"

Elspeth smiled. "Yes, two. Elizabeth and Peter. Peter lives in San Francisco and is involved with the internet and the law. Lizzie is raising my twin grandsons in Sussex and at night does website design. She is very good at the balancing act."

"Do you miss them?"

Elspeth had lived in America long enough not to be offended by Loren's directness. "Yes and no. We have all always been fiercely independent and intensely loving. Our times together are wonderful, our times apart filled with witty emails. I never feel far from them. But I also need my own space."

"Did you like being married?"

Elspeth might have thought this an intrusion on her privacy but then realised that Loren was not asking about her but more about the condition of matrimony itself.

"Yes, particularly at first. We were in love with the adventure of it, I think, and later I loved the children. Our life in Hollywood, where Alistair was involved in the film industry, was exciting, but in the end we had lived too often on the thrill of it. One day it ceased to be exciting for me but became rather shallow. Alistair and I had less and less in common. The children were grown and off and away. The purpose of Alistair's and my life together faded away. And our marriage did too."

Loren knit her brow. "Was that difficult?" she asked, as if the answer were of great personal importance to her.

'It still is sometimes but I've always had so much to do, so many people I wanted to meet and know, and so many places I wanted to see and be. I had a previous career in criminal investigation and was able to revive and revamp it when I left Alistair. When I met Lord Kennington, he offered me the perfect job to indulge all that I wanted in life. I've never regretted what happened. I wonder what the wee Scottish lass who set out from Perthshire for Girton College at Cambridge, as I did many years ago, would think of my life now. It is different from what I imagined but so much richer."

"Have you ever thought of marrying again?"

"No, I'm quite content as I am," Elspeth said with all the conviction she had before meeting Richard Munro on the previous Sunday morning. Inwardly she growled at the thoughts, much like unwanted termites, that had been wiggling around her in her mind since then.

Loren suddenly bleated out, "I thought about getting married once, but I didn't want to be buried in the needs of someone else."

"Oh, marry if you can. Don't expect it to be like your earlier experience. Every relationship is different. Most develop as people change. They can grow together or grow apart. I believe it is vitally important to recognise that any relationship, be it a love affair, marriage, friendship or parenthood, always involves two people. Both people have to invest in it. If the commitment on either person's side to make things work ends, the relationship ends. But that should not diminish either person. It's a tragedy when it does. It sounds like that's what happened to you."

"Yes. That and the fact that my brother was killed in a terrorist attack in the Near East when I was very young." Loren didn't specify which one, but Elspeth suspected it was the attack on the Marine barracks in Beirut, although she could not remember the exact date.

"I'm truly sorry," said Elspeth. She put down her mug and leaned over to rest her hand on Loren's.

"It makes me anxious when I consider any connection to a man," Loren said without moving her hand away.

"Yes, I can see that. Try to think of it differently."

The younger woman looked gratefully at the older one. There were hidden tears in Loren's eyes. Elspeth felt them even if she could not see them.

They sat quietly for several minutes in a comfortable silence, the way a mother and daughter can sit together without the need for conversation.

Loren spoke first. "My career keeps me continually moving. It's an adrenalin rush. But there are the moments in between when I think of having a serious relationship."

"As you should."

"You don't think it's wrong?"

"I do think it's right."

Loren grimaced. "A woman trained in the martial arts and crack marksmanship hardly seems a good squeeze. Too dangerous."

"Unless he could match you."

"What are you suggesting?"

"Nothing."

Loren suddenly laughed. "Oh, how I wish I had grown up around someone like you."

"I'm not so sure I would like anyone to grow up around anyone like me. Ask my children before you make any judgements."

Their tête-à-tête was broken by the harsh ring of Elspeth's mobile phone. Elspeth answered it. "It's your inspector, Loren. Shall I leave you alone?

Part 3

Message intercepted at GCHQ, Wednesday, 28 April 2004, 0005 GMT

Unexpected situation has developed. Change in plans essential. Contact Helios immediately for new instructions.
—Phoenician

29

Evan spoke urgently into his mobile, which had a direct connection to the police station. "The suspect leapt over the wall near Fort St. Elmo and disappeared into darkness. I need a spotlight and uniformed backup."

The reply was not what Evan wanted. "As soon as possible. Most of the forces are at the concert, but we'll contact several officers and they'll be there when they can."

A public concert in Great Siege Square off Triq Ir-Repubblika was scheduled for that evening, but Evan had forgotten that in rushing to chase Adam. Evan turned an ear towards the square but could not hear any music, but he remembered there were to be fireworks afterwards, which would require police vigilance.

Evan was faced with a dilemma. He had to decide whether to continue pursuing Adam Russell, scaling the wall himself and trying to negotiate a ledge on the other side, which he could just make out, or to assume that Adam had fallen to the pit below and was severely hurt or dead and he would have to call in more help.

He had chosen the latter course. Negotiating the wall was treacherous for a one-armed climber, and Adam surely had fallen far below. Evan listened intently for any movement that Adam might make, but he heard no sound other than the waves in the sea beyond.

Ten minutes passed before two police cars came screeching around two different corners and drew up to where Evan was standing. One car pulled up to the parapet and the driver cast his searchlight below. The light scanned the walls and the pit that yawned below. They could see nothing human, dead or alive, although large niches in the wall stayed in deep shadow. Evan instructed the officer in the second police car to go round to the other side of the pit to illuminate the parts of the wall that remained in darkness. Evan watched the car's light sweep back and forth. The only human forms uncovered were a couple in a compromising position who looked surprised and embarrassed that their tryst had become a matter of public scrutiny.

Evan was frustrated that his quarry had so quietly and so successfully slipped away. He rang the police station again, and had dispatcher issue an all-points bulletin. If Adam Russell a.k.a. Abdul Rashid were abroad tonight and visible, he would without a doubt be caught.

*

Adam had the cunning of a chased animal. He had been the brunt of so many attacks at the comprehensive in Peckham that he knew how to hide. Before he jumped over the parapet, he had seen that there was a small concrete shelf on the opposite side, perhaps a half-metre wide. The rough material of the parapet allowed a handhold. Someone who was not being hunted would have found crossing this ledge worrying. Adam, fuelled by pure fear, scurried along it. A heavy growth of brush protected him from view from above. He grabbed on to it and began lowering himself down the wall. Part of the way down he saw a small hole just large enough for him to press his body into. The foliage hid him from view both above and below. He knew from experience that once one found a hiding place, the best course of action was to stay absolutely still. From his nest he had heard Evan make his call to the police station and the police cars arrive. He saw the searchlights sweep the walls first from one side and then from other. He remained still and prayed that the lights would not find him. He was close enough from the parapet that he heard Evan swear in frustration.

Adam silently chanted, "God is good, God is great and Muhammad is his prophet." He gave himself to Allah's safekeeping and credited his escape from the police search to Allah's will. The lights that crossed his hideaway several times passed by so quickly that he was not discovered.

After the spotlights ceased, Adam relaxed but an explosion of fireworks interrupted his calm, and he almost fell from his hole. His heart took a long time to stop pounding, and he thought that this was what it must be like to be under enemy fire. He waited for what seemed a very long time. He recited all passages from the Qur'an that he could remember. He looked at the Rolex that Achmed had given him. The watch's glowing hands told him that an hour had passed. The fireworks stopped and the sounds of the crowds in the distance died down and then ceased. He waited another half an hour before crawling out of his space.

His legs were cramped, and he was shivering as the

evening winds had risen and his hideout caught the edge of the breeze. He wished he had brought his coat but he had left the hotel in panic. Having overheard Evan's conversation on the mobile to the police station, he knew it would be important to look different from the description the policeman had given of him. Despite the chill in the air, he shed his suit jacket and tie. He found a large stone to use as ballast, wrapped the clothes in it, and hurled the bundle down into the pit. He wondered who would find the coat of his suit, which cost eight hundred pounds, and his fifty-pound tie in the morning. He opened his shirt collar to expose the gold chain his father had sent as a gift and tried to ignore his trembling body.

He left his hollow, edging along to a gap in the parapet and crawled up into the street. He walked down the hill on a different road than the one he had taken earlier. He adopted a long slow, relaxed pace, although inside his heart was beating frantically once again. The small plaza gave way to a narrow street with rows of stone buildings on each side. As he strode further down the hill, he saw a sign 'The Red Rose British Pub' on a building with half-timbers applied to its limestone walls and a Union Jack flying in front. The temptation to enter a place was so great that he evoked the Christian Man-God of his mother and then asked for forgiveness from Allah. Then he slipped into the pub. Before his conversion to Islam, he had met his few friends at The Gull on a back street of Peckham. He recognised the odour of frying fish, the flicker of a football broadcast on the large-screen telly and a bar that could have been anywhere in the UK. He felt a sense of having arrived home in a place of warmth and safety.

The barmaid, who was well endowed and who accentuated this feature with a tight fitting, low cut black tee, looked up as Adam entered. It was now just after half past eleven and the streets outside were quiet. Several American tourists were sharing drinks in the corner and talking loudly over the rock music broadcast from large speakers at either side of the room. Adam did not hear any British voices at the bar or among the tables.

Despite his newfound Muslim faith, Adam ordered a pint of ale, took the glass up with both hands, which were still shaking from the cold, and drank down a good half of his brew without setting it down.

The barmaid looked at him strangely and Adam wondered if leaves and dirt hung on his clothes. He could see none.

"Just arrived in Malta?" she asked, leaning on her elbows and revealing a bit more of her bosom.

Adam looked away, feeling shy, and took another long drink. "Saturday," he said.

"First 'oliday 'ere?" she prompted.

"I…Yes." The early effect of the drink made him shake his head to clear it.

"Where yer staying?" she continued.

"Oh, eh, just up the street."

"Oh, the pension. Nice that one and good rates, for Valletta that is."

"It's OK," Adam said without correcting her.

"What's yer name? Mine's Eliza."

"Adam," he said, not wanting to use his new name.

Eliza gestured towards his glass. "Another?"

He nodded.

"Where yer from?" Eliza continued.

"London."

"Me, too. What part?"

"Peckham," said Adam and then regretted it.

"Me mum's from there. Fancy that."

Eliza continued her banter but Adam said less and less. He finished his second pint almost in silence. By this time he had forgotten his new found abstinence and ordered yet another. The American tourists left. At midnight Adam was finishing his fourth pint and asked for the toilet. There he collapsed.

When he came to, he was on his back on the floor, a bar of soap in his hand. He was so relaxed from his consumption of the ale that he had not hurt himself as he fell. He saw Eliza above him with a large pitcher. She must have poured water on his face. He had revived sufficiently so that she was able to get him on his feet and lead him to a small a room along the back corridor behind of the bar.

"We puts chaps 'ere that aren't ready to go 'ome," she explained.

She dragged him to a bed and he passed out again.

*

Evan returned to his flat at two in the morning, and for the first time since leaving the hotel he had a moment to regret the shortness of his dinner with Loren. He had had only snippets of official conversation with her since then. She was unlike any other woman he had met. He found her warm but tough, intelligent yet not conceited, athletic and beautiful. Mostly he felt at ease with her. As a younger man, he, like his father, had fought off women. After his disfigurement, he had considered himself damaged goods, and he did not want to see women's reactions to him when he turned towards them. He remembered Loren's expression when she had seen the scar. She appeared to be relieved. How odd he thought her reaction was. Was she relieved that he was something more than a handsome face? He thought so and was immediately glad. Since then she had touched his scar more than once. Each time it was a caress. In the past he would have put these feelings away as hopelessly sentimental. Things were different now, because of Loren.

He wondered about her. She seldom spoke of the past. Instead, she filled the present with excitement and vitality. He particularly noticed her keen powers of observation. She continually pointed out things to him on their runs together that he saw but did not notice. She made him more aware of small things, colours, textures, patterns, smells, even sounds.

What life path had led her to Malta from her beginnings in America? She had not said. Nor had she mentioned anything about her family or her friends there. She casually talked about living in France and said she preferred the European way of life to the existence she had led as a child. She did not say where that had been. What would draw a person like Loren to anti-terrorism? When he asked her about such things, she would laugh and say something bizarre, such as, "So I could come to Malta and share a magnificent dinner with you at this marvellous hotel." Evan wanted to be annoyed by her evasion but was instead captivated.

Evan's thoughts of Loren calmed him and gave him peace after a disheartening evening. He fell quickly into deep sleep.

*

Loren's thoughts as she lay in bed were disquieting. The day whirled in her head. She felt the frustration of a chase that was leading nowhere. She was torn about her feelings when Evan left the dinner table so abruptly. On one hand she recognised the necessity, on the other she resented the interruption. She pondered what Elspeth had told her about marriage and felt a deep sense of admiration for the older woman. Loren wondered if she had set Elspeth up as an ideal, and yet Elspeth had shown a self-accepting vulnerability that was new to Loren in personal relationships.

Vulnerability frightened Loren. She had hardened her heart because of her past and was determined that she would never again let feelings interfere with her life. Ending her engagement with Mitch had not been as difficult as she thought at first. Marrying Mitch was what was expected of her, the path her mother had set out for Loren early in her life. Life with Mitch, however, was not what Loren envisioned for herself. Her teenage years had been cast in sorrow when her brother, a marine, was killed in Lebanon. When she had been asked by the person who recruited her for Interpol to break all ties with her life in Washington, Mitch became an insignificant footnote but her brother's death still loomed large. She wanted to be the person who had entered the lobby of the Kennington Valletta four days ago. She wanted to be strong, independent and dedicated to her cause.

Then she had met Elspeth and Evan and Richard Munro and Conan FitzRoy and Magdelena Cassar. Each one of them instantly became enormous in her life. They all were flawed, alive, real, feeling, caring. Each was filled with vitality and commitment, and each was rich not with perfection but with imperfection. She loved Evan's scar— not his beauty. She cared for Elspeth's dedication to her career, someone who had left a marriage but adored her children without clinging. She envied Conan's exuberance. She adored Magdelena's talent and flamboyant lifestyle. She was intrigued not only by the high commissioner's old-fashioned ways but also his obvious transformation when he was with Elspeth. Her dreams were filled with all these people who swirled around her but whom she could not quite touch.

*

Before she went to bed, Bridget O'Connell asked for a six o'clock wakeup call. She took two sleeping pills that, combined with the wine she had drunk at dinner, put her quickly to sleep. As she drifted off, she hoped that the affair of her uncle's death would be concluded quickly and that she could return to her life in Rome without further trouble.

*

Elspeth was glad to be alone after Loren finished her tea and left the office. When Elspeth crossed the Atlantic four days ago, she speculated that Lord Kennington wanted her to look into another routine happening at one of his hotels. Usually he asked for her support when he felt a situation had arisen that needed, as Elspeth frequently put it, 'calming'. She went to a hotel, worked with the manager at smoothing over a prickly problem, flew back to London to reassure his lordship and took a few days off to see her

317

daughter and family in Sussex, visit her parents in Scotland or to enjoy moments alone in her London flat.

Normally she only handled internal affairs in the hotels. Seldom had she been so entangled in things beyond the confines of the back office. Even more rarely had she been involved in an affair that held so many past and present personal associations. This assignment was different and she felt rankled by its complexity. Her personal life was engaged to a level where her feelings were interfering with her professional judgement.

She wanted to call Richard but it was now well after midnight, and she could not remember if he said he kept late hours. There was nothing solid to report to Eric Kennington or Pamela Crumm so to call Pamela so late in the evening did not seem wise, although she knew Pamela slept only four or five hours a night.

She decided to call her son Peter in San Francisco, which would be an exercise in normality. She calculated it would be mid-afternoon there. She rang his office. He answered cheerfully and said he was late for a meeting but was glad she was safely back in London and to say hi to Lizzie. She smiled at his uninformed and loving concern.

She had no sooner ended her call than the phone rang. Richard was on the other end of her secure line. He sounded excited.

"We have just received a copy of an intercepted email from Tony Ketcham," he said. "They woke me because they thought it important. It reads: *Unexpected situation has developed. Change in plans is essential. Contact Helios immediately for new instructions.*"

Elspeth sat up in her chair. "Dickie, what could have

happened? When was the email sent?"

"GCHQ received it just before midnight GMT."

"But that makes Adam Russell's bit in all of this questionable, doesn't it?" She told him briefly about Adam's flight. "If Adam was the source of the new email, how could he have sent it? Are internet cafés open at this hour?"

Richard let out the sigh of a seasoned diplomat. "In Malta, I think not. Perhaps after they are more integrated into the EU it will be different. If we knew Adam's whereabouts in the last few hours, it would help answer your questions, of course. It's damnable that we don't. So we'll have to rely on you and Loren to pay even closer attention about what goes on at the hotel tomorrow morning. But, my dearest, of course you know that. Shall I come for tea at eleven o'clock and bring Evan with me? Will you rally Loren?"

Elspeth smiled at the endearment. "Yes to both," she said and then relented slightly, "although I shall miss breakfast on the terrace."

"So shall I," Richard said.

"Eleven o'clock then. Loren and I will be waiting." Not wanting to risk further closeness, Elspeth rang off, went to bed and slept fitfully.

At four in the morning the harsh ring of the phone woke Elspeth.

"Elspeth? René here. Our night security guard has just completed his four o'clock round through the car park. He found the night attendant slumped over in his booth. He seems to have been drugged."

"Drugged? Is he all right?"

"Pietru Para has called an ambulance. He asked them not to use their sirens, and therefore you would not have heard it. The attendant is on the way to hospital. Can you come to my office?"

"I'll be there as fast as I can."

30

Elspeth saw that their lack of sleep did not treat either her or René well. René was unshaven; she wore no makeup except a hasty slash of lipstick. They both wore clothing that paid no regard to fashion; he was dressed in dark trousers and a dark polo shirt that did not quite match in colour. Elspeth had pulled on dressy trousers but a casual knit top. Her shoes were wet because she had stepped in a puddle in the darkened garden; his were dry but his socks were odd.

She grumbled at the call at first but then was fuelled by a rush of both anxiety and excitement. At last there was some positive action. Despite the hour, it was a welcome relief from the guessing game that had played out until now.

Pietru was waiting for them in René's office. Coffee, juice, fresh croissants and fruit sat on one of the end tables. Pietru, just as a true hotelier should, had seen to the comfort of his senior staff even in this moment of distress. He poured coffee for them before supplementing the information he had given René over the telephone.

"At four o'clock, on his routine rounds, one of our security guards found the overnight attendant in the underground car park lying over his television monitor. The guard rang me immediately. The attendant was

321

unconscious and his breathing was shallow. After I had seen that he was safely on the way to hospital, I secured the car park, left a guard there and came back to the security monitors here in the back office," Pietru explained. "Ms Duff, normally we transfer the accumulated data from the cameras on to a storage tape early each morning and put them into the hotel vault."

Elspeth nodded, as this was a standard procedure in all Kennington hotels.

"This gives the night security staff something to do to stave off sleepiness as there usually is so little activity in the hotel after midnight," Pietru continued. "Last night's staff member told me that when he was doing this, he did not realise that the camera in the car park had gone black for about thirty minutes. He was quite shaken that he had not alerted me when the failure on the car park camera had first happened. He has provided me with the videotape that ran up until the power cut appeared. I have it here and will play it for you. I have not had time to review it myself because of my concern for the car park attendant."

"Pietru, before we start, what is the news from the hospital?" René's first concern was correctly for the safety of his staff.

Pietru took out his Blackberry and scrolled down through his notes. "They say that he was given a heavy opiate, probably in coffee," he said, and turning to Elspeth added, "One of the night kitchen staff takes a cup down to him at about three every morning."

"Do you have any new employees on the night kitchen staff?" Elspeth asked.

René shook his head. "None. Strange as it may seem,

night kitchen duty is highly desirable, as it is an easy second job. There is seldom much guest activity and the employees, except the bakers, generally can doze through their work hours until breakfast preparation begins."

"Who else has access to the kitchen?" Elspeth asked.

Pietru grimaced. "Probably anyone staying at the hotel. It would be more difficult for someone from outside because of the alarms on the unattended doors."

Elspeth shifted in her chair, her mind ready for action. "I would like to see the tapes, starting at midnight and up until the blackout."

Pietru pushed the video into a VCR on the racks near the security monitors. The eerie black and white world of the subterranean car park began to unfold. The videotape displayed the time as well as movements in the garage. There was no sound. The cameras were programmed to follow any motion but not to run when there was no movement. Once every ten minutes it made a slow pan of the rows of cars and then came back to rest on the entrance. For most of the night, all had been quiet.

Pietru fast-forwarded the tape to point where one camera suddenly swung around to the door of the lift as it opened. A smiling woman came forward with a tray with a steaming cup. She spoke soundlessly to someone beyond the camera, presumably the attendant. A hand reached out and took the cup. The woman looked to her left and, laughing, made her way back to the lift. The lift doors closed. Several minutes later the camera started to swivel towards the lifts and the tape went black. The time read 03:18:17.

"Who is the woman?" Elspeth asked, looking at René.

"Maria Gabriella," he answered. "She has been on the kitchen staff for the last four years. She is the widow of an employee who came here from the Kennington Rome after working there for many years. He died from emphysema, leaving her with two young children to support. We hired her shortly after his death. She has been a model employee," René said, apparently with instant recall of his employee's employment record. "Her job allows her to be with her children during the day, which she treasures. Pietru, if she is still in the kitchen, call her here at once."

Pietru nodded and left.

Maria was crying as she came in the room. Her tears fell from reddened eyes under dark brows. Her distress could not have been feigned. "Oh, *mama mia*. I do nothing wrong. I just take a cup of coffee to Giorgio. I do this many times. There never is trouble before." She threw her hands to her face.

Elspeth rose, approached Maria and spoke gently. "Was there anyone in the kitchen when you fetched the coffee?"

"Just the same people like always," Maria said with a cry of pain.

"The kitchen staff?" Elspeth prodded.

"*Sì*."

"Maria," René intervened, "did you see anyone in the car park when you went to give Giorgio his coffee?"

"Giorgio is in the *come si dice*, how do you say, the little house."

"The kiosk," Elspeth supplied. "No one else?"

Maria looked scared.

"No. *Nesuno*. No one." She lowered her eyes. Elspeth

believed her.

"Maria, you are to stay here at the hotel. Do not go away," René said in a soft but commanding tone.

"*Ma i miei bambini*? My babies?" Her worry dominated her tears.

"Stay, Maria. Call their grandmother. Go back to the kitchen and have Salvadore come here." Salvadore, René explained, was the night kitchen manager.

"Sì, *signore*, yes, sir." Maria fled the room.

While waiting for Salvadore, Pietru played the last part of the tape again. The cameras stayed at rest on the entry, except for the ten-minute check, until Maria had brought down the cup of coffee from the kitchen. No one came or left the car park after midnight; no cars moved.

When Salvadore arrived, Elspeth indicated to René that she would begin the questioning.

"Salvadore, do you know why I am here?"

"Yes, *sinjura*. To put in new security measures."

"Yes, and we also suspect that there may be some ..." she searched for the word, "some activities going on here in the hotel that may be dangerous to the guests. We believe that what happened in the car park this morning may relate to these activities."

Salvadore looked up, the wrinkles in his ageing face deepening. "What is it, *sinjura*?"

"We don't know precisely. We need your help."

"Yes, *sinjura*." Salvadore sat up a bit straighter.

"We see from the security tapes taken in the car park early this morning that Maria took a cup of coffee there. Does she do this often?"

"Not often. Usually Beatrice takes the cup down, but

Beatrice was not feeling well tonight and Maria asked if she could do it in her place."

"Maria asked?"

"Yes."

"Maria told us that she takes the cup down often."

"That is not true, *sinjura*. Maria usually helps with preparing the morning pastries and does not have time to leave the kitchen. Maybe once or twice before she took the coffee to Giorgio."

"Why would she ask to go down to the car park?"

"Ever since her husband died four years ago, Maria has had an eye out for a new husband. Perhaps she found Giorgio attractive."

Elspeth detected strain in Salvadore's words and wondered about its origin. Had Maria slighted his advances?

"Is he married?" Elspeth asked.

"Giorgio? No. He lives with his mother, who controls his life." Salvadore smirked in obvious contempt.

"Not a desirable husband if you have two young children," Elspeth said.

"No, *sinjura.*"

"Did Maria prepare the coffee last night?"

"No. Probably Manwel did that. He usually prepares the coffee, tea and biscuits for the staff during the night shift. He lays out a table with a fresh urn of coffee and hot water. He also prepares the trays for the staff in the other parts of the hotel. Beatrice takes the trays around during the middle of the night shift."

"Where are the trays put after Manwel prepares them?"

"On a trolley just inside the kitchen door near the lift."

"Who has access to them?"

"Just about anyone on the staff. But Manwel keeps an eye on them to make sure they are delivered to the staff before they get cold."

"Thank you, Salvadore. Wait here, will you? Pietru, telephone the kitchen and have Manwel come up here."

Manwel appeared several moments later. He was a small older man with dark olive skin, a large nose and gnarled hands.

Elspeth resumed her questioning.

"Manwel, what is your full name please?"

"Manwel Balbi."

Elspeth nodded, assuming the man was Maltese from his name. "Did you prepare coffee last evening for the attendant in the car park?"

"Yes, *sinjura*, I do that every night. I always put an extra sugar for him."

"Where did you put his tray last night?"

"On the trolley by the door. Maria said she take it immediately but she is not in the kitchen. I think she go use the women's toilet because she come back a little later and take the coffee."

"How long did the coffee sit on the trolley?"

"One, two minutes. Three maybe, no more."

"Did anyone come in the kitchen after you poured the coffee?"

"I think no. I go look for Maria. When I see her, she stand by the door and I tell her to take the coffee so it stay hot. She laugh a little and say OK."

"Was that unusual?"

"Maria laugh? Maria like to laugh. She laugh a lot. She like to flirt with the men. I think this is why she ask to take coffee to the car park."

"Thank you, Manwel. That is all."

Elspeth leaned back as Manwel left. "Salvadore, who else might have gone near the coffee?"

"I do not know. At that time in the morning, the kitchen is quiet. The bakers are waiting for the dough to rise and often go to the staff lounge to have a quick nap or a cigarette. The other tasks are usually done by three, and early morning calls do not begin until half past five or six."

"Thank you, Salvadore. Please leave a number where you can be reached after you leave the hotel today. We may have more questions. And don't discuss this with any other member of the staff."

"Yes, *sinjura*."

After Salvadore left, René, Pietru and Elspeth sat quietly for a moment.

Elspeth broke the silence. "So where are we now? From what has been said almost anyone could have slipped something into the coffee. While Manwel was looking for the flirtatious Maria, who was a substitute for the regular Beatrice, most of the rest of the staff were resting. Whoever put the drug in the coffee could have done so easily and remained unnoticed. But that person would have to know the early morning routine."

René nodded. "The moment of opportunity was short. The timing would have to be exact."

Elspeth agreed but she had heard that wording before. *Timing and precision essential.* "I think, René, we should question every member of the kitchen staff individually. Pietru, don't let any of them leave before we know where we can reach them this morning. There's one more thing. René, will you take me down to the car park, please. I may find something there that will be useful."

Elspeth's tour of the car park did not take long. Cars stood unmoving in their stalls and most of them had Maltese number plates. Elspeth noticed Conan FitzRoy's large Mercedes tucked in a dark corner at the end of one of the rows, several drops of water on its highly polished bonnet. She pointed this out to René.

"There must be a leak in the small window above," she said. "Is it going to be fixed soon?"

He frowned and Elspeth was not sure if this was because of the leak or her direction to him. After all, he was the hotel manager.

They surveyed the kiosk, which the security patrol still manned. Elspeth noted the video camera slowly following them around.

Suddenly Elspeth said, "We didn't look at the tapes after the blackout."

René looked puzzled.

"After the blackout, the camera began again. Please get me those tapes."

René spoke into his mobile and soon had the answer. "Pietru has the tapes in my office."

Elspeth became excited. "René, let's look at those tapes now. I think I have an idea of why this happened."

In the meantime Elspeth knew the hotel was slowly awakening. The morning staff would replace the night one. The concierge would come on duty and three people take up their posts at the front desk. The waiters would be in the breakfast room for those who wanted early morning refreshment. The coffee urns would be filled, the teapots readied and the final touches put on the morning buffet. No one aside from the kitchen staff would be aware that anything had ruffled the smooth running of the activities of the morning at the Kennington Valletta. Lord Kennington would have insisted on that.

31

"I can't stay to watch the tapes, Elspeth," René said. "I must make myself presentable and then instruct the morning staff."

"Of course, René. Leave me the tapes. I'll attend to them," Elspeth said, thinking she too should make herself presentable. Then she decided that despite her oddly assorted clothes the tapes were more important. She went into her conference room and locked the door. She took the tapes Pietru had given her and inserted one into the VCR under the television screen. She fast-forwarded until she came to the end of the blackout and watched the following minutes, frowning. At one point, she rewound the tape. She stopped the tape and looked one frame for a long while.

She finally drew back, straightened her stiff back, and gave out a small grunt.

She rose and called Loren's room. "How long will it take you to get to my office?"

"Five minutes," Loren said groggily.

"Good, take ten and call Evan. Get him here as fast as he can make it."

Then Elspeth took a deep breath, calmed her heart, and rang Richard.

He must have answered from a deep sleep.

"I told you my visit to Malta would bring mayhem,"

she said. "I hope you don't mind my making your life a bit more interesting." Elspeth remembered every word of their first breakfast together.

"Are you all right?" he asked with alarm.

"Dickie, I think I know what was exchanged but I'm still trying to figure out exactly how Conan FitzRoy's murder fits into the whole thing. It must. But I am almost certain about the exchange. Can you come to the hotel?"

"I have a breakfast meeting with Will Gaunt and his official party and then see Bridget O'Connell at nine. I want to see you, but I can't until half-past nine at the earliest. Will it wait? Will you talk to Loren and Evan?"

Disappointment flooded Elspeth.

"Of course," she said steadily, despite the need she felt to talk to him in person. "Ring me when you have finished with Bridget."

She stared back at the frozen image on the screen. That must be it, she thought but she couldn't be sure. The image was clear enough but the reason for it was not.

A knock came at the door and Loren entered at Elspeth's invitation.

"Look at this, Loren." She pointed at the big Mercedes parked in the corner. Then she rewound the tape to before the blackout. "Now look at this."

"It's Conan's car," Loren said.

Elspeth went back to the first frame she had shown Loren.

"Is it? Look more closely. Damn, I wish we could be sure. Do you see the wet tyre marks?"

Loren peered more closely at the frame Elspeth had frozen and nodded.

"It looks like Conan's car had been driven in after it had been raining," Loren said.

"Yes. But why?" Elspeth drew both of her hands through her unbrushed hair.

Elspeth picked up the phone and ordered coffee and pastries. Minutes later a fully laden trolley with a bowl of fresh fruit, a rack of toast, butter, jam, and array of cold meats and cheeses, a plate of sweet rolls and thermoses of coffee and tea appeared, DI Davies-Jones pushing the tea trolley into the room.

Elspeth nodded a greeting and turned back to the VCR. "Watch this." She ran through the tapes before and after the blackout.

When the tape was finished, Elspeth cried out an appeal, "Evan, how much do you know about technology? Can you blow up these images for me?"

Evan shook his head. "Not on this monitor. With a computer, yes."

Elspeth blew out her breath. "I think what was exchanged was the car."

"The car?" Loren and Evan said in unison.

"Loren, tell me again about the lorry that stopped at the vineyard," Elspeth said. "Would they have had time to switch Conan's car with another? Was the lorry big enough for a large car?"

Loren frowned. "I think so, although I only saw the truck from a distance. But when we got back in the car, Conan took the keys he had thrown on the dashboard, and started the car."

"But if one has a car's original key or its code, it can be duplicated, can't it?" Elspeth asked.

Evan nodded. "Usually the dealer does it when someone loses their keys."

"Can two cars be opened by the same key?"

Evan answered. "Technically, of course, although there are numerous safeguards against it. So you think the two Mercedes had the same key?"

Elspeth bit the corner of her lower lip. "Yes, almost certainly."

"Wait," said Loren, who was pouring coffee for herself. "I lost my lipstick case when Conan and I went to the vineyard. I was sure I'd dropped it under the front seat but, when we returned to the parking lot, it wasn't there. Since I couldn't find it, I thought I must have dropped it on the ground in the vineyard's parking lot. But if the cars were switched...?"

"At this point I think we shouldn't say if but rather why," Elspeth said.

Loren stopped with the coffee pot in mid-air. The hot liquid splashed in her saucer. "They check cars both coming in and going out of Malta to see if parts have been exchanged. That's what they said at the ferry."

Elspeth rubbed her eyes. "But if both cars came in to Malta, wouldn't they both be checked going out? Let me think this out."

"Perhaps there was some reason why our terrorists wanted FitzRoy's car particularly," Evan said.

"Or the other way around," Loren added. "They wanted Conan to have the duplicate car."

Elspeth stood up and turned off the VCR.

Suddenly she turned back to Loren and Evan. "Oh, damn," she said with a huff. "I fell into the trap face-first!

The Kennington Organisation and the high commissioner just facilitated the removal of Conan's car from Malta without it being thoroughly examined. So whatever is in the second car will leave here today on the ship with Bridget O'Connell."

Elspeth grabbed the house phone and called the front desk. "Has Ms O'Connell left the hotel? Did she take Mr FitzRoy's car?"

Hearing the answer, Elspeth swore again. "Damn, damn, damn. She was carrying a small bag and left in the Mercedes ten minutes ago. She sent the rest of her things directly to the ship." Elspeth checked her watch. It was a quarter to nine. Bridget would have to drive directly to the high commission to keep her appointment with Richard Munro.

Evan sprang up from his seat. "Let me have the police put out an APB."

"No, wait," said Elspeth. "Bridget will eventually take the car to the dock. There's no need at this point to alert her that we know the car is suspect."

She dug into her pocket for her mobile and rang through to the high commission.

"Sir Richard has not returned from his breakfast meeting," his PA informed her. "I will see he gets the message."

Elspeth rang off and growled. "What could be in the car? And what does the last email from GCHQ mean?" She recited the email message with Loren and Evan.

Unexpected situation has developed. Change of plans essential. Contact Helios immediately for new instructions.

Elspeth's brain whirled. Helios at the hotel. Was he

still at the hotel? Did he have anything to do with the drugging of the car park attendant the night before?

Out loud she said, "Helios, whoever that is, must have doped the attendant and taken the Mercedes out last night for some reason. That would explain the wet tyre tracks. But why? Probably the change of plans. What was the change? What was it?"

Elspeth rose and started pacing.

"Does it involve Bridget O'Connell?" Loren asked.

"I think so."

"Then she's in danger," Evan said.

"Yes," Elspeth answered. "More danger than she knows."

"I need to get to the dock," Evan said. "Loren, come with me."

"I'm coming too. I'll follow shortly in a taxi. First, I have an important phone call to make," Elspeth said. "I won't let Saieda beat me!"

*

Adam Russell awoke painfully. He was cold, his stomach and head hurt and he needed the toilet. He didn't recognise the room, which was small and dark; a ray of light came in through a window high up on one wall. He was still dressed in his shirt and trousers although his shoes were off. His eyes vaguely focused on them neatly arranged under a chair nearby. Adam felt for his wallet. It was gone. So was his Rolex.

"God is Great," he mumbled but at the moment doubted it. Then he saw the note. In large black letters it said, "The loo is down the hall. Yer things is in the safe in the offise. I'll be back. Eliza."

Adam found the gents and after taking care of necessities stared at himself in the small mirror over the sink. His eyes were red and puffy and the shaved parts around his beard had grown heavy. His shirt was wrinkled and smudged. He missed the coat and tie he had thrown away the night before but his gold chain was still around his neck. At least Eliza had not taken that so she probably was honest. He splashed his face with cold water and groaned.

He returned to the small room and sat on the edge of the bed, thinking how daft he had been. Had not his studies of Islam shown him that alcohol was evil? Would Allah be as forgiving as his mother, a Christian, would have been? He must ask the imam.

Now he wanted desperately to leave here. He was glad that his wallet, Rolex, papers and money was safe in the 'offise' but he wondered how he could retrieve them. He supposed he could wait, but had no idea how long it would be before Eliza returned. He was grateful to her but upset that she had not been more specific about ways to contact her.

What should he do? He could return to the hotel, but would he have to explain to anyone his behaviour of the night before? Could he simply walk into the lobby in rumpled clothes, unshaven and messy and ask for his room key? If he did, Adam felt that he might be suspected of wrongdoing, and he felt nervous.

His next idea was to call Achmed. He had put his mobile in his trousers pocket and found it still there. He could not get a signal and a message on his display said his battery was low. Why he had been so stupid and not

337

charged his phone the day before? Then he remembered his concerns that the Rashids might be using him, and decided they were the last people he should call.

Adam thought wistfully of his room above the greengrocers in Old Kent Road. Could he return there without the Rashid family finding out? Adam groaned again at his narrowing choices.

He could think of nothing to do but to wait for Eliza. His mobile told him it was 09:07:18. Then the display went dark.

He sat thinking and then rose to explore his surroundings further. Beyond the toilets were the doors to the kitchen and the bar but they were locked. There was a door to the outside that was self-closing. If he let himself out, he would not be able to get back in. He opened the door slightly and savoured the brightness of the morning and the coolness of April sea air.

Adam returned to the small room and put on his shoes, which made him feel more respectable. Undecided about his next move, he sat in the rickety chair and thought about the huge breakfast buffet at the Kennington Valletta. He forgot about his morning prayers.

Adam lay back on the narrow bed. To pass the time, he quietly recited lines from the Qur'an as well as he could recall them. Soon he ran out of material and considered his position. Over and over he told himself that he had done nothing wrong. His mother had taught him to consider his actions to see if they would harm him or others, and this lesson had become a part of him. When he first had discovered Islam, he had found it a gentle religion with ultimate faith in God. Certainly Allah would know he had not done anything that was hurtful to himself or anyone else.

Yet had he been led to do something criminal by his newly found family? Could it be that they were involved in activities that were not good and not kind to others? He could find nothing illegal in what he had been asked to do. Achmed and his father had asked him simply to watch everything that went on at the hotel and make note of it. That was not wrong. But why had he been asked? Was there anything that he might report that would be used to harm others? He, Adam Russell, no Abdul Rashid, had been so proud of his new family that he had not questioned why until now.

He would confront Achmed. Yes, that was the thing to do.

Adam wished that Eliza would return. He must have dozed off as he heard a church's bells strike twelve. He got down on his knees and recited the noontime prayers, although he did not know Mecca's direction. Then he spoke to his dead mother and prayerfully asked her to help him.

Help came in the form of Eliza, who emerged from the barroom door shortly after Adam had risen from his knees.

"There yer are. I thought ya'd want to sleep it off. Ya got a bit squiffy last night, with a few pints and all. I couldn't find yer 'otel key in yer pocket but I didn't want ya robbed or nothing. Yer things is in the safe."

"Eliza, where have you been?"

"My flat, where else? Miss me?"

"I need to get my things."

"Slowdown. I just got 'ere."

Adam drew up every bit of strength that his nineteen-year-old body could find and said with a very deep and loud voice, "I need my things."

"Right, o'course. Don't get yer knickers in a twist. They're in the safe in the office. C'mon. Whacha yer waitin' for?"

While hiding Adam's view of the dial, Eliza opened the safe and took out his wallet and watch. "'Ere's yer things."

"Thanks for what you've done," Adam said. "I usually don't drink so I'm afraid that last night I made a fool of myself. Please excuse me, Eliza. I'd like to give you something for helping me." He drew an English fifty-pound note from his wallet and gave it to her.

"Much obliged," she said obviously pleased. "Any time."

"I hope that there will never be another time, Eliza, but I'll tell my friends who might come to Malta that your pub is an honest place."

"Yer a good chap. They make 'em right in Peckham."

"I was a bit stupid."

"Aw, don't beat on yerself. You're OK. Lots of chaps do the same thing on 'oliday. Go back 'ome and forget about it. I won't tell."

"Thanks, Eliza."

"My pleasure. Come again." She said, wrapping the banknote around one of her fingers.

When he emerged from the pub, he was surrounded by the noonday street, people, cars and the hustle of an uncaring world. Disoriented, he found a taxi and directed the driver to the Kennington Valletta.

Adam asked for his key at the desk and the receptionist gave it to him. She gave no sign that she had noticed his day old stubble and rumpled clothes. He retreated to his room. The bed had been turned back and his copy of the Qur'an was laid on the bedside table. He picked it up and kissed it, as he had seen members of his mother's church kiss their bibles. "God is Great and Muhammad is his prophet. Thank you, Jesus."

Putting aside caution, he picked up his bedside phone and dialled Achmed's number.

*

After Loren and Evan left, Elspeth returned to her guestroom, showered and changed. She chose smart but utilitarian clothes, brown gabardine trousers, an emerald coloured tee, taupe suede jacket and flat shoes. She looked wryly at herself in the mirror and added a gold necklace. She hoped it would please Richard.

Returning to the conference room, she called and asked for the night hall porter on the floor where Bridget had stayed.

"Did Ms O'Connell leave her room at all last night after retiring?" she asked.

The answer was no.

Elspeth called the telephone operator and asked if Ms O'Connell had made any calls or used internet access the night before. Again the answer was negative, but in the days of mobile phones this meant little.

Next she rang René and asked for the early morning tapes of the corridor outside the kitchen. A waiter brought the tapes with a fresh thermos of coffee. Elspeth sat down to work, whirling through the tapes until she reached 02:45:17.

Several people came from behind the camera and went into the kitchen. At 3:01:05 a man whom she recognised as Manwel Balbi came out of the kitchen and put a tray with a coffee mug and several biscuits on the trolley that stood by the door. He returned immediately to the kitchen. Then Maria came out of the door. She looked up, smiled broadly in the direction of the camera and said something, but the tape did not have sound recording. Then Maria disappeared from view.

A man's back appeared. Elspeth thought she recognised the ill-fitting suit. He took the mug from the tray, dropped something in it and then turned to face the camera. Conan's driver—Seamus Riley.

Elspeth immediately called the reception desk. Mr Riley's bill had been paid in advance by Conan FitzRoy. They had not seen him go out but normally drivers used the exit to the car park.

She flew from her conference room. Finding René in his office, they rushed to Riley's room. No trace of the driver remained. Elspeth looked at her watch. It was nine fifteen.

*

Bridget O'Connell awoke impatiently. Even after having taken two sleeping pills she had slept badly, and was eager to have the upcoming day over with.

She rose and checked her mobile to see if she had any messages; she did not. She ordered breakfast in her room and prepared herself for the day. She had an appointment at nine at the British high commission where she expected to receive the papers for the removal of her uncle's body and effects. They would facilitate her leaving Malta with the minimum of bureaucratic intervention. Much as she disliked the British establishment and their ineffectual response to the crisis in Northern Ireland, at the moment she appreciated its respect for strict procedure. After her meeting she would drive directly to the dock.

She had already decided to take FitzRoy's car to the high commission. Her uncle was such a snob about cars. He always hired them from the most prestigious Mayfair leasing agents, although several times the cars were repossessed for lack of payment. Bridget more than anyone knew of her uncle's pretensions and his frequent lack of ability to finance them.

She found the key in an envelope Elspeth Duff had given her the afternoon before and took the lift down to the car park. The car stood where Seamus Riley told her it would be. Using the key, she opened the door easily and got in behind the massive steering wheel. She adjusted the wheel and seat to fit her size and nosed the machine towards the gate. She showed FitzRoy's parking validation to the morning attendant and turned into the chaos of early morning traffic in Valletta.

*

The Honourable Sir Richard Munro, Knight of the Order of St. Michael and St. Paul, Her Majesty's High Commissioner to the Republic of Malta, was not looking forward to his interview with Ms Bridget O'Connell. He trusted Elspeth's dislike of her and considered facilitating the transportation of the murdered body of his literary hero an onerous task. He would have preferred having breakfast with Elspeth on the terrace in Sliema or in a back room of the hotel.

Bridget was shown into his office precisely at nine. She wore the same long tweed coat and carried the same offensive attitude that Elspeth had told him she had brought to the Kennington Valletta the day before. Had Richard admired FitzRoy's writings less, he might have been haughtier. Instead he was excessively polite.

"Ms O'Connell, may I express my deepest regrets at your uncle's death. I have always enjoyed his books and had hoped to meet him for the first time this week. Unfortunately, I did not."

"Your Excellency—is that your title?" she asked.

"In the twenty-first century things have become more relaxed, and we don't use such exalted titles except at official events."

"I prefer to keep things formal since my visit here is formal. It's my understanding that you've arranged with the Maltese government for the safe-conduct of my uncle's coffin and his effects. I've booked passage for myself as well as the coffin aboard the HMS Oceania. The ship leaves this afternoon for Marseille and then goes on to London and Belfast."

The high commissioner took stock of this young woman. He did not find her as abrasive as Elspeth had suggested, but felt that she was being unnecessarily stiff. He did not associate this characteristic with the Irish. He decided that he would try to make her relax by engaging her in conversation.

"I understand, Ms O'Connell, that you are your uncle's next of kin."

"Yes, Your...Sir Richard. My uncle had several wives. The last few were mere trophies, so he was intelligent enough not to leave his affairs to them. I'm his only close relative and therefore I think he trusted me more than anyone else. My uncle was a self-centred man. He did not treat his family well. When my mother and father died, Uncle Kevin—Kevin O'Connell was his real name—felt some responsibility for me. Our relationship was not always easy. It softened as he got older, and realised not only that blood is important, but also that he was partly to blame for my mother and father's death. His acknowledgement of these facts brought us nearer together and that is when he made me his heir."

"I see," Richard murmured sympathetically, knowing that in doing so he might elicit more information, although he had detected something false in what Bridget said.

Bridget O'Connell shifted in her chair. Richard's warm words seemed to confuse her.

"When my uncle had his first heart attack, he was in a state of denial, which was true to type. He was incapacitated for several months and forced to restrict his lifestyle. He called me and asked that I come to London to be with him. He asked forgiveness. Isn't that an odd thing from such a pompous person?"

Richard nodded. "Perhaps."

"He was pompous, you know, but he was blessed with an incredible talent for making history seem real. After his first book, however, he chose to make the past come alive not for Ulster but for Malta and Cyprus and Vienna, almost as if he had never written about Northern Ireland. He forgot his roots."

By this time Richard realised that Bridget O'Connell was not speaking to him but was making a statement about her uncle's life that was bitterly heartfelt.

"Why should he forget who we were, the people of Northern Ireland, who have suffered so much? We should have been the biggest story in his life. But, no, we were mere riffraff, not the noble armies and navies of faraway places whose stories he could sell to the British and American public."

Richard could tell Bridget was dealing with anger more than grief, as Elspeth had suggested.

Bridget regained her composure. "I'm sorry to have gone on so with you, sir, as you are an official of Her Majesty's Government. It's rather a cry in the dark I know."

Richard felt some compassion for the young woman, which he had not expected.

"Yes, of course, my dear," he said without thinking. Bridget looked up at his address and scowled.

"Thank you for understanding, Your Excellency," she responded.

Richard was not too sure what to make of the remark. "I have made all arrangements necessary for your safe passage from Malta," he said. "The Kennington Organisation will be paying for the voyage as a final tribute to your uncle."

"That's what Ms Duff told me. I'm sure they're really doing this in order to keep everything out of the newspapers." Bridget's impoliteness had returned.

"Also as a courtesy to you and to Mr FitzRoy."

"Their greatest courtesy would be for them to

expedite my return to Rome as quickly as possible. My uncle cluttered his life with too many things and too many wives. I'm finding all this very difficult, as I have my own busy life to lead. Uncle Kevin never had much care for others."

"Here are the arrangements we've made for you," Richard said as he opened a sheaf of papers that lay on the desk beside him. "These are the papers that will allow the coffin to be loaded on the ship without customs inspection. The Maltese are quite paranoiac about cars. They have had rather bad experiences with cars coming in to Malta and being dismantled for the parts. Therefore they do tend to inspect cars that go out of the country to make sure used parts haven't been substituted for the original ones. I've asked the government to issue a paper for you that will bypass this inspection on my own word that your uncle's car has been in the Kennington Valletta's car park since he last parked it there. This should assist your boarding as well. His other things that you're taking with you will be passed through without a customs check. All of his personal effects have been searched by the police and therefore are above suspicion. I myself will come to the docks to make sure there are no last minute complications."

"There is no need for that. I'm sure the papers are in order."

"Even so," he countered. "What time does the ship sail?"

"At noon. The last boarding is at eleven. I've already made arrangements for my things to be sent to the ship and have just been awaiting these papers."

"I'll be at the docks at half-past ten. Until then, if I can be of any service, please feel free to telephone my office. Here's my card. My personal assistant will be able to find me."

Bridget took the papers and card from Richard, thanked him curtly, turned on her heel and left the room.

Strange, the high commissioner thought, she never asked about the police enquiry into her uncle's death. Could she have so little feeling for him? It would seem so. He sighed and felt that Elspeth was right about the basic rudeness of the woman who had just left.

The phone rang. It was Elspeth. Without prologue she said, "Can you get to the docks as soon as possible? I'll explain when you get here."

32

Before leaving the hotel, Elspeth called Scotland Yard. Detective Superintendent Ketcham came on the line instantly. Elspeth poured out her news and could hear Tony's grunts of agreement on the other end of the line.

"I think FitzRoy's car is being used to take something off of Malta. Bridget O'Connell may not know this. I think she is in grave danger from Seamus Riley," Elspeth said.

"Bridget O'Connell? Seamus Riley? My God, Elspeth! Do you know Bridget's full name?"

"I can get it from the hotel records. Give me a minute to open my computer."

Elspeth entered her password and scrolled down the hotel guest roster.

"Bridget Mary Margaret O'Connell. Seamus Riley seems only to have two names."

"Of course," he said. "It never dawned on me that FitzRoy's niece's name, a common Irish one, would be among the names on our most wanted terrorist list. Bridget Mary Margaret O'Connell is a leader in the extreme Ulster Defence Association movement. She has been the brains behind one of their top cells for a good number of years. I just didn't put two and two together fast enough because of the diversion of Adam Russell."

"Do you think she engineered FitzRoy's death?"

"Absolutely."

Realisation hit Elspeth. "She killed FitzRoy so she could get the car off Malta without it being inspected. How horrible. But why?"

"Get her, Elspeth! Use every means at your hands, Evan, Loren, Richard Munro, the Maltese police, all of them. And get what she has in the car. If nothing else, that will give us the evidence we need to detain her. Then we can find out why."

Elspeth arrived at the dock at Sengla to find that the Oceania was the only ship loading there. From the window of the taxi Elspeth could see the last few pieces of cargo were being hoisted into the hold. The sun bore steadily down on the pier, but the breeze off the sea kept the air cool. Customs officials, having apparently completed their final inspection, were coming down the gangplank.

As her taxi came to a halt at the gates to the docks, Elspeth saw Richard, Evan and Loren standing at quayside in the distance. An official in the shipping line's uniform was approaching them. Elspeth ran along the pier towards them.

"Where is Bridget O'Connell?" Elspeth shouted over the noise of the cranes.

"She's already on board," Richard shouted back. "Why?"

She gasped to control her breathing, and in brief sentences explain the situation to Richard, Loren and Evan.

"My God, she has tricked us! And I came down here to protect her," Richard growled. "She boarded about five minutes ago. The coffin was carried up the gangway and stowed in an area designated for sensitive freight. The car was loaded in the hold before that. They are set to sail within the hour. We must do something."

Evan hailed the shipping company official. "I'm Inspector Evan Davies-Jones of Scotland Yard under special assignment to the Maltese Police Department. The British high commissioner here can vouch for me and also for Ms Loren Axt and Ms Elspeth Duff who are assisting me."

Evan pulled out his warrant card. "We suspect that a passenger, Ms Bridget O'Connell, has brought on board some cargo that she is attempting to smuggle out of Malta. I want you to halt the departure of this vessel until we can search the belongings of Ms O'Connell and her uncle, whose body was just taken aboard. I am sorry to inconvenience you, but under the regulations of Commonwealth law you are obliged to honour my request." Evan later admitted that he was not certain this was true but it sounded reasonable.

"Not only obliged but most willing, sir," the official said. "Let us know what we can do. I'll notify the captain immediately."

"Inspector Davies-Jones," Richard spoke with the formal decisiveness that only comes when one has been in high positions for many years, "I have some authority here since this ship has British registration. I suggest that you let me board first and distract Ms O'Connell while you do your initial investigation. The longer we can keep her from knowing what we are doing, the more success we may have of finding what we are looking for. Ms Duff, come with me."

*

Evan turned to Loren. "Loren, follow me. I want you to examine the car and I'll examine the coffin."

Evan was loath to see FitzRoy's body again. No policeman enjoyed working with the remains of the dead. The Maltese mortuary, located in a country where the preservation of the body was part of the predominant religion, must have made FitzRoy's body presentable to some extent. Yet Evan considered an inspection of FitzRoy's cadaver with repugnance, even though he had performed this task in the past.

He rang the coroner and asked for his immediate presence on the ship. The coroner arrived in fifteen minutes and accompanied Evan to the special refrigerated compartment in the hold. They opened the lid of the coffin, and the coroner began a close examination of the body that he had seen newly dead only three days before. The coroner assured Evan that the body was as he had left it. Then they removed the body and examined the coffin. It was simple affair and did not require much dismantling. They found no suspicious objects and returned FitzRoy's body to his funereal packing crate.

*

In the meantime, Loren followed the officer in charge of cargo into another section of the hold. The space was dark, lit only by a string of low-level lights. The smell of stale salt water and ship's oil filled the space. In one corner was the Mercedes draped and chained to the floor. The official drew back the canvas that covered it.

"Do you have any tools available?" Loren asked. "I'll need to remove the panels on the car and if I find nothing,

I'll need to inspect any compartment where items might be hidden."

Loren silently went over Interpol's standard checklist for car inspections and with methodical carefulness examined each possible hiding place. She removed the door panels and the seats and finally the floor mats. The trunk of the car was dismantled; the spare tyre was checked. The tyres were deflated and various engine cavities were probed.

An hour's careful examination revealed nothing. The only thing she found was the lipstick case that she had dropped at the vineyard that had defied an earlier search.

*

Richard spoke quietly but pressingly with Elspeth.

"We already know that Bridget will be hostile. I think it best if we don't let her know that we know who she is."

"I agree," Elspeth said. "What about telling her that we have just received information that some of her uncle's belongings may contain items placed there by a known Arab terrorist whom Conan contacted on the last day of his life? This should confuse her if she is hiding something of her own."

"An excellent plan. Elspeth, sometimes I wonder ruefully about your ability to insert a twist in things, a talent you have always had as long as I've known you."

She grinned at him, despite the seriousness of the moment.

Bridget was alone in her stateroom when Richard and Elspeth arrived. The room had none of the graciousness of her room at the Kennington Valletta but Bridget looked more comfortable in it. She had shed her tweed coat and was dressed simply in jeans, a polo necked jersey and a cardigan. It seemed strange to Elspeth that this woman, who looked both vulnerable and defiant, should be a terrorist and a murderer. Had one seen her on a street in Los Angeles, one would have described her as a woman 'with an attitude' but surely not as an assassin bent on achieving her own political ends.

"High commissioner," Bridget said in acknowledgement of his presence. She did not greet Elspeth.

"I trust that you have had no trouble in boarding?" Richard asked.

"The papers were quite adequate." Bridget added no thanks.

"Ms O'Connell, as Ms Duff indicated to you at the hotel, we are concerned that your uncle was involved, at least inadvertently, with Arab terrorists here in Malta. He may have stumbled on to some information that these men don't want to become known. The police have contacted us and asked us to make one final search of his belongings that you have with you now. The ship does not sail for another hour so we would like permission to see your uncle's cases one more time. I trust you have no objection."

Bridget's dark eyes looked at Richard Munro without expression. Elspeth watched the Irish woman carefully for any tell-tale signs of wariness. There were none.

"I thought that the Maltese police and Ms Duff had already done this." Bridget looked sideways at Elspeth, who detected a hint of a sneer.

Richard was not deterred. "The police were looking

for signs of foul play in your uncle's death but not for information that might compromise a terrorist operation. They found nothing in the things Ms Duff gave you, and I assume we won't either. But when the Oceania sails, we will no longer have access to the items he had here in Malta. I hope you understand our concern."

"It's no concern of mine, high commissioner. I'm here to convey my uncle's body back to Northern Ireland. I've no interest in Arab terrorism other than I don't want to play any part in it."

"Then do we have your consent to see your uncle's cases one more time?" Richard asked.

"Do what you want. No matter what I say, you have already planned to do so. They're stowed in the hold, and I'm sure that the steamship company will comply with your request."

As they were leaving the stateroom, Bridget added, "You won't find anything. My uncle was very meticulous with his things and I've checked them all."

Richard and Elspeth returned to her stateroom half an hour later.

"Did you find anything?" Bridget asked.

"No, we must have been misinformed. Thank you for your cooperation. Please leave an address where you can be reached," Richard said.

"You can contact my uncle's solicitors. I travel frequently but they'll know where I am."

"One last thing, Ms O'Connell. May I see your passport?"

Bridget for a brief instant looked puzzled by the request. She fetched her passport out of her handbag.

"Bridget Mary Margaret O'Connell. That is a beautiful Irish name," said the high commissioner, with all his charm.

"Too Catholic for my taste. I don't know why my very Calvinistic mother and father decided to name me that." She showed no hint that that name might mean anything to anyone.

Richard followed Elspeth out of the stateroom and pulled the door to with a hard catching sound.

"Cool customer," Elspeth said out of the side of her mouth.

"Too cool," Richard said out of the side of his. "Way too cool."

*

Evan, Loren, Richard and Elspeth met in the captain's quarters to discuss what they had found or rather not found. Evan therefore had no grounds to arrest Bridget. Reluctantly they agreed to allow the ship to sail. Disembarking, they watched as it left the dock.

As it sailed, Loren said, "But there was something."

"What?"

"My lipstick."

Richard looked bemused. "What has your lipstick got to do with anything?"

"I dropped it in FitzRoy's car when we went to the vineyard but couldn't find it afterwards. I went back to the hotel parking lot after Conan and I had returned from the vineyard but it was not in the car. I assumed I had dropped it at the vineyard."

"Might you just have missed it?" Richard asked.

"No, it definitely was gone but just now I found it in

Conan's car in a place that I definitely had searched before."

"Which confirms there is definitely something questionable about the car," Elspeth said.

"Exactly. Elspeth, you guessed the car was exchanged. The car I just searched was FitzRoy's car, the one he drove to the vineyard. But it was not the car I searched when we got back at the hotel after our excursion."

"So where is the other car now?" Richard asked.

"I think that last night Seamus Riley took the duplicate car into hiding," Elspeth said.

Evan's eyes sparkled. "I just talked to Inspector Dom and told him to watch out for a large black Mercedes with British number plates. There can't be many in Valletta."

"And what about Bridget?" Richard asked.

"She can't very well leave the ship until it arrives in Marseilles. We have two days' time to find out the truth," Elspeth said.

Evan rang Inspector Dom and put his mobile on speaker.

"Evan," said Dom, "where are you?"

"At the docks with Ms Duff and Sir Richard Munro." He did not mention Loren. "Dom, what's happening there?"

"Conan FitzRoy's chauffeur, whom I recognise from the Kennington hotel when I examined Mr FitzRoy's car, is driving a large Mercedes towards the car ferry to Sicily."

"How do you know?"

"I'm following him."

"Arrest him. We believe he is smuggling something important in that car."

They could almost hear Dom smile.

"I am already on it," the Maltese said. The sound of his siren broke through both the Valletta traffic and Evan's phone.

33

Wednesday, 28 April 2004 – Day 5 Afternoon/Evening and Thursday, 29 April 2004 – Day 6 Morning

Bridget O'Connell stood on deck of the HMS Oceania and watched Grand Harbour recede from view. When the small figures on the dock that represented her send-off party—the British high commissioner, Elspeth Duff and two others whose names she did not remember—had finally disappeared from her view, she raised her arm in salute.

I pulled it off, she thought. I did it.

Almost. There was still the issue of the second Mercedes, but she trusted Riley would have no trouble if he followed her instructions to the letter. Now that she was transporting Uncle Kevin's car all the papers for the substitute car should agree when Riley went through customs. She told Riley to wait for two weeks before attempting to leave Malta. She would keep Riley informed. Brian Clancy, titular head of her organisation in Rome, might not be pleased with her last-moment double switch of the cars, but she had to stay ahead of Scotland Yard. She thought of Brian's warm body against hers. She would explain and he would understand.

A shock had gone through her when she had looked up and seen Evan Davies-Jones in the dining room. His face, so marred by the explosion of the bomb they had

359

rigged in the Minister's car, had been etched in her mind since she saw it in the press photograph when the Queen had recognised him for bravery. The photograph had been quickly withdrawn but Bridget's cell snatched up such things whenever possible. Had the injury to his face been less invasive she never would have remembered.

A sharp breeze blew across the deck, catching her blonde hair. The wind's coolness passed through her reminding her of the chill she had first felt when she had heard of her uncle's betrayal. It had all happened so unexpectedly.

She thought back to her childhood, the warmth of her early home in Belfast and her love for her parents. Then one day, when she had been staying for the night at a friend's house, they had heard a terrible blast and then the arrival of the fire brigade, sounds to which Ulstermen were almost inured. She and her friend had hidden under the covers and talked about growing up and joining the resistance against the IRA. The next morning Uncle Kevin had appeared, taken her away and explained that her mother and father were dead, victims of the blast. She was too young to understand fully. Uncle Kevin had taken charge of her guardianship, loved her and seen that she had a life that her parents could not have afforded.

As she grew, her understanding of the Troubles took on a new dimension. Despite the gentility that Uncle Kevin had wished for her, she became more and more radicalised, particularly after meeting Brian Clancy. He became her mentor and soon afterwards her lover. He trained her to hate both the IRA and any concession towards the Republic of Ireland.

One evening three years before in the back room of a pub near where she had lived as a child, she and Brian Clancy were celebrating the discovery of an IRA cell that they could target for extermination. The owner of the pub was serving their party. He was a well-known member of the Ulster Defence Association, and had frequently hidden its members in the attic above when they had been pursued by the police. He paused when introduced to Bridget.

"Are you Sean O'Connell's daughter?"

She acknowledged her parentage.

"Rotten thing his brother Kevin did the night of the bombing. He knew it was going to happen, you know, and he didn't tell your dad or your mum. He could have saved their lives and that of his pal Ryan Fitzpatrick, the one who was writing the book on the Troubles. After Ryan's death Kevin took most of Ryan's work, revised it and published it under his own name without mentioning Ryan. Not a nice man, your uncle."

Bridget stared at him stunned. Everything she had believed about the night her parents had died became unthreaded. If the pub owner was correct, Uncle Kevin had lied to her. And his first book? The only one about Northern Ireland, a subject he later shunned. Uncle Kevin had stolen his friend's ideas. He built his own life on the manuscript. No wonder he had changed his name and moved to London. No wonder he had assumed a persona so outrageous that everyone knew it was fake. The sham hid the real truth, that Conan FitzRoy was a fraud, and had betrayed his family and his friend. In that moment of discovery, Bridget had decided to kill him.

It had taken her three years of planning, but she had

done it seamlessly and had helped the cause of the Ulster Defence Association in doing so. She had fooled the authorities who were so focused on the Arabs that they had forgotten those near at home who wanted to stop any reconciliation between the north and the south of Ireland. She saluted the Mediterranean sky again.

She stood a bit longer on deck, and then, growing cold from both the wind and her recollections, went down to her cabin.

*

Riley eased the Mercedes out of their accomplice's garage just before noon. He thought of the night before when he had switched the cars.

After dinner, Bridget had come by his room. He let her in, making sure no one saw her. She told him that the original exchange of the car had to be reversed. The careful duplication of the vehicles in Rome, the split-second timing of the swapping of the vehicles at the vineyard last Sunday here in Malta and the roundabout email route they had set up for communication all went down the toilet. But he went along with Bridget, who was the brains.

How easy it had been to lure Maria away for a moment, and then slip the drug into the coffee that she carried downstairs. They all fell for his charm, the dark ones especially. Maria was such an ass. Her skin was swarthy and she had hair on her lip, not like his carrot-headed beauty back in Derry. Riley waited for ten minutes after Maria returned upstairs and then slipped into the car park where he found the attendant unconscious in his kiosk. He slid a cover over the lens of the video camera, which had not swung around fast enough to record his entry. Then he switched the cars.

As he drove out of the garage where he had left the car the night before, he thought of Bridget, Saieda. He had found out from the internet that Saieda meant "happy" in Arabic. Hardly our Miss or rather Ms Bridget. Tough as bullets and as deadly.

"Helios" she had called him. He looked that up too. Helios was the god who drove the chariot of the sun. Arrogant bitch. Did she consider herself the sun, centre of the solar system? He did not doubt it.

In Rome he had heard her talking to Brian Clancy. It was to Brian that Riley owed his allegiance. He knew Brian and Bridget were lovers but that Bridget had brains but no heart. He also knew that the Mercedes he was driving was padded with enough pound notes to finance a major operation of the Ulster Defence Association against the IRA. Enough pound notes to make him rich for the rest of his life.

She had told him to lay low. Malta, on Saturday, would become part of the EU. The bitch said to leave the car at their accomplice's garage and wait for two weeks, when she thought customs regulations would be eased because of Malta's entry onto the EU. She would come back to Malta, and they would drive the car across Sicily and Italy, through France and then on to England. Three borders, all within the EU. She told him there would be only light customs inspections, if any, but they still might be at risk at each one.

Riley had been a henchman all his life. First his father, who had drunk himself to death, and then his mother who died from having twelve children, then his wife and finally Brian Clancy, they all had told him what to do. He had never questioned it. Now he had a car filled with money.

His mind moved slowly as he dealt with Valletta's traffic. What if he just drove to the ferry and presented the papers? They were in order, according to Bridget. He could vanish into Italy. How would they ever find him?

Riley's mind was so occupied in his dream that he did not hear the police car behind him.

*

They were far out to sea when Bridget decided to retire for the night. The dinner she had eaten felt heavy on her stomach and the success of the day was strangely unfelt. Brian Clancy trusted Riley but she was not certain she did. She picked up her mobile to call Brian, but then thought better of it. She would talk to him when she reached Marseille. Her temple began to throb in the way it always did when she sensed danger.

Sleep evaded her. She rose and went on deck as the sun rose. It was cold and she wrapped her tweed coat around herself. On the lightening horizon, she saw motion. She watched as slowly, like a cloud of locusts, three seagoing helicopters made their way west towards the ship. As they came closer, fear grew within her. When she saw the 'POLICE' and a French flag stencilled on their sides, she knew she had nowhere to hide.

How could such a perfect plan have gone so terribly wrong?

34

Friday, 30 April 2004 – Day 7 Late Afternoon

Pamela Crumm showed Tony Ketcham into Eric Kennington's Office.

"Lord Kennington will be with you shortly," she said, vaguely implying that the detective's visit was an inconvenience. The Kennington Organisation tolerated the police but was not thrilled by their presence, even on the successful conclusion of a case involving murder at one of their hotels.

Pamela returned to her own office, and before closing the connecting door watched Tony Ketcham stand by the windows and stare down to the street below. She wondered what he was thinking. Had the affair in Valletta, which had occupied so much of their time for the last week, been an important case for him or just one in a long queue? Would he take all the credit for it at Scotland Yard or would Evan Davies-Jones get some too? She hoped the glory of the arrests made in Malta and Marseille would be shared. In any event, Pamela wanted to meet Evan after listening to Elspeth's glowing words regarding his ability and marred good looks.

She returned to her computer and put on headphones. She started typing rapidly, although only gibberish appeared on her screen.

The owner and president of the Kennington

Organisation arrived ten minutes late for his appointment with Tony Ketcham. Through her headphones, Pamela heard Lord Kennington apologise for the unreliable nature of London traffic, but he appeared to be in a good mood. He was always exuberant when his security staff resolved troublesome issues at any of his hotels.

Pamela knew Eric would ask her to send lavish flowers to Conan FitzRoy's funeral in Belfast, and make sure that the obituaries all said that FitzRoy had died in Malta without mentioning the Kennington Valletta. His lordship had sufficient sway with the fourth estate that his wishes were almost always carried out after he had promised the editors free meals at the Kennington Mayfair. Only a Belfast tabloid said that the death had occurred 'at the hotel where Mr FitzRoy was staying'. The article also stated that Mrs FitzRoy (the fifth) when asked where FitzRoy had died said she couldn't remember if it was Malta or perhaps Corsica or Crete. One of those hot, little islands in the Mediterranean somewhere.

Lord Kennington offered Tony Ketcham tea, which he accepted politely. His lordship did not offer coffee. He had often ranted that afternoon coffee was a foreign invasion and did not sanction it in his office, although he served the finest Jamaican, Kenyan and Arabic coffees at his hotels.

"Now, detective superintendent, will you tell me what happened exactly? Elspeth Duff kept us informed as things unfolded in Malta, but so much has gone on since Wednesday that I'm not certain about the actual sequence of events. But wait a moment, Ms Crumm was involved as well and is privy to all my business affairs. I'd like her to hear as well."

Pamela took off the headphones and entered Lord Kennington's office through the connecting door. She did not presume to pour herself a cup of tea, as she kept a thermos of the best Kennington Jamaican coffee concealed in her desk.

"I am glad that you can join us, Ms Crumm. We appreciate the help you were able to give us in the FitzRoy investigation," Tony Ketcham said. Pamela smiled at the compliment. "I'll bring you up to speed as much as possible. Had it not been for Elspeth Duff's insight, we might never have discovered the truth," Tony Ketcham said.

Eric Kennington and Pamela Crumm sat silently as Tony recounted Bridget's plot but when he finished Lord Kennington burst out: "What a fiendish thing and what a devilish woman that Bridget is. She might have succeeded. I feel sorry for old FitzRoy. He never had a chance."

"On the contrary, Lord Kennington, he had every chance in the world," Tony Ketcham said. "He had too much of an ego to see that his own niece had turned against him. Many years ago he chose his path and that led to his own destruction as well as the destruction of those close to him, including Bridget O'Connell."

Pamela closed her eyes and in her heart she knew that FitzRoy had always been a tragic figure. Yes, life was a much fuller thing than any fiction.

Tony Ketcham continued, "Lord Kennington, I want to thank you for assigning your staff and particularly Elspeth Duff to this case. The coordination of our team in Malta along with Elspeth, René LeGrand, Pietru Para and the entire Kennington Valletta staff helped expedite the solving of this crime. Each one added bits of information like pieces of a puzzle. Finally Elspeth put them together as a whole."

Lord Kennington nodded.

"I enjoyed seeing Elspeth Duff again," the detective superintendent said as he rose to leave. "She always has had such a good mind, and was the first one who suspected a direct link between FitzRoy's murder and the exchange of the cars. Tell her we are grateful."

Pamela showed the detective superintendent out and was about to return to her office when Lord Kennington called to her, "What about this Arab fellow?"

"Adam Russell checked out this morning. René LeGrand tells me he seemed enormously relieved to be gone," Pamela said. "René arranged that the hall porter give him a very handsome copy of the Qur'an and assurances that he would always be welcome at the Kennington Valletta. René was left with the distinct impression that Adam would not return under any circumstances. Poor fellow."

"Not poor fellow at all," said his lordship. "What right had he skulking around my hotel?"

"Evan Davies-Jones contacted Achmed Rashid after Adam was cleared of suspicion," Pamela said. "Achmed admitted that the Rashid family was considering a takeover of the Kennington Valletta, and they had sent Adam there to see if it was a desirable place to stay for rich young Arabic men. Adam said that hotel was totally unsuitable."

"The nerve! Cheeky young man! My hotel not suitable? What effrontery!"

For Pamela Crumm had difficulty in keeping from

laughing before she returned to her office and shut her door.

*

In Malta, Elspeth invited Evan, Loren, René and Richard into her temporary office and poured out the coffee she had ordered for them all.

"You have all contributed so much to this case," she said graciously, "that I thought it only right that you all should be aware of the events that happened in the end. Evan, why don't you start with the police?"

"Inspector Dom arrested Riley as he was attempting to get the second Mercedes on the ferry," Evan said. "Although the car's papers were in order and the engine checked for replaced parts, Inspector Dom demanded that the car be thoroughly searched. When the customs officials removed the door panels, they found British notes amounting to over two million pounds. Riley was arrested and taken to police headquarters."

Elspeth took a sip of her coffee and said, "Riley was not the fanatic that Bridget was, and did not have her intelligence. He had the sense to know that he had a better chance confessing his part in the scheme and facing imprisonment in Malta than he had in braving Bridget after the scheme failed. Riley had been a part of the exchange from the first. He confessed that the money had been gathered in cash bit by bit from many sources and brought to Malta, where it was put in a number of small bank accounts in Bridget's name. The cash was to finance the Ulster Defence Association's criminal activities. Bridget said she felt Malta was an unlikely place anyone to monitor these small financial dealings, and she had arranged to have the full amount of all the accounts put into the second car, which was then switched with the innocent one FitzRoy had brought into Malta. Bridget had thought that the entrance of Malta into the EU would have eased customs inspections. Bridget had not explained why the second switch, although Riley thought Bridget must have found a flaw in her original plan.

Evan added, "Riley had told us about the plot to exchange the cars, but he wasn't aware that FitzRoy died from other than natural causes."

Elspeth nodded. "Bridget knew FitzRoy came to the Kennington Valletta every year and she chose the hotel as the venue for his death."

Evan added, "Detective Superintendent Ketcham told me that after being caught, Bridget confessed that she hated her uncle after she discovered his actions that led to the death of her mother and father. Bridget joined the Ulster Defence Association, and had made it her life's mission to avenge her parents' deaths. She was determined to get revenge on the IRA, who engineered the bombing that killed them, and vowed that she would destroy FitzRoy for not warning her parents of the threat."

"Bridget was clever", Elspeth said. "By the time she devised FitzRoy's murder and the transfer of the money in Malta, she had already plotted a number of violent crimes against the IRA. Scotland Yard knew of these but never had enough concrete evidence to take her into custody. Her last endeavour here in Malta served two purposes: to get rid of her uncle and to transfer money to Belfast. Perhaps if she had settled for one or the other goal, she wouldn't have been caught."

Richard, who had been quiet until now, asked, "But what about the cars?"

Evan explained. "Bridget planned the exchange of the two cars in minute detail. She had Riley lease a Mercedes of exactly the same model as FitzRoy's from the same agency in Mayfair. The agency has identified Riley's photograph to confirm this. Riley drove the car to Rome before FitzRoy arrived. When FitzRoy visited Bridget in Rome, his car was photographed, so that any scratches, dents or other anomalies could be duplicated. Riley volunteered to serve as FitzRoy's driver after his usual driver was struck down with food poisoning, administered of course by Bridget. FitzRoy and Riley motored leisurely down the coast of Italy and on to Sicily. An accomplice, the addressee on the emails, drove directly from Rome to Catania and brought the duplicate car on to Malta days before Riley and FitzRoy arrived."

Loren frowned and asked, "What did all the emails mean?"

Evan turned to her and answered, "We think Phase One was the preparation of the cars in Rome. Bridget arranged for a duplicate computerised key for Conan's car and made sure the key would work in both cars. Her plans were almost upset when Conan announced he might stay at the Hotel Saint John. She talked him out of it in the end, but had to convey this to her sources here in Malta, thus the plain text mention of the Kennington Valletta in the original communication. This was her first false step. If she had not done this, Scotland Yard would never have contacted the Kennington Organisation."

Loren, who had been silent up to now, spoke. "Phase

Two took place when the cars were traded while Conan and I were touring the vineyard," she said. "Remember '*timing and precision essential*'. The lorry with the so-called puncture pulled up, blocking the view of the Mercedes from the house. The cars, each bearing the same number plate, were quickly switched. Conan, believing the vineyard site was safe, had thrown his keys on the dashboard. The only thing Bridget did not account for was that you dropped your lipstick case and could not find it in the substitute car."

"Many's the slip twixt the lipstick and..." said Richard, who grinned.

Elspeth gave him a sideways glance, grimaced, and went on. "The murder, which was Phase Three, was arranged in Rome as well. Conan made no secret that Bridget organised his packing for him. Bridget knew that FitzRoy was planning eight days to get to Malta and therefore she put the cyanide-laced capsule in the pocket of his medicine bag and dated the packet to be used the day after he arrived. This gave FitzRoy time to visit the vineyard, which he always did when he came here. In fact, Bridget had set up the appointment with his old friend Roberto and knew the exact date and time."

Putting down his cup, Richard asked, "Who was Helios?"

"Seamus Riley," Elspeth explained. "The emails were written by Brian Clancy, Bridget's co-conspirator and lover. Brian was probably Phoenician, and sent the emails through an accommodation address originating in Jeddah. It was imperative that Bridget, alias Saieda, keep in constant contact with Brian about the progress of the mission in Malta and then Brian conveyed the information to their other accomplices here."

Elspeth gave a crooked smile. "After Bridget, thanks in part to my intervention, got clearance to take Conan's car off Malta without going through customs, she planned to have Riley drive what appeared to be her uncle's car, which was loaded with the money, on to the boat bound for Marseille. By the time they reached Marseille, Malta would be a member of the EU and therefore Bridget, correctly or incorrectly, assumed the car would not have to go through a strict customs search there. If there were complications, she could produce her papers from the British High Commission and the Maltese government. Afterwards Riley was to fetch FitzRoy's real car, which was to have been hidden in a local garage, and take the car back across to Sicily."

"Which obviously didn't happen," Loren said.

Elspeth nodded. "All might have progressed without a hitch but for two things. Bridget didn't know that the British government intercepted the emails and therefore was aware of the possibility of the exchange. And then, as she sat having dinner with Riley, Adam fled the dining room, and she turned around and saw Evan. I'd seated Loren and Evan behind Adam and I was behind Bridget. I hadn't thought that Bridget would see Evan or would recognise him."

Loren and Richard looked puzzled.

Evan came to the rescue. "I'd never seen Bridget before that evening nor had I been aware of her terrorist ties, but she had seen my photograph in the papers when I went to Buckingham Palace. When she spotted me in the dining room, she immediately assumed that I was on duty and might be aware of who she was. Bridget knew she would be getting her safe passage papers from the high commission in the morning, but if I was following her, the safe passage might be rescinded. Bridget felt she had to devise a new plan. The combination of conceit and panic on Bridget's part was her undoing. Knowing that FitzRoy's car might now be searched before being loaded on the cargo ship, she had to improvise. She rushed down to Riley's room and told him to switch cars back again so that the car she took on the Oceania was FitzRoy's original car without the money in it. As a result when Loren examined the car on board the ship she found her lipstick. It was such a small thing with such big consequences."

"But what about the second car that was padded with money?" Loren asked.

"Bridget advised Riley to keep the car in hiding until she could conceive of some other way to get the money to Sicily without it being discovered," Evan said. "But Riley got greedy, hoping to take the money for himself. He decided to drive the car off the island immediately, unaware that Inspector Dom was watching out for it. Bridget might have evaded detection from involvement in FitzRoy's death but Riley implicated her in the exchange of cars in order to get a reduced charge. At Interpol's request, the French police met the Oceania before it docked this morning, and arrested Bridget on board."

"Yes!" said Loren making a fist.

"I think the saddest thing about the whole case," Elspeth said, "was that one of the last things Conan FitzRoy did was to go out and buy Bridget a very expensive pair of gold earrings. Inspector Dom found these in a small box in his room. The assistant in the gift shop at the Hotel Saint John confirmed that was his five o'clock appointment. The irony is that Bridget was, I think, the only person in the world that Conan really loved."

*

When the others left the conference room, Elspeth spoke to Richard quietly. "Dickie, will you stay on for a minute?"

He looked at her but her face conveyed no emotion.

She handed him a folded piece of heavy Kennington hotel stationery. He took it and unfolded it. Inside he saw Elspeth's large handwriting. She had written a London address that he recognised as being in Kensington, with a phone number and an email address.

"I thought you should have that in case you ever needed to contact me," she said and then smiled broadly at him. "Only if you need to."

Tucking the note in his pocket, he took her hands gently in his and said, "Only if I need to?"

"Yes, only if you need to," she said and then added. "Or want to."

Epilogue

Magdelena Cassar swooped down on her guests.

"Darlings, so you return. In triumph, I am assured. Elspeth, you have brought these delightful people back into my life and have made this day complete. Come, come, Teresa has made lunch for us to be served on the balcony."

Elspeth was reminded of the efficiency of a border collie as Magdelena shepherded her along with Richard, Evan and Loren into her home. They were all laughing and talking by the time they reached Magdelena's cavernous great room. The Baroque splendour and the freshness of the Maltese sea air that filled the room reflected the happiness of the moment. Magdelena Cassar had the talent to make such things happen.

In the daytime, the view from the balcony revealed the arid charm of the Gozitan landscape, the golden rock faces of the cliffs and the splendour of sea beyond. It being May, spring flowers were sprouting in every spot where water and good soil had found a home. Soft orange bougainvillea clung to the balcony rails, the colour of the flowers heightened by its contrast the blue of the Mediterranean.

"Now come, my dear friends and enjoy the peace of Gozo after your days in the urban pollution of Valletta. Why my fellow countrymen have such a love affair with car exhaust, overcrowded housing and general urban blight, I do not know. Yet I would not want them flocking over to Gozo and spoiling what we have here. Can anyone imagine a more perfect place than this?"

The lunch table had been set out on the balcony. Everything about the setting had a touch of delight: a brightly patterned tablecloth of colours that were reminiscent of Matisse's later works, freshly picked flowers strewn with careful abandon among the place settings of Italian pottery and persimmon-coloured napkins were folded like a bishop's hat with lopsided tails.

Magdelena offered them a chilled local dry white wine. At first it cut the palate, but a second sip provided a coolness that was perfect for the warm spring afternoon.

While waiting for lunch, Magdelena sat at her piano and invited Elspeth to join her on the bench next to her. The others spread themselves on the sofas in the great room. Elspeth looked at their faces and somehow knew they all felt a great ease in the presence of this grande dame. Magdelena touched the keys lightly. Each of the guests seemed to fall into a private reverie, perhaps thinking of the intense days in Valletta and the success of their dénouement. Elspeth wondered if each of them was saddened by the beautiful music and felt the finality of the moment.

*

Richard Munro looked across at Elspeth, who was seated on the bench next to her aunt and was turning the pages of the musical score. He remembered the days in Scotland when Elspeth had been fifteen and Magdelena a bit of a scandal in the family. Richard wished he could go back to that time. He would have changed things had he been able. Would Elspeth have altered things as well? The awkwardness and enthusiasm of the gangly schoolgirl had morphed to the grace and vitality of a middle-aged woman who had opened to him over the last five days. He had fallen in love with Elspeth when they were young, and when he saw her puzzling over the front door of his home on Triq It-Torri a week ago he had fallen in love with her again.

Tomorrow she was flying back to London. He had carefully put away the paper she had given him with her London address and phone number, although he had long since committed its contents to memory. At Marija's restaurant, she had challenged him by saying he might not want to renew her acquaintance when they had finished working together, but he wanted to be with her even more now. Would he follow her to London and ask her to come back to Malta? He doubted she would consent, but at least he now knew how to find her.

*

Elspeth let her mind float back over the years. She had sat at this very piano bench so many times in the past. In the act there was a stability of love and of remembrance. Heartbreak and happiness had accompanied her here to Gozo throughout the years. She did not know how old Magdelena was, but Elspeth wanted her to be eternal, to sit here and play music until there was no more time.

Elspeth felt a happiness she had not felt in years, and wondered if it had anything to do with Richard Munro. The vigour of life in Lord Kennington's employ suddenly seemed less compelling than in the past. What assignment would Eric have for her when she returned to London tomorrow? She would insist on spending several days with her daughter Lizzie and her family in East Sussex or taking a trip to Scotland to see her parents, but she knew Eric would be impatient for her to return to work.

Elspeth let her thoughts wander from the music and raised her eyes to Richard. He smiled and, having just turned a page, she looked at him and smiled back.

*

Evan felt the onset of separation. He was scheduled to stay on in Malta to handle the final details of the FitzRoy case, and then would return to London within the week. Tony Ketcham had told him his next case would be in Edinburgh and involve a suspected group of Hamas activists who were secretly negotiating with an underground group of Scottish gunrunners for arms to send to Palestine. Edinburgh in the spring would not offer the Mediterranean beauty of Malta. This time he would be posing as a disaffected terrorist, maimed in the explosion of an incendiary device, so his circumstances would be rough. A week ago he might have relished this. Now the crisp bite of the cold wine and the tender chords of Magdelena's music filled him with a sense of mellow inertia.

Evan looked at Loren, who was sitting on the sofa opposite him. He had met a woman called Alicia Kent who had revealed she was from Interpol. The superficial beauty of the rich American girl had dissolved into the toughness of a trained professional. She and Evan had become a team. Their five days together had been a symphony of action, commitment and closeness. Yes, closeness. She ran and moved and thought as easily as he did, but he felt no competition. He wanted her to come to Edinburgh with him, to explore being together more fully. He knew she would not.

*

Loren at first got lost in the music. The pure beauty of each note filled her. She let her mind float. She felt a deep contentment that she had never known before. She could stay here in Gozo forever, she thought, listening to the music and sipping the cool white wine, forever and ever, with Magdelena Cassar and Elspeth Duff and the high commissioner and mostly with Evan Davies-Jones. She smiled at the illusion. Alicia Kent would disappear once she got on the plane at Luqa Airport, and Loren Axt, at her handler's insistence, would no longer exist once she landed in Lyon.

*

Magdelena finished the Chopin etude and broke the reveries of her guests. "And now we must have lunch."

Her guests did as bidden.

After they were seated, Elspeth raised her glass. "To Adam Russell," she said.

The rest looked puzzled.

Elspeth laughed. "He led Loren to the information about car smuggling. Had he not bolted from the dining room, Bridget might not have recognised Evan and changed her plans. Should we recommend Adam for a commendation from Scotland Yard to thank him for his part in the apprehension of a heinous terrorist?"

"No, perhaps not," Richard said kindly. "He might not understand."

Author's Appreciation (First Edition)

A Murder in Malta is the first of a series of Elspeth Duff mysteries. Written at night after I returned home from work, the book took several years to complete. It has had numerous revisions thanks to input from many friends and colleagues. I am particularly grateful for the assistance from friend and author Judith Horstman, who read the novel in its early stages. She urged me to keep writing and has helped me with subsequent drafts. Writing instructor Margaret Lucke also read the manuscript and showed me how to refine it. I received many useful suggestions from Shannon Kelleher, Janice Seagrave, Edy Raby, Jerene DeLaney, and Shelby and David Ingram in the United States and Jocelyn Jenner and Caroline Johnson in the United Kingdom. Special thanks and love go to Ian Crew, who has encouraged me from start to finish, and who accompanied me to Peckham to see where Adam Russell might have lived.

So many people in Malta assisted me when I visited there in April 2004. I particularly want to acknowledge the help I received from Mark Fenech at the Castille Hotel in Valletta, Police Constable Brian Farrugia of the Maltese Police, George from Euro Cab on Malta and Margaret of Peter's Mini-Bus Service on Gozo.

Author's Notes and Appreciation
(Second Edition)

Since the publication of *A Murder in Malta* in 2014, I have wanted to issue a second addition that would correct the mistakes in the first and freshen up the text. I was urged to do this by Gim and Ian Crew and am grateful they did so. Without their support I would not have done this.

The book is a bit shorter but the plot and characters remain the same. Much of the material about the characters and the hotels is reflected in future books in the Elspeth Duff mysteries.

Since the book's first edition, I have visited Malta again and found it changed since Malta's ascension to the European Union. The original text was written in the early days of this century and recounts Valletta and Malta as it was then. I regret the changes that have taken place there but I am certain most Maltese embrace them.

I have tried to stay true to the technology current then, VCRs, DSL (forerunner of broadband) and Blackberries mentioned are now out-of-date, which makes one appreciate the world we live in today,

Special thanks go to my editor Alice Roberts and my proof-reader Beverly Mar .

Ann Crew is a former architect and now full-time mystery writer who travels the world gathering material for the Elspeth Duff mysteries. Visit *anncrew.com* or *elspethduffmysteries.com*.